A symphony of i

... This story from t

could hardly have been dreamed ... The strength of character the two young lovers exhibited to reach out and grasp freedom are universal for mankind and inspiring to the reader of this page-turner ... It will have you wondering if this wouldn't make a powerful screenplay. (Tony Copple)

A great read, and I highly recommend it,

... This story is so multi-dimensional that it should relate to any reader and provoke instances of self-reflection, just as it did with me. Anyone who desires deeper insight into what life and people really are, and have the potential to be, should read this book. (Jindrich Novak)

A gripping read.

A true story of love conquering all! ... Highly recommended! (Kate Hart)

Required Reading!

... Those of us who have grown up in North America don't appreciate what we have; we take for granted that freedom is our right, not a privilege. This book should be made a compulsory reading for every young person (and most adults) ... (R.Beadry)

Captivating story of love and determination.

... This romantic story provides unique insight into the everyday life of Michael and Danna that is in many respects similar to many people anywhere in the world but in other respects unimaginable for most people in democratic free world. ... Once you start reading you will be unable to stop until the end.

(bookworm)

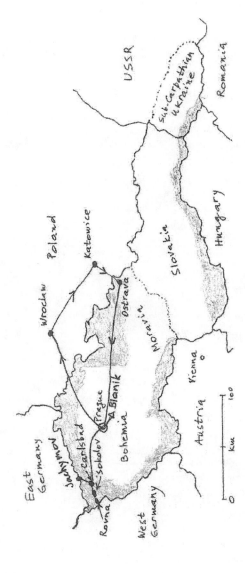

Locations important in Allegro Appassionato and in Andante Cantabile.

(Shaded area: Predominantly German or Hungarian speaking population prior to 1945)

To captain Von Trapp
Jiri Soukup
Dec, 30, 2013

ON MOVING MOUNTAINS

by Jiri Soukup

This book is based on a true story that happened long ago, when there was no Internet, no cell phones, and no credit cards. Typewriters were still the norm, and computers were room-sized machines used for mathematical calculations. All characters are fictional.

www.soukup.ca

Magic Well Publishing
P.O.Box 344, Richmond, ON
K0A 2Z0, Canada

Feedback to the author
OnMovingMountains@gmail.com

Book website and blog
www.soukup.ca/onmoving.html

Printed by CreateSpace
an Amazon company

ISBN 978-1482547559

Hanka, thank you for your unwavering support and help with this project which took much longer than we expected.

I also want to thank many people who helped me when collecting the material and editing the manuscript, in particular late Jenny Bennett, Meghan Soukup, Joan Gamble, and Martha Bohm.

The cast:

Love pentagon, all about 30 years of age:
    Michal and his wife Zora, children Rita 5, Filip and Liza 2
    Danna and her husband Ivan, daughter Lenka 3
    Lída, divorced, children Tibor 5 and Emma 3

Prague office where Michal and Danna work:
    Radim, department manager
    Olda, colleague and friend
    Xavier, mining engineer, before retirement
    Comrade Director, close to 60
    Comrade Schmidt, Party chairman, former RAF pilot, 50

Ottawa:
    Dr. Matheson, geologist
    Mr. Wellington, high security agent in Immigration Canada
    Young Allan and Kathy Kraemer, Michal's landlords.

Important characters who never or rarely appear on the scene:
    Ťapka, leader of the illegal Scout troupe,
    Michal's parents
    Danna's father, international chess master, retired
    Danna's mother, living in Argentina
    Mrs. Fuerst, Zora's mother
    Ivan's father, judge

and a long line of interesting characters Michal meets on his journey and who help him unselfishly like the Presbyterian minister and his wife that share with him a can of soup and the last piece of bread in the tourist camp of Rome, Italy.

The places:

The story starts in 1970 Prague, two years after the Soviets re-established their grip on that part of Europe., and follows Michal to Ottawa, Canada, back to Prague, and then around Europe.

The music:

If you are not familiar with the composers and their work mentioned in some parts of the book, you can play or download samples of this music from www.soukup.ca/onmoving.html.

Contents:

ANDANTE CANTABILE

PRESTO

Appendix: Brief history of Czechoslovakia
which you won't find in any textbook

Allegro Appassionato

"A woman looking for a husband
is the most dangerous of all carnivores. "
(G. B. Shaw).

1. TURTLE LADY

Michal wakes up. It's dark, he doesn't recognize the bed, and the terrible din of the two antique alarm clocks ringing simultaneously is unbearable. He kicks off the blanket with an unfamiliar feminine scent, and tries to think. Both alarm clocks read 4:30 a.m.

Now he remembers: He placed the alarm clocks on the metal tray. If he slept in, the consequences would be unimaginable. He is still in Prague, hiding in the apartment of his good friend Lída, but where is she? Why did she leave before he arrived late last night?

So far I outsmarted police, he thinks. Could they still get me just before the departure? And how could all this be happening to an ordinary, law-abiding, thirty-two-year old computer programmer?

Leaving the country without a proper permit is a crime punishable by years of harsh jail.

He tries to think slowly and clearly.

It is June 26, 1970. His wife Danna and his adopted daughter Lenka are already in Canada, and his bus tour to Yugoslavia[1] departs in ninety minutes. Rumour has it that getting to the West through Yugoslavia is less dangerous than crossing the heavily guarded Czech border.

He jumps up, washes his face, grabs his two bags, and tiptoes out of the apartment. If neighbours report him, Lída would be in grave danger.

His steps echo through cold, empty streets. For such a long time, he tells himself, I had been searching for a soul mate and now, when I have finally found her, who would expect this kind of adventure?

It is that early morning time when streetcars are not running yet,

---

[1] Under Marshal Tito, communist Yugoslavia included Serbia, Croatia, Bosnia, Slovenia, and Macedonia.

and streets are completely empty. Even late-night drunkards are already in bed. Suddenly, infinite sadness stirs up in his heart. He is leaving his country never to return! He is leaving his children, his parents, and all his friends! And yet this is all he wants, something he and Danna orchestrated so carefully.

He has no inclination to reverse his decision, but these feelings surprise him.

The first sunlight floods everything around him. The park is alive with birds, and chirping sparrows search for food and lost feathers. They hop around, bathe in puddles, and shake themselves dry. He opens his eyes and sees minute details: wrinkles on the birds' legs, uncombed feathers, grains of sand, and leaves of grass with tiny drops of dew. Two sparrows fight over a string, and Michal can see its fibers.

Unaware of the time passing, he is musing. Poor birds, they live all year under the street signs and in the crevices of houses. And just like the people who inhabit those grey houses, these birds know no other country. They never fly south.

A sweet scent of blossoms rises from ornamental bushes, and he thinks of the workers who built the park long before cars were invented, and how they had worked on their knees to set the cobblestone pavement. What would they think if they knew that he would desert their city, the wonderful city where he was born and which has no equal?

He arrives at the bus stop holding back his tears. A group of people in holiday attire and straw hats is already waiting beside a pile of suitcases. He examines his reflection in the glass door of the waiting bus: A slim, tall figure with a Tartan-canvas suitcase in one hand and a worn-out duffle bag in the other, short brown hair, fashionable black-framed glasses, blue-checkered shirt with rolled-up sleeves, jeans, and old sneakers – he isn't like the others but could still pass as a tourist. "Hey, professor, do you know the time," one of them greets him.

Feigning coincidence, Michal glances at everybody's eyes. Are the STB agents already here?

The state secret police, STB, is the sister organization of Soviet KGB and German STASI. Its agents can – on a whim - detain, torture, and jail anybody without letting the family know where the person has been taken.

There ought to be some agents – their eyes cruel and cold, like closed shutters hiding their souls, he reminds himself. They have not arrived yet.

He hopes that before this "two-week holiday" is over, he will be in Italy or Austria.

Two drivers arrive and open the door. Michal climbs aboard, and takes the seat he had selected while pacing outside the bus: Not the front row where he would be the first to face immigration officers, but close enough to the door that he could easily run out if that could be of any help. From his window, he will see the border guards before they would enter the bus.

Others follow Michal, shouting and signaling with their hands. Take that seat, not that one, the one over there – they push through the narrow aisle with their bags and suitcases.

The two drivers will take turns at the wheel during the thirty-hour journey. The bus has no restroom and no air-conditioning. "Please, leave the windows open," one of them yells.

A skinny woman pushes her way through, throws her bags onto the rack, drops into the seat beside Michal, and straightens her short cotton skirt with both hands.

He looks at her with pity. By the time we'll get to Split, he is thinking, you won't worry about your clothes being pressed.

"Travelling alone?" She smiles at him, and her eyes pause at his wedding ring.

A woman looking for a fling – that is the last thing I need now, Michal thinks. Or is she working for STB?

"My wife got sick at the last minute," he repeats the story he told the police.

"I am sorry," she says in a tone, which gives Michal the impression that she has got the wrong message.

There is a long pause.

As the bus takes off, Michal pulls out the worn copy of Kipling's

Kim. His mother gave him this book as a charm for his dangerous journey, and the thought whether he will ever see her again returns to his mind.

He has read *Kim* many times, and he opens it randomly on the page where Kim and his lama board the train to Benares.

"Have ye room within for two?" lama said.

"There is no room even for a mouse," shrilled the wife of… " and my lap is full of seventy times seven bundles. Why not bid him to sit on my knee, Shameless?"

How fitting, he thinks, looking at the crowded bus. Not much has changed since those days.

The woman interrupts again. "What's your profession?"

It would be impossible to sit with someone in the narrow seat for a day and night, touching shoulders and hips and without saying a word. With resignation, Michal stuffs *Kim* into the bag under the seat.

"A software programmer. And what do you do?"

The woman is not as young as he first thought. Small wrinkles on her neck and the skin on her hands tell him she must be over forty. The boyish haircut, simple white blouse, beige skirt and good makeup make her look younger. She has an air of nervousness about her.

"I am a technician in a lab; we breed meat-eating turtles." Her eyes are brown and sad.

Michal can't resist. "What? No turtles live in this country. Why would you breed them?"

"If we understand how they hibernate, it may help people survive adverse conditions. They live in water, and they are so cute," she goes on and her eyes glow with excitement. "They take food directly from my fingers."

"Have they big teeth?" Michal looks at her nicotine-stained fingers. She has no cuts or scars.

"They have no teeth. Their jaws have a razor-sharp edge, and they are very fast."

"You feed them with your fingers?"

"Of course not," she laughs, "I use forceps."

"You have an interesting job."

"It's not only the turtles," she says. "We have such a great team."

"And how big is your team?"

"Actually, it's just the two of us. You might know Dr. Černý – he is a world authority on turtles. Have you seen his latest book?"

She takes a deep breath and a dreamy expression crosses her face. "He is handsome, a good dancer, and he knows everything about the arts. He writes poetry, and is a good tennis player."

"Is he married?" Michal asks cautiously.

"Unfortunately," she says in a hard cracking voice. "He considered divorce some time ago, but his wife wouldn't let him go."

"Can you two at least travel together?"

"We never do. One of us has to feed the turtles," she smiles. The turtles are her fate and her curse.

After three hours, Michal and the lady are chattering like two old friends. Michal is getting a feeling that her affair with her boss has reached a dead end, and she is on a hunt for another man. He needs to shake her off.

He pulls out his wallet with the pictures of his children. "These three are from my first marriage, and this is Lenka. I adopted her recently. I pay so much alimony that, without my wife's income, I'd live on bread and water."

That would deter any other woman but the turtle lady is unshakable. "Lovely, cute kids! You don't have a picture of your wife, do you?"

"Sorry, I don't," Michal lies. That picture is too sacred to share.

He turns toward the window and watches the passing grey countryside, the forsaken country ruined by communists, the country he has decided to leave. His face shows no emotions, yet he is burning with love. It's only six months since he married Danna, and he knows that, somewhere across the ocean, she is thinking about him. What a difference, he muses, from the miserable existence of Dr. Černý and this lady, who is spending her life with turtles because she loves him.

After several brief stops, the bus crosses the Hungarian border and then, late in the night, from Hungary to Yugoslavia. Soldiers in strange uniforms run around the bus and shout in a language, which Michal does not understand. The tour guide collects passports, the guard checks them, and the bus takes off into a country with a different, spicier smell.

Michal can relax again. This is a routine border crossing within the Communist Block, he is thinking, but if the police in Prague noticed his disappearance, they could notify the Hungarian border guard and pull me out.

The night is tiring and long. Passengers compressed in narrow seats sleep in contorted positions, trying to maintain an illusion of privacy. Michal attempts to sleep, but keeps waking into the warm summer night. The bus rolls through a dark moonless country.

With first light, one by one, people wake sweaty and exhausted. To beat the foul taste in his mouth, Michal pulls an apple from his bag. His eyes are dry. The bus windows have been open all night, and the warm air is blasting his face.

Outside, he sees mountains covered with small hills peppered with mounds of rock, and all this passing by like giant green waves covered with thorn bushes. There must be a lot of vipers, he thinks. Crossing the border in mountains like this would be deadly.

"A strange landscape," turtle lady says. "Now I understand why Germans never defeated Yugoslavia."

"Everybody hates Germans," she adds after a while.

"Not all Germans are bad, my wife is half German," Michal says quietly.

If there is anything he is eagerly awaiting, it is the sea, the surprise of its colour, the salt in the air, the mysterious, ever-changing sea. He looks around the bus. Everybody is unkempt, but the tour guide looks downright funny with her glasses tilted to one side.

At noon, the bus finally stops in front of a small hotel, and Michal staggers out into a lazy, holiday atmosphere. He has never been this far south – the sun is directly above his head and objects cast no shadows. The rush and nervousness have ceased – even the group of Czechs ready to board the bus home seem insignificant. The two-story hotel, able to accommodate a busload of tourists, stands in silence and the sea is whispering. A long island shelters the bay and, on the other side, above the village rooftops, is a chain of mountains: green at the bottom, abruptly changing into grey fields of loose rock, and above them teeth of white cliffs reaching for blue sky without a single cloud.

A gentle breeze moves red-and-white tablecloths in the dining area under majestic chestnut trees, and the sound of dishes being washed and stacked filters from the building. Everything else in sight is pure white and reflects the sun's glare with unforgiving forcefulness.

He turns his head toward the commotion by the bus, and hears the voice of the tour guide.

"All men travelling alone will stay in room ten, all women in room two. Bělička and Zrzavý families will stay in room three …"

Instinctively, Michal grabs his luggage, hurries across the garden, and takes the wide staircase two steps at a time. He finds door ten and pushes it open. The evenly spaced rows of beds give the impression of an old hospital or army barracks. He hesitates for a second, throws his luggage onto a bed near one of the window, leans against the wall, and looks outside. He does not want to leave the room until the other men arrive, and territories are established.

The street below the window is so narrow it seems to him that if he stretched his arm, he could touch the roof across the street. Several backyards over, a donkey is braying laboriously. A fly crawls over the window frame and small patches of grass grow between the fieldstones, which pave the tiny street.

What should I try first, he is thinking – the airport or the Italian consulate? I must let Danna know that I am here. How could I call Canada without being noticed?

One by one, other men arrive and follow the same pattern. After a moment of hesitation, they throw their suitcases onto an empty cot, and either join Michal at the window, or sit down on their beds.

"Here we are," one of them says.

Michal is not sure what it is about them, but the last two men appear different. He glances at them without making eye contact. Something in their faces or in the way they walk?

And I thought it could be the turtle lady, he chides himself. If they search my luggage when I am not here, they won't find anything, he assures himself. But I must not talk in my sleep, and that is hard to prevent.

> *"The world is a large, smooth sphere,*
> *round thus never ending"*
> (Prologue to 1960's Czech spy movie "Skid")

2. MICHAL MEETS DANNA

Major upheavals, both on personal and political level, often begin inconspicuously – as a brief eye contact, accidental touch, or a few words with irreversible consequences. Michal's adventure which changed not only his life but his entire being, began on May 14, 1968, when the Prague radio news was generally positive – no threats or no imminent wars in this part of the world.

By seven a.m., still half asleep, Michal was clinging to a leather loop suspended from the ceiling of a crowded tram. He was not thinking of love or of the mountains it can move. His brain was not in gear yet. He watched his hands grasping the leather, and how similar they were to the hands of his father.

Except for his curious, insatiable eyes, Michal blended well with the morning crowd. For several years, his exercise had consisted mostly of lugging groceries, children, baby carriages, and wet laundry baskets, but he still could sprint after a streetcar he had just missed, and catch it at the next stop. He liked to be tidy and clean, and his clothes were always comfortable and practical. His short, brown hair, grey slacks, and blue-checkered shirt contributed to his inconspicuous appearance.

When he stepped out at Charles Square, the warm sunshine brought him out of his daydreaming. The pale-blue sky and the blooming forsythia and lilacs contrasted with the gloomy architecture of the Ministry of Mines. Michal did not work for this horribly bureaucratic ministry, but for the Research Institute of Mining located in the same black-marble building. It looked like a tomb, with cracks and stains of dog urine along the bottom of its walls.

The main entrance was the only part of the building that still maintained the illusion of majesty from the pre-communist times. It led to a grandiose staircase built for diplomats and foreign visitors, with red carpet, brass railings, and a crystal chandelier. At that door, he met Danna.

"What are you doing here?" she asked.

"What are *you* doing here? I have been working here for two years!"

"I'm starting today."

A voice interrupted them. "You two know each other?"

They turned and saw Michal's boss, Radim.

Radim's gentle, brown eyes eclipsed his physical appearance – short legs under a suit hanging loose on his frame, long nose, large ears, and scrubby black hair.

"We keep bumping into each other in odd places," Michal said smiling, and a view of the Vltava River flashed before his eyes. How old was I, he thought, twenty? He saw the landscape deserted before winter and yellow leaves floating on the river – everything so quiet that he could hear the leaves rubbing against the bottom of his boat. Like a ghost, Danna emerges from the mist, her hair dripping with water. She lifts her hand in a silent greeting and, after a few powerful strokes, her kayak glides out of sight.

He looked at her now. The same determined smile.

Something has changed, he wondered and looked at her again. The same shoulders and the bearing of a gymnast, the tanned face, a few early wrinkles around her eyes as if she lived in mountains. Her black curly hair is short, but she is not a tomboy. She is not tall but has an exquisitely feminine figure with full firm breasts, narrow waist, and muscles playing under the dark-blue skirt. She wears a plain white blouse, no lipstick, her ears not even pierced – as if she understood that adding any ornaments would cause a sensory overload. But what makes her so different now? The radiating glow of her face!

"Radim, was it you who hired Danna?" he said.

Radim answered in his staccato Ostrava accent. "Yes, but she still does not know how odd this place is – at least for electrical engineers and programmers."

Danna watched Radim and Michal – they acted like good old friends, not as a boss and his subordinate.

"His father taught me philosophy and formal logic in high school, and he . . ." she pointed to Michal with a grimace, "he taught me math at the university. And here I am ready to work in mining."

She turned to Michal. "Do you still have that little sailboat?"

Already in her engineering class when always surrounded by boys, she had developed a friendly, matter-of-fact way of dealing with men without sexual undertones.

"I sold it. With three kids, I have no time for sailing …"

"I thought you only have one daughter."

"We had twins last year. …" He glanced at Danna's hand. "And you are married? "

"Ivan from the calculus class your taught is my husband, and our Lenka is almost two."

Radim gazed at Danna and Michal, both radiating energy, confidence, and youth.

"Let's go in," he said. "We'll miss the eight o'clock meeting."

During the coffee break, Michal slipped out to check the nearby grocery store. It was the Prague Spring, and the newspapers wrote about building the new *communism with the human face*. Czechs were free to travel, but basic groceries were still hard to get. Whenever the delivery truck arrived, a line would form – for oranges, apples, liver, pork or whatever came in. That morning though, no truck was parked at the store and, inside, clerks idled by empty shelves.

While waiting for the light to change at the crosswalk, Michal found himself standing beside Victor. Unable to resist the opportunity to surprise the old friend, Michal nudged him with his elbow. "What's new?"

But it was Victor who had astonishing news. "I am leaving for Canada tomorrow."

"How have you managed that?"

"A one-year fellowship," Victor smiled as if he had outwitted not only Michal but the entire world. He winked, and said in a low voice ". . . and it could be forever – my wife is going with me."

"Listen, you have to tell me more," Michal pleaded.

The light had long changed from red to green. "Idiots, you are blocking traffic," a man with beer on his breath said, trying to navigate the crossing.

"Write to the National Research Council, Ottawa, Canada," Victor said, striding away.

"Wait! What's the full address?"

"That is the full address!" Victor shouted over the stream of pedestrians that already separated them.

That evening, Michal typed the letter and dropped it into the mailbox without expecting much to happen.

> *"Peace is neither booty nor a gift."*
> (V. Nezval)

3. SOVIET INVASION

In August of that year, three curious things happened. First, the mailman brought a long blue envelope bearing the logo of the National Research Council. The envelope had something exotic about it – perhaps the soft touch of the paper or the smell of its glue, Michal stared at it for several seconds before cutting it open.

It contained an application form, a glossy brochure packed with openings in every possible field, and a letter asking for a resume, diploma, and a list of publications. Excited, Michal filled in the form, copied the documents, and sent it by registered mail the next morning.

"Can't you do something more useful?" his wife Zora said while cooking dinner. "How many of these letters have you mailed, and nobody ever answers?"

Under her apron, she wore a fashionable dress and sophisticated makeup. She was a professional photographer, and did not compromise on her appearance even while housebound since the twins were born. Since Michal worked in mining, his salary could support the young family comfortably.

Three days later, in an evening course Michal was taking to improve his English, he discovered a children's rhyme which, in some deeper way, expressed his inner turmoil – Zora and he gradually but unstoppably losing each other, while on the surface everything running as usual and the clock ticking. *Engine, engine number nine, going down Chicago line. If the train falls off the track, do I get my money back?*

On August 21, the telephone rang in the middle of the night. The phone was in the hall of their prefabricated apartment, and the ring volume had been set to carry over the household noise during the day. At night, the bedroom door was open, and the racket startled Michal out of his sleep.

Zora looked at the clock on her night table and covered her head with a pillow. "Whoever's calling, tell him to go to hell. He'll wake the children."

Michal staggered to the phone and lifted the receiver. "We have been invaded," a raspy male voice said. "The Soviet Army is in Prague."

"That's a stupid joke, especially at this time of the night," Michal said ready to hang up. "How could they get here so quickly?"

"Open the window and listen!"

Michal left the receiver dangling from the wall, went to the kitchen, and opened the window: A dark, warm night and a distant roar of tank engines – now and then a steel belt scratching the pavement. He returned to the phone, but all he heard was the dial tone.

Three steps to the bedroom, and he turned the radio on.

"Calling for help! Calling the entire world! Without provocation, we have been brutally invaded." Then sound of machine-gun fire.

"What are we going to do?" Zora sat up in the bed.

Michal watched her for a second, thinking how vulnerable she looked in her lacy pink sleeveless nightgown – a lock of hair across her face, the fashionable slim blonde she always wanted to be, even in the middle of night. Her eyes projected fear. She sat, staring forward, and unable to decide what to do.

Tanks are roaming the city, Michal thought, and our one-year-old twins and four-year-old Rita are peacefully sleeping in the next room.

He remembered WWII – air raids, deafening barrage of cannons, bullets ringing on the cobblestone pavement under his feet. The lesson he had learned was that one has to react quickly.

"This may be a matter of survival," he reflected. "Fill all the pots and the bathtub with water, and count the cash we have in the house. The banks will be closed. I am going to figure out what's happening outside the city."

He went back to the phone. One hour later, when he returned to the bedroom, Zora was asleep. She woke up and propped herself in the bed. "Michal, calm down, it's not so urgent."

"You are too young to remember the war. We may be soon without water. People will storm the stores and, within hours, there will be no food.

"The entire country is quiet except for Prague," he continued. "Get as much sleep as you can. I have to be at the supermarket before it opens."

When the store opened, Michal worked fast. He was lucky. He found powdered milk, rice, pasta, flour, several canned meats, bread, apples and carrots. It was not a matter of choosing, he simply grabbed whatever was there. Other shoppers worked with the same fervor, and the shelves were emptying rapidly. Yet it was all orderly, no looting.

At 8:10, Michal called his office.

Radim, answered the phone, and his voice was calm. "Don't come here. The transportation system is a mess, and nobody is working. The few people that showed up are listening to the radio or went to Wenceslaus Square to see the tanks."

It took the entire day to figure out what had happened. A

neighbour said she saw three tanks passing by. Shortly after that, there was the sound of machine-gun fire, and three ambulances sped toward the hospital. Another friend returned from Wenceslaus Square where he saw dozens of tanks. The façade of the National Museum was full of bullet marks and many windows were broken, yet nobody seemed to be hurt. The radio did not report any wounded, but stopped transmitting for several hours. Then the broadcast continued from a different location.

How the tanks had gotten to Prague was at first a mystery, but then the radio explained that Soviets had flown them in. Every night, the Prague Airport closed between midnight and six in the morning. The guards placed barbed wire barricades across runways, and turned off all position and navigation lights, but on the day of the invasion, at two in the morning, the Soviets dropped paratroopers who took over the control tower, removed the barricades, and activated the lights. After that, transport planes loaded with tanks began to roll in. At dawn, the artillery was already set at strategic points around the city, and the Red Army was pouring into the streets of Prague.

The Czech Army offered no resistance. The Soviet government claimed it sent the tanks to counter an anti-Communist takeover. Everybody knew that was a lie, but any resistance would have helped the Soviets to justify the invasion. People crowded along the sidewalks and shouted at the Soviets, in Russian: "Go home, we are your friends, not enemies!" For twenty years, the Russian language had been taught in Czech schools and the younger generation spoke better Russian than the boyish crews on the tanks. These troops from Siberia knew nothing about the political situation in Europe. They were told this was a training exercise. They had fear in their eyes and commanders with cocked pistols at their backs.

In the general confusion, accidents happened. Tanks flattened cars left in their way or because the steel belts slipped on the cobblestone pavement. In one or two cases, people were inside the car. Some pedestrians fell under the tanks some, were shot accidentally. One student doused his clothes with gasoline and set himself on fire as a protest against the invasion.

Michal only heard about these horrific events, but he witnessed how people tried to climb the tanks and soldiers fired in the air and at the adjacent buildings. He instinctively ran for cover at the entrance of the nearest house.

In a small, quiet street, a Soviet soldier approached a Czech girl. She tried to run away, but after a short chase the soldier grabbed her by the shoulder and produced a crumpled envelope. "For God's sake, please, mail this to my parents," he said in Russian.

She stopped shaking and stuffed the envelope into her handbag before anybody could see it. Not sure what to do with it, she brought it to Zora and Michal. The three opened the envelope and cold sweat ran down their backs.

Dear Mom and Dad!

My heart is breaking, but I may never see you again. We have been sent to Prague and, most likely, we will not return to our normal base. If you receive a letter that I have died on duty do not believe it! Most likely, we will be transferred to a special camp, so that the public never learns what really happened here. You know how this works: Our country is big, and a few people or the entire battalion can easily vanish. I miss you, and I love you.

Forever, your Vasia.

Michal posted the letter but was most doubtful that it would ever reach the parents.

At the Ministry of Mines, a Soviet sentry came to confiscate the few rifles that People's Militia kept in the stockroom. As the sentry passed through the reception area, a noisy old refrigerator kicked on. Instinctively, a short stocky soldier grabbed his submachine gun and fired through the appliance. Nobody was hurt except for two bottles of vodka the secretary kept for foreign dignitaries.

The Soviets tried to take over the Prague radio station. With tanks all over the city and no resistance, this seemed like a trivial task, but with short interruptions the Czech broadcast continued calling for help in English, German, and Czech.

When Michal called the office the following day, Radim told him that the Austrian Embassy was giving visas to anybody who would come. "Most people from our office have already gone there," he added.

Zora frowned. "I am not going anywhere."

"Nobody knows what's going to happen. We may just get the

visa in case we need it. I'll be careful …" Michal was already searching for his and Zora's passports.

He returned six hours later, waving the passports victoriously. "The streetcars are operating, but not on their regular routes. You simply board the next tram, and ask the conductor. The line at the Austrian embassy runs around the entire block, but it moves quickly. Three clerks are giving stamps hastily. Just have the passport open …"

He sat down. "There are huge lines at every gas station. It is clear that the West is not going to help us. Our western allies sold us out to Hitler in Munich, then to Stalin in Yalta, and they are not going to risk a nuclear war for this little country which has no oil and with its uranium deposits depleted by the Soviets."

Zora stared at him with a dirty diaper in one hand and a half-empty nursing bottle in the other.

"I know it's scary, and hard to decide what's best to do," Michal continued. "I saw the exit highway. Streams of cars are leaving westward – cars packed with families and suitcases on the roofs. You can't get on a westbound train. This is a mass exodus … Are you ready to go?"

She shook her head. "The radio reported an accidental fire exchange between the Soviet and Bulgarian troops. Polish and East German armies are crossing the country. Nobody knows what's going on. It's too dangerous to take the children out."

"Borders to Austria and West Germany are completely open," Michal pressed on.

"That may be just a rumour or, perhaps, it was true yesterday but not anymore. What if the Soviets are waiting at the border and shooting everybody who attempts to cross?"

"Another reason why I don't want to go," she continued without looking at Michal, "… is that we almost separated last year. If we run to a foreign country and then we split, what would I do there with three children, you perhaps without a job and no family or friends to help? "

"You know what will happen after the dust settles, it will be similar to what happened after 1948. We will never travel to the

West. All of us, including you and me, will be called to an interrogation where we will have to prove that we did not support Dubcek. And if we fail, we will lose our jobs, and will be sent to coal or uranium mines. Do you want our children to be brainwashed at school, to be raised as dedicated communists? Do you want to live again in the fear that, for no reason, the police may kick out down door and drag us to jail?"

"At least, we must get out of the city before a war breaks out," he continued when he saw that she was not responding. "We booked a vacation on a farm … Perhaps we can start sooner."

"Can we take my mother?" Zora revived and sat down onto a chair. "We can't call the farm. Long-distance lines are down."

"Call your mother, and get everything ready. I will drive to the farm, and check whether the roads are clear." Now or never, Michal thought. Emotions aside, we have to get out of here.

He took the car to an abandoned field at the edge of the housing development, and practised bailing out of the car door about a dozen times, as he had seen it in movies. He jerked the door open and rolled out shoulder first into the ditch. Soviet tanks took up the full width of the road, and he wanted to be ready in case he would meet a tank, head-on, or would he run into gunfire.

Gas pumps allowed each driver only ten litres, so Michal suffered through four long lines to get enough fuel. Early next morning, he fastened his seat belt, and took off with a sense of adventure. By avoiding major arteries and busy crossings, he reached a Soviet checkpoint safely before leaving town. An ominous display of tanks and army vehicles massed ahead on the hilltop, and a line of cars waited for clearance.

Several patriots waving Czechoslovakian flags ran along the line advising drivers that the Soviets would confiscate guns, radios, and cameras. Some of them offered to store such items until their owners would return to the city. For those leaving permanently, they smuggled the articles around the checkpoint free of charge. After a short conversation with one of them, Michal decided that he could trust them, but had no such articles with him.

The Soviet soldier who stopped Michal's car two hundred yards later was clean cut and all business. Michal answered in Russian but the soldier still frowned from under his cap.

"Open the trunk, please! Lift the back seats! Do you have any guns?" He searched under the seats, and looked into the glove compartment. "You don't have any luggage?"

In a minute, Michal was free to go. Ahead, as far as he could see, was the lush summer countryside flooded in sun, and no signs of war. At the first intersection, someone had removed every road sign, and replaced them by a single big arrow pointing toward the East. It read "Moscow 2000km."

Good joke, Michal thought at first but he soon got lost. He had no map, and his memory of the route was not as good as he had thought. Frustrated, he returned to the intersection, took new bearings, but got lost twice more before he reached the farm.

The little whitewashed farmhouse sat at the edge of the village, with only a strip of grass separating it from the Sazava River. Village children splashed above the wooden weir, and the stone mill across the river appeared distant. A row of old willows offered cool shade and fields of wildflowers stretched as far as he could see.

He thought of his little Rita and her dark wise eyes, how they will collect berries and pebbles together. He imagined himself beside her in the tall grass, watching the clouds changing shapes.

When he opened the farm gate, a goat looked inquisitively from the shed, and chickens announced his arrival. The old farmer greeted him with a smile. "All other people cancelled their reservations, and with a young strong man like you, we'll feel safer in this time of war. Bring your family as soon as you can." The farmer's wife dried her hands in her blue apron, and brought them big mugs of coffee and a fresh pie.

4. UNDER A TANK GUN

Michal stuffed all he could into his small Škoda car: Rita sitting between him and Zora who had Filip on her lap. Zora's mother held Líza on the rear seat, surrounded by diapers, baby food, toys and clothes. On the roof, they tied two cribs and a roll of blankets. The car windows displayed various items Zora and her mother fetched at the last minute.

After closing the last door, Michal turned back to his mother-in-law, Mrs. Fürst: "Mom, if you and Zora were not as slim, we'd never fit into this car."

Not even a faint smile, he thought, she is not fifty yet and such a stern face, always working even on weekends, her hair with a touch of grey tied into a little bundle.

Over the eleven years Michal had known her, he learned she did not know much about science or fine arts but, even under the communist system, she knew how to make money and then get services and commodities completely unavailable to other people. She was a manager of a large government-owned restaurant, and she worked there seven days a week, including nights when she tended the bar. Zora grew up with her grandparents far from Prague, and joined her divorced mother as a teenager when the grandparents became old and ill.

The mother was practical and efficient, and was equally hard on herself as on those around her. She never explained how she did it, but in spite of surprise inspections and audits, she regularly supplied Zora and Michal with bags of restaurant meals or prime cuts of meat. *'If you don't steal at work, you rob your own family'* was the popular saying of the time, and though Michal did not like it, only a fool would have objected, especially to his mother-in-law.

Zora's mother used to be proud of Michal, but since she had noticed the signs of marital problems, she had distanced herself from him. Aware of her presence behind his back, Michal concentrated on driving, constantly checking for possible danger from different directions.

They were already on a peaceful highway out in the country when Michal had to slow down: A column of soviet tanks, as wide as the road, was travelling ahead – in the same direction as they were heading. No imminent danger, he thought at first, but then he looked in the rear view mirror and saw a tank hanging right on his tail!

"How did the tanks get behind us?" he asked, but Zora had no clue. The tank ahead blocked the view, and the tank behind was so close that its gun reached over the car roof. At sixty kilometers per hour, Michal was afraid to touch the brakes. Czechs lined along the road shook fists at him, and a rotten tomato landed on his windshield.

"Zora, please, place pillows against the windows in case stones begin to fly," he muttered without taking his eyes from the tank ahead of him. "They think we are helping the Russians."

At a sharp curve, the tanks slowed down. Michal swerved onto a side road, and waited there until the last tank passed. They reached the farm without further incident, seemingly happy and relaxed, but the tension of an uncertain future remained like an ominous cloud.

Zora began to organize the kitchen, while her mother and the children were petting rabbits and a baby goat in the yard. Michal brought in the last suitcase and put his arm around Zora's shoulders.

"Don't touch me," she shook him away. "I can't stand you!"

"This isn't the time to fight. I still love you."

"To be with you all the time drives me nuts.

"This is the second time you agreed that we won't separate, that we will give it another try, but you are not exactly trying."

"Look in the mirror. It's your face, I hate you."

"You are torturing me. I stopped playing cello because you did not like its sound. I stopped painting after you kicked a hole into my best painting. My parents let us live with them when we had no place to stay, and you never even thanked them. Instead, you declared that your children are not their grandchildren. And then, of course, you flirt with everybody around. What else do you want me to do?"

"The flirting was an innocent fun, I have never been unfaithful."

"You flirted with my best friend and seriously damaged his marriage. That is not at all innocent. It also tells everybody that you don't love me, that you are looking for someone else."

"Maybe I am …"

"For three years, you've been sending me away. You sleep with me in the same bed, but when I reach for your hand, you push me away. I love you and I love the children, but you are stretching my limits." He stood for a few seconds looking for the right word. "Be careful! My love has been steadfast as granite, but even granite – if you hit it with a hammer many times in the right spot – will eventually crack."

A cheap melody poured from the transistor radio. Michal was so angry he could not find words to express his feelings. He grabbed the little black box and smashed it on the floor.

Zora dropped to her knees, collecting the fragments. Tears were running down her face, the speaker still producing a strange gurgling sound. "How typical of you! You always destroy what's dearest to me," she sobbed. "This was my only friend – it played music for me all day, it told me all the news …"

"Sorry. I just grabbed the first thing in sight."

"Go away, get of my sight …"

Zora's mother pretended not to notice anything. Four days later while washing dishes after lunch, she suddenly declared: "The radio says everything's back to normal. You are on vacation, but I must return to work."

What a vacation, Michal thought.

"I'll give you a ride and check in at my office tomorrow morning," he said after a pause.

Rita was watching the conversation. "Daddy, are you going away?" she said with a worried look in her eyes.

"I will be back tomorrow night, but let's go for a walk first. Help me with Liza and Filip."

That meant catching the twins and fastening them in the stroller. He started with Líza, who was as quick as a monkey, but by the time he picked up Filip, she squirmed out from the harness, crawling away and giggling. Rita caught Líza again, and together with Michal, they pushed the stroller onto the field road outside the gate. The troubles instantly faded away.

Michal whistled his favourite melody for the twins, and Rita found a bright-green tree frog with round transparent fingertips and golden eyes. They patted its back – gently with one finger –

before placing it back onto its leaf. They watched swallows swooping by, and munched on wild raspberries that grew along the path. There were no signs of foreign armies, and nobody was angry. It was a perfect summer day with the scent of freshly cut hay.

When they returned, Michal helped Zora's mother into the car, threw his bag into the trunk, and without addressing anybody in particular, uttered "I'll be back tomorrow night," and stepped on the gas pedal.

"I didn't want them to cry," he said after a while.

His mother-in-law stared silently out the side window, and Michal drove thinking how he and Zora, happy and not married yet, had eloped for two weeks of camping without telling their parents about it.

Was I blind then, he thought, or did Zora change so much? And is Filip going to be all right? The previous winter, after three ear infections, his temperature began to rise uncontrollably, and Michal and Zora took him to the hospital.

Filip was placed to the intensive care. His brain was infected and no antibiotics were working. "To be honest," the doctor said, "his chances are fifty-fifty."

"Can we at least see him?" Michal asked.

"Only his mother, and just for five minute. He is in a critical condition, and his immunity is low."

Michal paced the bleak hospital hall. The air, saturated with the smell of disinfectant, was difficult to breathe. A child's screams echoed down the hall. Was that Filip?

Zora returned, devastated. "You should see his translucent face, his red, semiconscious eyes, the tubes connected into his shaved skull." Then something hard flashed through her eyes. "I thought about how I could save him … and I promised to God that if Filip lives, I would sacrifice my love for you."

"Listen, this is *our* child. Together, we have to save him. Why do you set him against me and me against you?" A cold wave ran down his back. "This curse of yours may end up like a Greek tragedy."

She held her face in her hands, and her shoulders convulsed. "I don't want him to die."

Later that night, Michal returned and parked his car across from the dark hospital with one lighted window on the third floor. Was that the room where Filip was fighting for his life? With his eyes closed, Michal kept sending all his energy not only to Filip, but also to all the anonymous children suffering in that hospital. If only a small part of this love could reach Filip, he thought, it may pull him over the edge.

At daybreak, he woke up with the steering wheel in front of his face. Light snow covered the windshield; someone left a line of footprints along the sidewalk. Michal turned the on the ignition and took a deep breath. At noon, the doctor called: They had found the right drug; Filip would live.

Feeling overwhelmingly grateful, Michal vividly remembered Filip returning from the hospital, smiling and clutching his stuffed squirrel in his arms.

"Drop me off at the next corner," his mother-in-law interrupted his daydreaming. "I expect you for dinner tonight."

"Thank you," Michal said, Filip's pale face still on his mind.

> *"All above, and all below*
> *if you understand, you will be happy."*
> (old witchcraft)

5. MARRIAGES BREAKING DOWN.

What happened next burned deeply into Michal's memory, but like everybody else, he did not talk much about it. The Soviet Army began to withdraw to their camouflaged camps, and tanks vanished from the streets. Soviet-controlled media talked about the process of normalization and everybody knew what it meant – the country had been defeated.

Michal's attention turned inward, trying to understand what had happened to him. The cornerstone of his existence – his marriage – was in ruins. When he arrived at the office, he found Radim sitting with his feet on the desk, reading a newspaper.

"I am still on vacation, but I wonder what's happening here," Michal said. "I also want to look again at the program that crashed last week."

"Most people are still at home, without taking a leave of absence. Those few that show up, don't work. They gossip, listen to the radio or read books."

Radim and Michal shared a small room where their desks had been pushed together, facing each other. They were constantly aware of what the other one was doing, of his every move, expression of his face and changes of mood. Two swivel chairs, a small file cabinet, and a drawing board in the corner completely filled the remaining space. A large apartment-style window provided plenty of light and, in summer, plenty of fresh air when it was fully opened.

The grey cloudy day outside reflected the mood inside the office when Michal entered. He dropped his bag on the floor, sat down, and stretched his legs under the table.

"If everybody stops working, the country will grind to a halt."

"Our research has no immediate impact but if factories and farms stop – that would be a disaster . . ."

The phone rang and Radim lifted the receiver. "You want to paint the kitchen? Now when we still have tanks around the city? And the bathtub tap is broken? Can't you get a plumber to fix it?"

Michal understood. Radim was talking to his ex-wife. Radim's face turned pink and then red as he listened to a lengthy explanation. Finally, he took a deep breath and said meekly "All right, I'll be there tomorrow."

He hung up, and they both sat quietly for a long time.

"I have not told this to anybody else," Michal broke the silence. "Zora doesn't love me anymore. I still can't believe it. And whose fault is it anyway?"

"I've asked myself the same question, but I don't know the answer."

Michal leaned across the table. "If we had no children, it would be so simple. I would give her anything she wants, and I would start again – perhaps a bit ruffled but free as a bird ... but to abandon the children is like tearing my heart out, an incomprehensible nightmare."

He continued. "I have a feeling that, in spite of our differences, we will stay together until something unexpected happens – something so extraordinary that our lives, our entire existence would be at stake. We both love the children."

Radim shook his head. "I don't know what's going on. Everybody is getting separated or divorced. Friends, neighbours, relatives ... And look at those court battles for money and children!"

As their thoughts ran on, the conversation turned into two independent monologues.

"For marriages which are not absolutely solid, this Soviet takeover can be the last straw; they may collapse into a pile of shards without warning."

"Or is our generation just growing older?" Radim reflected. "In the beginning, all our friends were paired. Since one couple separated and began to search for new partners, it has been like an avalanche – one marriage collapsing after another.

"Except for a few lucky ones, like Danna," he added.

"Perhaps I am a hopeless romantic," Michal said looking at the floor, "but I believe in a heavenly match – a relationship so firm that no outside forces can disturb it."

"Have you noticed," Radim continued with his theory, "how women change after their first child? Is it the stress of giving birth, the pregnancy, or the new lifestyle? They don't even seem aware of it," he waved his hand; "they are busy with more important things."

Michal grinned. "Playing the devil, it crossed my mind whether it isn't better to marry a woman with a child. She is not going to change. Why does everybody want a virgin?"

"Men change more gradually than women," Radim said pensively. "We dance between family and work, fight for territory and power, compete in sports – but I tell you, the true success is at work. Work also brings the money you need for the family."

Michal played with his eraser, pondering. "Men work more and more, and the more successful you are, the more women like you. But you spend less time with your family, and some invisible ties break down. These minute intangible changes pass unnoticed at first, and later it's too late ..."

"Women really don't need us," Radim maintained with a grim face. "They can earn their living. They can raise children without us. It is not easy, but it can be done. Marriage has become a temporary arrangement."

Michal looked straight into Radim's eyes. "You see, even you with your pragmatic attitude, are a dreamer. We search for true love, the soul mate who can read our mind. Bodies and souls entwined. It does not happen often, but it may happen, and we insist it must happen to us. Like in a lottery or in a gold rush, the chances are slim, but the rewards are out of this world.

"That's what we seek, but very few find love so deep," Michal continued. "Regardless, two people in love, whether married or not, are something so special that the rest of us should tiptoe around them."

"Come down to earth," Radim put his newspaper down. "You should have been a preacher. Remember, you are not even separated yet, and what is ahead for you is not pleasant. I fed children at night, washed all the diapers, cooked half of the meals, stood in grocery lines, and for what? She found a new man, asked for the divorce and, at court, she got the children. We are like drones, just like drones ..."

"But what is the reason?" Michal asked.

"In our society, men and women have the same rights, same pay for the work, and same access to schools. Women have the one-year maternity leave on 75% salary. We have free daycare. We do not pay anything for the doctor, dentist, or hospital. In all that, we are ahead of the West, but we have lost our freedoms. And because mothers and children are revered by both public and the government, we are not equal at the divorce court."

"After all, we are not biologically equal," Michal, said with a grin.

They sat quietly, then Michal returned to where he left off. "One should never play with love; it's a game with fire. I heard people saying *I will not love you if you do this or that*, and it actually happened. I saw entire lives destroyed by someone who introduced two people as an experiment: *Will they fall in love? And what will happen next?"*

Without answering, Radim folded the newspaper, and they turned to their work.

At four, Michal was getting ready to leave for home, one arm already in his coat. "It seems to me," he suddenly said, "that love can reach multiple levels. Except for reading about it, most people cannot comprehend the heights and the depths to which it can take you. Perhaps they experienced something unusual, but was it true love? And even if they think it was, could there be something better?"

"That's a dangerous thought," Radim looked up at Michal with surprise.

> *"Like a coin silently given to a blind man,*
> *my autumn here you come ….*
>
> (K. Toman)

6. TRIP TO POLAND

On October 25, Radim summoned Michal and Danna for a brief meeting and began with a mysterious smile. "Would you like to visit Poland for a few days?"

"I'd love to go," Danna replied instantly. "What would be our assignment?"

Michal just stared at Radim, thinking. What is the catch? Only the higher echelons travel abroad on business.

Radim leaned back in his chair. "Sokolov mine needs a computer, and the ODRA company in Wroclaw announced a new, desk-sized model. It is transistor based, and it resembles the latest IBM model. We would not need hard currency …"

Compared with the Russian vacuum-tube-monstrosity Danna and Michal were using, this sounded like a great leap of technology, but Michal had his doubts. "You want to use a *Polish* computer?" he said hesitantly.

"You two can judge whether it fits our application. From Odra factory in Wroclaw, you'll continue to Katowice. The Mining Institute there has been using the new model for three months and they are willing to share their experience. Michal, the company will reimburse you for the use of your car."

"This means at least three nights away from the kids," Michal said. "Let me talk to Zora."

"And what about you," Radim turned to Danna.

"Ivan's mother offered to take Lenka if we ever need it. I should be able to go."

On October 30, when Michal entered Danna's office ready to take off, the technician asked with a knowing smile: "How many nights are you going to be out there together?"

"Book separate rooms," the secretary looked up from her typewriter. "Don't scrimp on that item!"

"Did Zora and Ivan approve this?" someone else added to the heat. "Or are *they* going together for their own private trip?"

Michal's ears burned, and Danna was incensed.

"Idiots," she whispered to Michal and banged the office door behind them.

They drove in silence, melting away the atmosphere of the office. Brown and green fields decorated the countryside and the scent of freshly plowed soil lingered in the air. The intoxicating, pale blue sky reminded Michal of distant places. "On days like this," he said, "I believe that if I stood on a hill with my arms stretched out, I could fly."

"I'd like to see just that." Danna covered her mouth to hide her smile.

"You should see our Rita," Michal said after a while. "She called her babysitter an ugly old witch. The poor lady thought that we had set Rita against her and did not come to babysit for several days."

"Our Lenka did something similar," Danna said. "She locked her babysitter in our bathroom, and dropped the key into the babysitter's handbag where nobody expected it to be. She peed her pants, and when I arrived home, she was standing in a big puddle, saying repeatedly: 'Oh my Lord, oh my Lord!' That was exactly what the baby-sitter was saying behind the locked bathroom door."

"Listen," she looked at the dashboard. "Are we going to get gas before we reach the border? Is your gauge broken?"

It read EMPTY.

"Let's hope we'll make it to the top of the next hill," Michal said. The engine sputtered but then returned to its regular hum. They reached the summit and a view of a magnificent tableau of fields opened, with only one building – a gas pump at the bottom of the hill. The engine gave its last kick, Michal shifted into neutral, and the car rolled silently down the hill until it stopped some thirty meters from the gas station. They jumped out and pushed the car to the pump. "Hurray, we've made it."

They departed with their adrenaline still rushing. Michal turned on the radio and a fast samba filled the car. Danna tapped the floor with her foot: "Do you like dancing?"

"I do. Why?"

She looked at him. "I love dancing."

"But I'm hungry now. Should I stop at a restaurant?"

"Don't bother," she reached into her bag. "Do you want a cheese sandwich or a ham sandwich?"

"The cheese one, please, but I didn't expect this kind of treatment."

"I always take extra food with me."

The radio switched to another tune. "I don't like rock-and-roll," she said. "It's primitive and vulgar."

"It's popular, but I don't like it either," Michal glanced at her. "When I dance with a girl, she is my partner. I can't flip her around like a sack of potatoes. "

The road ascended into mountains and when they reached the Polish border, it was already getting dark. Grey clouds covered the sky and a cold, persistent drizzle made the road slick. The road continued through a strange countryside, pitch black with hostile empty roads and foreign traffic signs. Danna stopped talking, and stared into the darkness.

"Could you stop somewhere, please?" she said after a while. "I have to go to the washroom."

Like two long fingers, the headlights of the car followed the wet road and bare grey fields. "I haven't seen a restaurant or a village for a long time," Michal said. "Not even a bush or a clump of trees to hide, but I will find you something."

He drove kilometer after kilometer, through the same scenery, dark ditches full of water. And then he forgot.

"Stop now, you sadist!" she shouted in despair.

The car screeched to a halt. Danna jumped out, ran across the ditch and out into the field. Michal headed in the opposite direction. It was so dark that, except for the headlights, he barely could see the car across the road.

She returned giggling and laughing. "Did I scare you at least?"

"Yes, you did. I'm sorry."

"That field served me better than a stinky public restroom. But I will mess up your car," she said, trying to clean the mud from her hiking boots.

"Don't worry about the car. Get in. It's pouring!"

They reached Wroclaw by ten o'clock, found the hotel, and sleepily checked in. As they turned toward the main staircase, a Dixieland band began to play down the hall. Michal felt the rhythm of his steps subconsciously adjusting to the beat, and Danna's eyes lit up.

They stopped. Something intangible bounced between them.

"Perhaps not tonight," he said.

"Yes, when Zora and Ivan are with us," she added.

He looked at his key. "Good night, I am on the third floor."

"And I am on the second. I'll meet you here tomorrow at seven."

7. HAPPY PLACE

Michal and Danna found that the new computer was superb – it was small, fast, and the software included a library with 0/1 linear programming they needed. They discussed the delivery terms, drove to Katowice, and checked into another hotel. The next day, their colleagues in the Mining Institute confirmed that both the hardware and the software worked flawlessly, and they were finished by noon.

"Is there anything interesting around here?" Michal asked one of the engineers. "It is too late to drive back to Prague, and we have the afternoon free."

"This is an ugly industrial town, with no tourist attractions except for old mine shafts. But you must see Wiesołe Miasteczko[2]."

"And what's that?

"A park with sport grounds, a lake, and amusement rides. I like it for its trees and lawns. We don't have many trees in this polluted region."

"Danna, would you like to go," Michal asked.

"Why not?"

Michal parked the car at the edge of the park, and they set out at a brisk pace without thinking about any particular direction. "It feels good to walk after sitting for almost three days," Danna said.

Michal rolled up his sleeves, and took off his boots.

"You look a bit weird," Danna said. "It may look like summer, but the ground is already cold."

"I love to walk barefoot – at least for a while."

"What's your favourite part of the country?"

"South Bohemia around Tabor, with its lakes and marshes where you can wander for days without seeing a soul. I like large bodies of water."

"That's the mosquito hell," Danna said. "I prefer mountains."

---

[2] literally Happy Place, but translates as Fair Grounds.

They walked fast until they were out of breath, then sat on a bench. Danna leaned back and watched the moving clouds.

"Life is full of strange coincidences," she said eventually. "For example, take astrology. What do you think about Hřebačka?"

"He became a celebrity after he predicted the day of the Soviet invasion in a newspaper long before it happened," Michal said while putting on his boots. "And in those days, most people couldn't imagine that Soviets would use force against us.

"I played with astrology for years," he continued. "I even wrote a computer program which did all the calculations, but I could neither prove nor disprove it. It works remarkably well for some people like me, but it completely fails for others. My life always changes when Uranus transits a house cusp in my chart. And for two days before the full moon, I tend to wander at night like a tomcat. I always get my best ideas before the full moon."

From the technical discussions in their office, Danna knew that Michal's weird ideas were often intriguing and deep. She liked his boyish playfulness and curiosity, and she felt he was the most trustful and reliable friend. "This is a strange conversation between two engineers," she said, picked up a dandelion puffball, and examined it from different sides. "What is the house cusp?"

"A house cusp is one of the twelve angles related to the hour of birth. When Uranus moved through my twelfth house, I lived like an artist. I painted everywhere I went – at home, on the streets, in dancing halls, at university lectures. When it was moving through my first house, I married Zora, stopped painting, and began to teach math. And now, it's in my second house. I got the job in mining and my salary doubled. The second house represents money."

"This doesn't sound very scientific. When do you expect the next change to happen?" she grinned.

"In a year and a half," he said after a few seconds thinking. "I also exchanged several letters with Hřebačka, who offered to analyze my chart. Do you know that he is also an engineer?"

"And what was his prediction?"

"He wrote that I will achieve professional recognition and

honours, but will be in danger of imprisonment."

"And when?"

"He did not say, and I burned his letter. I don't want to think about it."

"I've heard bizarre stories about your painting," she said after another while.

"I know. Someone saw me on the street painting at night. It was pouring. I held a flashlight in my teeth, and the raindrops were mixing with my oil paints. My classmates made fun of me for several years."

Slowly, as the evening descended, the grass turned wet, and the breeze, pleasant and warm until then, strengthened and grew colder.

"Don't you miss your children?" she said.

"I do, and you?"

"I'd like to see what Lenka is doing just now."

"It's Friday. Why are we wasting our time here?" Michal was bursting with energy. "It's only five o'clock. Let's cancel the hotel."

"Imagine how happy Zora and Ivan will be if we arrive earlier, but how long would it take?"

"Eight hours if there is no fog. Let's go!"

8. ONE BLANKET

They returned to the hotel, checked out and, on leaving, Dana noticed a bottle of Cinzano wine in the shop window adjacent to the hotel. In Prague, one could purchase that hot item only in western currency. Happy they found such a good gift, they quickly bought two bottles and immediately took off.

As the red disc of the sun slipped under the horizon, a crimson curtain with glowing columns of yellow began to rise. With awe, they watched the fascinating spectacle.

They passed cemeteries lit with thousands of candles – entire hills that looked like intricate jewels. Hundreds of people prayed in each cemetery, their silhouettes and black crosses against the red sky.

"I wonder," Michal said, "is there something to celebrate?"

"It is the first of November, the All Saints Day, the Night of Dead," she whispered.

It's about death, Michal thought, but not entirely sad – only a mystery of time. A full moon rose, and its milky light flooded the valley. Michal turned the headlights off.

"Isn't this against driving regulations," Danna said.

"Just for a minute," Michal said. He could see clearly, as if it were day.

The road lined with silver trees reflected the moon and a metallic haze shivered in the sky.

"This is a magic night," Danna said. "It feels like a dream."

Michal turned the lights back on. The road ascended into the hills, deeper and deeper into a white mist. Grey ghostly villages came into view and vanished again. After a busy day, both Danna and Michal were exhausted. Except for a shabby pub with a flickering light, no hotels or restaurants remained open that late at night. Danna fell asleep, and her chin bobbed up and down as the car hit potholes.

Michal stopped beside the road, and gently reclined her seat. She mumbled something in her sleep, smiled, rolled into a blanket Michal gave her, and fell asleep again. Her feet protruded beside the gearshift. She had taken her winter boots off, and her socks reeked. One of the socks had a hole showing a toe. Michal kept glancing at the socks as he drove on. Not exactly feet of a respectable young lady, he chuckled.

His attention returned to the road. He was tired, but a warm feeling that he was taking good care of this young mother helped him guide the car through the treacherous night. But then he hit his limit. First he realized that he was weaving like a drunk, then he caught himself driving along the left side of the road. Finally, his tired brain began to create phantoms. He saw them walking along the road, but when he reached the spot nobody was there. He stopped and tapped Danna on her shoulder: "I'm sorry. I need a nap."

The frost-covered car stood at a deserted fork in the middle of nowhere. They both had winter coats, but only one blanket – an embarrassing situation. Would it be proper to sleep under the same blanket? He did not dare to ask.

"It's not a big deal," she said as if she knew his thought. "If we turn back to back, we can share the blanket." They reclined both seats, turning the car into a double bed, and covered themselves with the blanket, sweaters, towels, and anything they found. In seconds, they were asleep and they slept like logs.

Two hours later, they woke chilled through. The car seemed to levitate in a white mist. Michal got out of the car, but was not sure where the sun was rising and where the pavement ended. The light had saturated the air and reflected in all directions. His teeth began to chatter.

Danna also crawled out, her joints cracking loudly. She rubbed her hands, and began to jump around the car like a stiff little bear.

Michal turned the ignition, and the car began to breathe warmth. Danna joined him, and they made it to Prague before the city woke up.

Michal dropped her off at her door.

"Good night, I mean, good morning," she laughed, and waved at him with the bottle of Cinzano. With a smile, Michal answered by raising the bottle he was bringing for Zora.

On Monday, the technician teased them again: "And where did you say you spent the last night? And did you stop in Paris?"

When others laughed, Michal and Danna shrugged their shoulders. They looked at each other and smiled.

9. PETR AND HIS PIPE

Business frequently took Danna to Ostrava, a dirty industrial town reminiscent more of a conglomerate of rusty pipes than a settlement inhabited by people. In winter, even the snow was black and the rooms of the best hotel where Danna usually stayed had a rather unusual view – she never figured out whether the psychedelic metal structure was a chemical factory, a coke plant, or an industrial scrap yard on the bizarre background of steep hills of mine tailings.

Over the centuries, countless mines and steel mills had taken over the entire district, and the Prague Institute had a sizable branch there. The coal of that region, both on the Czech and the Polish side of the border, had the superior quality needed in steel manufacturing, but the obsolete mines were notorious for leaks of methane and frequent explosions. Danna coordinated a project monitoring the mine gases and tracking the personnel within the underground shafts and tunnels. With the seams of coal a mere three feet tall, miners often worked horizontally, flat on the ground. surrounded by running water and falling rocks. No women worked in the mine but Danna had been through such places a number of times.

A few weeks after the trip to Poland, Michal noticed that Petr, one of her Ostrava colleagues, began to show up at the Prague office rather frequently. Petr was a mysterious character. A black beard covered most of his yellowish face, and deep-set eyes made him distant and sad-looking. Michal did not like him from the first day they met.

Petr smoked a pipe incessantly, taking it out of his teeth only for rare moments. When he spoke, he spat short ironic sentences interrupted by long breaks, in which he drew on his pipe. After a few drinks, he relaxed and recited numerous anecdotes, presenting them slowly and without the slightest change in the expression on his face. The aroma of his exotic tobacco lingered around him, leaving a trail of scent as he passed. His fingers trembled and, most of the time, he appeared buried in his thoughts. Two sounds betrayed his presence; the noisy sucking of his pipe and a mouse-like scratching sound when he cleaned it.

When Petr came to a meeting, he and Danna moved as if they performed a complicated dance. Michal could feel the forces that connected them as they moved around the room without looking at each other, in circles and complicated patterns, the field passing through furniture and people and becoming stronger as the distance between them diminished. At every meeting they ended up sitting beside each other. Nobody else seemed to notice.

During one particularly lively discussion, Michal noticed Petr's and Danna's hands on the table, touching by the tips of their small fingers. Their eyes had a glassy look as if they were hypnotized, and when Michal looked across the table, he saw Radim's eyes focused on the two fingers. Could Radim be interested in Danna?, Michal wondered. He is much older than Danna, but he is divorced and she is definitely attractive.

Before leaving the office, Michal asked Radim whether Petr was married.

"Yes, he is," Radim mumbled while rummaging through his papers. "But he must have some problems. Nobody has ever seen his wife."

Michal was shocked. He would have sworn that Danna was happily married, but now it was clear she was not! She would not fool with someone just for fun – that would be completely out of character for her.

> *'I saw a young gypsy girl*
> *With the tread of a fawn.*
> *Her lithe form lived on my mind*
> *All the day long, all the day long."*
> (L. Janacek, The diary of one who disappeared.)

10. DANCING THEIR SOCKS OFF

For January 6, the mining society organized an out-of-town convention.

"On the night of the Three Kings? What a dumb idea!" Michal said when he first heard about it.

He liked to watch neighbourhood kids parading door to door dressed as the Three Wise Men – Kašpar, Melichar, and Baltazar – the general commotion and the boys wishing everybody health and a prosperous year.

"We would have to get up at a ridiculous hour, and the roads will be slippery," he said.

Nevertheless, on January 6, he was waiting at the corner,

watching the bleak dark avenue with the first purple stripes of the still distant morning. The wind blew pellets of frozen dust across the pavement, which rang under his steps as he walked in circles to warm himself up.

The luxury Tatra car arrived with fogged, frozen side windows and everybody was already there: Vlado the company driver, Danna, Petr, and Radim. Michal took the front seat the others had left for him. Danna and Petr probably wanted to sit beside each other and Radim wanted to watch them. Also, the front seat was not the safest place in the vehicle. The short, tanned, and sinewy Vlado used to be a professional car racer.

He was also a womanizer of the highest order, no female who crossed his pass was safe from him. He had affairs everywhere he went, long or short and at any time of the day. The irony was, Michal thought, that Vlado was the only one in that car who seemed to be happily married.

Vlado was shifting smoothly and overtaking other vehicles. The sleepy passengers spoke little. Ahead of them, near the East German border, was the mountain town Jachymov with its uranium and silver deposits, ski resorts, and health spas.

They finally got there, and the convention hotel squatted in the snowdrift below the highway. Fresh, untouched snow covered everything in sight including an abandoned bandstand. Michal imagined the blare of the brass band, and streams of relaxed guests rounding the promenade under the summer sky. Now, the entire spa appeared deserted and small. The usual convention sign either was either nonexistent or covered by snow.

Vlado separated from the group at the reception desk. Nobody had noticed where he had found the young waitress in a black velvet dress and short white-laced apron. Holding her around the waist, he was whispering in her ear.

After a brief search, Radim and Michal found the conference hall which was still empty. The antique ballroom with crystal chandeliers and walls of ornamental mirrors had the air of past glory. "It smells like an old attic in here," Danna said, entering behind them.

Rows of hard, black chairs lined the parquet floor. On one of them, Michal suffered all day listening to inane papers while repeatedly falling asleep. It seemed that the world's most mediocre minds had converged at this place to thrash old, useless ideas to death. In Russian, German, and Czech, the speakers confused facts with complicated theories that nobody could untangle. After the morning ride in the cold car, Michal was hypnotized by the monotonous voices, and had to use all his willpower to keep his eyes open

When the last speaker finally finished, it was already dark outside. Another foot and a half of snow had fallen. Like little kids, everyone pitched snowballs. Radim rubbed his red hands and looked at the sky. "It's certain we won't be back before midnight. Why don't we have dinner here?"

"There is a dance in the town hall," Vlado said, as he reappeared.

"Where have you been all day?" Radim asked.

"You have to allow some fun for the poor driver," Vlado faked a humble face. "I am not allowed to drink … What else could I do?"

Roads and sidewalks disappeared under the snow, only narrow trails crisscrossed the town from one door to another. Radim took one of these trails up the hill and, in a line, others followed behind him.

Michal wondered what he was doing in that snow in a jacket and a tie. I'd rather have my parka and a pair of good mittens, he thought. At least I have good winter boots.

With his hands buried in his pockets, he bent to enter the low door of the pub. The room was charged with energy and voices. Dense cigarette smoke formed clouds along the black wooden beams of the ceiling. Michal took off his foggy glasses and ran his finger over the grain of the pine table they found.

The waitress had no menus: "Sorry, guys, we don't serve hot meals, but the wine is excellent and you can have some appetizers."

"Cod liver on rye with raw onions for everybody," ordered Radim. "I haven't had that for years. And two bottles of Three Gracias. Petr, do you remember? That's the smooth Slovakian wine."

"Have you heard the one about the Russians in the zoo?" Petr began.

Everybody around the table added a few anecdotes, but after several rounds only Petr and Michal continued, trying to outdo each other with a better tale.

The audience was rolling with laughter, but Radim watched Petr and Michal intensely.

After countless jokes, Petr gave up, and sat silently with his eyes down, sucking on his pipe. Michal felt dizzy, and the bottles were empty.

The waitress returning from the cellar left the door open, and the sound of the live band playing filled the room. "Who'd like to dance a bit?" Vlado said.

"I don't know, it's getting late," Danna reflected.

"Zora will be worried," Michal said, looking at his watch. "I have to go home."

Radim stood up, holding on the back of his chair. "Nobody is waiting for Petr and me. It's up to you two."

"All right, just for half an hour," Danna said reluctantly.

"Half an hour won't hurt anybody," Michal said, and he led the group down the steep stairs into the cellar. Dim lights suspended from rough-stone walls barely lit the dancers who packed the room tight. Except for the musicians crowded in one corner and a few people squatted on rough little stools along the wall, everybody was dancing.

Petr paid for another bottle of Three Gracias, and asked Danna for a dance. Michal sat with a glass of wine, watching them dancing like two jerking machines. He did not know why, but it irritated him immensely. After three dances he pushed through the crowd to them: "Excuse me, Petr, may I have a dance with Danna?"

From the moment he took Danna into his arms, Michal danced as never before – like a leaf in a breeze, like a dancing flame. They moved as one body, and under the same spell. They danced foxtrots and blues, Viennese waltzes and slow waltzes, tangos, rumbas and cha-chas, polkas and Charlestons. Michal realized that they were making new steps and new dances for each piece of music. "You are a fantastic dancer," he said.

"It's all you," Danna exclaimed. "I've never danced like this before."

They kicked off their boots, and went back to the floor. Soon, Michal's socks had large holes, and the soles of Danna's stockings were completely gone. Nobody else in the cellar seemed to notice.

Petr retired to his pipe. He sat with Radim and drank one glass of wine after another, staring with no particular interest at the mass of moving people.

Now Vlado became impatient. "It's time to go," he called. "Midnight."

"No way, not yet," Danna and Michal shouted from the floor, without missing a beat.

"You said 'half an hour' and you have been dancing for two and half hours."

"It's all your fault, we wanted to go home. Now you have to bear with us."

"All right, until one o'clock. But not a minute more," Radim decided.

For a while, Michal and Danna danced without a word, in a unity of body and mind they had never experienced before. They both had felt that something like that might exist but, until that very moment, it was only an abstract notion like a wish or a dream. Now, suddenly, it was there like a beam of light. Beyond intuition and logic, Michal knew instantly, and with the absolute certainty, that he found his soul mate, his destiny. Oh, Danna, he thought, who would expect that it would be you!

He needed only one additional proof. He danced Danna into the opposite corner. His voice was trembling. "Danna, would you be mad at me if I kissed you?"

In Danna's eyes, he saw thoughts flashing by. "No, I would not," she said slowly.

They united in a long kiss, their eyes open.

All this is possible because we both feel the same thing, Michal felt. Suddenly, the world is different. We are inseparable. I belong to Danna and she belongs to me. It is like a fairy tale.

Back in the car, Danna sat in the front seat, with Michal behind her. Radim curled to sleep at the other end of the long back seat of the luxury car and Petr stayed in Jachymov to catch a morning train directly to Ostrava.

The car quietly cruised through the night. Red and green reflections of the panel lights danced on Vlado's face. Like a machine, his eyes probed the darkness and the road ahead of him. As usual, he drove fast and completely focused.

Radim's eyes were closed, but did he only pretend to be asleep? For the moment, Michal cared little about what Radim might think. In his mind, he was alone with Danna, flying through the winter night.

He placed his hand on her shoulder and stroked the lobe of her ear. Through the gap between the backrest of her seat and the car door, he reached forward and gently touched the side of her chest where the breast started. Without turning her head, her whole body, every inch of her skin was responding: "Yes, it's me. I belong to you. I love you as much as you love me."

> *"Four rivers run, four rivers run,*
> *and a circle around them ..."*
> (V. Nezval: Atlantis)

11. MARRIAGE PROPOSAL

The next day at work was feverish and tense. Radim, Michal, and Danna arrived at eight, exactly on time – not because of the office rules but as a matter of pride. After partying and drinking, they always pretended to be functioning as usual, but this time even their colleagues who did not participate in the convention seemed irritated and running mindlessly around. Radim had already finished his second cup of coffee, and Michal, with his sleeves rolled up, opened the window. "The heating system must be out of control," he declared watching the waves of hot dry air flowing into the minus twelve degrees Celsius outside.

Several times, when lifting eyes from his papers, Michal found himself gazing directly into Radim's eyes. Why is he staring at me?

Is he so foolish as to think that Danna would be interested in a thirty-nine-year old man?

Danna entered the room several times for various reasons: She was looking for a mug she had left there the day before the trip, she wanted to see how Michal filled his expense report, and she asked Radim for a telephone number in Ostrava. Once she stopped behind Michal, reading a program listing over his shoulder. She never used any perfume but had an air of freshness about her.

Her physical proximity overwhelmed Michal's senses. He could think of nothing but her. He sensed the shape of her body behind his back. His hands trembled and his eyes scanned the paper but the characters blurred as his mind raced in circles. "It still isn't working, is it?" she said, but noticed Radim was watching her, and left without waiting for the answer.

Before Michal joined the Institute, the Ministry expanded the offices into adjoining, originally residential buildings. Michal's office still had a once fashionable, opaque-glass door with floral patterns etched along the edges. It displayed the silhouettes of people approaching the door or crossing the hall. Tuned to the bouncing rhythm of Danna's footsteps, Michal's mind subconsciously recorded her path through the rooms adjacent to the hall – her office, the secretary's room, computer lab, lavatory, and the office where Michal pretended to be working.

Fifteen minutes later, Michal came to her office with an excuse that he wanted to borrow her Fortran manual, but her office accommodated four people and, as usual, she wasn't there alone.

At eleven, Radim stepped out. Within seconds, Danna rushed in and began to rummage through the drawers behind Michal.

"Yesterday, we drank too much," he said without changing the position of his body or lifting his eyes. "Never mind …"

In that instant Radim returned. He swung the door open as if trying to surprise them. Michal, prepared for something like that and still in the same position as when Radim had left, kept staring into his listing. After searching through the drawers with her head down, Danna picked up an armful of files and left, closing the door behind her with the heel of her right foot.

With all his might, Michal tried to invent something that would allow him to see Danna alone, to finish their conversation. Perhaps during the lunch break, he thought. The hands of the wall clock above Radim's head moved unbearably slowly. It took fifty-two infinite minutes before Radim got up and went to the next office. After some shuffling of feet and laughing in the hall, the elevator door closed, and it was quiet. Danna and Michal met in the hall. They had to speak quickly.

"Of course we drank too much," Danna started exactly where Michal had finished before. She was nervous and not quite herself. "Never mind what happened yesterday," she whispered.

Michal had to temper his voice: "That's not what I meant. Never mind that we drank. I love you. I'd like to marry you one day."

From that moment, everything happened very fast: Shock in her eyes, her mouth half open, a click of the door handle at the end of the hall, and both of them darting back to their offices.

12. TWO SOLITUDES

Deep inside, Michal and Danna were profoundly changed, but on the surface, they lived as if nothing had happened. Their colleagues had not noticed a thing, except for Radim who sometimes stared intensely at Danna or Michal, probing their eyes.

Every day after work, Michal took the tram home, out of town and a long way up the hill to a plateau with modern apartment houses, where he and Zora had a small but comfortable second-floor apartment. Considering the notorious shortage of housing, this was a luxury to which Michal had not yet fully adjusted. He loved the open views and the ever-present wind carrying the scent of paint, of fresh concrete, frying onions or of goulash being cooked somewhere down the street.

His friends already knew not to call him at home. Once he arrived, the household sucked him in. With the twins in the carriage and Rita holding his hand, he pushed through the snow to the supermarket. On the way back, he and Rita watched snowflakes descending from the sky and discussed such important things as why airplanes need wings or what alarm clocks are made of. He usually tied the baby carriage to the tree in front of their house – the jumping twins could easily tip it over – and he took the stairs two at a time, deposited the groceries upstairs, and came down again quickly.

In summer, he would play with the children in the sandbox behind the house, but in winter they walked around the block until Zora called from the window that supper was ready. Then came the usual chores: feeding the children, bathing them, and putting them to bed.

At nine, the communal laundry opened for those who wanted to wash beyond the regular bi-weekly schedule, and Michal retreated to the basement with baskets of diapers. While waiting for the cauldron to boil, he studied or read technical papers, constantly wiping his fogging glasses. After boiling the diapers, he ran both diapers and the children clothes through the washer, and hung them on the clotheslines in the dryer room next door. When he returned upstairs, Zora was already sleeping.

Danna's world revolved around an old apartment house, with the architecture that makes the cores of Prague, Vienna, Budapest or Warsaw so similar. Her windows overlooked the corner of two quiet streets lined with starving locust trees, but with construction and facade repairs in progress, scaffolding and cement-stained wooden planks blocked the last rays of sun that could possibly reach the ground-floor apartment.

The flat belonged to Danna's father, an international chess master, a short, dark, inward looking man who kept only one room for himself. He came and left at odd, irregular hours, and needed the kitchen only for making his coffee or storing a roll of salami in the fridge. As Danna explained to Michal on their trip to Poland, communists expropriated his small printing shop, and labeled him a capitalist. He worked as a night guard in a factory, but never complained about his meager salary. "It is a perfect job for me," he once told Michal. "I can play chess with myself all night without being disturbed."

This house, in which Danna lived since she was six, was not far from her office, and if you saw her bouncing gait and smiling face on the way to work, you would understand how much she enjoyed this half-hour walk through streets filled with shops, people, and traffic. She also liked her work with people and the constant challenge of computer programming.

When she returned from work, glowing Lenka ran into her arms, shouting "Mama, oh mama!"

At the back of the hall stood Danna's aunt Mara, hands on hips and smile on her wrinkled face. She babysat Lenka during the day, and the black dress she always wore emphasized the greyness of her hair and the gauntness of her body. "Lenka, sing for mama the new nursery rhyme you learned today," she said with a pride.

As Danna would cook dinner, Lenka would bring a big cardboard box representing a make-believe kitchen stove. Danna would give her a carrot, and after Lenka meticulously cleaned it with a nylon brush, Danna would lift her so she could add the carrot to the soup on the stove and watch the boiling brew for a few seconds.

Ivan, six feet seven inches, arrived just before dinner, and he ate fast. Danna watched the shirt hanging on his square shoulders, his sinewy tanned face and unmanageable crew cut. Sitting at the table, he did not appear particularly tall.

Ivan's basketball team played in a league, and they trained every night. After the practice, the team stopped in a pub, and he often returned late, not drunk but light-headed. Before Lenka was born, Danna watched the games or took off with the boys to the mountains, but now she was bound to Lenka and new work. She also needed more rest.

Michal was often thinking about Danna and Ivan. Why did they drift apart? Did they marry too young? Were they more friends than a husband and wife?

From Danna's casual comments, Michal sensed that Danna expected a more romantic relationship and, at the same time, she wanted Ivan to share the household chores with her. She also mentioned that when the Soviets invaded Prague, she wanted to emigrate but Ivan was reluctant.

That still isn't enough to split them though, Michal thought. Danna is honest and loyal to her friends. Something more serious must have happened, something that cracked her marriage – perhaps not noticeably but irreversibly.

Only much later, Danna told him how Lenka was born. Eight days before the due date, Ivan was leaving for a three-day tournament abroad, and Danna pleaded with him to stay.

"Don't worry, everybody says that the first child always comes late," he said with a smile and left for his tournament.

The next day Danna went into labour, and a neighbour took her to the hospital, where she gave birth without family or friends.

When Ivan returned, he continued with his sport activities and mountain climbing. He was proud of Lenka but could not give up his friends, and his attitude did not change even when Danna returned to work. "Come with us to the mountains on the weekend," he would say on Friday nights. "Both Aunt Mara and my mother offered to babysit Lenka."

"But I want to be with her," Danna said, close to crying. "I miss her while I am at work. Besides, I have to prepare meals for the next week. And who is going to do the laundry and cleaning? I need your help."

"You are hopeless," he would say angrily and slam the door. This would repeat every weekend with increasingly hostile undertones.

What a contrast with the feeling of unity I feel, Michal thought. He was aware of the invisible thread connecting him with Danna at all times, of their yearning to be together. To share the daily chores would be a blessing, he felt.

Several times a day, Michal scribbled letters to Danna, pages long or short poems, telling her how much he loved her and how beautiful she was. He passed the folded letters to her under his hand or inserted them into a book. Danna read them, then tore them up quickly and put them in the pocket of her skirt. Such a lovely thing, yet so dangerous, she thought as she felt the paper shreds against her thigh before she disposed of them safely, down the toilet or into a street basket on the way home.

13. RESTAURANTS AND CAFES

What Michal and Danna longed for most was a quiet corner where they could sit talking about ordinary, unimportant things, about the joy of being together. They yearned to share their thoughts and the extraordinary beauty they felt, but there was no opportunity to meet, and it dragged on like that for weeks.

Unexpectedly, it was the Ministry of Mines that rescued them. Czechs like to eat a lot, in both quality and quantity, and at least in those days, most inhabitants of Prague would have considered a sandwich lunch a form of punishment. Each month, Michal and Danna bought a sheet of subsidized coupons, which entitled them to a good, three-course lunch in the company cafeteria.

This was not some meager catering service. From early morning, the cooks were busy preparing everything from scratch and, exactly at noon, the crowd already waiting at the door quickly filled the serving room. The aroma of marjoram and potato soup filled the air, accompanied by the sound of banging pans from the kitchen. Stacks of steaming plates waited on the counter, and people pushed in the lines and squabbled over the tables. It was hard to carry a bowl of soup across the room without spilling it on someone's back. Everybody knew everybody else, and if Danna and Michal sat at the same table two days in a row, rumours would circulate instantly.

And it was like that every day, until the ever-important director of the Institute called a general meeting. After he finished his introductory praise of the government, the Party, and *our big brother – the USSR*, he said "Comrades, as you know, our cafeteria is overcrowded."

Sure enough, Michal thought, the price of lunches is going up.

But the director went on. "Our Institute and the City of Prague are issuing discount vouchers. You can have lunch in any restaurant for half price."

"And what will happen to our cafeteria?" someone asked.

"It will continue as usual."

While most of their colleagues remained faithful to the cafeteria, Danna and Michal slipped out of the office separately, and met several blocks away. "What a coincidence," Michal would grin, "are you going for lunch?" Danna's eyes flickered with mischief.

They always met on a different corner, chose a random direction, and walked off quickly. Each day, they tried a new restaurant, never the same place twice – small family diners, large beer halls, fancy places for foreign visitors, Old Town underground cellars, and cafes where they could hide behind the leather partitions of the long-gone era, whispering and holding hands.

Even in the communist times, Prague was a large bustling city, and chances of being seen at noon far from the office were minimal. During the first three months, it happened only once, and Michal had an explanation ready: Their work at the computer center took a bit longer, and they decided to grab a bite on the way back to the office.

At one of these lunches, Michal stopped eating and watched Danna's face. He felt as if the entire universe curved around them like a large transparent bubble. "Danna, I am so happy I've found you," he said quietly. "I thought I had already lost faith that two people could match like this."

"One minute I'm happy, and the next one I'm depressed," she reflected. "There are four children in this game." Tears rolled down her face. "Do you know where we are heading? You are married. I can't take you away from your children? I can't take Lenka from her grandparents and Ivan."

He held her hand in both of his hands. "I'd have to leave Zora even if you were not here. My personality is crumbling; I am losing my kindness, my empathy… She has made me to do terrible things."

"You? What have you done?"

He let Danna's hand go, and stared at the surface of the table. "First it was my Scout leader, Ťapka[3] – my best friend and mentor who taught me so many things. He was already at the retirement age, when Police descended on him, took away his comfortable villa with a large garden full of apple and cherry trees, and exiled him to a dilapidated German house in the polluted, industrial region of Northern Bohemia. At that time, we had only Rita and we lived comfortably, but Zora did not approve sending him any money. When I wanted to help him move and renovate his new place – only for a couple of days, I begged her – she made a big fuss and I caved in.

---

[3] "Little Paw" in Czech

"I sent him a letter that I am thinking a lot about him, and he answered in the most positive way. Raising your family and your scientific work, Ťapka wrote, require all the physical and mental resources you have. Go for it with all your heart. This is the real purpose of the life. And if you sometimes think about me, I cannot ask for more. Your success is my success."

"We should visit him together sometime soon," Danna said. "He must be a wonderful person."

"I am sure he would like you. I can hear him saying *Michal, this modern, adventurous girl is the right companion for you. How did you find her?* but it's too late, he passed away last year," he said, his eyes full of tears.

"Then it was my parents," he continued when he collected himself. "Zora never liked them, but without being provoked, she suddenly declared that I must never take our children to them. After months of discussions, I resigned. The two-year-old twins have never seen their grandparents, and Rita hardly remembers them. Can you imagine how much this hurts my parents? From time to time, I visit them without telling Zora about it.

"And with my brother, it was the same thing. Zora was nasty to his wife, and I have not talked to him since. She antagonized my entire family. I am like a drowning man trying to save his life. I have to leave Zora before she asks me to kill someone as a proof that I love her," Michal said holding his head in his hands.

"You must have loved Zora very much," Danna said quietly.

"Perhaps, but now I know that love can have many other dimensions."

"… but you still live with her."

"… only because of the children."

We have discussed this many times, Michal was thinking. What would be best for my three children and for Lenka? And this cruel and false-hearted legal system makes everything more difficult. Our marriages are dead, but if we stopped hiding, we would lose our children and be financially ruined.

"This isn't our fault," Danna said as if reading his thoughts. "We are not cheating. We don't want any luxuries – just a bit of food and a roof above our heads, but think what they will ask us in the court? How will we explain what happened? Nobody can fully understand this indescribable chain of events that brought us to this point – who said what and how one thing followed another."

"Long before we danced in Jachymov, I had a violent confrontation with Zora," Michal returned to the subject of children, "and she shouted at me that if I leave her I will never see my children again."

"I love you more than I can say," Danna reached for his hand, "but I can't risk losing Lenka. I'd rather go through hell. I'd rather stay with Ivan."

A wave of infinite sadness overwhelmed Michal. Imagine the tragedy of our love lost, he thought, lives turned into mediocre existence, and this unbelievably rare opportunity entirely wasted. It also dawned on him that he may be the one who would pay the ultimate price – losing the children. He looked at Danna.

She is at the beginning of that long journey which took me several years, he thought. I must not pressure her. It would not be fair, it could be also counterproductive. She needs more time. And with my children, he concluded, it's not over yet. I will do everything I can to keep them.

All this turmoil and thinking lasted only an instant, as if a shadow passed over Michal's face, followed by a faint smile. "Your exceptionally strong maternal instinct is one of your great qualities," he said. "I've watched how completely strange children come to you, hold your hand, and tell you their secrets."

"It would be wonderful if we could keep Rita, Filip, and Líza," Danna answered the question he did not dare to ask. "I always wanted four freckled boys. They would not be freckled and not all of them boys, but we would have instantly four children. I would be delighted…

"… yet I am afraid of Zora," she continued. "She will use her children as a weapon to destroy our love."

"Trust me that I won't allow anything like that," Michal said and kissed the tip of her nose.

"What did we do out there, what did we do?
We just talked about our love ..."
(Czech folk song)

14. KISS ON THE NAVEL

"I need to improve my English for reading technical papers, and the two-week course in Ostrava would be perfect for me," Michal said, placing the application form on the director's desk. "Please, could I go?"

The director stared at him suspiciously but Michal maintained his innocent look. He could not tell the director that he had applied for a Canadian fellowship.

"This is an immersion course in *oral* English," the director looked at him with a fatherly expression, "but since you represent us at international conferences, you'll benefit from it anyway."

He signed the form and passed it back to Michal.

Ten days later, Michal flew to Ostrava and started the course in an upbeat mood. However, by the end of the first day his head was buzzing. From eight in the morning to ten at night, with only short breaks for meals, he was subjected to a crossfire of questions that required immediate answers, in English, and not a word in Czech. He also missed Danna more than he could imagine, He realized that, by his own request, he was separated from her for two weeks, without his car and eight hours by train from Prague. The course even ran on Saturday, but Sunday was free.

Every night, he wrote a long letter to Danna, *poste restante* to a post office on her way to the work where neither the post master nor other customers would recognize her. She could not write to him, and only once during the first week he found a reason to call her office and hear her voice.

Perhaps I could catch a plane to Prague tomorrow when we have no lessons, he thought on Saturday morning, but when he opened his wallet, there wasn't enough cash.

I must get there one way or another, he decided. Ivan would leave for the mountains, Lenka would be at her grandmother's, and Danna would be at home alone.

On Saturday night, he rushed to the train station. Danna hates weekends in the empty apartment, he thought, and I will surprise her and cheer her up.

With hundreds of travelers swaying in their sleep, the overnight express carried Michal toward Prague. All night, he sat half asleep. Flashes of outside lights briefly illuminated the lonely vigil of smokers and the bleak-faced soldiers in the aisle travelling across the country on a three-day pass. The rhythm of the train reminded him of a drum, each phrase ending when the wheels hit the switch. Faster, run faster, he prayed. I want to be there.

In the morning, he called from the payphone: "Hi, how are you?"

He could hear Danna almost breaking off the receiver cord: "Is it really you? Where are you?"

"Oh, I'm here, just around the corner! May I come in?"

It is risky, he thought, but if neighbours saw me, I could easily deny it. It couldn't be me, I would say later. How could I get there from Ostrava?

With mixed feelings, he entered the apartment building. He had been there before, but hadn't noticed its menacingly cold walls. What if Ivan returns unexpectedly or a relative drops in?

He sneaked past the janitor's door and pressed the doorbell. I am a fool, he thought, a fool entering the lion's den. Then he saw Danna and his worries melted away.

The red jogging suit she wore at home flashed behind the door as she peeked out before letting him in. "I didn't expect any visitors," she said playfully.

"Is anybody here?" Michal whispered

"Don't worry, everybody's gone."

Like two somnambulists, they walked into the middle of the living room. A cool draft lifted the curtains on the half-open window as Danna threw her arms around Michal's neck. "What magic has brought you here?"

"It's only for a few minutes. I have to catch the train back. Do you still love me?"

She pulled herself closer to him, stretching on her tiptoes. Michal felt more than saw the small gap that opened under her top. Unable to resist, he bent and kissed the warm, perfectly shaped navel. "You are beautiful. Are you aware of that?"

She shook as if a wave passed through her body. Surprised, Michal looked up.

"Please, let me go! Return to Ostrava," she sobbed.

"It was a tender little kiss. I meant no harm," Michal straightened and moved his hands to her shoulders. "Please, don't cry. I came to bring you joy, not sorrow."

"I am happy, but can't resist the temptation."

Just happy to be together, they sat on the edge of the sofa, a foot apart, and talked in low voices about what had happened during the past week, what Lenka did, and about the spectacular sunrise that Michal watched from the train.

Twenty minutes later, Michal was gone. He left no trace, and even Danna wondered whether he had truly been there.

15. TELEPHONE CALLS

Simple things always work best and the method Michal and Danna developed for calling each other was a good example. They had telephones at their homes, but those were useless when Zora or Ivan were there.

As long as Zora did not notice, Michal could call from the street phone outside of his house without being conspicuous. All his neighbors had party lines and used the street phone when the lines were busy. Michal usually ran out for a few minutes while washing diapers after dinner.

The conversation between Danna and Michal always started the same way. When Danna answered *Danna speaking*, it was a signal that Ivan or someone else was there. Michal hung up without a word.

A simple *Hello* meant *I am alone – talk, please talk!* Sometimes, they exchanged only a few words, sometimes they chattered for hours until Ivan came home or impatient neighbours waiting in a line began to bang the telephone booth.

When Ivan picked up the phone, Michal waited quietly until he hung up. It was a strange feeling to hear Ivan's breath from the cold metal receiver, repeating: "Who's there, damn, is anybody there?"

Michal felt sorry for Ivan who had lost and was not aware of it yet. On some evenings, he traveled across the city and circled Danna's block just to be closer to her. Sometimes he called her from a payphone: "Danna, can you come to the corner of Řipská and Kladská streets exactly at ten thirty-five?" Never the same spot, never the same hour.

"What, now?" she was startled, "I don't know. Someone might see us …"

"In ten minutes exactly. At least for a few seconds, please! It's a warm summer night. I'd like to see your eyes."

She arrived out of breath, avoiding bright spots under the street lamps, and checking the sidewalk behind her frequently. Nobody followed her; only her footsteps echoed through the empty street.

As she approached the corner, she slowed down. Where was Michal? At the last moment, he stepped out of the shadow of the house. "Come, if we stand here nobody can see us."

"Is such a short meeting worth of two hours of your travelling? I have to be back in five minutes. Lenka is there alone."

"She is already sleeping, isn't she? Give me one kiss to prove that you still exist. One kiss for good night, and I can go."

16. PARTY MEMBERSHIP

The afternoon sun was falling on Michal's desk, and the room was unusually quiet. Radim was gazing into a technical report without turning its pages, and the technician who came to work at the drawing board had probably dozed off. Cigarette smoke rose in a vertical line from behind the board when the phone ring startled all three of them.

Michal was the first one to reach the receiver and he instantly recognized the secretary's voice: "Comrade director would like to see you. Yes, right now."

This means trouble, Michal thought. He got up and ran down the stairs to the director's office. The secretary pointed to the open door: "He is waiting for you."

The director took off his reading glasses, and placed them on a pile of paper in the middle of his desk. "Please, take a seat." He was smiling as he moved his chair to the side of the desk to be closer to Michal. It looked as if the matter were delicate and private.

"Comrade, I have to tell you something important."

Michal had already guessed what it was going to be. He was prepared for a lesson on the morals of socialist citizens, about the importance of marriage and, in short, that he was behaving badly. He seated himself comfortably and, without changing his expression, stared at the director, patiently waiting for what was to come.

"Comrade, you manage our most important project which has already gained international recognition. Only the Kiruna mine in Sweden has a system comparable to what you developed in Sokolov."

Come on, Michal thought, get to the point! "I believe so," he said cautiously, "but we still have a long way to go."

"You are thirty-two. It's time for you to consider an application to the Communist Party. As one of our best scientists, you should join the organization that truly governs our country. You should participate more actively in our political life."

This is the last thing I need now, Michal thought looking at his feet. He thought of all the people taken away by the STB. Some never returned, some reappeared years later – with grey hair and failing health, unwilling to tell what had happened behind bars.

I already decided this three years ago, he was thinking. When they told me that I could not become an associate professor unless I entered the Party, I left the university and went into mining. I cannot join an organization that tortures innocent people.

Then it crossed his mind that if young people like Danna and he joined the Party, they might be able to change all that. Radim and the administration manager Olda were party members and still loyal and trustworthy friends.

At the same time, he felt a growing sensation of repulsion. He thought of Jan Masaryk, who would have become the next democratic president in 1948, and who was pushed out of a third floor window by communist thugs He also recalled a pensive evening when he and Ťapka, the Scout leader, were sitting at a campfire alone. Michal asked him why all his front teeth were gold.

"I was interrogated twice," he said, "by German Gestapo during the war, and then by STB. Germans broke my teeth, but Communists were much worse ..."

I can't have anything to do with this Party, Michal thought looking straight at the director. This was a different, more disturbing trouble than he had expected.

"You probably know," the director continued, "that your position assumes Party membership. This is one of the most important decisions of your life. If you decide to apply, and I hope you will, we will have to test you first."

"This is a great honor," Michal lied without blushing, "but also a big surprise." The second part of his statement certainly came directly from his heart. "I'll let you know soon."

The director was beaming. He owed his career to the Party. He was a member of the Communist Party Assembly, a body of representatives more important than Parliament. A powerful man who played dirty politics, but at that moment, Michal almost believed he was innocent. The director smiled, and took Michal's hand into his own soft, sweaty hands.

"Don't rush, Michal, think about it ... ," were the last words Michal heard as he passed through the black upholstered door. I hope the Canadians will reply soon, was his only thought.

*"The great pleasure in life is doing
what people say you cannot do."*
(Chinese fortune cookie)

17. FELLOWSHIP

In the middle of February, the snow was gently falling. The mailman delivered a simple white envelope with a Canadian stamp, and Michal examined it slowly from all sides, before cutting it open. The letter started with: "You have been granted a postdoctorate fellowship in the Geological Survey of Canada, Ottawa, for one year, starting on September 13, 1969."

What? Geological Survey? Haven't I selected computer science and electrical engineering? But why not, was his second thought. I would be glad to take anything as remote as medicine or submarine exploration – just to get out of this damned place.

Without even mentioning the letter to Radim, he went straight to the director, who against all odds approved the trip and wrote a personal recommendation to the Minister of Mines. With this letter, Michal received a leave of absence, and had an exit visa in his pocket in the unbelievable time of only one week.

After almost a year of idle waiting, he felt dizzy from the speed in which all this happened. It also amazed him how he bypassed the police screening and filling in all the required forms and signatures. The director must be a more powerful political figure than we thought, he mused. He must be thinking that I would never defect with my family back in Prague but, and that is a big *but*, do they want me to bring them some sensitive information, to become a spy? Michal had heard about such cases.

I have seven months, Michal counted on his fingers, enough time to bring Danna to Canada as my wife. Anyone of sound mind would have told him that this plan was simply impossible.

18. MOTHER AND MINING

After work, Michal stopped at his parents, who lived in the same kind of five-floor apartment houses that Danna did. Outside, the light brown stucco was deteriorating, but inside people kept nice, cozy apartments with the window frames freshly painted.

His mother, still in her office suit, opened the door, and Michal noticed the grey streaks in her brown hair. She looked tired, but her round face smiled.

"Daddy is still at the school," she said. "Come in for a coffee and cake – it's your favourite, with poppy seed filling."

"We have not had a nice chat for years," she added without mentioning Zora's attitude.

He took his coat off and made himself comfortable in the kitchen.

"Something was telling me today that you would show up," she said bringing the cake, still warm and dusted with sugar. "How are the twins? We'd love so much to see them, especially Daddy. He loves children, all children …"

When Michal did not answer, she changed the subject: "For the longest time I've wanted to know what are you doing in those mines? It seems to me that you had a great academic career in electronics and computers. I know you too well – you wouldn't go to mining just for money."

He took a big bite of the cake, and after he swallowed it, he said: "You don't have to be a mathematician or a mining expert to understand what we are trying to do. It's all in Sokolov, close to the German border, and the enterprise consists of four open pit mines, a coal sorting plant, a briquette plant, and a power station. The rail yard has more tracks than the railway station in Prague."

"That sounds interesting. Please, go on!"

"Imagine the change from the theoretical work I did at the university. In the mine, we are trying to control hundreds of people, and an incredible amount of machinery. It is real, sometimes too real, with dirt and smoke and hard physical labour. The land out there is like another world: Large cavities open the ground, so wide and long that one could hardly see the other end. Black and brown scenery with huge smokestacks on the horizon, piles of coal and uprooted soil, and coal dust on everything in sight. It's like a moon landscape and very much like hell. It's dark and hot inside the briquette plant. The floor vibrates under your feet, you can't hear your own voice. Steam leaks and whistles blow and you have that physical feeling of being close to fire.

"If you stood at the edge of a pit," he continued, "deep under you, you would see the enormous excavators loading the railway cars. These enormous machines are like steel castles. Powered by electricity, they pull a heavy cable behind them. They look like big beasts, like dinosaurs on a leash."

"I almost can see it," his mother laughed. "Go on."

"Railway tracks spiral up the pit. The loaded trains slowly puff up the slope, toward the storage bins where they unload the cars with a big bang. From the bins, a never-ending stream of coal, one meter wide, flies on conveyor belts into the plant where it is crushed, screened, and sifted from belt to belt by hundreds of monstrous machines, until it spews out at one of the outputs. The coal quality is different with every shovel and it changes with time. In the power plant, the changes of coal quality may crack the furnace walls. In the briquette plant, the shiny square briquettes may crack and break into pieces. And you can imagine that customers who order pea-sized coal for chemical processing are not happy when the train arrives with ten-centimeter lumps of coal."

"But how is it all controlled now?" his mother shook her head.

"The control depends on a single man – the shift supervisor. Like a blind army general with several telephones on his desk, he sits in a quiet room and receives messages about everything that is happening. He tries to visualize the entire operation, he feels in his fingertips all the mills, trains, and the streams of coal, and he fires his orders back by telephone. Usually, everything is fine until something unexpected happens. When a train goes off the track or a shovel moves into a new location, the man is in trouble. The output fluctuates wildly, the rail yard is flooded with cars, and money is pouring out of the window."

Michal finished his coffee, ate two more slices of the cake and after praising its exceptional taste returned to his narration.

"We placed a minicomputer beside the supervisor's desk, and we feed it with data about everything in the mine. At any time, the supervisor can print a detailed summary in neat tables. The computer optimizes the production, the blending of the coal, and the movement of the trains. It only prints a recommendation of what's best to do, though. The supervisor makes the final decision, and issues the orders. It's not completely automatic, but it works best for them that way."

She swept the crumbs from the table. "I'm sorry I'm too old to get into computers. Does your system save a lot of money?"

"That's the beauty of this optimization," Michal said enthusiastically. "Imagine, if you improve the production by one percent, you save millions of crowns. From the mathematical point of view, it's all routine stuff: mixed-integer programming, blending, capacity calculations and the scheduling of trains. We are also trying to control the production to fit day-by-day contracts. That's the new part, which stirred interest abroad.

"And besides having so much fun," he said, "I am paid three times as much as I was at the university. But I'd better go, Zora will be angry."

19. XAVIER

Radim authorized the overnight trip to Sokolov, but Michal had orchestrated the whole thing.

"I need two people to collect coal samples in the processing plant," Michal explained to Radim, "and it has to be a morning shift. Collecting samples near moving belts is dangerous at night."

"When do you want to do that?" Radim looked at him without a hint of suspicion in his eyes..

"This Friday suits them the best," Michal replied in a firm tone. It was a little lie. He had selected the day when everyone in Radim's department was busy, except for Xavier and Danna. The mine administration only approved the date.

"That means you have to travel on Thursday, and stay overnight." Radim scratched his head. "I am short of people. Couldn't you do it with only one helper?"

"I need three people including myself," Michal insisted. If he agreed to one helper, Radim would give him Xavier.

"One person will scoop the samples and fill plastic bags. The second person will prepare labels and mark the location and time. And the third person will haul the samples in a wheelbarrow. This is a big job: One-kilogram sample every minute, for eight hours, that's about half a ton of samples. Also, we cannot interrupt the sampling even for one minute, and if one person has to go to the toilet …"

"I can only give you Xavier and Danna," Radim said.

"That will do," Michal said after a moment of faked hesitation. After months of running and hiding with Danna like hunted deer, he envisioned a long velvet night at their disposal.

Having Xavier along, Michal thought, would be a good cover. He imagined Xavier, his kind face, jacket and trousers hanging on his skinny frame, shadows under his eyes, black bristle-like hair, and black dots of embedded coal marking his face. Xavier was a real miner who had spent his life underground. He had seen tunnels collapse and rows of stretchers being carried out of the shaft. Close to retirement, but still vigorous and strong, he had been a chain smoker all his life. He liked to drink but nothing made him drunk. If Xavier is with us, Michal thought, nobody can object, not even Ivan.

Xavier rarely spoke of his wife, but from his indirect remarks Michal sensed a depth of devotion. He also had noticed how eagerly Xavier returned from every business trip.

"This is my third marriage, and I cherish everything in love," Xavier once had said. When Michal told him about the trip, Xavier smiled with his yellow teeth. "With Danna and you? I would be delighted."

Before accepting the assignment, Danna went to her friend Běla. Before the two had married, they had raced on kayaks, and they still shared intimate secrets.

"It is a new, fascinating world, and it's drawing me in like fast water. I'm scared," Danna said. "What should I do?"

"My dear," said the older Běla. "You are in for big trouble. If you go, it will be the end of your marriage."

20. LONG VELVET NIGHT COMING

When Danna arrived at the bus terminal that early March morning, Xavier and Michal were waiting in the middle of a long line already boarding the bus. Frost covered railings, wastebaskets and everything in sight, damp wind chased streaks of fog around the lamp posts, and travelers huddled in their coats, shivering.

She found a window seat, Michal sat beside her, and Xavier across the aisle. The bus took off, but they soon discovered that the heating was broken. They had overcoats and winter boots, yet their feet were freezing.

"This is like an fridge on wheels," Danna said, while trying to scrape the ice from the window. "I can't see anything outside."

When they arrived in Sokolov, the sun broke through the clouds and fresh snow covered the ground. The spring was in the air, and children with toboggans ran around the city park. Xavier took his winter hat off. "With this warm breeze," he said, "the snow will be gone in a couple of days."

Once they checked into the hotel, they returned outside in a happy mood.

"Let's build a snowman," Michal shouted, and began to roll a ball which quickly picked up thick layers of the wet snow along with dead leaves and old grass. "Look at the tracks I am making. It looks like tank tracks all over the lawn."

"You and your tanks," Danna laughed, and threw a snowball directly at his chest. "Let me help you haul the next ball up. It's too heavy."

Xavier joined them. Together, they added and shaped more snow, and plastered gaily as if working with clay. "It's not a snowman," Danna laughed. "It looks like a polar bear."

"Well, let's make it a bear," Michal said, forming an open mouth, and inserting two sticks for fangs. The bear sat on its hind legs with its paws up. Danna made claws from short twigs and eyes from pieces of coal that had fallen from passing trucks.

"That's the prettiest snowman I've ever built," Xavier laughed.

"You mean a snow-bear," Dana tickled the bear under its chin. "Look, how cute it is."

Michal walked in a big circle and measured the proportions of their creation. "My mittens are wet, and I'm getting cold," he said.

"Let's go in. I'm hungry." Danna breathed into her hands.

The modern hotel where they were staying was the only respectable accommodation in Sokolov, but it lacked the class of a similar hotel in Prague or any other large city. Cheerful curtains in the lobby contrasted with fingerprints along the walls and a trail of black footprints on the red runner on the stairs. The imitation Oriental rug in the waiting area had a hole where someone had dropped a cigarette butt and, in spite of charming Scandinavian furniture, the rooms suffered from a cold, lonely atmosphere. Perhaps they needed interesting wallpaper or a picture on the institutional white walls. The view of backyard shacks with piles of coal and construction debris was not terrific either, but the washrooms were spotless and the bedding was clean.

Sokolov was not a tourist attraction. The hotel served business travelers and tourists passing through, but the restaurant catered to the local miners, who made good money and had nowhere else to spend it.

The three friends changed into dry clothes and met downstairs. Candlelight dinner was served in three crowded halls. In one corner, a group of noisy young miners guzzled beer. The menu listed many delicacies and the best wines from Yugoslavia, Romania, Morocco, and Italy. "Any drinks with your meal?" the waitress asked routinely.

Michal and Danna looked at each other and asked for water. They never had talked about it, but after the dance in Jachymov they wanted to keep their minds sharp and clear.

Xavier, who remembered many wild parties thought 'them drinking water?' but without lifting his eyes from the wine list, he ordered a carafe of the red Romanian wine.

All three sat without saying a word until the waitress brought the meals. While feasting on Wiener schnitzels, Xavier and Michal discussed the next day's plan. Rowdy miners at the draft table called for yet another beer, and half of the hall joined them in singing.

When travelling, company policy required employees of the same gender to share a room. It kept expenses down, improved camaraderie and enforced good behaviour. Following Xavier up the stairs, Michal whispered to Danna: "See you later," then – loudly for Xavier to hear it – he told Danna: "Good night. We'll wake you tomorrow at five."

Doors banged, one on each side of the hall, and the long corridor fell quiet again, with stuffy air, dim lights, and two rows of white doors.

Xavier did not wash himself, only brushed his teeth, changed into pajamas, and climbed into his bed. He was tired and sleepy, but turned on his nightlight, and began to read an old paperback with bent corners and the front cover missing. Michal noticed the black hair of Xavier's chest protruding from his half-buttoned pajama top.

Xavier paid no attention to Michal who, fully dressed, stretched across his bed, stared mindlessly into some technical papers, then dropped them on the floor beside his bed, and studied patterns of cracks in the coarse ceiling.

After suffering for what felt like several hours, Michal concluded it made no sense to wait until Xavier fell asleep. He got up, mumbled some ridiculous excuse, and left the room without looking in the direction of Xavier's bed.

> *"On the most silent path in the meadows,*
> *I wait for thee.*
> *You'll feel great in my arms,*
> *Ascending Heavens with me."*
> (F. Šrámek)

21. LONG VELVET NIGHT BEGINS

Michal did not go straight for Danna's door. The sound of his steps would have betrayed him. He followed the red carpet to the lobby, checked the newspapers displayed on the edge of the reception counter and examined the prices of chocolate bars behind a locked glass window.

After fifteen minutes of poking around, he returned on his tiptoes and scratched lightly on Danna's door

"Is that you?"

"Yes, it's me."

The door quickly opened. Even with the heating fully on, the room felt chilly. They moved two chairs close to the window where mittens and socks were drying on the radiator. They sat side by side, with their feet resting on the radiator, hugging their knees and staring out the window at the dark backyards. Walls of the old apartment buildings towered against the sky, with lights in their windows switching on and off in an irregular pattern, some glowing yellow and some dark red.

After a while, Michal got up, turned on the light, closed the curtain, returned to his chair, and placed his arm gently around Danna's shoulders. They now faced the white curtain and the radiator still warming their feet. Is there a divine plan, Michal thought. Our paths have touched so many times but always divided again.

Danna looked at him. "Why did we have to wait until we both married someone else?" After a pause, she continued: "If you knew who I really am, you would not even want to talk to me again. My own family called me *that German brat*."

"How could anybody to be so cruel!" He pulled himself closer to her. "You are the loveliest German brat I've ever met, but tell me."

"It's a long story. You really want to hear it?"

"Yes, please, I do."

"My mother actually is my stepmother, and I am not sure who my father was. Before the war, three million Germans lived in Bohemia."

"That many? In the school, they just talked about the German minority. "

"Six million Czechs and three million Germans. My true mother, an attractive woman at the age of sixteen …"

"Just like you …," Michal said with a smile.

"This is not funny," Danna slapped him on his wrist. "Even people who hated her never disputed that she was very pretty. She came from a small town west of Prague. Her Czech father, a dressmaker, died of tuberculosis, and her German mother struggled to keep the family going. Reportedly, my mother seduced her teacher, was kicked out of school, ran away from home, and became a street vendor in Prague. In a café, where my thirty-nine-year-old father regularly played chess, she sold him shoe laces one night, and the next day she moved into his apartment. In just a few weeks, they married."

"I know your father is a chess master, go on."

"My father's family objected adamantly. The war already started, and marrying a German was a disgrace."

"But she was only half German," Michal said.

"She spoke both languages, but sided with Hitler. This was my father's second marriage, and it lasted only a year. The two remained friends and met frequently after the divorce.

"Then my mother found a new boyfriend," Danna continued, "a German clerk who, after a short affair with my mother, was drafted into the army and sent to Greece. Before I was born, my mother traveled to Vienna, so I would have a citizenship of a German-speaking country."

"Considering the circumstances, it was a smart move," Michal said. "German-speaking Austria was neutral, and regardless of who would win the war, you would always end up on the right side."

"On my birth certificate, my name was Freya, not Danna, and there is no recorded father. After I was born, the German clerk married my mother by proxy and swore his paternity while dying in a military hospital. Imagine my mother, she was just twenty-two. As a widow of a soldier who died in the line of duty, she received a small fortune and opened a factory which manufactured felt inserts for the boots German soldiers needed in Russia. She employed many Jews and though she claims she saved their lives, they were also cheap labour. When she met her current husband, a Czech lawyer, her business was booming.

"When the war ended, the Allied Command approved the Czech proposal to *relocate all Germans back to Germany*. It happened on short notice, and allowed only twenty-kilograms of luggage. All Germans – even those who lived there for centuries and did not support Hitler – were driven from their villages untouched by the war, and shipped by train to bombed-out cities across the border. Nobody talks about it today, but along the way, many were robbed of gold and other valuables they carried with them. Thirty thousand Germans died because of beatings. Within days, Falkenau – later renamed Sokolov – became a ghost town. When all this happened, I lived with my German grandmother near Prague."

"Now I understand the spirit of sadness which surrounds this area," Michal said. "Deserted villages, deteriorating houses, coats and work boots still behind the unlocked doors, gates to overgrown gardens hanging on one hinge. Even now, twenty-three years later, I always drive through as fast as I can."

"My mother and her lawyer husband were now in trouble," Danna continued. "Maybe, he was innocent, but how many decent Czechs worked at the courthouse during the occupation? My mother owned a factory and had sympathized with Hitler. If this had come out in public, they would have been mobbed. You know how people hated every German after the war. My mother and her husband also feared Russians. Russians raped women and treated Germans like dirt."

"All wars are terrible," Michal sighed. "Think what the Germans did to the Russians."

"I know. My mother chose to run through the woods to the American Zone. It was a long and dangerous journey. They had to avoid towns and any contact with people. For her four-year-old daughter who spoke only German, she thought the safest passage was with the Red Cross train and accompanied by her mother, my grandmother. That was a big mistake!

"Before she departed, she paid a visit to my father, the chess player. She gave him her bank books with her savings and begged him to take care of me, claiming that after all I was his daughter.

He asked her to marry him again. As a Czech citizen, you would not have to leave for Germany, but she would not hear of it.

My father then went to his first wife Marie and asked her for help. He always remained friendly with his ex-wives. Marie was on the committee which organized the transports. It was easy for her to remove me from the list since I was his daughter. Later, under the name Danna, I received Czech citizenship. When my grandmother came to the transport with me, soldiers took me from her arms and pushed her, screaming, onto the train."

"Your father was not stupid. He must have had some reason to believe you were his daughter."

"My mother must have had two lovers around the time I was conceived. Later, my father married my stepmother who, to me, is really my mother."

"What happened to your mother?"

"When my grandmother arrived without me, my mother was devastated. With no diplomatic ties between Germany and Czechoslovakia, she had to travel illegally to Switzerland to apply at the Red Cross. She wrote to the Czech government, but the replies were always the same: I was adopted, in good care, and would not be released to her. Later on, she had another child, and now she lives in Argentina."

Danna continued. "I don't remember her face except from pictures. Since my sixteenth birthday, she began to send small photographs or passport pictures, always sad-looking and exhausted. Twice a year, she sent small amounts of money that helped me through university."

"When I was six," Michal recalled, "I had a German classmate who had hundreds of plaster soldiers in various positions – with machine guns, cannons, and trench mortars, all in proper uniforms – German, English, and French. After school, we staged battles on his living-room carpet while the radio was reporting on the fighting at Stalingrad and on the Western front. It annoyed me that the German army always had to win, but my parents instructed me not to resist."

Michal went on with his recollection: "At the time of the Prague uprising, in May 1945, I was already eight. The war was over, Berlin was defeated, but not less than a kilometer from us, the SS units were pulling people from apartment buildings – men, women, and children, everybody – and machine-gunning them down. These SS units were moving in our direction, and we sat in our cellar listening to the street battle above us – German planes flying over and dropping bombs, sometimes close to us, sometimes further away. For three long days and nights, we wondered whether we would be next.   I still can hear the march the radio played, intermittently calling for help in Czech, English, and Russian.

"After the Russians liberated Prague, someone had to put back the pavement and the cobblestones that people ripped out to build barricades against the German tanks. I always thought that only Germans can be cruel, but then I saw this eighteen-year-old Czech with a red Revolutionary Guard sign on his sleeve. He cracked a four-meter long whip at old, grey Germans repairing the pavement and failing from exhaustion. The grandmother of my friend was one of them."

Still in the grips of his old memories, he continued: "I often think of my parents who had to go through all this hell with two little boys, for six years, always ready for evacuation, running to the cellar several times a night. At the time of the air raid on Prague, in February 1944, I was sick at home with whooping cough. When the siren sounded, I ran into the apartment hall and seconds later all the windows of our apartment caved in. When I returned, my bed was full of glass, and the four-story apartment house across the street was missing – only a deep, smoking crater was left.

"As a child, I wasn't afraid of being blasted away, but I had nightmares of being engulfed in fire. It also bothered me greatly that all adults in the cellar carried a gas mask, but there were only adult sizes. What would I do in a gas attack? My mother told me I'd pee on my handkerchief, and breathe through it. I remember her eyes. "That's what Germans told us", she said. "I guess it's better than nothing."

"I tell you," Danna returned to her story, "I was upset when my mother left, and I was upset when soldiers took me from my grandmother's arms, but I was totally out of my mind when they took away my fox terrier. He had been my dog since I was a baby and I loved him. It was my only security in this world. I cried, had tantrums, and did not talk to anybody for several weeks."

Michal held her tightly, tears rolling down his face.

22. LONG VELVET NIGHT CONTINUES

Lost in their thoughts, they slowly returned to the reality of the white hotel room. The socks had dried. "No words can express what I feel," Michal heard himself saying. "I love you, and want to be completely yours – more than any words could say."

"Yes, I feel the same way," she said and lowered her head to his shoulder. For some time they sat entranced, staring into the white curtain that kept the darkness out.

"I will shower first," Danna rose. She said it as if sharing a secret, touched Michal's back, stretched her arms, and closed the bathroom door behind her.

Michal sat on the bed with a taste of sweetness in his mouth. Every inch of his body longed for Danna, but he was full of doubts. Zora had told him he was a lousy lover, and Danna mentioned that Ivan taunted her of being cold in bed. Now he had only one simple wish – to make Danna happy.

He watched the frosted window near the ceiling that separated him from the bathroom and listened to the shower running in waves like heavy summer rain.

He was not sure what to do. He undressed to his shorts, folded his clothes over a chair, and sat on the bed, waiting for what seemed a very long time. He was getting cold.

Danna emerged from the bathroom wrapped in a towel, bringing with her a cloud of hot steam. Michal was grateful that she had something on. He kissed her lips and touched her cheeks with his fingertips. Her skin was hot and moist.

He showered fast. He could not wait much longer.

His uneasiness thawed when he stepped out of the bathroom. Danna removed the pillows and blankets from the bed, left all the lights on, and was in the center of the white bedsheet – on her tummy, one foot up in the air, and completely naked. Except for her bottom, she was hiding most of her beauty, and like a mischievous child, she turned her head toward him. She was more beautiful than any woman Michal could imagine.

When he stretched out beside her, she turned and opened to him and took him into her arms. It was all simple, everything was written in her eyes, like a miracle, like a melody they had known forever – they, who had almost given up the search, there it was, the love of gentle giving and receiving and unlimited trust.

23. BRIQUETTE PLANT

The next day, they moved like in a dream. Xavier and Danna scooped up coal dust from the conveyor belts and from tin transportation ducts into plastic bags and closed them with wire ties. Michal marked the bags and transported them to the chemical laboratory in a wheelbarrow. They worked mechanically, as if they had performed this task for years, not fully aware of where they were or what they were doing.

In blue coveralls and a red scarf, Danna looked like one of the factory workers, her face smeared with coal dust, but even when watching her from behind, Michal could see an unmistakable difference in her movements. She was graceful yet not soft, like a spring loaded with energy, and Michal felt the invisible bond between them. At one point, Danna planted a quick kiss on his mouth, then turned around as if nothing had happened.

On the way back to Prague, they sat in the middle of the bus, holding hands, not worrying about Xavier who read his book at the back of the bus as if nothing had happened.

"When I came back last night, the lights were on and he was sleeping with the book open on his chest," Michal said.

"He is not dumb," Danna mused. "By now, he must have a fairly good idea of what's going on. He's not going to tell anybody."

"And if he does, who cares?" Michal said and leaned his forehead against her shoulder. "Let's enjoy the two-and-half hours we still can be together."

They cuddled closer to the window, and watched the winter countryside moving by like a movie: People in scarves and tuques, horses pulling carts, and a layer of mist halfway up the tree trunks. Their cheeks touched, and the snow outside glowed before the red setting sun.

On this bus crowded with miners in heavy winter gear, they whispered for the first time how wonderful it would be to have a baby. "A tiny baby of our own. Can you imagine?"

24. LEAVING ZORA

Michal opened the door and his children ran into his arms, yet he felt as if his entire world had changed. The planets left their orbits and Zora, more alien and remote than he could ever imagine, sat in the kitchen. He felt he had no choice, he could not stay with her any longer.

He would never abandon the children, and the question was not whether he should leave Zora but where he could move. In this city of more than a million people, there wasn't a single apartment or a room for rent, not even a wet basement without windows or a cottage close enough to the city that he could commute by car.

In the next few days, he called his friends, relatives, and neighbors, talked to janitors idling at entrances of buildings, and offered a generous bonus for any advice that would lead to a rental, but all in vain. Eventually, a high school classmate Vašek suggested: "… and have you thought of Lída?"

Perhaps it was a streetcar passing by, but when Vašek pronounced her name, a long tremor shook the ground. "Lída? Isn't she married?"

"She divorced recently, and has a spare room. With two preschool children, she may be glad to have someone around to help."

This brought Michal back to his high school years – tall, slim Lída dressed in plain dark colours. Lída calm and distant, her acute mind always focused and engaged. People who met her for the first time looked up in surprise, when they first heard her soft, contralto voice that rang like a bell. And when she talked, Michal remembered, it was like someone playing Debussy in the background. Her long, black hair and large almond eyes resembled girls from Gauguin's paintings. At the graduation ball, Michal had met her mother – and ordinary looking Czech, but what was the nationality of her father? Had he died young, divorced her mother or perhaps never married her? Lída had never mentioned anything about him.

"That's interesting," Michal said, "so she is also divorced."

"Her problem is that men admire her, but they lose confidence in her presence," Vašek said, and scribbled two addresses and a phone number on a store receipt he fished out from his pocket. "She does not have a telephone. Try to call her mother."

When Michal dialed the number, Lída answered the phone.

"Lída, it's a long story," he said. "I need help. Where can I talk to you?"

This was a rather strange introduction after not seeing each other for years, but she grasped the situation instantly. "Come here to my mother, yes, right now! It's all right."

After a short search, Michal found the house and pressed the bell on the correct door. His mind was not working normally. Facing the unfamiliar door, he felt as if he had a fever. He heard several people shouting inside about who should answer the call. Then the door half opened, and Lída appeared in a bathrobe, her hair dripping wet. Soapy vapour was coming through the door, and an overloaded washing machine was shaking inside the apartment hall.

"Lída, I can't live with Zora anymore. I have to move out. May I stay with you for some time, or would you know about someone who might have a room?" Until he started to talk, he was not sure what he would say, but pressed by the circumstances, he chose the bare truth.

She looked behind Michal as if projecting her thoughts onto the dirty wall of the stairwell above his head, and slowly reached into her bathrobe pocket: "Here is the key. See you tonight." And she closed the door.

As if he were in a hypnotic state, Michal drove home and packed his belongings. He cleared his part of the closet and threw the armful of clothes in the back of his car. Then he carried out three boxes of papers that were of no value to Zora: engineering textbooks, dictionaries and his university notes. He also took one comforter, one sleeping bag, his old small tent, paint box, and cello. It was amazing to see how little he owned at the age of thirty-two, after a successful career and nine years of marriage.

He feared a violent confrontation. Well before Danna appeared in his life, the day after discussing separation, Zora turned on the gas stove without lighting it, and called his office, speaking in a dying voice. In those days, gas appliances had no automatic shut-off valves and all three children were with her and in grave danger.

With her, one never knows, he thought, but taking the car should not be an issue. We had already agreed that if we ever split, I could keep the car. Considering the large unpaid loan, it isn't a great asset, and Zora was to keep the apartment for the children.

He had known that leaving the children would be hard, but it was much harder than he expected. He had to block all his emotions and let his brain guide him out of this mess. Even then, it took every bit of his determination to finish what he had started.

The children asked Zora: "Mommy, what is Daddy doing?"

She was frowning. "He is leaving us."

The children jumped up from their lunch, and hung onto his arms with their sticky little hands. They pleaded with their innocent eyes bewildered by what was happening "Daddy, don't leave! Please, stay with us!"

Michal loved them immensely. Is it safe to leave them with Zora, he wondered again. But the psychiatrist insisted that Zora is a good mother, and that she only becomes violent in my presence.

And even if the unthinkable happens and Danna leaves me, his mind was exploring all possibilities, I cannot stay here. I have to leave, and this painful step is unavoidable. Postponing it would not solve anything.

He took all three children onto his lap. "I love you very much," he said and petted their heads. "I am not leaving you, and I am not leaving town. I will see you often."

Then he gently took them off his lap and ran down the stairs unable to see through his tears. He jumped into the car and drove away, afraid to look back.

> *"Sublime, not remote, and mysterious,*
> *in silence lives the rose."* [4]
>
>   (Adolfo Bioy Casares).

25. LÍDA

Soon, Michal and Lída had a smoothly running household. Except bedrooms, they shared everything – expenses, cooking, and washing. Jointly, they took care of Lída's two children, Tibor 5 and Emma 3. Michal picked them up at the day-care center when Lída worked long hours.

This style of coexistence implied a certain level of closeness. The two toothbrushes in the bathroom – side by side and almost touching. Lída's panties tumbling with Michal's T-shirt in the washing machine. Michal himself acquiring the scent of Lída's household.

After dinner, when the children were in bed, he and Lída sat in the kitchen. Dirty dishes stacked on the table, clothes and wet towels scattered on the floor, and both of them exhausted.

"Today, I filed for divorce," Michal said.

"That must be hard for Zora," Lída said. She has three children, and she is out there alone."

"For several years, she kept asking me to leave. I also have my limits." Just the thought made him angry. "I wanted to bring the children here last weekend, and I cannot repeat where she told me to go. She wouldn't even let me to see them …"

"What she has been saying may be one thing", Lida reflected. "But what she means may be entirely different. She still loves you."

"Perhaps - in her strange and devious way. More likely, she is just mad that she can't control me anymore."

"That may be true," Lída began washing the dishes, "but don't forget the children."

On the kitchen counter, next to her pots and pans, Lída kept the most important item of her household – an old stereo, which

---

[4] In Spanish, this sounds like beautiful music: *Sublime, no lejana y misteriosa, con el silencio vivo de la rosa.*

continuously played classical music while chores were done, the washer was going, the children were fighting or did not want to eat. Frequently, Lída and Michal would become motionless or continue mechanical tasks such as drying dishes while absorbed in the music.

"It reminds me," Michal said, "how I played with my toys under the piano while my father played the Pathetic Sonata – its music thundering around me and taking over my body and mind."

Michal had brought some of his records with him, and they played their favourite pieces for each other, often modern music not frequently performed. They played Carmina Burana, Ballad of the One-Eyed Sailor, or Poulenc's concerto for two pianos and, every so often, they moved the needle several grooves back, replaying a few of bars and pointing with their fingers into the air to indicate a special chord or a breath-taking melody, sometimes singing along or replaying the music in their heads without producing a sound.

This went on until exactly eight p.m., at which time Michal put on Tchaikovsky's piano concerto, and sat silent, with his ear close to the speaker, without paying attention to anything else. On the other side of town, and exactly at the same time, Danna was listening to the same spellbinding recording by Svjatoslav Richter. It was like a prayer.

One evening, after the music stopped, Michal was sitting in the quiet kitchen contemplating his peculiar situation: I am legally married to blond, fashion-conscious Zora, but I live with tall, dark Lída and her world of abstract beauty, yet the one I love is straightforward Danna, with her short curly hair and athletic body. All three are educated and smart, but each is different; all three grew up without a father. An outside observer may think that I love three women, but Zora is history, and Lída is an exceptional friend – but only a friend. Danna has everything: She is a born adventurer and fun to be with. She is a great thinker, yet unassuming. She is sensitive and kind, practical and fast, full of energy and life. But these are just words. Zora has, or had, some of these qualities, and Lída has many of them. Yet when Danna touches my hand, I know she is the woman – and I say woman not girl, because she is a strong woman and a great mother – with whom I want to be with until the end of my life.

At night, Lída always left her bedroom door open, and Michal regularly passed by her bed when closing or opening the window in the children's room after his late night's work, or when checking a child that had a fit of coughing or talked in its sleep. He stopped and looked at Lída's peaceful face, herself sleeping like a child, in a plain cotton nightgown, and with her hand on the pillow above her head. When Michal had a high fever and barely could walk, she moved his bed to the kitchen so she could be there with him. She undressed him, washed him, and changed his bedding, but there was nothing physical between them. They shared only thoughts and beautiful music.

Michal told Lída how much he loved Danna and Lída listened to him patiently. She passed messages between Danna and Michal and treated Danna as her good friend. When Lída enrolled in an English class, Michal thought that she wanted to improve her professional skills. It did not occur to him that, perhaps, she wanted to join him in Canada if Danna changed her mind and returned to Ivan.

When Tibor and Emma called Michal 'Daddy' one evening, Lída lost her usual calm. "Michal is not your father," she shouted at them. "He is our friend. Please, call him Michal!"

Rumours began to spread that Lída was having an affair with a married man, but she carried her head proudly, and said not a word.

> *"My body shivers steadily*
> *Just like the wolverine in the ZOO,*
> *My bear, I yawn merrily,*
> *Why have you bowlegs too?*[5]
>
> (author's brother)

26. FINLAND

Michal was aware that, for a long time, Ivan and Danna had been booked for a ski expedition in northern Finland. He did not know any details, but as the departure drew near, he was getting

---

[5] The Czech original: *Chvěju se celý po těle tak jako rosomák v ZOO, medvěde zívám vesele, pročpak máš nohy do O?*

increasingly uncomfortable.

"If you love me, how can you join him for a holiday?" he asked Danna. "It just isn't right."

"I have been agonizing over it since our night in Sokolov," she sobbed. "This trip has been organized and paid for by our friends from Finland. We hosted them in Prague, and ran the entire Vltava river with them on kayaks. Another Finnish couple is going with us, total of six people. If I don't go, I would not only spoil the trip for all these friends, but I would also waste their money. For safety reasons, six people is the minimum size of the group and the bookings are non-refundable.

"The second problem is," she continued, "that I have not approached Ivan about our separation yet. I am afraid that he will be angry, and I don't want to hurt him. If I don't go, I would have to tell him now without waiting for the right moment. I'd better leave it until we come back."

"I accept your reasoning, but I still don't like the idea of you going with him," Michal said. "It will only make everything more complicated."

She put her hands on his shoulders and looked into his eyes. She radiated humility and kindness. "If I could follow my heart, I would just take you by the hand, and walk away from all this with you, but I have my responsibilities. All this is my fault and Ivan needs time to agree with the separation. If I want to keep Lenka, I have to proceed cautiously."

"She collected herself. "The good thing is that we will sleep in simple log cabins with only one common room – not a place for Ivan to make any advances."

"But you will sleep in a hotel at the beginning and end of your journey …"

"Yes, but that isn't much different from sleeping in the same room at home, is it?"

At the beginning of April, Danna found herself on a ski trail with two weeks of supplies on her back. After pushing through deep snow twenty, sometimes thirty kilometers a day, the group camped in primitive huts with a fire pit in the middle of the floor.

During the freezing nights, they took turns tending the fire.

With every muscle of her body sore, she stared at the glowing embers, her mind fleeing to Michal. Surrounded by the dark mass of sleeping bodies, she could not write him a letter. And even if she wrote one, how could she send it from this remote location in the midst of frozen lakes and snarled northern trees. She tried to send him her thoughts – can you hear me, my dear? What are you doing right now?

Under physical stress, problems reduce to basic needs. She had to eat, sleep, and survive the cold. There was no urgency to solve anything else. She enjoyed cutting the untouched snow of long frozen lakes, and she pressed on thinking of Lenka. She skied and skied, as if she were going to ski like that until the end of her life.

> *"Have no fear, just have no fear*
> *Listen to Sebastian Bach*
> *And hear the fugue we'll play.*
> *When the time comes ..."*
>
> (F. Halas)

27. A BACH FUGUE

No letters came from Danna, not even a postcard. Michal sank into despair. Could it be that Danna returned to Ivan? he thought after the hours and days of unbearable, passive waiting. Why didn't I object more strongly to her departure?

If only he knew about the blank postcard Danna carried in her pocket, waiting, in vain, for an opportunity to scribble "I love you" and immediately post it! He was thinking about the places where she and Ivan slept, and his imagination went wild.

For several years – since Michal had noticed the first cracks in his marriage, he watched deteriorating marriages around him, and he arrived at a conclusion that worked with the precision of a mathematical theorem: *The first serious lover interfering with a marriage is usually the casualty.*

He woke one morning with the idea that his case fit this theorem. Ivan had not had an affair yet, and Michal was the first serious lover Danna had had.

She may still return to him, he worried, but later when she

divorces him, which she undoubtedly will, she will marry someone else. I will be the casualty.

Danna is not an ordinary woman – she will not follow this pattern, he was assuring himself. She loves me as much as I love her. In his heart, however, he was not completely convinced.

In Prague, spring had begun. The snow melted, and a warm breeze dried the streets. Out of habit, people still wore overcoats but they did not button them up. At the Prague Conservatory, one of the large dusty windows was open, and the sound of an organ was pouring out like a waterfall. Michal stopped in his tracks, and looked up: No sign of life behind the window except for music descending in waves, interwoven voices singing and the organ thundering. As if the mighty God were playing there, he thought, as he stood in the middle of the sidewalk with his mouth open. The music carried both sadness and joy, all human emotions, the entire world

There was a short pause, and Michal thought of clapping and shouting Bravo! but then another fugue gently started. He leaned against the wall like a man waiting for a date and listened intently. People passed by in both directions, but nobody seemed to notice the music. He wanted to call someone to witness this miracle – Danna, Lída, his father or mother, someone to share the music with, but the concert would be over before they could come. Oblivious of streetcars and trucks passing through the busy street, he listened until the music stopped, then lowered his head and quietly walked away. The music kept playing in his head for several hours.

28. THE WINDOW

Danna returned with a tanned face and a distant expression. Michal noticed that something had changed, but was afraid to ask. Danna told him 'of course I still love you', but in the same breath, she said that Ivan needed more time. Michal had a feeling that the precious link between them was withering away. He had never been as desperate in his entire life.

This feeling of a sudden gap can only be two-sided, he thought. Danna did not say anything, but it spooked her out of her wits.

Michal's sad eyes haunted her at night, and she realized that she could not make everybody happy. Either Ivan or Michal would be hurt, and waiting would only prolong the agony. In two days, she approached Ivan.

"It was absolutely dreadful," she told Michal the next day. "He began to shake. It was a pitiful picture – this tall, strong guy falling to pieces, his eyes reflecting the broken dream of the happy home, cheerful wife, and cute little daughter – all lost within a dreadful second."

"What did you tell him?"

"I said that our marriage had not been great lately – and you know that was an understatement – and I asked whether he would consider splitting up."

"And what did he answer?"

"He said 'No way, you must have someone else', with a threat rumbling in his voice. I told him I am attracted to another man, but that's not where it started."

Michal saw Danna's ears turning red, and droplets of sweat formed on her forehead.

"I wish the whole thing would resolve quickly without anybody getting hurt," she said. "Ivan is not the best husband, but he does not deserve to be punished like this."

The rules of the game in Danna's household changed. Ivan quit basketball, came home every night and never let Danna out of his sight. One day he came to her office and had a chat with Radim.

When Danna returned from work that day, he was already there and told her as a matter of fact: "I am still your husband and if someone pokes his nose into our marriage, I'll break his neck."

Every day he apologized to Danna and pleaded with her to reconsider her decision. He talked her into going with him to a marriage counselor and sent her to a gynecologist thinking that her aversion to him might be a result of some medical problem. She kept telling him that it all made no sense, but went there just to prove her point.

With Ivan at home, Michal could not call Danna in the evenings.

On such uncertain nights, driven by the desire to be closer to her, he came across the city and circled her house, waiting and watching. Sometimes the draught through the open windows of her apartment stirred the curtains, giving Michal snapshots of the life inside. From the dark street, the apartment was like a lighted stage, and unless Michal stopped or made circles that were too short, nobody paid attention to him.

He usually saw Ivan reading a book, or Danna in an apron behind an ironing board; Lenka at the dining table pointing her spoon up above her head and Danna explaining something to her about the food. Sometimes he saw an empty room – just like an empty stage waiting for the actors to continue the play.

On one starry night filled with the scent of locust trees, he saw a picture that almost drove him out of his mind. Only a night table light was on. The red sofa was unfolded into a double bed and Danna was already there, rolled in a blanket. Dressed in striped pajamas, Ivan was searching for something in the room.

Michal felt as if a rock had landed on his heart. He passed by the window and immediately turned on his heels to catch another glimpse, then crossed the street to where he could stand for a few seconds without rousing suspicion. Ivan climbed over Danna into the same bed, reached over to the lamp and turned the light off.

Michal did not know what to do. He paced up and down the street. Was this the way Ivan was getting his last chance? Did Danna lie and live with Ivan as if nothing had happened? Was Ivan winning her favours? Michal darted toward a street phone. He wanted to call them and get them out of that bed, but abandoned the idea. He could not tell Ivan and Danna what to do, whether she loved him or not. Perhaps she does not love me anymore, he thought. He had an urge to howl like a wounded animal.

When he arrived at Lída's, he was mentally exhausted and looked like a drunkard.

The next morning, he caught Danna alone in the office. "You didn't tell me that you still sleep with Ivan in the same bed!"

She did not even question how he could know that. "Don't be upset. I didn't say I wouldn't. It doesn't mean anything." Michal read her smiling face and realized her innocence. "We don't have any other bed, and we use separate blankets. We have been sleeping like that since Lenka was born without anything happening. You don't have to be afraid of anything."

"I have been there," Michal was not sure how to put it. "This will end in a disaster. He may think that your NO means YES, that you tease him just to be conquered. Some women are like that. You are testing his limits."

Five days later, Danna called late at night and she asked Michal to meet her in the street not far from her house. "Please, come soon!" She was crying.

When he met her thirty-five minutes later, she still had horror in her face. When she began, "It's finished between Ivan and me, absolutely finished ..." Michal already knew what had happened. She had no chance against Ivan. Her pleading to his senses, her crying, her anger, nothing had changed his mind. "I am not on the pill, and I could be pregnant," she said and covered her face with her hands.

I can't blame Ivan, Michal thought. Is this a punishment of the gods? Long ago, I made a similar mistake with equally devastating results. And I also did not want to hurt Zora.

"He still loves you," he said, and wiped Danna's tears with his fingers.

He could never have predicted how he would react to such a situation. He had thought he would became violent if anybody touched Danna, but he was stunned by how everything happened so predictably. He had scored against Ivan, but the price was higher than he was ready to pay. He rocked Danna in his arms. "Don't worry," he whispered. "One child or two, I'll love you the same."

Within one month, Danna filed for divorce, and things began to roll with unprecedented speed.

29. MICHAL MEETS IVAN

Danna and Michal met several blocks from their office on the way to yet another lunch.

"I told Ivan that it's you I love," Danna said. She announced it in the same uninvolved voice, as if telling him that she had bought two kilograms of potatoes.

"What! Are you crazy?"

She looked at him innocently. "He has to learn sooner or later."

Two hours later, Ivan called Michal and asked him for a short chat.

"I can meet you at your factory reception desk, tomorrow at eleven," Michal replied, his heart pounding. Hopefully, he thought, Ivan will calm down overnight, and he will behave rationally if we meet near his office.

When Michal arrived at the factory, an old guard looked at him over his glasses, called Ivan through the intercom, and continued reading his newspaper. He had a big nine-millimeter gun at his hip, but looked so frail that he would have had a trouble loading it, let alone firing it. He would be of no help, Michal thought, if Ivan wants to kill me.

There were no chairs in the hall and Michal's nervous pacing irritated the guard.

Ivan delayed his arrival. He evidently wanted to show how little he cared, but when he appeared in the corridor, he couldn't restrain himself any longer. He barged in, and gestured toward the door. "Let's go outside."

Michal had not seen Ivan for several years and he had forgotten how tall and muscular he was. He came in an old shaggy sweater with frayed sleeves. His crew cut was not combed to any particular side, and he moved in long strides keeping his lips tight. Both men avoided eye contact except for brief moments.

It felt as if winter had returned. The sidewalks were empty and nobody was in sight. Gusts of cold northern wind swept the neglected streets around the factory and low dark clouds raced through the sky. A peculiar pair, they strode silently in the middle of the road, several feet apart. Ivan was like an engine building up steam with the safety valve shut off, and Michal kept a safe distance.

Trying to release the tension, Michal offered the first sentence: "You asked me for a chat. Why?" He tried to sound cool, but his voice trembled. After he said it, he was sorry that he had broken the silence.

For Ivan, it was as if a dam had broken. He began to spill everything he had been mulling over for the last twenty-four hours. "I have respect for you … you used to be my teacher … and now Danna is telling me that she loves you."

He looked straight at Michal. Michal met his gaze with a neutral, calm expression. If Ivan knew how far things have gone, he would accuse me more directly, he thought.

"I've made many mistakes," Ivan rumbled on, "but she is still my wife. Promise that you will not interfere with my marriage. Can we shake hands on it?"

They reached the wire fence at the end of the street, hands freezing and teeth chattering. They turned around and Michal felt he had to play it straight.

"I'm sorry," he said. "You and Danna have reached the point of no return. I've been through something similar in my marriage. You have no other chance. If it's not me, it will be someone else. Like it or not," he went on bluntly, "I do love Danna, and there is nothing I can do about it. You can beat me to a pulp, but it won't change anything …"

With this last statement, Michal kept an even greater distance from Ivan, who swayed as he walked, his fists pressing on his hips. They reached the factory gate. With his hand on the door handle, Ivan uttered: "You better watch it. If I find anything between you two except your platonic thoughts, I'll finish you quickly."

30. KARATE CLASS

When the factory gate closed behind Ivan, the weather suddenly felt surprisingly pleasant. Michal looked at the sun peeking from behind the clouds and checked his watch. Nobody was waiting for him at the office, and a brisk walk appealed to him more than taking a streetcar. As he walked, he kept thinking about Ivan's fists that looked like sledgehammers. He took a detour and stopped at a karate club, where he knew the instructor.

"It's not a good idea to join right now," the instructor said. "The class is preparing for the national championship, and the training is tough."

"That's exactly what I need," said Michal, undeterred. "I want to learn karate as quickly as I can."

"Come tomorrow, but don't forget that these guys are ten years younger than you and they are in good shape."

Starting the next day, Michal sweated with the class through countless push-ups, sit-ups, and dart runs. He jumped up and down three flights of stairs on one leg, ran around the gym with a 95 kg student over his shoulders, rolled and fell on mats and on the parquet floor, three hours a day, five days a week. He had never thought he could endure so much.

When Zora heard about it, she was furious: "Stupid idiot! If he has a heart attack, who will support the children?"

Michal was getting stronger but he was not learning anything about fighting. One day after class, he pulled the instructor aside: "I have to tell you the truth. This big guy may want to kill me. Can you teach me something practical quickly?"

The instructor grinned. "I thought there must be something like that. Is it about a girl?"

"About his wife."

"You? That's a new twist!"

The short instructor, still in his kimono with a black belt, sat down on a chair with its backrest between his legs. "First of all, get it out of your mind that he is stronger than you are. State of mind is all that matters in a fight."

"Maybe in theory," Michal talked to the floor, "but if you saw us standing side by side, you'd understand my problem."

The instructor contemplated a bit. "Rule number one: You must avoid the fight. Talk him out of it, postpone it, and run away from him if you can. He who leaves intact wins. It's not worth losing an eye or having a broken spine for a woman. What if he has a knife?"

"Have you ever been in love? If it meant losing her, running away is not an option."

"I see this all the time," the instructor nodded. "Intelligent, smart men blinded by love. Tell me more about him."

"He is about two meters tall," Michal showed with his hand, "his shoulders are this wide, and I think he is right-handed. Good at basketball and mountain-climbing, but he has not done any martial arts. A graduated engineer, sloppy in his appearance, speaks slowly in a deep voice; when excited he may stutter a bit. He does not smoke, but has a few beers here and there like everybody else. He likes the outdoors. A loner, but honest. He always keeps his word."

"A guy like that may beat you up, but he won't kill you unless by accident. His arms are long, and because he plays basketball, his reactions are fast," the instructor analyzed the situation. "He is not going to attack you from the back – it will be a face-to-face, one-on-one encounter.

"I will teach you one punch and one kick. Let's start with the punch," he said after a short pause. "It's a matter of speed. Raise your hand, and I will try to hit it. Move the hand away when you see I am ready to strike."

Every time the instructor hit, Michal's hand was still there.

"If you can't move the hand away," the instructor explained, "you can't protect your body. I can hit you wherever I chose.

"Before you strike, you must be ready in the launching position and you must get there inconspicuously – while you talk, or at the beginning of your encounter. Neither your body nor your eyes must give away that you are ready to strike. Then suddenly, you explode into this tremendous hit." The instructor's fist suddenly sprang out and hit the wall with unbelievable speed. The brick wall shook and patch of plaster fell to the floor.

"Your right leg forms a firm base, and as your arm moves forward, you turn your fist. When you finish the turn, the arm is straight, locked into a stiff position, and it delivers a hard blow. At the time of the impact, your entire body is behind your arm, and your arm is like a steel rod. Try it on a mat first."

He suspended a mat on the wall and Michal punched it for several minutes. "Curve your fingers to protect your thumb, and make your fist flat so you won't hurt your knuckles. Try to hit the wall, but gently first."

"The kick is similar, but you aim for his shin, which is excruciatingly painful. Even with a tall adversary, it will give you enough time to run away or knock him down with a solid punch. Practice the kick on a lamp post out in the street. You stand casually like this, and then suddenly – bang. At the end, again, the leg must be stiff, and the mass of your entire body is behind it."

"And remember," the instructor emphasized, "you have to practise this for weeks, several times a day. Place a towel on the wall first. Later, you will punch a bare wall. Come every day to show me your progress."

Michal stopped coming to the karate classes, but he practiced diligently until all this became second nature. One day, after an argument with Zora, he felt an urge to punch something. He hit a particle-board wall, and his fist went through.

Ivan never attacked. He went from jealous rage to quiet depression, from throbbing pain to false hope and, because he never saw Michal and Danna together, he began to wonder about his own sanity. It even crossed his mind that his suspicion could be a mere illusion. In the meantime, Michal and Danna kept hiding carefully. They knew that even the slightest indication that there was something physical between them could have a devastating effect at both their divorce hearings.

"I am afraid of forest. In high noon forest,
Lover can't bear his heart…"
(Fráňa Šrámek, Splav)

31. SCENT OF SUMMER FOREST

Since the divorce application was filed, Danna felt free and without obligations to Ivan. For her, just as for Michal, marriage implied deep unconditional love; it was relationship so special and sacred that whether it was approved by a priest or a town clerk was irrelevant. Using the same logic, if the love ceased to exist, the marriage automatically dissolved, regardless of whether the divorce was already approved in a court of law.

Ivan and Danna adhered to their daily routines, but Danna left whenever she wanted. Before such departures, she gave Ivan instructions about Lenka or about the dinner in the fridge – without any guilt, just as she would have told a babysitter or her mother-in-law.

When opportunity arose, Michal and Danna drove out of the city in search of secluded places, and became experts in pulling the car from muddy gulches, sand dunes, or dead ends full of boulders and roots where it was impossible to turn.

On one memorable afternoon, they left after work, each in a different direction. Michal aimed for the car he had parked in a small street not far from the office. The early summer sun hurt his eyes. People rushed from work, cars blocked the traffic, and drivers blew horns and swore at one another. Making sure that nobody followed his car, Michal turned several times through the adjacent streets then stopped at a quiet spot, as if searching for something in the glove compartment.

With perfect timing, from the opposite direction, Danna came out of the crowd. She slipped into the car, turned her face away from the curb, and Michal stepped on the gas.

"It feels great to sit beside you," she said.

They had no exact plans except driving north, somewhere out of Prague, to the flat sandy countryside with patches of woods and lush pasture where rivers meander slowly through water lilies and cattails. This was not cottage country and the chance of meeting a vacationer or a hiker on a workday afternoon was virtually nil. Frogs were singing in the marshes, and bees were busy collecting honey.

"You have beautiful eyes," Michal said.

"Watch the road." She kissed him on the cheek.

He followed the highway for about an hour, then turned into a small, grassy forest road. Clearly, nobody had passed through there for at least two weeks. The road changed direction, narrowed into a trail, and ended on a sandy meadow surrounded under a big pine. Danna jumped out of the car, stretched her arms, and took a deep breath. The air had the scent of summer forest, of dry grass and bark baking in the sun. Crickets buzzed in the grass and jade-like drops of the tree gum dripped from the pine needles. Michal noticed the line of Danna's breast, and the aroma of her body.

A dense growth of young spruce surrounded them in all directions, and Michal pulled the car right inside it. Unless someone searched for the car, it was hard to notice. Then, with a blanket under his arm, he pushed through the thicket and Danna followed him with a provision bag over her shoulder.

The trees formed small openings with fragrant floors of dry moss and strawberry leaves. No voices, no steps, no sounds of human activity.

"These little meadows are like little private rooms, each nicer and more inviting," Danna whispered.

They rushed eagerly into the next one and the next one, until the scent of strawberries overcame their senses.

Michal took Danna in his arms. "This is far enough. Let's stay here."

They shed their clothes quickly, and embraced in full sunlight, naked . . .

The sun sank behind the treetops, but their little room was still warm. Stretched out on the blanket, they watched the shadows growing longer. Only the sky had not changed – light summer blue and without a single cloud.

Danna knelt on the blanket, unzipped the bag, and pulled out a round object wrapped in a checkered cloth. "This is for you," she smiled, holding a watermelon with arms stretched like an Egyptian goddess. Michal took it from her as if this were some religious ceremony, rummaged through the bag until he found a knife, and sliced the melon in half. It was still icy cold; dew rose along the cut like tiny crystals of sugar. He kissed her naked breast. "You are the most beautiful woman in the world. Are you aware of that?"

"What do you think?" Danna laughed, spitting the seeds into the grass around them. "Is this going to be a watermelon patch next summer?"

Somewhere behind the trees the sun crossed the critical line. The temperature began to drop, and the ground grew damp. They collected garments scattered in the grass and dressed quickly. "We'll have to cook some dinner," Michal said.

"I have a pack of chicken legs back in the car," Danna remembered, "but for a barbecue we need a better place. This forest is too dry."

They drove the car from under the bushes, back over the highway and, without looking at the road map, they continued westward on a dirt road that lead them straight into the sun. Little puffy clouds rose on the sky, the sunset turned purple, and the night was descending.

They crossed a stone bridge over a creek and all they could see ahead were large abandoned fields on both sides of the road and the ribbon of the road vanishing in the evening haze.

"If not the world, today's journey ends here," Michal said and stepped out of the car. "The ground's hard like a landing strip. We can drive anywhere we want."

He climbed back into the car and, guided by Danna, drove over the wild mustard and ragweed, away from the road. Earlier that summer, the creek must have overflowed its banks. A layer of dry, cracked mud covered the ground, and clumps of muddy debris hung on the lower branches of the willow and aspen bushes along its shore.

Together, they quickly pitched Michal's tent. Michal ran to the creek, broke twigs here and there, returned, and started a fire with one match without using paper. Then he ran to the creek again, came back with two big branches and a rusty wire, sanded the wire with a scrap of the sandpaper from his car, bent it to form a crank, spiked the chicken legs on it, and tested that the crank would turn on the forks of the two branches that he had pushed into ground.

While he was doing this, Danna unpacked the sleeping bags, arranged them inside the tent, filled the teakettle in the creek, found two old bricks under the bridge, set the teakettle on them, peeled and sliced a cucumber, and sat beside Michal watching the fire.

"You really are an experienced camper," Michal said.

"How many times have *you* done this before?" she grinned.

"Thousands of times during my ten years of Scouting."

"Ten years?" Danna turned to him." Scouts were banned by Germans until 1945, and then by the Communists since 1948. It can't be more than three years."

"It was a secret troop. I owe them almost as much as I do my parents."

"Do you know what you could get for that?"

He was staring into the fire. "Severe beating and ten years in a Communist concentration camp."

"Michal, you always surprise me with something. Your mother did not have an easy life with you. Tell me more about this troop."

"When the radio announced that Scouts had been disbanded, I was twelve. You can't imagine a more dedicated little Scout. I lived for the Scout ideals, their field trips and for the adventure."

"Sometimes, you are still like a little boy."

Michal gave her a gentle jab with his elbow. "I went to our clubhouse but it was already sealed. A pink proclamation from the Communist Party taped on the door condemned Scouts as a military, subversive organization promoting imperialistic aggression.

"You would have to be a Scout to understand our pride, our devotion. During the war, many Scouts including Ťapka – I told you about him – joined the Resistance; many were tortured or killed by Nazis. Besides survivor skills and love of nature, we were raised in high ideals such as service to others, democracy, and the right to justice and freedom. It was unthinkable that we would give all that up."

Michal bent down, blew several times into the fire, and continued: "Several months later, Ťapka opened the Division of Young Sailors in the local yacht club. This group of twenty-four carefully screened boys (none of our parents was in the Communist Party) trained on sailboats and competed in regattas, but otherwise did all the other things that Sea Scouts normally do. We had no uniforms and never used any Scout symbols. The word Scout was strictly prohibited even in our private conversation – if anybody heard it, we could have all gone straight to prison. From the old rituals, we maintained only two: We shook left hands and flew our original flag with the Scout lily removed."

Michal slowly turned the crank. "We built our boats, and made month-long expeditions every summer. As a skipper, at the age of fourteen, I was responsible for planning, provisioning and cooking, as well as the life of five other boys. We went through wild rapids and mill shoots regularly."

"You knew how to cook at fourteen?"

"We had the entire year to prepare for each trip. My mother taught me to cook. For a month, I either cooked or helped her cook all our family meals. I could cook soups, meat, dumplings, and pasta, anything you can imagine. On trips, when we had enough time, we even baked pies in an improvised stone oven.

"The training was quite rough though: Always on the go, always running, getting up at night and taking off for a twenty-kilometer marches, surprises and night games, athletic races … Some of my friends think it was perhaps too rough – a bit like marines."

"Did you have to bear arms?"

"No, never. We trained to survive under any condition but our motto was to help others, not to kill. It was the Communist Youth that trained with rifles and fake hand grenades. We knew well though how to penetrate guarded territories, move through woods or cities undetected, or how to swim under water. Any of us could cross the country with only a knife in his pocket."

Danna was staring at the stars. "And is your group still active?"

"The police interrogated Ťapka several times, but could not prove anything. Then they expropriated his villa and, as I told you, exiled him to a polluted town near the German border. Later, he suffered a heart attack, lost most of his vision, but never gave up. I still have his letter about the old handcart he loaded with quality books from local bookstores. On paydays, he pulled this *library on wheels* from one factory gate to another and sold the books with a small markup. *I am not only able to support myself*, he wrote me in one of his letters, *but I also promote good literature to these factory workers.* "

"And what happened with the other Scouts from your troupe?"

"Most of them left for the West. Victor, the last one I talked to, was leaving for Canada over a year ago. He gave me the address for the National Research Council."

With a blanket over their shoulders, they watched the roasting chicken, the juice dripping into the ashes. "This is the strangest campsite I have ever been to," Danna drew closer to Michal. "So rugged and still so cozy."

"Nobody's going to look for us here," Michal laughed. "We're camping like two gypsies. Did you steal the chicken?"

"Not this time," she laughed. "Did you bring any bread?"

"No, I thought you'd bring it."

They ate the chicken with their fingers, laughing.

"I wonder why you are so hungry," Danna looked at him with foxy eyes.

"I wish I had a mirror," Michal laughed. "You smeared grease and ashes all over your face."

"You should talk! Go see your face in the car mirror."

"We can't wash now. It's dark, and the shore is muddy. The flashlight battery is dead."

"You can wash in the tea," Danna laughed, "if there is any left."

They crawled into the tent. "What a pain, these single sleeping bags," Michal complained. "I've been looking for a double since I met you. They just don't make them. What's wrong with a double sleeping bag?"

"Ask at the office meeting tomorrow morning," Danna giggled.

"Your nose is cold, I'll warm it up." He kissed her all over her face.

"Good night! We have to rise early to be at work on time."

They woke with the first signs of light. Low-lying fog covered the fields as they washed in the creek, brushed their jeans and shoes, packed the tent, and started the engine.

"We don't have time for breakfast," Michal said.

"This was the nicest camping trip I have ever been on," Danna passed him a cold apple.

"I only wish I could be with you like this all the time," he said while driving back to the road.

He drove with Danna leaning on his shoulder. The sun came up like a red sliver above the morning mist, then trees and field flowers slowly changed from purple-grey to their true colours. By the time trees and shrubs turned to bright green, they were back at the office.

"I am not dead, I am in love."
(Adolfo Bioy Casares)

32. MYSTERIOUS BLANÍK

The myth of Mount Blaník had puzzled Michal since he was a little boy. Everybody told him that there was nothing to see out there, one among many hills covered with dense trees and brushes, two hours southeast from Prague. No tourist attractions, nor parking lot or information sign.

The old myth has it that inside Blaník lies an army of knights, ready to defend Bohemia in its darkest hour. The mountain will open with a thundering noise and King Wenceslaus – bearing the white and red Czech banner – will lead the knights into a battle to defend their homeland. No enemy will be able to resist their magic force, and Bohemia will be free again.

Surprisingly, Bohemia's darkest hour had not arrived yet. In 1621, Austrian Habsburgs defeated the Czechs. Twenty-seven Czech leaders were publicly executed, and their spokesman had his tongue cut out before being decapitated. German became the official language, and during the 300 years that followed, Czech Protestants were tortured and killed by Jesuits. In the mid 1800's, the Czech language was resurrected, and in 1918 an independent democratic republic was established. Hitler's army occupied Czechoslovakia in 1939, and the nation's elite were sent to concentration camps by the thousands. The communists took power in 1949, and the Soviets invaded in 1968. Was this not bad enough? Are there more dreadful times yet to come?

The myth says that treetops will dry all over the mountain. A dry oak at the summit will turn green, and the spring under the eastern slope will become a torrent. The enemies will be so numerous that they could trample the entire Czech kingdom with the hooves of their horses.

The legend makes no sense. King Wenceslaus loathed wars. Instead of fighting German King Henry, he bought peace for 300 silver rods and 300 steers – to be delivered yearly *until the end of all times*. Many Czechs, including his brother Boleslav, refused such serfdom. Eager to get Wenceslaus's crown, on September 28, 929, Boleslav with three armed men confronted him on his way to morning Mass. Wenceslaus wrestled the sword from his brother, and ran for the safety of a nearby cathedral. One of the assassins caught up with him at the church door, and the 28-year-old king died hanging onto the door ring, with a dagger in his back. The church declared him a saint.

At one of their lunches, Michal told Danna: "The last symphonic poem in My Country[6] is about Blaník. I'd like to explore that mountain."

"It sounds romantic," Danna smiled. "Let's go there next weekend."

On the Saturday, Ivan took Lenka with him to his parents and, after lunch, Michal picked up Danna several blocks from her

[6] Má Vlast (=My Country) is the set of six symphonic poems by B. Smetana. Well known Vltava (Moldau) is the first one.

house. Fog and drizzle spread over the entire region, but it was cozy and warm inside the car. The weather had another advantage: Most people would stay indoors, and the countryside would be deserted.

The rain descended in tiny drops, and drivers adjusted their speed to the low visibility. Wipers moved back and forth with a monotonous sound. Nobody was passing.

Michal drove through small villages and towns that surrounded the city, then entered cottage country with wooded hills along the Sázava River. Had this been a sunny day, voices of bathers would be heard across the river, the air would have smelled of freshly caught fish, and suntanned bodies of volleyball players would have glowed in the sunshine. But on that day, nobody was there. An old steam engine pulled an empty train along the river and gave a long whistle before it entered a tunnel.

By that time, most cars had left the highway and the drizzle turned into a downpour, smearing the grey scenery. Michal and Danna recognized Blaník as soon as it came into view. An unmistakably gloomy air surrounded the mountain and the trees covering its slopes had a distinctly dark colour. White vapours rose from it in narrow vertical columns.

"Are you sure the mountain does not swallow people at this time of the year?" Danna said.

"Don't go in," Michal teased her. "Remember, those who had entered reappeared only a year later!"

Numerous forest roads circled the mountain, but no road led directly to it. They traveled in circles, until the narrow road took them to a grassy field. The downpour changed to steady drizzle again. They got out of the car, and Dana touched the ground with her hand. "We can't camp here. The ground is soaking wet."

Michal embraced her, their bodies touching from lips to toes. "I'd like to camp soon."

"Look over there – an old logging road," she pointed forward. "We can drive deeper into the forest, and sleep in the car."

"That depends on how soon we'll get stuck. Let's try it."

Danna put on her raincoat and walked ahead of the car, pointing to protruding rocks, roots, and potholes. Michal gingerly followed her directions until the road vanished. The car stood in the middle of a flat, wooded area, and they could not see any road, not even looking back in the direction from which they had come. The trunks of big, tall trees stood in rows wide enough for Michal to drive anywhere he wanted, but their crowns connected overhead. The wet, black bark of the trees contrasted with the bright yellow leaves accumulated on the forest floor. As if the leaves illuminated the place, the light was coming from the ground, not from the sky.

Michal turned the engine off, stepped out, and took Danna around her waist. "Don't move and listen!" There was a deep absence of any sound except for tiny drops falling, and a scent of decaying leaves.

When undressing inside the car, Danna worried. "Could someone see us here?"

"At night? In this rain? Nobody will be here except for wild pigs and possibly some deer."

"I don't like even a doe watching me like this," Danna laughed.

"Don't raise your little legs then …"

"I can't help it," she covered his face with kisses.

The next morning, when Mother Nature forced them to leave the car, they could not stop giggling. The rain had stopped, and the car stood in the middle of forest, visible for miles. Assorted clothes hung on the car windows – Danna's blouse, Michal's jeans, a striped duffel bag. Danna's bra had been forgotten under the rear window and, inside the car, it looked like a burrow. Everything out of order – sleeping bags, blankets and socks, wet running shoes, and an unfolded tent.

Danna came out in her panties, wearing Michal's sweater. Her feet were wet and cold. "If that's the way squirrels spend their rainy days, I don't mind. We should stay in the car a bit longer."

Several hours later, they drove back over the leaves, until they found a marked trail. The sun broke the clouds, and the forest awakened. "We must get to the top," Danna said.

"Absolutely," Michal laughed.

While ascending the hill, they met a group of students, and four other couples. Michal worried at first whether these people might know Danna or him, but as they chatted, they soon forgot about it and walked holding hands like ordinary lovers.

33. WEEKEND WITH CHILDREN

Two weeks later, the office phone rang. Radim picked it up and made a sour face: "It's Zora." Michal reached for the receiver, mentally shifting from his work to some new convoluted nonsense.

"Michal, it's me. You will have the children for the weekend and we have to discuss the logistics."

I'd love to have them, Michal thought, but then it crossed his mind that this could be the kind of trap only Zora could conceive.

"Wait a minute," he replied. "Last time you talked to me, you said that you would not allow a scoundrel like me anywhere near them. Besides, it's Thursday. Don't you think I may already have plans for the weekend?"

"Then change your plans. You have always claimed you want the children. I'm going to Vienna, and will be back on Sunday night."

Now Michal understood: Zora's mother had bribed someone to get them a weekend shopping spree to Austria, and Zora needed a babysitter.

"All right. On Friday, after work, I'll take them to my place."

"Absolutely not! You'll stay here in my apartment over Friday night, and for Saturday and Sunday, I have arranged a cottage near the Sázava River. The cottage owner is a friend of my mother's, and he promised to make sure you are treating the children properly."

Here was the trap. Zora did not know about Danna, but by forcing Michal and his girlfriend – whoever it was – to split for the weekend, she was trying to plant a seed of discord between them.

The idea of getting the children for the entire weekend was irresistible. "So you've already arranged to leave tomorrow, have you?" he said.

"Yes, the bus leaves at five p.m."

"How can I reach the cottage owner?"

Zora gave him the man's phone number, and Michal called him right away and met after work. The man was about sixty, bald, and looked like a carpenter.

"Would you mind if I bring three more children and two friends of mine?" Michal asked.

"Does that include your new girlfriend?"

As Michal expected, the man was well informed. "Oh, no – just two more single parents. We all have sleeping bags."

"We have two bedrooms downstairs, and with the sleeping bags, twenty people can fit in the attic. Let's have fun," he winked at Michal. "Bring your friends along."

> *"The night spread its golden hive*
> *over the evening groves."*
> (V. Nezval)

34. ANTS AND FIREFLIES

Most cottages in that region were packed on small lots along the river, but some were on the hills overlooking the valley. The car climbed the curves through a dense forest until the view opened wide. There, at the top, the grass was dry and tall and field flowers were blooming. The road passed a small sand pit and then, in the middle of nowhere, met a dozen of squared gardens separated by hedges. Each garden had a large cabin.

When the car stopped, it looked as if it exploded. Michal opened the door, and numerous packages rolled out. Five children between two and five crawled out, Michal and Lída unloaded more stuff. The cottage owner and his wife were already standing at the gate. "Welcome, welcome! Bring them all in!"

Passing through the gate, gave Michal a sensation of reducing the entire world to one of these green squares filled with the aroma of recently watered flowerbeds on a hot summer day. Everything essential was there – apple orchard, cold frame, two beehives, iron tub for collecting the rainwater, and a vegetable garden with rows of strawberry beds. The sky was blue, and what was beyond the hedges was irrelevant. The children fell in love with the attic, and climbed up and down the ladder until the adults chased them out into the garden.

At that moment, a second car arrived. A young, chubby man and a saluting girl of five marched through the gate like an army. The man played a guitar, and they both sang with great gusto:

The ants are marching one by one, hurrah, hurrah the little one stopped to suck his thumb, hurrah, hurrah.

The ants are marching two by two, hurrah, hurrah, the little one stopped to tie his shoe, hurrah, hurrah.

The ants are marching three by three ...

The man danced around, and greeted the cottage owners with a pirouette.

Michal laughed. "This is Olda[7]. He needs no introduction. We work at the same place."

The program was simple. The three parents supervised the six children. Only minor problems occurred: one child stepped on a bee, another cut her finger, a toddler fell backward into the tub. The parents washed diapers, and improvised cooking. By noon, everybody was tired.

Olda and Michal lined up the children in a row, and washed them with a garden hose, while Lída and the wife of the cottage owner prepared lunch under an old apple tree. With full stomachs, the adults ached for a nap, but the recharged children began to chase each other around the garden again.

Michal got an idea. "Olda, could you read something to the children?"

"Sure. Did you bring any books with you?"

Lída reached into her bag and pulled out *Ferda the Ant*. In this book, a smart, mechanically talented ant who can fix or build anything encounters other characters from the insect world.

---

[7] Pronounce [ol-da] with 'ol' as in Oliver.

Children loved the story, and parents knew it by heart.

Olda shouted: "Hey, kids, come here and sit beside me, so you can see the pictures."

The cottage owner and his wife leaned against the tree trunk, and listened intently. They used to read the same story to their children, but had not heard it for some twenty years. Lída lay on her back and watched the moving clouds. Olda read:

A young boy followed a trail through the forest, and he whistled to himself.

The boy would have whistled until the end of the forest, but a rustling sound blended into his melody. Is it raining? The boy stretched his arm and looked at the sky. The sky was clear like the cover of a new schoolbook. What could it be? Under a tall spruce was a gigantic anthill, almost as tall as the boy himself, with ants running all over. They were making the rustling sound.

Michal fought his drowsiness with little success, but the next paragraph woke him up:

At the top of the anthill stood an ant wearing a red scarf and a small knapsack. He held Karl Marx's Capital in one hand, and a smooth spruce needle in the other. He called out: "Comrades, watch out! In the name of the Victory and Communism!" And he sat down on the needle, and rode it down as if it were a sled.

"That isn't in the book," Michal said. "I remember this section."

"I only changed a few words. It makes the story more interesting," Olda said with a serious face. "Children, do you like it? Should I continue?"

"Yes, please, do!" the children were glued to his words, and Olda went on.

In the book, Ferda gets lost, and it begins to rain. Enormous drops plaster the poor ant, and he searches for a shelter. Finally, he runs into a snail sleeping inside his house. The ant knocks politely on the door, but the snail is most unfriendly and rude. In Olda's interpretation, the story took a new, interesting twist:

Ferda saw a brass plate on the door: Comrade Brezhnev. Great, he thought, he will give me the shelter I need. He knocked on the door, but you should see what happened! The front of the house lifted, and a grim face with big black eyebrows came out: "Get lost, you revisionist, you imperialist puppet, you bourgeois parasite!" The head was very angry, and was spitting in all directions.

Olda had changed the innocent children book into a political satire. The ants worked hard trying to meet the five-year economic plan. They went for the May Day parade, and talked about their dedication to the communist cause. When the cricket's radio broke, Ferda fixed it so well that he could even tune in Radio Free Europe. All of the insects gathered at his house to listen to the great American music.

The children listened with their eyes wide open. The adults shook in bursts of laughter until they hit the ground, exhausted. "You are a born comedian, Olda," the cottage owner was drying his tears, while holding his stomach with his other hand.

After dinner, Michal told the children: "Once a year, on St. John's day, there is a magic night called Midsummer Night, and it happens to be tonight. On this night, fireflies[8] come out in great numbers. There will be night moths and June bugs, and chestnut blossoms will stand all over the trees like pink candles. If you are good today, you don't have go to bed early tonight. We'll go to the woods to see the fireflies."

"We will be good, we will be good," they shouted and jumped around him.

The parents washed them, and pulled warm pants and sweaters over their pajamas. The sky was already changing and bats began to fly. Children and adults, hand in hand, formed a line across the field, and followed the narrow road into the dark woods. In his palm, Michal felt a little hand shaking with excitement and fear.

"Are you afraid of something, Rita?"

"Of the wolves."

"There won't be any wolves tonight. This is a night of good magic."

As the crowns of the trees closed above them, thousands of fireflies came out in bursts and processions, swirling around them and flashing their tiny lights. Children and adults alike watched them, bewildered.

---

[8] in Czech, fireflies are called St. John's flies.

"Have you ever seen anything so beautiful?" Lída whispered.

The next day at noon, the sun was far too strong, and Lída called from the kitchen: "Michal, we have run out of milk. And look how filthy the children are."

Even Michal was tired. "Let's leave earlier and avoid the traffic."

They thanked the cottage owners, and the children waved from the car window long after the gardens and cabins disappeared behind the hill.

"How did you like the weekend?" Michal asked them.

"It was great!" they shouted, but after a while they complained about thirst. The car was small for so many people. Their faces were red, and Lída's little boy asked to pee just as they drove to the vicinity of Zora's apartment.

"Why don't we stop there?" Michal said. "We'll wash them there in all the modern comfort."

"I don't like it," Lída shook her head. "You know Zora."

"Zora won't return until late. It will be quite a chore to wash them in your place. The water heater is broken."

"If you insist," Lída said with a grim face, and looked at the windows of Zora's apartment. "I have a feeling we are heading into a disaster."

Michal ran upstairs and unlocked the door. The apartment was empty. They started to wash the children immediately. Michal worked in the bathroom while Lída dressed and undressed the five children in the hall. The vinyl floor was covered with puddles and piles of dirty clothes, the water in the bathroom ran full throttle, and the sound of splashing water filled the small space. Nobody spoke much.

Then the bell rang. To Michal, who answered the door with soapy hands and sleeves rolled up, Zora appeared like a phantom. She wore a purple and yellow knitted dress that hung on her like a potato sack. He noticed she wore no bra and looked pitiful with green eye shadow and a strange hairdo. Knowing Zora, it was the latest fashion, but Michal hardly recognized her.

She was pale with anger, and words came out of her mouth like rapid gunfire: "Get away from my place, you swine, you shit, you slut with no morals ..." she shouted at Lída. She purposely screamed with the apartment door wide open, making a show for the entire house.

Lída grabbed her children, and covered their ears. "We have to go, this lady must be out of her mind," she said, and ran with them down the stairs as fast as she could.

Michal darted after her, but his three little ones clung to his arms, water dripping all over the place: "Daddy, please, stay with us! We don't want you to leave!"

Michal closed his eyes, and saw the fireflies and their reflections in children's faces. He saw the laughing children and Lída caring for them over the weekend.

"I hate you so much that I could kill you!" Michal heard himself telling Zora, "Why do you have to spoil everything?"

Zora sat in the kitchen, silent. After seeing Michal when passing the children to him before her departure for Vienna, she decided to reconcile. She spent the entire weekend trying to make herself more attractive. She bought a portable stereo and took an earlier bus, planning to surprise Michal with the expensive gift. She was in the apartment already when Michal arrived, but when she saw the crowd coming in, she panicked, ran up two flights of stairs, and hid on a public balcony. After a while, unable to stand the humiliation any longer, she came down, and rang the bell.

When Michal arrived at Lída's, she was already there. Her face looked tired, but she was not angry.

"I apologize," Michal said. "It was a dumb idea to go there."

35. BIRTHDAY GIFT

Michal paid no attention to his birthdays, and celebrated those of people dear to him only because he saw that it mattered to them. He could not understand what difference it would make whether he was in this world thirty-two years or thirty-two years and eleven days.

He was perplexed when, at one of their lunches, Danna gave

him a miniature box wrapped in dark-blue paper with small silver stars. Her hand was trembling. "Happy birthday."

"I forgot, you are right. Today is my birthday."

He slowly unwrapped the box. This looks like a ring box, he wondered. Why anything so expensive? What would I do with a ring?

Two small cuff links made of sterling silver sa side by side on a silky, white cushion. He took them out, and examined their shape and geometric engravings.

"Danna, they are so elegant!" He tried one on his sleeve. "I have never owned any jewelry except my wedding band."

"I noticed ... I wanted to give you something different, something you don't have," Danna smiled.

He kept the box in his pocket for the rest of the day, taking the cufflinks out when nobody was around, examining them in the light, trying to imagine how Danna selected them and touched them with her fingers.

36. ANOTHER BIRTHDAY GIFT

When Michal returned home – he called Lída's place his home because it was his registered address – he helped Lída to feed the children, and then they ate dinner together and talked about work. When they finished, Lída cleared the table and brought out her briefcase.

"I have a little birthday gift for you," she said quietly while looking sideways, as if it was something not even worth mentioning.

"How did you know it's my birthday?"

"From your identification card," her eyes laughed. "But listen, this is an unusual present. Will you accept my conditions?"

"I will, unless you ask for the impossible. Come on, I'm curious!"

She took out a book. "You can read as much as you want, but you mustn't copy anything, not a single word. Tomorrow morning, I have to return it. The source of the book is my secret."

"I accept, pass it on." When he looked at the front page, he cried out: "Where did you get this?"

He began to read. Holding the book in his hands, he recollected that many years before, he had read this very a collection of science-fiction stories. He had forgotten the title of the book, its author and the publisher, except for one story that still fascinated him.

In this story, two young brothers find a battered metal container with a strange toy – a frame with randomly arranged strings, which allow many beads to move around the frame. All the beads are blue except one, which is red. The boys play with the toy until they discover that one sequence of moves causes the red bead to disappear. Neither the boys nor their parents understand that the toy came from the future; its purpose is to teach children four-dimensional space and time travel.

Eventually, the boys abandon the toy and begin to build a contraption from scraps of wood, strings and pieces of wire in the middle of their living room. After being preoccupied by this for several days, the younger boy suddenly shouts: "Look! I have it. He changes something in the construction and crawls through one of its holes followed by his brother. Their father hears the commotion, looks over the newspaper he is reading – only to watch helplessly how the boys vanish.

Shortly after Michal had moved with Lída, he had mentioned how he had searched through libraries and bookstores, but the book had eluded him.

Now, he was reading the story over and over again. "I am not allowed to write anything down?" he asked. "Not even the publisher or the author?"

"Remember, you promised," Lída laughed. "Not a single word! After I return the book, no trace should remain."

37. CAR ATTACK

What Michal did not expect on his birthday was that Zora would show up – and especially not in the middle of the night.

Zora frequently asked for the car to take the children for a medical checkup, visit her mother, or for a weekend outing. Michal never refused, but often had problems getting the car back. Zora pretended that something had broken down, the car was in a repair shop, or she simply refused to return it because she 'would need it for another couple of days'.

Alone on the warm rainy night, Michal was still sitting at his desk. Except for a circle of light under his lamp, everything around him was in darkness. The doors throughout the apartment were open. Lída slept peacefully after a busy day, an open book beside her bed as it had fallen out of her hand. Michal could hear the breathing of the two children and peeked into the nursery room. The little girl smiled and mumbled in her dream.

He was absorbed in his latest idea – a computer made from thousands, perhaps millions of tiny, identical cubes pressed into a large block. The internal logic of such a computer would not be fixed and unchangeable. Like the human brain, the computer would remember logic as a path connecting these cubes. He was excited. Such computers would be universal and more reliable. If, by repeated learning, each relation were stored as multiple independent paths, such a computer would keep working even if some blocks began to fail. It could monitor its own health, and repairing it would be easy: A robot could disassemble the block, test individual cubes, replace the faulty ones, and put the block together again.[9]

Outside, torrents of water gushed down in vertical lines. Large oily drops rolled down the leaves that touched the black iron of the balcony railing. Through the open balcony door, the scent of soil and wet flowers was rising from the garden. The entire street was already sleeping, except for two windows across the street, where only a dim, diffused light penetrated the curtains.

---

[9] In 1960s transistors just replaced vacuum tubes, but integrated circuits had not been invented yet.

He was trying to implement the basic cube with threshold circuits[10], and it seemed to him that he already had it. Then, suddenly, his ear caught a new sound. A car was coming down the street, and it sounded like his car.

The car slowed down, stopped in front of the house. The sound of the doorbell rang through the entire house. Again and again. It was Zora. Then a blast of the car horn tore through the street.

Lída ran into the room, tightening her housecoat: "Is she insane? She'll wake up the entire street."

As typical for Lída, she was not even upset, only tired of making another decision in the middle of night.

Michal went to the balcony, and half whispered across the garden: "What do you want?"

"I want to talk to you," Zora insisted from somewhere below. She sounded impatient and angry.

"That's the last thing I am inclined to do now. If you are drunk, you shouldn't be driving. Go home and get some sleep."

The answer was more horn blowing. Lights went on across the street, and Michal could hear windows and shutters being opened. A voice asked into the night: "What's going on?"

This is another blow to Lída's reputation, Michal thought.

He pulled slacks over his pajama pants, slipped into his running shoes, threw on a raincoat and ran down the stairs.

It rained so hard that the first jump from the house toward the garden gate felt like diving under a waterfall. He passed through the gate, saw Zora's face in the open car window but, without stopping he took a sharp turn and ran along the street. He hoped to lead Zora away from the house.

The trick seemed to work. The sound of the engine changed from idle to a slow acceleration, and the car lights began to move. After two blocks, the road would come to open, recently ploughed fields. His glasses were so wet that all he saw was a black wall of falling rain. Then he noticed that the car did not follow the road. It

---

[10] Threshold circuits were precursors of neuron nets.

followed him!

How long ago was it, he thought, three years? That night, he woke up and saw Zora standing beside his bed with a large carving knife in her hand. Her eyes had a strange glare, and pointed somewhere above his head with erratic, uncoordinated movements. He wrestled the knife from her, and never told anybody about the incident, but for several months, he stayed on guard, waking at the slightest noise and keeping an eye on what Zora was doing.

The car drove on the sidewalk, faster and faster. With no time to think, he ran along the fences ready to jump over like a torero running away from an angry bull along the wall of the arena. Using the few trees that grew along the curb as a cover, he aimed for the fields, and dashed over the mud, not straight but veering to his left. That took him out of the car lights for a few seconds. By the time the car reached the corner, Michal lay flat between the furrows, pressing his face down.

He rested on his arms in a push-up position trying to avoid contact with the wet soil, but the cold water was slowly seeping onto his stomach and chest.

The car stopped and Michal felt Zora's eyes peering from behind the rain beaten windshield. Then the car slowly turned, using the headlights as a searchlight. It stopped again and after a while it started toward the main road.

Michal got up and watched the red taillights heading back to the city. He was wet through, covered with mud, and angry. I should report this to the police, he thought. If I am killed, they will have some clues who did it.

He had no identification on him, no money, not even coins for the payphone. He looked himself over under a street lamp at a nearby bus stop. Striped pajamas showed at the bottom of his pants and from the sleeves of the raincoat. The coat had a tear under the right arm and was plastered with mud. Water splashed in his shoes. As he was washing his hands in a puddle, a city bus arrived. Hesitantly, Michal approached the door and whispered to the driver: "I am in distress. Please, could you take me to the police station?"

The driver stared at him for two long seconds, then waved his hand: "Next please!"

Michal huddled in a corner, as far as possible from the other passengers, who clearly felt no urge to sit closer to him or address him.

At the police station, the atmosphere was leisurely and quiet. The ceiling light was off, but a brass lamp illuminated the desk across the counter.

Just like my father's desk, Michal thought. The brass lamp with the green glass shade, papers arranged in neat piles, the same teak desk with a small bookshelf at the back. He almost expected his father to appear at the doorway, wearing his reading glasses and an old pullover with leather patches on the elbows. If his father were sitting at the desk, correcting assignments, he would have lifted his face and narrowed his eyes trying to see Michal across the dark room: "What's wrong, Michal? Sit down and tell me."

A young, sharply dressed sergeant came through the door, turned on the light, and offered Michal a cup of coffee: "Comrade, calm down and tell me what happened."

Michal described his absurd experience while sipping the coffee, and the sergeant meticulously recorded details onto a police form.

"Are there any witnesses?" the sergeant asked. "Can anybody confirm that it was your wife? What was the car number? Did anybody get hurt, and was there any property damage?"

"Nobody's injured, and no property damage except for my raincoat. But, comrade, it was an attempted murder. Please, at least record that!"

"Can you prove it?"

"I am a recognized scientist. Do you think that I ran out into this rain in my pajamas, rolled in mud, and came here by city bus – just for fun?"

"Comrade, we get all kinds of weird people. This looks like a family dispute, and because neighbours did not complain, it isn't even a case of public disturbance."

"Please, could you lend me the bus fare, so I can get home?"

The sergeant gave him a stamped bus ticket. "I am sorry I

couldn't help you".

The trip in a bus full of people returning from theaters and concerts was humiliating. They stared at Michal and gave him a wide berth.

Lída was still up, and Michal narrated what had happened. She listened tentatively, then nodded her head. "It's sad," she said. "She still loves you."

38. VRTBOVSKÁ GARDEN

Non-negotiable deadlines and unexpected complications made the weeks before the departure torturously hectic, affecting Michal's state of mind. He worried about many details that were beyond his control and could upset his plans.

On a hot August afternoon, he met with Danna on a bench in a quiet corner of Vrtbovská Garden. This less known yet immensely beautiful garden consists of steep terraces that rise high above the Small Town[11], and they did not have to worry about someone overhearing their conversation. Down below them, the red roofs and centuries-old palaces and churches radiated heat, but where they sat, in the shadow of the fountain with two baroque giants locked in an eternal fight, a cool breeze blew through their hair.

The thought that he might never sit on this bench again filled Michal with a quiet nostalgia, but he quickly suppressed the feeling. Without paying attention to the spectacular panorama of the river, he pulled a small piece of paper from his pocket and passed it to Danna.

August 29 - project delivery;

September 9 - my divorce;

September 15 - departure for Canada;

September 30 – Danna's divorce.

"The airline allows twenty kilograms," he said, "but the Institute will pay for the excess luggage. I have about ten boxes, ten

---

[11] Prague has two old quarters: Small Town (Malá Strana) between the castle and river Vltava, and Old Town (Staré Město) across the river.

kilograms each."

"That's not exactly travelling light."

"This is not travelling, this is moving. I have to take copies of all my publications, dictionaries, textbooks, manuscripts to be published, office reports, and Russian and Czech technical books that may not be available in Canada. We will need sleeping bags, a tent, an ax and good winter clothes. We won't be able to buy anything for a long time. I also need my dark suit and my dress shoes in case they send me to a conference."

"All this isn't critical," he said and took Danna's hand. "What worries me most is how you will get there with Lenka. Whether you are divorced or not, Ivan must approve her exit visa."

Danna searched through her handbag and took out her passport. "Ivan must approve any new application, but look – I already have an exit visa in my passport, and it includes Lenka. Last year we planned a trip to Switzerland, and then we didn't go. The day I am divorced, I can take Lenka, fly to Zurich, and meet you at the airport."

"Forget the divorce, and fly with me on September 15. They will condemn you and call you all kinds of names, but the court will divorce you automatically."

"But, legally, I might lose Lenka. Can you imagine the mess of having her in Canada and Ivan claiming her custody? I want to close my past properly."

"But what if your divorce isn't granted?

"I'd have to wait for another hearing."

"My gosh!" Michal pressed his hands to his forehead. "Think about possible consequences! I couldn't live without you for the entire year."

"Don't worry," she comforted him. "The divorce will be granted."

"How can you be so sure? What are your chances in the court where your father-in-law is one of the judges?"

"He is the most honest man I've ever met, and he is not handling my case."

Michal shrugged his shoulders. He imagined the austere face of Ivan's father who, shortly after the Communist takeover, was exiled to an outpost near the German border. On a pitiful salary for more than a decade, he supported his family in Prague while visiting them only on weekends. Later, he was reinstated in Prague.

"I am sorry to disappoint him," Danna said. "He loved me like his own daughter."

39. PACKING

Burning bridges is always hard, especially if you designed them and built them with your hands. On Saturday, Michal went through the closets and drawers in his room, and he searched Lída's attic. This left him with two piles, one marked *garbage* and the other *Canada,* plus his cello and a box of sheet music including the complete J. S. Bach Suites that he had manually copied from his teacher because they were not available in the stores.

Along the opposite wall was a collection of his own sculptures and paintings, some thirty oils, some over a meter long, wax and clay busts, and a large plaster cat. These items had survived his previous purges, and he felt they deserved to be spared.

He set the paintings along the walls, and studied them for about an hour. Then he got up, carried them to the car, and spent the rest of the day making a tour of his friends. "Take only those you really like," he said at each stop. "I'm not asking for money, but you must hang them on a wall. If you get tired of them, I want you to return them to me when I come back from Canada."

Michal did not mind giving away his life's work – this was the best way to protect it from being destroyed by someone who might not appreciate it.

After leaving his cello and the music scores with his parents, he called Zora: "I am leaving soon, and it is not good for any car to sit unused for the entire year. You may also need it for the children. If you promise to take good care of it, you can keep it until I'm back."

If I remain in Canada and Zora has the car, he was thinking, the police would not confiscate it. It is most unlikely that I will ever return, but if I do, the car will be waiting for me here.

"That's unusually generous of you," Zora said. "When can I have it?"

"I will leave the car at the airport parking lot. Olda will bring you the keys and the car papers on September sixteenth.

40. STILL PACKING

In the evening, when Danna opened the door, Michal was sitting on the floor of his office surrounded by boxes.

"I brought Lenka to help us," she said. "How did it go at Customs?"

"I just don't have enough patience to repack everything," Michal said. "All boxes must be under ten kilograms and accompanied by a typed form, with each item including books individually listed. The forms must be signed by the director, and have his stamp. The officer even questioned why I am taking sleeping bags and hiking boots for a business trip. And here is a little detail: I have to pay a deposit equal to the full purchase price of each article. For my old tent and hiking boots? Where I will get all that money"

Michal opened the first box and began to repack it into smaller cartons while Dana recorded each item. Lenka stuck her little nose into every parcel, unrolled the entire spool of string, and tied the four chairs to the coat hanger that stood at the corner. In the box with the camping gear, she also discovered Michal's old frying pan, and set it on one of the boxes, pretending it was a kitchen stove.

"This is just the first box, eight more to go," Michal said. "I don't think we can finish them before I depart for Canada."

Danna put the writing pad down. "Why are we wasting the precious time that we can spend together. Let's go to a theater or concert."

"Marcel Marceau is in Prague, I saw a poster," Michal said. "But who's going to pack the boxes?"

"I'll finish them and send it all off after you leave. Now, please, drive us home! Lenka is ready for bed."

41. TYPEWRITER

The Institute threw a good-bye party for Michal, and as Michal guessed, Olda was behind it. The director took off his jacket and, all smiles, delivered the toast at the general meeting of the Institute:

"Michal, we are proud of your success. Good luck in Canada! Have fun and learn a lot, but always remember that your home is here. You will be representing our Institute and our entire country. One year will pass quickly and, on your return, we expect you to share your experiences with us.

We have been looking for something practical, something that would remind you of your old friends and your motherland. We thought you might like this …"

From under the table, he pulled out a flat black case. Michal could not believe his eyes. The director passed him a new portable typewriter, something Michal had always dreamed of but never had the money to buy.[12]

He opened the case and unwrapped the plastic. The cold metal parts were shining, and the new cylinder smelled of rubber. Nobody had touched the keys yet.

The director continued: "It's good for both English and Czech – it's keys include Czech diacritics. For you, it will be easier to type your letters; for us, it will be easier to read them. We hope to hear from you often."

Behind the director, Olda was grinning. The audience clapped and shouted *Hurrah*. An avalanche of thoughts thundered through Michal's head. Can I accept this gift while planning to defect the country? Can I betray my friends? But if I tell them, I will never get out.

In half a second, he was back on guard, but still truly moved: "Thank you, comrade director, I am most honored. I did not expect anything like this."

---

[12] At those days, computers were used for computation, not for text processing.

42. DIVORCE

Several days before the divorce hearing, Michal stopped responding to the chaotic events around him. With his mind detached and calm, he began to concentrate on this focal event through which everything had to pass and after which everything would be different, yet what would happen exactly was impossible to predict.

He hired a divorce lawyer who made a few obvious suggestions, but he didn't help much or give Michal any hope. He warned that divorces with children required several hearings and usually dragged on for years. If both parties wanted to divorce, it could save time.

Michal called Zora three times, but her answer was always the same: "I didn't ask for it, I don't want it."

Last time she added: "And I will make it as tough for you and Lída as possible."

"Leave Lída out, she is not my girlfriend."

"Or whoever it is," said Zora and hung up.

When preparing for the court hearing, in his mind, Michal rehearsed many times what Zora would say, his reply, and the judge's contemplating face, but he had never been in court, and such details were difficult to imagine.

On the big day, he arrived dressed in the gray suit he usually wore to work. He only added a tie and polished his shoes, trying to look decent, modest, and above all not rich.

He circled the court building several times until he freed himself of negative thoughts. I'm coming to negotiate and not to accuse Zora of anything, he told himself, but within seconds of entering the building his nightmares became reality.

The dark, gloomy hall with the scent of old leather depressed his spirit. The building, only a decade old, had already developed the atmosphere of the ancient courts from old Prague. The image of Kafka's *The Trial* flashed through his mind. Somewhere there must be files, he thought, that nobody has touched for years, files filled with fears and tears of desperate people.

Three judges in long black robes passed by and Michal thought about the forces that brought him to this place. Nobody committed any crime, just two people have to part – a sad story, but their private matter only.

He tried to turn the brass handle of the courtroom door, but it would not move. The door was locked, and the secretary next door told him: "Wait in the hall. You will be called when it's your turn."

Outside the door, he counted thirteen black seats arranged in a circle.

Why this number, he wondered. All chairs are empty except for the two on which Zora and I are sitting – as far apart as possible from each other, and not looking into each other's eyes. Eleven empty chairs is also a prime number. Former friends and lovers which give me shivers, now foes in the court of law.

Michal concentrated on Zora's mind: You have to agree, you must agree …

Zora lit a cigarette, her fingers trembling.

She did not used to smoke, Michal thought, but why she is wearing furs, gold bracelets, and a big brooch? In warm, summer-like weather? And where did she borrow the furs?

Perhaps, this unpleasant waiting has its purpose, he reflected. It is so painful that some couples may actually reconcile.

The ominous silence on both sides of the door bothered Michal most. He got lost in his thoughts again, revisiting the hair-raising experiences and the good times he had had with Zora. No, he could not imagine returning to her. The nine years they spent together floated away like a strange dream.

He sat up straight in his chair, thinking. A battle is starting, and I must defend myself.

With a click, someone unlocked the door from the inside, and the secretary called: "Both parties of the divorce application for Mr. and Mrs. Sedmý, please come in."

As a routine politeness, Michal paused at the door with a gesture, but Zora uttered "After you" and, with an angry expression, stomped her foot. Michal entered before her.

The room wasn't what he expected. It did not look like the court halls he remembered from the movies. A wooden barrier divided him and Zora from the judges, who sat on a raised, velvet-covered platform. They sat so high they appeared to be floating in the air, halfway between Michal's head and the tall ceiling.

Are they going to play gods, he wondered.

The secretary had a small desk on the side of the barrier where Michal and Zora were sweating, and was ready to record the proceedings.

Neither Michal nor Zora was accompanied by their lawyers. They had agreed that lawyers would only make everything more complicated, besides being outrageously expensive. Rain started outside, and the room, bleak under normal conditions, turned colourless and grey.

Michal stared at the presiding judge, a majestic woman with long grey hair hanging over her enormous black robe, and he thought he had been transported to the age when mothers had ruled primordial tribes. The two elected judges, one on each side, asked a few questions, but all three judges talked to Michal and Zora not as equals, as if from a great height, and in the abstract voice of justice. The communication was one-sided. Michal and Zora were there to be examined and tried.

That woman will side with Zora, Michal worried.

After a formal opening, Michal and Zora swore that they would tell the truth.

"Mr. Sedmý, you applied for the divorce," the presiding judge said. "Please, explain your reasons."

Michal had prepared his speech but, at the last moment, decided replace some sections:

"Dear Honors, Our marriage has not been working for more than two years. We have almost separated twice already. Living together has been unbearable: We quarrel, have violent exchanges, and Zora has attempted suicide. We do not live as husband and wife anymore, and our marriage has lost its meaning. We have three children, but even for them the divorce is the only possible solution. The atmosphere of hatred and constant fighting is detrimental to their development. I love them immensely, and I would like to keep all three of them. If that is not possible, please, give me the custody of at least one child. Our neighbours can testify that I can take a good care of all three children."

When asking for "one child" Michal was thinking about Rita. He could not ask for all three children. If he got them, he felt, Zora might attempt suicide again. He did not want to destroy her.

When the judge turned to Zora, she exploded with emotion. The secretary's hand worked fast, trying to catch every word Zora was saying. Zora stood like a flame, her eyes burning with hate. She described Michal as the lowest of all creatures, a beast who should not be permitted anywhere near her children. Michal was not surprised, but the judges leaned forward with their mouths open. When Zora finished, she glared at Michal as if she had flattened him, and declared: Providing sufficient alimony is granted, I agree with the divorce."

Michal's offer to pay Zora $100 a month while he would be in Canada impressed the judges. Multiplied by the current rate, it was more than Michal's full salary. It was tax free and twice as much as most judges were making.

The judges recessed, and left Michal and Zora on their benches, facing the barrier. The room was cold like a funeral parlour. They sat recollecting the expressions of the judges, their questions, weighing hardness and compassion in their eyes, but neither could guess what the verdict would be.

The judges returned and everyone stood up. The woman in black hit her desk with the wooden gavel, and articulated the decision in a metallic, impersonal voice.

"The marriage of Michal and Zora Sedmý is declared dissolved. All three children are given to the custody of their mother. Mr. Sedmý will pay alimony of 480 crowns monthly for each child, plus 480 crowns monthly to his former wife."

At their last meeting, the lawyer explained to Michal the usual formula for calculating the alimony. The husband's salary after tax was divided into parts: one part for each child, one part for the wife, and three parts for the husband. This would allow Michal to keep three-sevenths of his salary.

Michal had gone through similar calculations at home. He immediately recognized what had happened and raised his hand: "Your honour, my salary is 2,800 crowns and, as a divorced man without children, my tax will be 860 crowns. With the total payments of four times 480, this leaves me 20 crowns per month."

The judge looked at her papers. "Your payments are based on the six-month average of your income, 4,466 crowns per month."

"You included a large bonus for finishing a project. I have not received any other bonus during the four years of working with my current employer, and I do not expect any in the foreseeable future. I cannot live on twenty crowns per month! It is not enough for a bun and a glass of milk per day, not to mention the rent."

"If you are not satisfied, apply for another hearing," the judge said, her eyes turning cruel. When it came to money, she was clearly merciless.

"And what about my visiting rights?" Michal asked.

"Usually, parents can negotiate that themselves. If you can't, we will call another hearing."

Out in the hall, Zora stuck her tongue out at Michal. "Now you have what you wanted! You'll work for me like a slave."

Michal turned away, walked out of the building, and took a deep breath. The rain had stopped. The street was still wet, but the air had an unusual taste of lightness. Michal looked at the sky, and felt happy, humble and happy, outrageously and still quietly happy, so happy that he, the atheist, thought of kneeling in prayer under a starving linden tree right there, at the corner of two busy streets.

The amount of the alimony was irrelevant. In one week, he was leaving for Canada, and $100 would be only one-seventh of his salary there.

And even without getting the custody of the children, they should be able to visit us in Canada," he thought.

43. PANTOMIME

Big posters on every corner announced the Marcel Marceau's performance. Prague had a famous school of pantomime, but this was an opportunity of a lifetime. People were coming from across the country to see the great master.

Michal pressed his black suit, and went for a haircut. Danna bought a pair of expensive Italian shoes to match her navy-blue velvet dress, and spent two hours at the hairdresser. Going to a theater, together and in formal attire, felt to them like being reincarnated on a different planet. They strolled proudly arm in arm, enjoying this ordinary pleasure that had been denied to them for such a long time.

During the performance, they held hands and, united through their interwoven fingers, they allowed the pantomime to carry them out of the theater building, to the sun, butterflies, and trees.

In two short hours, and still not completely back from the magic they had just experienced, the theater door spilled them out into an unusually warm night.

"It would be sacrilege to ride a street car now," Michal slipped his right arm around Danna's waist. "Let's walk through the old town."

It was not completely dark yet. The gaslights had just turned on, and after the brief shower before they came out the street pavement reflected the sky. A street vendor flooded the entire neighbourhood with the aroma of his grilled sausages.

"Where are we?" Danna asked. "In Paris or in Prague?"

Instead of answering, Michal made a graceful, mime-like gesture with his left arm.

At the bottom of Wenceslaus Square, the evening traffic pushed through the narrow street. Streetcars waited in long lines, cars blew horns, and the vehicles inched through the mass of people – all disregarding signal lights. Shoppers crowded at store windows sparkling with lights, neons illuminated the walls of local houses. At this spot, Prague looked like a true cosmopolitan city.

As Danna stepped into the street crossing, the narrow heel of her new shoe caught between two cobblestones. Her ankle twisted, and she fell to her knees. Michal helped her up and back to the sidewalk. She leaned on the house wall – pale and in pain.

"I should take you to emergency," Michal said.

"I'll put a cold compress on it, it will be fine tomorrow. Just take me home, please."

Michal flagged a taxi and helped Danna in.

By the next day, the ankle had swollen, and Danna could not walk even with a cane. In the evening, Michal drove her to the hospital. A nurse at the emergency desk checked her in, and helped her through one of the white doors.

Michal paced the large hall, looking at the bulbs in the green ceiling. What if the injury is serious, he thought. I am leaving in three days.

After what felt like an infinity, the nurse opened the door: "Are you her husband?"

"No, not husband," Michal blushed. "A friend."

"She has a broken ankle. Can you take her home?"

"Yes, I have a car."

At the same time, another nurse pushed Danna into the hall in a wheelchair. Danna had a broad smile on her face, and waved at Michal with a crutch. Her leg was in a cast.

44. KITE FLYING

Danna had never been to Lída's place – she did not even know what it looked like from the outside. Without talking about it, Michal and Lída had developed an understanding that it would be best if Danna never showed up at their door. It kept Lída out of the two marital disputes, and shielded Danna from possible accusations at her divorce hearing.

The key figure in this consideration was Lída's landlady. When Michal came to register his new address, the landlady noticed in his identification card that he was still married. Since then, she had been giving Lída a hard time.

During the first few weeks, whenever Michal or Lída passed through the hall, the landlady opened her door and shouted obscenities at them. Later, she would open the door only slightly, stare at them through the gap, then slam the door shut. If the door did not open, Michal knew that her haunting eye, enlarged by the lens in the door peephole, was looking at him, and he simply ignored it.

Two nights before Michal's departure, when both children were already in bed, Michal and Lída sat down to a dinner, but Lída sat motionless, staring at the fork beside her plate.

"Michal, why don't you bring Danna and Lenka tomorrow?" she said. "They can sleep over if they want to. We'll place a mattress on the floor in the nursery room for Lenka."

Michal put his fork and knife down, and looked straight at her: "Are you sure?"

Their eyes met.

"Yes, I am." Lída said. "I have thought about it for a long time."

"And what about the landlady?"

"You are leaving in two days, and after that, who cares. On your last day here, I want you to be happy."

"Danna will like the idea," Michal whispered to himself.

They ate, cleaned the table, and washed the dishes without saying a word.

"Good night, Lída, and thank you," Michal broke the silence before going to bed. "You always amaze me."

The next day after lunch, Michal brought Danna and Lenka over in his car. He ignored the landlady staring from her window, ran upstairs, and returned with Lída, and her children Tibor and Emma; they had been anxiously waiting for twenty minutes.

After getting everybody including Danna with her cast into the car designed for four passengers, Michal waved at the landlady with a smile, and drove away – beyond suburbs, to a windswept plateau high above the Vltava River, where the blue untouched sky stretched in all four directions and rabbit trails crisscrossed the grassy fields around protruding rocks. The strong, cold wind carried the first signs of winter, but near the ground and protected by the car, the sun gave enough warmth to feel comfortable.

With Tibor's help, Michal launched a kite which he had made for this occasion, using bamboo splinters from an old ski pole. "Hold it tight, and release the line slowly."

Danna sat by the car door, warming her cast in the sun. "Look at him," she turned to Lída. "Boys remain boys."

Michal added more string. The kite picked up the upper wind and began to pull straight up. Michal could barely hold it.

"Is the kite higher than the airplane over there?" Lenka asked, pointing across the river.

"I don't know," Michal said, his eyes full of tears. He thought of his three little ones and wished they could be with them.

Danna and Lída did not talk much either. Lída sat with Emma in her lap and watched the kite until it was so small that nobody could see it. An empty string curved up against the sky.

"I am out of string," Michal called. "All three rolls are out. Let's send the kite a letter!"

He cut a small square of paper, made a hole in the middle, and threaded it on the line. The wind picked it up and pushed it higher and higher toward the kite somewhere high in the sky.

Danna touched little Emma's nose. "It looks like summer, but fall is already here. The soil smells of dry grass and mushrooms, and the children's noses are getting cold."

"I'm hungry," Lenka declared.

"Let's go home," Michal said and reeled in the kite.

While helping the children into the car, Michal instructed them: "When we get to the house, you must be quiet like mice. No jumping or yelling! You know the old landlady, she gets very upset."

When they arrived, the children whispered, "Like a mouse, like a mouse, . . ." and tiptoed across the garden. Lída and Michal helped Danna, who hopped on one leg.

When they entered the house, Danna found it difficult to climb stairs with her new cast. "I will carry you upstairs," Michal said, swept Danna into his arms, and started up the stairs.

The door beside them opened, and the landlady stood there opening and closing her mouth as if she were choking. At the same time, Lenka dropped her collection of sand buckets and plastic molds, which rolled down the stairs with a clatter. When the old lady recovered from her shock, she yelled "Sodom and Gomorrah, just like that …" and she slammed the door so hard that a piece of plaster fell off the wall..

When everybody was inside the apartment, Lída locked the door and the children laughed and ran around in circles. "We made it, we made it."

"Imagine, how happy she is going to be," Michal said, "when she learns that I have left."

Danna stood in the apartment hall, absorbing the scents, sounds, and the spirit of the place. "So this is where you spent the last six months," she said in a whisper.

After dinner, they retired early. Lenka giggling and whispering secrets to Lída's children in the nursery, Lída saying "Good night," and closing the door between her bedroom and the kitchen, Danna and Michal choking with laughter while trying not to disturb the others.

"Look," Danna whispered after she fell out of the bed. "This is a single bed, and we are three – you, I, and my cast."

The following morning, Michal was shaving in the bathroom with the door open, whistling a tune. Lída came in, and looked at him closely: "Danna, look at him! He is cheerful and happy. I did not even know he could whistle."

Danna slapped him on his back. "Yes, you're supposed to be sad today."

"How can I be sad when I am with you?"

When Michal, Danna, Lída, and Lenka were standing outside,

with the car's engine already running, Lenka asked Lída: "You're not coming with us to the airport?"

"No, I won't," Lída said in an empty voice.

Until then, she had never shaken hands with Michal; now she offered her hand.

"Thank you for everything," Michal said. "I will never forget you."

"Farewell, and the best of luck!" Something switched in Lída's eyes, as if a light went out.

She turned around, and without looking at Michal or Danna, she entered the house and locked the door behind her.

"Let's go," Michal said.

At the airport, Danna forced herself not to cry, but her eyes were red and her voice was raw.

"Don't be sad," Michal tried to cheer her up, about to cry himself. "Imagine us, together and in Canada," he whispered in her ear so that Lenka would not hear it.

Danna broke into tears: "And will I ever see you again?"

Michal embraced her, with Lenka standing between them, holding Danna's hand. Her head was bent backward as she looked at Michal with her big eyes full of questions. Michal noticed her, bent down, and kissed her. "Be a good girl and help your mom. I'll see you soon."

From the stairs of the aircraft, and then from behind the thick window, Michal waved at the two lonely figures on the observation deck. They could not see his hand at the window, and waved blindly at the plane. The plane roared down the runway, became airborne, and rose rapidly in a smooth curve, leaving a trail of smoke.

After the first moments of desperate emptiness, Michal's optimism returned: I have a lot to do. I have to prepare everything for Danna and Lenka to come.

With sharpened senses, he tried to see the land the plane was passing over, but clouds covered everything and, with mute droning, the plane hovered in the blue space between the heavens and the clouds.

He closed his eyes and imagined Danna and Lenka at Customs. An impatient officer was checking the list of items Danna had made, while she hopped back and forth on her one leg bringing parcel after parcel. Lenka was playing on the floor with a large ball of twine which caught the legs of the old lady waiting beside them, ripping a hole in her stockings.

Scherzo

45. CANADA

Leaving Danna for three weeks – and possibly more!! – was probably the hardest decision Michal had ever made. This step is absolutely essential, he assured himself. I have to start the new job, find a place to stay and prepare everything for Danna and Lenka.

In his heart, Michal was an explorer of new ideas and new places. His favourite book from his childhood was the four-inch-thick 1890 treatise of Enrique Stanko Vráz about the jungle and tribes along the Orinoco River, which he discovered in the attic of his late uncle. Michal's other heroes were Captain Cook and Luis Pasteur, and only a few things gave him the euphoria he experienced when he first heard about the Van De Graaf generator or discovered the concert for two pianos by Francis Poulenc.

Sitting idly in the soft airplane seat drove him out of his mind. He went through the brochures in his seat pocket, studied emergency exits and the use of the oxygen mask, and laughed at the pictures of fashionable flight attendants sliding down with a smile after an emergency landing. He tried his broken French on the old lady from Quebec on his left, then got up and explored the plane. He peeped through the half-open door of the pilot's cabin, examined the food storage bins and the bar in the kitchen, walked the aisles and checked the faces of the other passengers. Then he returned to his seat, took his shoes off, ignored the on-board movie, and wrote a long letter to Danna.

After hours of being slouched in the narrow seat with his eyes closed yet not sleeping, he straightened up and raised the window shade. The silver clouds were gone. He stared at the dark, metallic globe with tiny white wrinkles, guessing that the three little specks with the widening lines behind them were some cargo ships or destroyers. The plane flew over bare land, rugged beyond imagination, then came the blue ocean again, and finally the new continent.

Imprinted on the flat land, a pattern of complicated waterways dominated the view. The trailing edges of the wings curved down, and the plane's body began to shake. They prepared for landing.

Like a stream of molten gold, the river stretched from the sun all the way to the horizon. The air and the land, the river and the sun, all gold – only the shades were different. In the suspense of landing, he watched parking lots packed with toy-like cars; highways slid through the city in geometrically perfect loops.

The Promised Land, he thought.

He thought about pilgrims who had knelt on this ground, kissing the soil. When he descended from the plane, he stood on the tarmac and slowly sampled the incomprehensibly clean air which tingled the inside of his nose. The wind carried air of vast, unlimited spaces. It had the taste of freedom.

Michal took numerous moving sidewalks, passed through Customs, and took another short flight before he finally retrieved his suitcase from the conveyor belt in Ottawa. People who had arrived with him embraced relatives and friends. He stood there alone, not sure where to go next.

The only cash he had on him was seven dollars in single dollar notes. Idiots, he thought, who else could send someone over a quarter of the globe with so little money?

"Comrade, the Canadians are paying for your fellowship. You don't need more money," the clerk in the Czechoslovak State Bank had told him.

Feeling lost in the unfamiliar airport, Michal remembered a letter from Dr. Matheson he carried in his pocket. He pulled it out and read it carefully again.

Dear Michal,

Thank you for your letter accepting the postdoctorate fellowship in our department. From the previous correspondence with the National Research Council, you know that this is a one-year assignment. For the first three days, we booked you a room at the Lord Elgin Hotel, Ottawa, starting on September 13. Please, call me on 992-8470 the morning after your arrival.

Looking forward to meeting you

Dr. I. E. Matheson, Department Head

Michal stepped out through the revolving door into a cold, windy night. Except for a few street lamps, it was completely dark. Such a strong steady wind, he thought. How far is the city? Will seven dollars get me there? What if there isn't any Lord Elgin Hotel? What if this isn't the right city?

Twenty minutes later, the airport limousine dropped him at the hotel entrance. The chauffeur set his luggage at the curb: "This is the Lord Elgin Hotel, sir. That will be three dollars."

The receptionist smiled when she saw Michal's worried face. "Here is your key, Dr. Sedmý. The room has been prepaid."

Michal picked up a free city map in the lobby, and followed the bellboy. After the Spartan simplicity of the communist hotels, the luxury of the room was overwhelming – everything spotless like new, piles of thick towels, colorful linen and quilted bedspreads, letterhead paper and several pens, matches, shampoo and a sewing kit, colour TV, electric alarm clock, rich velvet wallpaper, good modern paintings on the wall, and a leather armchair beside a comfortable oak desk.

You would not find even one of these items in the Sokolov hotel, Michal thought, and that is one of the better hotels I remember.

He sat down carefully on the edge of the bed that had the scent of a distant field meadow, and examined individual items with his fingers. He had not eaten any dinner, but decided to wait until morning before spending his last money. He opened the curtains and stared at a dreary picture of backyards with black bare walls which contrasted with the luxury of his little room. Oh, Danna, why are you not with me?

46. FIRST MORNING

He woke to full daylight and looked at his watch. It showed 11:40, and he was so hungry that getting food became his prime motivation. He dressed quickly and ran down to the lobby, only to find that he had forgotten to set his watch to the new time zone. The reception counter was closed, loaded ashtrays sent a pungent smell through the lobby, and the iron grate over the restaurant door was locked. He slipped out through the back entrance.

The city was still sleeping. Buses went by empty, the stores were closed, and his own steps echoed through the street. Two blocks away, a menu posted at the window of a small Italian restaurant listed spaghetti and meatballs $2.50.

He could afford that, but the lights inside were off and the door was locked.

After exploring the neighbourhood, he gave up and returned to the hotel lobby, where the aroma of freshly brewed coffee surrounded him instantly. The hotel restaurant had opened.

As soon as he sat down, a waiter came in with a menu, bowed to him, poured him a cup of coffee, and stood beside his table with a white napkin over his arm. For a brief moment, perhaps as a result of being so desperately hungry, Michal saw everything around him with great clarity and depth: His own tanned hands against the white tablecloth and the silver cutlery, the surface of the coffee reflecting the window pane, the steam from the cup rising up in a straight line.

He roused from his daydreaming and studied the menu, while the waiter stood motionless beside him. "Egg with toast," Michal finally decided. "Only one egg," he emphasized with one finger.

According to the menu, two eggs and the toast were $4.35. He had exactly four dollars.

"White'r rye?"

"One egg," Michal repeated, at loss what the waiter meant.

The waiter brought in the breakfast, and Michal ate slowly, enjoying every morsel. But when he saw the bill, his face turned red.

"Why $4.17? The menu says $3.50."

"The coffee is an extra 40 cents, sir, plus 7% tax."

Michal had never heard of the tax being added. With the coffee, it was $3.90 and, in his opinion, if something cost $3.90, it cost $3.90.

"This is embarrassing," he said. "I have only four dollars. I planned to give you a 50 cents tip. Instead, I am 17 cents short."

"Four dollars will do," the waiter smiled. "Don't worry, a few cents makes no difference."

With a full stomach, Michal felt better. He went back to his room, and dialed the telephone number from the Matheson's letter.

"Welcome to Canada!" This was the first time Michal heard Matheson's melodic voice. "I have already called you … Someone is coming to pick you up … No, you don't need any transportation, he has a car . . ." Matheson spoke slowly, and Michal understood every word.

47. MATHESON AND KRAEMERS

The man who showed up twenty minutes later in the hotel lobby looked just like Michal – he could have been his brother. "Dobrý den," he said in perfect Czech.[13]

"What? Are you Czech?"

"Dr. Matheson thought it would be easier for you. I am Pavel Janota, a postdoctorate fellow like you and returning in twenty-nine days. I am counting every day …"

"You don't like it here?" Michal instinctively trusted no one who wanted to go back.

"My wife is waiting for me. It's a year since I left."

That placed Pavel into a completely different category; but Michal still did not trust him. "My English isn't so bad that I would need an interpreter," he said defensively.

"You have to start at the administration office, which is on the other side of the town. Using a car will save you time."

At the administration office, Michal was glad to have Pavel with him. They both were busy explaining now in Czech then in English Michal's family situation. Michal received a cash advance of $480, and the clerk told him that his monthly salary would be $560, tax free. After sending $100 to Zora, it was not a great fortune.

"And what about my fiancée?" Michal tried the new word,

---

[13] Good morning

which summarized best his relationship with Danna. Back in Prague, couples did not formally engage. They dated until they simply decided to marry.

The clerk shook her head. "Since you are not married already, we can't pay her airfare. There is a regulation about that."

How will I raise the $520 for her ticket and $260 for Lenka? Michal worried as Pavel drove him to his new office.

Pavel parked the car in front of a large brick building and led Michal several floors up.

Michal had never seen anything like Matheson's office – the room was literally covered with books. Books were crammed vertically and horizontally to fit the shelves along the walls, were heaped in piles and on several large tables. Rows of boxes stretched under the shelves, and a large pyramid of books dominated the room near the door Michal entered through.

He also noticed many maps, field laboratory equipment, a pair of mud-covered hiking boots, and a row of small jars with yellow and black sand. Rock samples of all colours and shapes covered every inch of the remaining space.

Matheson sat in the middle of all this in a swivel chair with a computer printout in his hand. He was short, blond, about forty, with a tie and unbuttoned collar – completely different from how Michal imagined him from his letters. He looked more like a clerk than the geologist who regularly camped in high Arctic for the entire summer.

"I am glad you've made it," he said and shook Michal's hand. "I hope you'll help us optimize the use of our helicopter."

"That sounds most intriguing. What do you want to optimize?"

"Each summer, we explore vast areas of the arctic with a helicopter, which collects rock samples on a three-and-half kilometer grid. The winter before the sampling, we bring the helicopter fuel over the frozen ground and store it in caches which, in summer, become our temporary camps. The entire operation is quite expensive and we would like to know the ideal size of the cache and the best pattern of collecting the samples. For example, should the helicopter fly in concentric circles around each cache, or is it better to fly in straight lines radiating from it. And how could we apply such strategies to our square grid?"

"I am sorry you could not bring your future wife with you," Matheson changed the subject. "I understand your political situation. Last year, the Geological Congress was in Prague, and I witnessed the Soviet invasion from my hotel window on the Wenceslaus Square... But now you have to find some accommodation. Your hotel has been reserved for five nights."

"Heavens, that leaves me only four days!" Michal said. "It takes more than four years in Prague, and you still need good luck, right connections, or pay a hefty bribe."

Matheson laughed. "It's much easier here. Just get a daily newspaper and look for apartments to rent."

Michal bought The Citizen, and he immediately noticed another difference. In Prague, ads gave a box number, and were answered by mail. Here, they listed telephone numbers.

There were three pages of apartments for rent, and Michal marked those with the monthly rate of $100 or less, but when he dialed the first number, he ran into language difficulties. What he caught sounded like "Yes, I have ... grrrr ... it is good ... grrrr ... in the bathroom has been replaced. Are you ...?"

"Thank you!" he said politely and hung up.

After a bit of thinking, he dialed the next number but reduced the conversation to bare essentials. "Hello, I'd like to see your apartment. Please, could you spell your address? When would I come? Probably today or tomorrow."

That worked, and when he had all the addresses written down, he located them on the city map and drew a path, which connected them in a large loop. Then he immediately took off, on foot. This not only saved him the bus fare, but in three days, he also knew the city well.

The prices reflected the apartment quality and the location. For $50, he could have an unfurnished bachelor apartment on a street, which looked a bit rough; a modern efficiency on a clean but noisy street was $100, and anything fancier was beyond his reach.

On the third day, he was exploring the suburbs by bus. He easily found the first address, 259 Springland Drive with the name "A. & K. Kraemer" on the mailbox, and pushed the doorbell.

A young man of medium height with wide shoulders and square face opened the door and led Michal downstairs. "I am Allan. We rent the basement room and charge fifty dollars."

One peak inside the room and Michal knew that he had found the right place: A narrow pine bed, chest of drawers, student's desk with a wobbly chair, and a large, ground-level window. The room so small that Michal could only pass along the bed after pushing the chair under the desk – yet there was something deeply pleasant about it. The afternoon sun made the room cozy and warm. The window was open, and the room smelled of fresh linen, resin and dry autumn grass.

"You'll have your own bathroom, and we can share the kitchen. If you want to watch TV, you are welcome in our living room. We'll treat you like a member of the family."

The last sentence touched Michal's heart. He was lonely and needed friends more than anything else.

"Come upstairs, and I will tell you more about us…. This is Kathy," Allan said, and placed his arm around his wife's shoulders. "And this is Claire," he pointed to a five-year-old girl with wise brown eyes who had been hiding behind Kathy. "I teach at Carleton University, and Kathy is expecting a baby. Renting the room helps us to pay the mortgage."

In spite of his serious appearance, dark hair and black spectacles, Allan had something boyish about him. Tall, blond Kathy, radiated a strange mixture of nervousness and strong will. In spite of her pregnancy, she was elegant in her loose, light-green dress.

Isn't that strange, he thought. Her face and body language resemble Zora. She is like her twin.

"Nice to meet you," he said cautiously.

"You have to see my canoes," Allan pointed to the garage. "You cannot live in Canada without having one."

They took a red cedar canoe down from the rack and in the most serious manner examined its canvas and ribs.

"I love this one," Allan said. "I've had it since I was a teenager."

Michal noticed scratches and dents that had been carefully repaired.

Children from the neighbourhood played hide-and-seek around the garage. "Look at this little girl," Michal said. "She is like my Líza. I wish she and Filip could be here with us."

"The bus stops at the corner every five to ten minutes," Allan said, returning to practical matters.

"I've checked the bus connection already," Michal said. "It goes directly to my office. It's all perfect. I'll move in tomorrow."

48. MAPLE LEAVES

Michal's first days in Canada were like a dream. He saw people talking but comprehended little of what they were saying.

Two blocks from the Kraemers, in a large garden under tall oak trees, he found a nursery school where happy, healthy-looking children played in the most harmonious way. This would be a perfect place for Rita, he thought. Since Michal arrived, he was thinking about her visit.

Each time he entered a supermarket, the abundance of food shocked him: Endless meat counters, fresh vegetables, and piles of tropical fruit. Once he counted thirty-seven different types of cheese. He wished his friends in Prague could see it.

The first two weeks in Canada were also like a dream, because time stood still. Every day, he sent Danna a letter, but nothing came from her yet. Back in Prague, the police employed thousands of informants who read letters crossing the border, and Michal knew it would take two to three weeks before the first letters from Danna would arrive. In Canada, this appeared totally absurd, but when writing to Danna, Michal always remembered that his letter would likely be analyzed by some scummy informant.

Michal's route from the bus stop to his office led under a canopy of majestic maple trees. On these cold crystal mornings, he was thinking about Danna while dragging his feet through the radiant red leaves that covered the street and enjoying the scent of autumn rising all around him. One of these mornings, he threw away all precautions, and sent Danna a letter with one of these leaves:

Dear Danna,

Let this red leaf be my messenger.

This is the free world, which has no boundaries or limits. You can fly with the wind. It's impossible to describe — you'll have to experience it yourself. Every day here is a miracle. I think about you wherever I go. I remember the touch of your hand, the sound of your steps. I love you …

49. NEW APARTMENT

Across from the Kraemers, a newly built apartment complex posted a large sign: "CAMPEAU APARTMENTS - OPEN MODELS". Every night, at the sunset, twelve floors of glass glowed like gold, and at those moments Michal dreamed of a place where he and Danna could live. He imagined how magnificent the view would be from the upper floors, but when he read that the building had an indoor swimming pool, he ran across the street to see it.

"I'd like to see your apartments," he introduced himself at the rental office. "My family is coming from Europe soon, and we will need more space than the room I am renting now."

Through plush carpeted halls, the salesman took Michal to the elevators. Every button, every screw was made from brass or stainless steel and soft music played as they rose to the tenth floor.

When they opened the door of the new apartment, the view surpassed anything he could imagine.

I wish Danna could see this! he thought. To live here would be like paradise!

He took off his shoes. Everything was new: the kitchen range, the avocado green fridge, the bathtub, the tiles and the vinyl floor. In the kitchen, the salesman noticed pinches of sawdust along the counter and a white spot on the sink tap, and he quickly rubbed it off with his sleeve

"Everything is top quality, sir."

He opened the sliding door, and Michal stepped out onto the balcony. Even on this autumn afternoon, the rough concrete floor radiated the heat it had accumulated during the day. The surrounding area, including the river, lay under them like a map. A light breeze carried a scent of the distant fields. Michal leaned over the railing and took a deep breath. "How much is this unit?"

"Two-hundred-dollars a month, sir. This is a special. We just opened the sales."

Michal could not believe that his low salary would allow him such a luxury. "When my wife arrives, I will definitely take it. How long can you hold it?"

"Considering how serious you are, we can hold the price for three months."

50. GRASSHOPPERS

On the first weekend, Michal was sitting in his room thinking about Danna.

Her divorce hearing will be in ten days and I cannot do anything about it. The letter I just posted will take two weeks to reach her. What could I do to shorten this agony of infinite waiting? I could explore the countryside!

He packed a sandwich for lunch, and took his usual bus line out of town. He hoped to find a country road, which would take him to open fields where he could stretch under a tree, watch the sky, and dream of what Danna was doing. To his surprise, around Ottawa, field roads were completely missing. All he found were paved highways with fences along the grass-covered ditches.

He walked three hours out and three hours back without finding a field road. At one spot, a bull came running toward him from behind the fence, head down and foam at his nostrils. Michal ran for safety, not sure whether the fence could stop the beast.

He had not seen a single person on foot. Three times, different cars stopped and the drivers asked him whether he needed help; each time Michal politely explained that he was only out for a Sunday stroll.

He also noticed unusual creatures along the road. Every few seconds, a strange insect flew up from under his feet. It had wings like a butterfly but flew fast, and when it landed, it disappeared in the grass. He couldn't find a trace of it even when combing the grass with his hands.

After playing this game awhile, one of the bugs landed on the pavement. It was a grey grasshopper, quite different from anything Michal had seen before. It did not jump—it flew—and its white wings showed only when it was flying. He caught two more specimens and put all three into a plastic bag left over from his sandwich.

When he returned to the Kraemers, he wondered who could appreciate his little discovery, then recalled that Radim's son collected insects. After a short search through his room, he found a used Styrofoam cup, punched holes into its plastic lid, and carefully transferred the three grasshoppers in it. He wrote Radim's address directly on the cup, and added in big letters DO NOT OPEN – LIVE INSECT. He reinforced the cup with Scotch tape, added two airmail stamps, and unaware of the Customs regulations for transporting live animals and especially insects, he dropped the whole thing into the mailbox across the street.

Only much later, he learned about the upheaval the grasshoppers caused in Radim's office. When the cup arrived – surprisingly intact – Radim lifted the lid to see what was inside, and the three grasshoppers instantly flew out. The entire staff including the director's secretary searched behind furniture and crawled underneath the desks, but they never found what had arrived in that cup.

51. CHEVROLET BEL AIR

On his project, Michal worked with geologists and chemists from around the world – Scots, Australians, Indians, South Africans and Chinese. They spoke English, but when waiting at the lunch cafeteria, Michal suddenly heard in crispy Czech "… but if they had a pork roast with sauerkraut and real dumplings – that would be something."

He laughed, looked at the two characters behind him and added, also in Czech, "I wouldn't mind either."

Later, at the table where skinny and short Dr. Kopal ate with his hat on, Michal learned more about them. Long before Indiana Jones, Kopal searched for minerals in the jungles of Africa and South America. Even when eating, he was alert – his quick, sharp eyes always following the conversation.

Big, burly Dr. Kytička worked on mining operations from the Arctic to the tropics, managing heavy machinery and rough, adventurous people. He spoke slowly and in spite of his appearance – grim face, unruly hair, and bushy eyebrows – he had a good sense of humour. Both fellows had defected right after the Soviet invasion and they already knew everybody around.

What a coincidence – such funny names, Michal thought. In Czech, Kopal means 'digger', while Kytička, even more funny, means 'little nice flower'.

"Why don't you buy a second-hand car?" Kopal said after Michal described his situation. "It does not cost much and if you have to sell it, you'll get the money back."

"Could I afford a car?"

"Janota needs to sell his 1962 Chevrolet Bel Air. He drove you in it – it is rusty, but it runs well. You may get it for under $300."

"American cars last forever," Kytička added, "and Janota is one of us. He would not sell you a lemon."

Three days later, Michal was the proud owner of the metallic blue Chevy. He parked the car in front of the Kraemers' house, opened the hood, and studied the huge V8 engine. Then he closed the hood, and took a series of pictures for Danna and Radim, using the Kraemers' house as background. His pictures did not show the bare tires, the white stuffing that protruded from a large gash across the front seat, and the chrome peeling from the controls. The driver's door had rusted through along the bottom, and when the car approached sixty miles an hour, it began to shake. Michal loved it anyway.

It is amazing how much easier life is here, he thought. When Dana and Lenka arrive, we will live in a new apartment, have a car, and all that from my meager fellowship salary.

52. RIDEAU CANAL

On the second weekend, Michal helped Allan clean the garage.

"This uncertainty and waiting is dreadful," Michal said, as they were carrying the canoe out of the garage. "I try to do good work at the office, but everything beyond that is just to kill time. I am preparing everything for Danna's arrival, but it all may be in vain if her divorce is not granted"

Allan said "Would you like to take this canoe out for a day?" Allan said.

"That would be most wonderful. I was thinking about it, but I did not dare to ask."

"Then help me tie it to the roof of my car, and I will take you to the river tomorrow."

On Sunday morning, the two unloaded the canoe onto a deserted beach. A loon cried and dove under water.

"I couldn't believe we are in a city," Michal said.

"That's what's wonderful about Ottawa," Allan replied and passed him a paddle. "When you return, tie the canoe to a tree, and come to get me."

"Would anybody steal it?"

"No, not here," Allan laughed.

Wind blew patches of mist across the bay and Michal was glad he had brought a warm sweater.

"Should I go upstream or downstream?"

"This is all flat water," Allan said. "Going upstream will take you out into the country. Downstream," and he pointed into the fog, "will bring you downtown, near the Parliament buildings."

Michal turned toward the city. He knew that the best view of any town is from water, but it puzzled him how any river could take him to the Parliament. Isn't the Parliament at the top of a hill? The mist surrounded the canoe, and Michal listened to the voices of the river. Somewhere ahead of him, he heard the sound of falling water.

He pulled the canoe ashore and followed the sound on foot, along the bank and across a road, which connected to a short bridge. What he saw gave him goose pimples. Under the bridge, water was falling over a dam into a deep gorge. Covered with foam, the violent current tumbled between two enormous rocks, each the size of a whale. The blasts of air carried the spray up and. He felt the taste of the river on his lips.

Flat water – in Canadian terms, he thought, and he explored the shore in the other direction, to a canal that led into a lock. He portaged the canoe around the lock. Meanwhile, the sun rose and the fog dissolved. The canoe whispered as picturesque houses and autumn trees reflected in the smooth water around him. He could smell river, fish, and the decaying leaves. The hum of the city was barely audible. At some spots, steel ladders allowed Michal to climb up the wall and explore the park above the canal. He reached the Parliament buildings with his hands and knees dirty from rust and slime that covered the ladders. The view was rather unusual: The canal ended at the top of a hill, and all he could see ahead was the blue sky with a few scattered clouds.

He tied the canoe to the railing, and went ahead on foot, only to discover another strange thing. Nine huge locks marched down the hill like giant steps. This is unreal, he shook his head. I must bring Danna here in a canoe one day.

With the wind at his back, the return trip was more comfortable, yet something subtle had changed. The canal had an air of sadness. Michal mused about the colours of the trees, fleeting views, about the canal itself.

Life is so short and transient, he thought. I won't be able to show this to Danna. It will never be the same again.

He drifted along, his eyes absorbing the last days of autumn. The wind and the sky were telling him the winter would arrive soon.

He ate his lunch sheltered under a willow tree, its branches already bare. The food that he brought with him was an experiment and culinary adventure. Never before he had seen or tasted vacuum-sealed jellied beef tongue, sliced like a salami, or the white, spongy bread so different from the rye bread he grew up on. The bottle labeled "orange" contained a liquid, which tasted remotely like the orange juice he had expected, and he knew dried figs from Europe, but had never heard of cookies with fig filling.

"I am sorry," Allan said when Michal arrived. "I never thought that, in that fog, you could have gone down the Hog's Back Rapids."

53. GOOD NEWS, BAD NEWS

Two days later, the persistent ringing of a phone woke Michal in the middle of night. He sat up in his bed, not sure what was going on, but then he realized that Danna might be calling. The only phone in the house was at the top of the stairs.

He jumped out of bed and ran up, taking three stairs at once. When he lifted the receiver, the stair railing was still rattling from hitting it as he charged up the stairs.

"Is it you, Michal?" Her voice sounded as if it was passing through a long narrow pipe under the ocean.

"Yes, it's me. What's new?"

"It's great to hear you. I am at the post office. Your first letter arrived this morning. We have just three minutes. We have to keep this short."

"I've been sending you letters every day, but I have not received anything from you. The mail is ridiculously slow. I am thinking about you wherever I go."

It is so slow because the damned informants read our letters, Michal thought while watching every word he said. Most likely the conversation is being recorded.

"The good news is that my divorce has been granted," Danna said. "I also have the custody of Lenka."

"Hurray!" Michal shouted.

"If you read the court decree, you would not even talk to me," Danna said. "I am a deplorable, unfaithful woman who destroyed an otherwise perfect marriage."

Barefoot and hastily wrapped in housecoats, Allan and Kathy

had tiptoed in and watched the expressions on Michal's face, trying to guess the outcome from what Michal was saying in fast, incomprehensible Czech.

"The bad news is," Danna continued, "that the government canceled all the passports."

She said nothing about her exit visa to Switzerland, but Michal understood. She lost it with the old passport. She was stuck and could not leave the country.

"If we get married, you may be allowed to visit me," Michal said after a few seconds of thinking. "Perhaps, we could do it over the telephone. Check with the police and I will ask at the Embassy here. There must be a way …"

"Three minutes," the operator said. "Please, hang up."

Michal was sitting on the hardwood floor with the telephone receiver in his hand. He gradually began to notice his surroundings and Kathy with Allan staring at him from two meters away.

"What happened?" Allan said. "Is she free?"

The three discussed the situation, right there, in their pajamas and housecoats. "Don't worry," Kathy was confident. "We'll help you to get her out."

The Kraemers went back to sleep, but Michal threw himself onto his bed with eyes open. Plans and ideas swarmed in his head.

54. CZECHOSLOVAK EMBASSSY

The clerk at the Czechoslovak Embassy acted as if Michal suddenly fell from the sky. "Why all this rush? In a short year, you will be back to Prague."

That took Michal's breath away. The clerk was like a piece of wood. Rarely had Michal felt such a lack of communication – perhaps the clerk was not only trained to control what he was saying, but also to block his emotions. Or was his brain disconnected?

"Can we marry over the telephone? I've read an article about a couple who did that," Michal started over again.

"Comrade, it will take a year, whatever you do," the clerk moved closer staring into Michal's eyes. "It takes six months just to prepare the paperwork."

After two weeks in Canada, the word "comrade" already felt like a slap in the face.

"And even if you marry, she will have to wait another six months for the exit visa. If she ever gets it . . . Didn't you say she divorced only a week ago? That sounds suspicious."

Michal backed away from him. He felt the conversation was entering dangerous territory.

The clerk saw that he could not get rid of Michal unless he offered some hope. "Fill in an application for her visit, and state that she would come for the purpose of marriage," he said. "You can try."

Michal filled in six forms, wrote a short resume for Danna and himself, and stepped out onto the sidewalk. Looking back through the row of maples, the gloomy building with iron bars protecting its windows appeared inconspicuous on the quiet, residential street.

Like a prison, Michal thought and spat on the ground.

55. CHURCHES

Secretly, Michal began to visit churches around Ottawa. If any of my friends followed me, he smiled at his thoughts, they'd think I have gone crazy.

He did not believe in a God one could pray to, the God of gold decorations, the God who brings wars upon ordinary, innocent people. If there is any God, he thought, I would be part of It, and It would be part of me. The ultimate guidance must come from Nature.

Michal also agreed with what his father had taught him; he wanted to be good because he chose to be good, not from a fear of some abstract God. His sensitive mind helped him detect places where people of noble thoughts had gathered, and he was constantly on the lookout for such spots – not merely churches – because they gave him a sense of purity even when nobody was present.

Until Michal came to Ottawa, he did not know there could be so many religions: Presbyterian and Anglican, Catholic and Orthodox, Unitarian and Lutheran. He visited a mosque and a synagogue, a Japanese shrine and a French convent, but he was thinking of a wedding and none of these places satisfied him.

One day after work, he walked down Bank Street, away from downtown and across the bridge over the Rideau Canal where he noticed a small church surrounded by trees. Dense ivy covered the sandstone walls, a wrought-iron gate guarded the entrance. There was something pleasant and inviting about it.

The sign said South Westminster. He had never heard of that denomination and, with a humble feeling, he entered. The church was empty. A flood of sunlight entering through the stained-glass windows formed a cloud of light in the middle of the hall. The walls and ceiling, benches, and altar were all made of natural wood.

He sat down in one of the pews, lowered his head, and closed his eyes. This place is not preoccupied with death, he felt. It breathes energy and life. Through a half-open window, the sound of chirping birds kept coming in.

"Are you looking for something, young man?" The minister stood beside him. "We close the church after the service."

"I'd like to have my wedding here, but it is complicated. My fiancée is still in Europe. We both have been divorced - had civil weddings only. This time we'd like it to last forever."

"Do you believe in God?"

"I believe in a Great Spirit, but I don't belong to any church. I studied the Bible and Eastern religions. According to our birth certificates, I am a Protestant, but my fiancée is a Catholic. Does it matter?"

"It complicates matters slightly. Why did you choose this church?"

"I've seen many churches. No other church in town has a comparable spirit. I cannot describe what it is."

The expression of minister's eyes changed from intellectual

curiosity to compassion and kindness.

"I'd like to meet with both of you before I promise anything. Bring her in when she is in town."

56. CZECHOSLOVAK EMBASSY AGAIN

Every day during the lunch break, Michal stopped at the Czechoslovak Embassy. The guard and the receptionist recognized him instantly. The answer was always the same: "Nothing new, no message from Prague."

"Is there anything that could speed it up?" Michal asked the clerk.

"Nothing," the clerk said bluntly. "I sympathize with you, but I have told you that your chances are slim. I don't know anybody who could get a visa under similar circumstances. Is she expecting a baby?"

"I hope not," Michal sighed. It would have to be Ivan's baby, he thought.

Danna cried all the way through their next telephone call. "You know how it is," she was sobbing. "With the shortage of apartments, I have no place to go. Ivan is living here, in the same apartment, and since you left, he is making advances toward me.

"Everybody else tells me that you will never come back. I am like a flower without water, only half-alive. I cannot bear this anymore!"

"Let's give it two more weeks," Michal said slowly. "If you don't get the exit visa by then, I will return to Prague."

"Would you really do that?" Danna instantly replied.

From her voice, Michal could hear how she began to smile. "Yes, I promise. We will be together soon. I love you."

57. SELECTING WEDDING RINGS

The same day, Michal went to Birks, the largest jewelry store in Ottawa. After looking at the gems and watches in the windows for five minutes, he gathered enough courage to enter the store. Inside, arrays of cases displayed pairs of wedding bands arranged by colour and style.

Diamonds and intricate ornaments are not for us, Michal thought, and after an hour of moving from one case to another, he found a pair of plain simple rings, elegant, and geometrically perfect, in light yellow gold.

"How much are these?" he pointed with his finger. He had saved $100 from his last salary cheque, but after buying the car and sending the payment to Zora, he did not have much left.

"$120, would you like to try them?" the sales clerk said.

"Yes, but I don't know the size of my fiancé's finger."

"Then bring her in," the clerk said. "Sizes are difficult to guess."

"How large is your hand?"

Michal examined her hand, trying to project an image of Danna's fingers over the clerk's old skin. "Just a minute," he said, as if he had a better idea.

This was a large store with a complicated pattern of counters; at least a dozen assistants talked quietly to other customers. Michal walked amongst them as if searching for something under the glass counter but, at the same time, he scanned the hands of all the women.

"Excuse me, madam," he approached a woman of about forty who was looking at a set of expensive china. "I'd like to ask you for a favor. Could you try on a ring for me, please?"

"You seem to have the right sized fingers," he explained, when he saw her perplexed expression. "This is for a girl who is in Europe, and I am not sure about her ring size."

The woman accompanied Michal to the wedding band counter, smiling. She wore no jewelry on her hands.

"Wow! A wedding band," she exclaimed. "Who is the lucky girl?"

"The most wonderful girl you can imagine," Michal blushed.

"Look, this one is perfect," the woman looked at her hand with dreamy eyes.

"Good luck to both of you," she said after a long three seconds, and reluctantly pulled the band off her finger.

The clerk watched everything from the distance, and frowned at Michal's manners. "What do you want to engrave inside the bands?" she asked when he brought the band back to her. "Please, write it down here, in capital letters."

Michal wrote carefully: DANNA in the bigger band and MICHAL in the smaller one.

"Is that all?" the clerk was disturbed again. "There must be a date – the date of your wedding."

"We don't want any date. Besides," Michal hesitated, "we don't have a date yet."

"What? No date? Then buy the bands later when you know the date."

"I need them now. Can't you just engrave the names?"

That was too much for the poor clerk. "That's not the way it's supposed to be done," she shook her head. "Will you pay in cash?" she said as if she did not trust Michal.

"Yes. When will they be ready?"

"I suppose, in one week."

"Please, I need them soon."

This was clearly beyond the clerk's comprehension. "Not before tomorrow afternoon," she said, and turned away from him.

58. TINY PARCEL

Next day, with the bands in his pocket, Michal went to Janota. "When are you leaving for Prague?"

"In two days. I've packed everything already."

"Could you take something small for my girlfriend?" Michal took out the smaller ring. "It's gold, which means trouble on the border."

"Anything to cheat the government," Janota smiled. "Pass it on!"

"She is having a rough time, and this may cheer her up." Michal said and pulled out a photograph from his wallet. "This is the only picture I have, I can't give it to you. Will you remember her face?"

"Don't worry. I will deliver it to the right hands," Janota laughed.

Four days later, in Prague, the entrance guard called Danna. "Comrade Engineer, someone is looking for you."

Danna dropped her papers and trotted down the stairs.

"Are you Danna?" Janota recognized her instantly.

"Yes, I am. But I don't know you …"

"I came from Canada yesterday," Janota produced a tiny parcel. "Michal asked me to give you this." After smuggling the band in his shoe, Janota wrapped it nicely and tied a silver ribbon around it.

"Thank you!" She balanced the little box on the palm of her hand. "Did he send any message?"

"No message, only this parcel," Janota said mysteriously. "Have a nice day!"

Danna pushed the elevator button and, while going up, ripped the paper and opened the box. A wedding band, and the inscription read: MICHAL. She began to cry, tears of joy running down her cheeks.

The elevator stopped. She stuffed the paper and the box into her pocket, wiped her tears, and walked out of the elevator and into her office. She felt like telling everybody about it but, instead, she sat down at her desk and stared into her papers.

Radim stepped in looking for something and looked at her face. "Has anything happened?"

"Nothing important, a friend dropped by."

59. PROSPECTING FOR GOLD

One day, when Michal had nothing on his mind except Danna and how to get her across the border, Kopal and Kytička came to his office.

"Would you like to join us on a prospecting adventure this weekend?"

"You know my situation – I have no time for recreation."

"Prospecting is no recreation – it's hard work. Besides, you cannot do anything over the weekend. All offices are closed."

"What are you looking for?"

"Copper, uranium, possibly gold."

Michal thought for several seconds. "I always wanted to see the true Canadian wilderness. Tell me more about it."

"As the Earth cooled," Kopal said as in a tone as if talking to a bunch of university students, "it shrank like a dried apple, with ridges and cracks in two perpendicular directions. The map of the ocean bottom demonstrates the idea."

He also said that the Earth magma, rich in heavy metals, had oozed to the surface through these faults, and showed Michal a large map of Canada with all the known deposits marked in different colours. The dots formed a system of horizontal and vertical lines.

"Where two lines cross," he explained, "there ought to be a deposit."

Using this method, he had discovered two copper deposits in South America, and one in Malaysia. On his map, two such lines crossed on a small island, in the middle of a lake three hundred and fifty miles north of Ottawa.

"We have to get across the water, and we need your help. You know everything about boats," Kytička said.

On Friday night, the three drove to the warehouse of the Geological Survey of Canada, which in itself was already an adventure. They started with the clothes: Each selected a heavy parka, a pair of work pants, winter boots, mittens, and a woolen cap. Then they brought in an aluminum boat, an outboard motor, a small all-terrain vehicle with six balloon wheels, and many small items such as rope, oars, axes, a chain saw, a pick and a shovel, and a heap of canvas bags for the rock samples.

Michal was looking at the growing pile. "How are we going to carry all that?"

"You'll see," Kopal laughed. Seconds later, Kytička drove in with a big van.

The cart, the boat motor, and the supplies fit inside the van. Then, with some difficulty, they lifted the boat, and tied it to the roof.

"Ready to go?" Kopal stroked the dashboard. "I will take the van with me, and pick you up in the morning. Be ready at five."

It was still completely dark when they crossed the bridge to the province of Quebec. In the predawn gloom, Michal watched the flat fields turning into rugged hills. The road took sharp turns along the cliffs overhanging the Gatineau River. Other drivers passed them in narrow places with absolutely no visibility, and drove with disregard to traffic signs and the lines on the road.

"Those French drivers ..." was the only thing Kopal said after one such close encounter.

The river wound its way through the valley below the road. Its water was black as if it sprang from marshy grounds, and it ran fast. Michal saw white rapids and numerous logs coming down with the current. In one place, logs jammed the entire river.

Woods of magnificent timber lined the next stretch of the road. "Look, the slope along the road is full of berries, and what a poetic name," Michal pointed to a road sign. "Lac des Poissons Blancs."

"These hills are rich in minerals," Kytička said and took out a Geiger counter. It stayed at zero until the road cut through a hill with exposed red rocks on both sides. The needle jumped up half the scale.

"Just traces of uranium, not profitable to mine," Kytička mumbled to himself.

After four hours of driving, they reached La Verendrye Park, closed and deserted for the winter. The parking lot was empty, and the lake full of dead trees looked like the end of the world.

"This isn't the wilderness I imagined," Michal said. "It is depressing and gloomy, but still the most powerful beauty I have seen."

Oh Danna, he thought, you would be in your element here.

They stopped on the shore of the lake but quickly returned to the warm cabin of the van. The temperature was dropping, and a chilling wind ruffled their faces. Despite of layers of clothing, Michal felt the cold air penetrating to his stomach and chest.

Kytička scanned the sky in a slow, sweeping motion. "Turn on the radio. We may get a snowstorm." Low leaden clouds moved rapidly overhead.

"In October? You are joking," Michal said.

"You are in Canada, not in Bohemia," Kopal said with a worried face.

The storm arrived with an unprecedented force. Snow covered the road within minutes, and drifts began to build. A curtain of white flakes reflected the car lights, but Kopal kept driving. All three men sat with their eyes glued to the road barely visible in the white darkness.

When they reached Val d'Or, the snow stopped. "This is gold country," Kytička said. "That building over there is a gold mine."

From the car window, the shaft tower and the rusty buildings looked shabbier than any mining operation Michal had encountered. Paint peeled from the houses in the adjacent village, barns were falling apart; a beaten up corner store looked dirty and fields were full of stone.

"With all its gold, this part of Canada isn't very rich," Michal reflected.

It was dark when they checked into a cheap motel in Rouen, all three in one room with only two beds. Michal spread his sleeping bag on the floor.

When Kopal woke them in the morning, Michal's entire system revolted against rising again at a ridiculous hour and leaving the warm room. Like a robot, he followed the others to the van.

According to the map, no road led to the lake, but after thirty minutes of driving around, they found a logging road that took them to a meadow which bordered on the lake. Two inches of snow covered the grassy, frozen ground. Kopal drove off the road and straight toward the lake. Gray open water separated two wide strips of thin ice – one along the shore where they were standing, the other one around the island.

"Hurry up, before we get another snowstorm!" Kopal shouted.

With Michal's help, the geologists unloaded the van and rolled the cart out over two planks. Its red plastic body and black rubber wheels contrasted with the fresh snow, which covered everything in sight.

"Can this be useful even in the snow?" Michal reflected. "It looks like a boat, but it isn't amphibious. It has a drain hole in the bottom."

Kytička pulled on the engine cord, but nothing happened. They all pulled a dozen times each, with the choke on and off, until they were sweating. Finally, the engine started with a roar.

"The noise is terrible," Michal complained. "Leave the devil here!"

Kopal and Kytička ignored Michal, threw their hammers and sample bags into the cart and jumped in. Michal joined them reluctantly.

Kytička drove toward a rocky ridge covered with young forest. As they reached denser growth, the cart got stuck.

Kopal began to blaze a trail with his machete. In the arctic parka and his city hat, he was a bizarre figure. The hat, bleached by tropical sun, had lost its shape long before, but it was still a city hat.

Michal and Kytička pushed the cart, until the bigger trees stopped them. They could not continue unless they used the chain saw.

The geologists abandoned the cart, climbed up the ridge, and started to break the rocks at an unbelievable speed. It looked as if they wanted to pulverize the entire hill with their hammers. Occasionally, they mumbled Latin names, and showed each other a rock fragment as if it were a treasure. After two hours, it became boring.

"Have you found anything interesting?" Michal asked.

"No, not yet," they said but, from their expressions, Michal thought they must have been on a verge of a great discovery. He browsed through the brushes and found fields of blueberries frozen under the snow. He also found a rabbit trail and footprints of a wolf which had strayed out onto the ice and back to the shore.

"No signs of bears?" Kopal shouted.

"With the noise you are making, I can guarantee there will be no animals within ten kilometers range," Michal shouted back, and began to carry the growing pile of samples to the cart.

The two stopped breaking rocks, and stared over the water at the black cliffs along the island shore. "What a pity we can't get there!"

"Who said we can't? I can break through the ice. I used to do this with my little sailboat every winter. "

They returned to the van, took the boat off the roof, attached the motor and pushed the boat toward the lake like a sled.

"Get in," Michal said, when the boat reached the ice. "Sit on the side and push with one leg. When we reach thinner ice, the boat will break through."

Against all expectations, when they broke through, nobody got wet. The boat sat in the ice tightly, unable to move or turn in any direction. Starting the motor did not help. Kytička slammed one oar against the ice. The oar split into two parts, but the ice remained intact.

"We have to break it like an icebreaker," Michal said. "Let's move astern, push the bow on the ice, prop the boat against the ice with the oar, and then move our weight forward."

Using this method, they broke a long, jagged path halfway across the white surface. By then, the ice was as thin as a sheet of glass. It also cracked like glass, but with more water around the boat, the method of breaking the ice stopped working. As they moved backward, the boat moved forward, but when they shifted the weight forward, it slipped back like a pendulum. The water around them was filled with fragments of ice that jingled when they disturbed the water.

Now with the island within reach, Michal saw birches on its shore. His nose was dripping and his hands were purple. "Let's use the motor," he decided.

The boat rammed forward, first slowly crunching the ice then accelerating quickly. The propeller made a white turbulent path in the dark, oil-like water.

When they thought they had already conquered the ice, Michal waved his arms. "Stop the motor!" The thin aluminum was caving in at the waterline. "If we are not careful, we'll sink any minute. Shift the weight back to get the weak spot above water."

Aware of the danger, they moved the boat gingerly back through the path of broken ice, until they reached the beach where they had started. They loaded the equipment into the van, crawled into the cabin, and Kytička started the engine.

"You still have enough energy to drive all the way home?" shivering Michal asked. "In this snow? All night?"

"This is Canada. You just get used to it."

At four a.m., they arrived in Ottawa.

"What is my share of the gold?" Michal said.

"Exactly one-third," Kopal said with an equally serious face. "We haven't found any."

"Better daring forehead than a large homestead."
(Czech proverb[14])

60. PREPARING TO LEAVE

In similar situations, most people – and Janota was a good example – obediently served until the end of their assignment. Others never returned to the communist hell, hoping that their families would eventually make it out. And those few who opted to return prematurely did so with a grudge; they were missing the opportunity of their life and ruining their careers. They knew they would never get out again.

Michal's reaction was different. He did not have to agonize over the decision; he simply followed his heart. He was relieved. A clear executable plan replaced the vague uncertainty that had tortured him since he had left Prague; he was not defeated. He had no doubts that, one day, he and Danna would return to Canada. It was only a matter of time.

After some hesitation – this was an unpleasant thing to do – Michal knocked on Matheson's door and explained that he would like to take a leave of absence.

"I finished the program, which simulates the helicopter sampling," he said and placed a report on Matheson's desk. "The problem is solved."

As usual, Matheson remained relaxed, only his eyes grew alert. "You are free to go," he said after a short pause.

"Danna can't come unless we get married." Michal added, feeling guilty for upsetting Matheson's plans.

"I'd like to meet her one day," Matheson said, "but you may never have the luck to get her out. You may not get out either."

"I am leaving my books and clothes in my office, packed in boxes. If I don't make it, could you please send them to Prague?"

"If you need any help, call me from Europe. Wait a minute …" Matheson searched in his papers. "I was afraid of this. The funds

---

[14] "Lepší drzé čelo než poplužní dvůr"

are allocated for one year only. If you return after September thirteenth next year, your job will be gone."

Michal's next visit was to the Czechoslovak Embassy. He did not expect much from going there, and his anticipations proved correct. After telling Michal that there was no news in his matter, the unpleasant clerk told him: "If you return to Prague, your exit visa will expire. You may not get a new one ..."

"Big deal," Michal said just to annoy the clerk. He did not depend on him anymore. "The Ministry of Mines will help me again."

"I doubt it," the clerk shrugged his shoulders, as if he knew more about it.

The third visit of the day was not the mere formality Michal expected. The usually smiling woman at the National Research Council was frowning. "We can't stop you, but you are wasting the money somebody else could use. You will never make it back. And who will pay your airfare?"

"I will pay it myself," Michal said. "I am sorry to cause difficulties, but I have to go."

"If you leave on November twelfth, you'll get the last paycheck on November eleventh. It will be $160."

Michal hated money. He always thought in projects and inventions, and financial rewards arrived effortlessly while he was having fun. Now his fate was a matter of dollars and cents.

"I thought my paychecks are $560."

The woman explained that, from September 13 to November 12, Michal was entitled to two monthly salaries $600 each, and because he already received the $480 advance and one $560 paycheck, it left $160. She closed Michal's file.

"If you don't finish your fellowship properly," she said, "you'll also have to pay the original airplane ticket."

When Michal arrived at the Kraemers, Allan invited him for dinner. "You look tired," he said. "Stop worrying."

"The airline has the twenty-kilogram luggage limit – not enough even for my most important papers," Michal said. "I also need the airplane tickets for Danna and Lenka, but I don't have enough money."

"Forget your problems for a while, and enjoy the meal. I even baked a cake for you," Kathy said as she placed a steaming roast and vegetables on the table.

"We already discussed this," Allan said and glanced at Kathy when they finished the dinner. She nodded approvingly. "We'll keep your room for two months before we rent it to someone else. If you can't make it in two months, you still can come to our house. For the first few days, we'd put mattresses on the living-room floor."

"I don't know how to thank you," Michal said and looked down, but Kathy noticed the tears in his eyes.

61. BANK LOAN

The problem with the airline tickets was not only the amount of money, but also the fact that a ticket across the Atlantic had to be paid for in dollars. Once Michal returned to Prague, he was obliged to exchange all foreign currency to Czech crowns. If he wanted to buy transatlantic tickets, he had to purchase them in Canada. He also needed the more expensive, open-date return tickets.

Shortly after his arrival in Canada, Michal had opened an account in a small branch of the Bank of Nova Scotia, two blocks from his office. Besides the government employees, the branch served a bustling Italian community nearby. When coming to the bank, Michal often waited in a line with short, stocky men who had weathered faces, rough hands, and worked on roads and construction sites around Ottawa. On holidays, Italian flags flew the entire length of Preston Street, and a sign on the bank door read PARLIAMO ITALIANO.

Michal also remembered another sign – LOANS AVAILABLE – and, in midafternoon when the bank would be least busy, he paid a visit. "I'd like to apply for a loan," he said at the counter.

A man in a dark suit and red tie led Michal to a cubicle, and presented him with a business card which read: Ian Watson, loan officer. He used the word 'indeed', had a mustache, and looked British.

"How much do you need, and for what reason?" he said and unfolded the application form.

Michal looked around the cubicle: An old desk with a torn green paper mat, three squeaky chairs, and dirty wall-to-wall carpeting curled up at the corners. There wasn't enough light. The person who will give me a loan must trust me, he thought. I have to tell him the truth.

"I am here for a one-year postdoctorate fellowship. My wife and daughter are still in Prague; their exit visa has been canceled. I am returning to Prague, and will bring them out – legally or not. Since Soviets invaded our country last year, there is no hope…"

Watson listened without a slightest change of expression in his face.

"Once I return to Prague, I am obliged to exchange all my money for Czech crowns but, for overseas flights, all airlines accept only hard currency. I need three open tickets from Prague to Ottawa, and I have to buy them now, before I leave Canada. I already researched the fares. Air France has the best prices: $520 return, 50 percent child discount. I need $1,300."

Watson smiled. "With all due respect to your education, it seems to me ..," he searched for the right words, "… that you are not familiar with how banks operate in this part of the world."

"You are correct," Michal smiled back. "Please, tell me."

Watson gave him a twenty-minute lecture about stocks, mortgages, investments and loans, checking and savings accounts. Michal took off his sweater and listened intensely.

"You have no equity to back up the loan," Watson said at the end. "I sympathize with you, but you must see it yourself – I can't give you the loan."

"You would be taking no risk," Michal instantly replied. "It would be the most secure loan you've ever arranged."

"How's that?"

Michal looked at Watson's interest tables. "For a five-year loan, at eight percent, the monthly payments are $26.30. You said you can deduct the payments from my checking account automatically. I will leave $350 on my account, which will provide payments for more than a year."

"And after that?"

"I will be back in a year, and if I am not, I will return the tickets at the Air France office in Prague. They can deposit the proceeds directly to your bank. And if I get shot crossing some borders …"

Michal's voice faltered for a split second. He included this possibility to make his argument complete but, for the first time, he realized that this also was, though quite remotely, a possibility. "… the loan includes a life insurance policy."

Looking straight into Watson's eyes, he continued. "I cannot cheat you. You have my fate in your hands. If you contact the Czechoslovak embassy and tell them about my loan, I'll rot in a communist prison for at least ten years."

Watson leaned back in his chair, and looked at Michal for several seconds. "Let me talk to the manager."

He returned in five minutes, smiling. "The loan has been approved."

Michal left full of energy and optimism, and headed straight for the Air France office. Then he called Danna, and told her that he would arrive on Saturday, November 13, at eleven in the morning.

"I can't wait until you are here," she said. "I am afraid something will spoil it in the last minute.

"I found eight grey hairs when I was looking at the mirror today," she continued. "It's all this stress."

"Place a sign DANNA on your coat so I can recognize you at the airport."

"You and your jokes. Aren't you sorry to leave Canada?"

"The only thing which matters is that we will be together again. I love you."

62. MR. WELLINGTON

Michal hesitated for several days, and even when he entered the elevator at Canada Immigration on Laurier Street West, he still was not sure whether he was doing the right thing.

The elevator cabin was crowded with people from all corners of the world – everybody going to the ninth floor, all trying to avoid eye contact with others in the elevator and staring at their feet or watching the floor indicator above the door.

The ground floor was all marble and chrome, but the ninth was like a beehive – simple, busy, and functional. In the waiting room, all chairs were taken; some people sat on the windowsill, some leaned against the wall. A big sign informed the newcomers: REGISTER HERE.

Michal joined the line and watched the registration procedure. The receptionist wrote each name into a big book, while handling incoming telephone calls.

Two young men behind Michal spoke Russian. They could be diplomats coming for their regular visa, Michal thought.

"Your name?" the receptionist asked.

To prevent people waiting around him from hearing his name, Michal opened his passport. She carefully copied his name. "The purpose of your visit?"

Michal glanced left and right, then leaned closer to her. "I have a one-year visa, but I am leaving for Prague the next week. If I leave Czechoslovakia illegally before this visa expires, may I re-enter Canada?" he whispered.

Her eyes quickly scanned the bystanders. Nobody noticed anything. The two Russians continued in their conversation. She dialed a number, and a short, gray man stepped in from behind a partition: "Please, come here. You don't have to wait.

"Make yourself comfortable. How can I help you?" he said when he took Michal to a cubicle where nobody could hear them. Then, with a warm smile, he quietly listened to what Michal had to say.

Halfway through, he apologized for interrupting. "Your case falls under a different jurisdiction. You ought to see the head of our special department, Mr. Wellington." He wrote the directions, address and the telephone number on a card.

Michal followed the directions across the town, frequently looking back and assuring himself that he was not being followed. When he reached the special department, he was out of breath.

Mr. Wellington welcomed him like an old friend. "Come in, they already called about you."

An air of prosperity surrounded Mr. Wellington: The large office with light Scandinavian furniture, his unique green and ochre peppered tweed suit that matched his green eyes, and the woven tie with a small golden pin. He was tall, with the complexion of a redhead, but his hair was blond like sun-bleached straw.

He offered Michal a comfortable armchair and a glass of water, then pulled his chair from behind the desk so that they sat face to face and close to each other.

Everything around Mr. Wellington matched perfectly, except for his shoes. He sat with one leg over another, and his shoe suspended in the air attracted Michal's curiosity. It was a brown sport shoe probably size eleven and half, with a thick leather sole that had been repaired at least twice. A map of numerous wrinkles covered its upper, and had the shoe not been meticulously polished, one could have called it an old casual shoe.

This shoe is a key to Mr. Wellington, Michal thought. The plush image is only a mask. He imagined the distances this shoe covered day by day, through dust and morning dew. He also imagined the loving care with which Mr. Wellington polished his favourite shoes. He must have a large family, Michal decided. Why else would he be saving money by not buying new shoes?

Behind Mr. Wellington, a huge bay window covered the entire wall. From his chair, Michal saw no houses or trees, only blue sky and small cumulus clouds slowly moving across it.

It almost appears, Michal thought, as if Mr. Wellington controlled things from outer space or interviewed people up in heaven.

Michal narrated the truth with all the tricky details – about his first marriage, about Danna and their work in Prague, about his wish to stay in Canada and the difficulties to bring her out. And then his main question: "If, by some miracle, I succeed in escaping with Danna and Lenka, would we be admitted to Canada?"

"I've loved Canada since the day I arrived," he said at the end. "I'd like my children to grow in freedom and peace."

This is bizarre, he thought. During the entire conversation, Mr. Wellington never asked for any identification.

When they stood up at the end of the visit, Wellington held Michal's hand, looking into his eyes. "Michal, Canada needs people like you. You are welcome to return – any time. If you encounter problems, any Canadian embassy or consulate will help you. Just mention my name …"

"If this leaks to the communists, it can cost me my life!" Michal said.

"There is no record of your visit, and I will keep my mouth shut. Good luck with your trip."

Michal walked out intoxicated by his success, little white clouds still dancing in front of his eyes. If there is one person I can trust, he thought, it is Mr. Wellington.

63. GROCERY STORE

Michal was packing for winter and, possibly, for many months to come. He sold the car, pulled his suitcase from under the bed, and filled it with his clothes and personal items such as the hunting knife and the flashlight he took everywhere with him. When he put the suitcase on Kathy's bathroom scale and added two small dictionaries, he was already over the luggage limit.

He did not weigh his winter coat and the hiking boots. The weather was not cold yet, but he planned to wear them to reduce the check-in weight. His project notes, publications collected for his colleagues in Prague, and unpublished manuscripts did not fit the suitcase; he packed them into a canvas carry-on bag, together with his camera and personal documents.

Then he took out the gifts that he had stowed in shopping bags under the bed: A fashionable French beret and a shawl he had bought for Danna in Montreal, two 24-ounce bottles of Canadian whiskey – one for Radim and one for the director, a carton of Phillip Morris cigarettes for Olda, a big collection of chocolate bars, coffee, souvenirs for his parents, and an eight-inch doll for Lenka.

He had no special gifts for his children. In the toy store, he contemplated buying a stuffed giraffe and an elephant that Líza and Filip would have loved, and he almost bought a new edition of Mother Goose with gentle, Japanese-style illustrations for Rita, but then he remembered that Zora made it clear: If he attempted to visit the children, she would call the police immediately. He knew her well enough – she would discard any gifts, and that would upset the children.

I will be back in Canada in about two months, he thought. That's not enough time even to start legal proceedings about visiting rights. And keeping away from Zora will be essential – she would spoil our escape plans if she knew how.

He placed the doll on the top of the heap, and tried to imagine how Lenka would like it. The doll looked like a real, smiling baby, had a raggedy body, white dress, soft nylon head, and when placed in a horizontal position, she closed her blue eyes. The blond hair looked like it was really growing from her head. When Michal saw her in the shop window, he immediately thought that Lenka would love it. The store clerk told him that the doll was popular because girls could comb her long hair, and rearrange it in a variety of styles. She was also small enough that a three-year-old could easily cuddle it and carry her around. Michal took her from the pile, and pulled the ring on her back. She cried several times like a baby.

He remembered that, when departing from Prague, the airline agent had only weighed his suitcase and not the carry-on bag. He stuffed the dictionaries, the flashlight, one bottle, and other heavier items into the deep pockets of his winter coat, and packed the suitcase to exactly 19.7 kg.

The remaining small items must go into the carry-on bag, he decided. I can wear the two sweaters and take them off after I board the plane.

He had to sit on the suitcase to close its zipper. The carry-on bag was as heavy as a stone. When finished with packing, Michal took his camera and went to the local supermarket. He was just focusing the camera on the meat counter, when the store manager came rushing in.

"What's wrong? Please, don't take any pictures."

"Look at this wonderful display," Michal said. "Sirloin and T-bone steaks, pork, veal, lamb, chicken and turkey, salmon and liver."

"What are you going to do with those pictures?" the manager was still suspicious.

"It's for my family in Prague. They wait in line for meat – if there is any meat that day, and there is no fruit or vegetables except, perhaps for potatoes and carrots.

"Look over there," Michal continued. "It is November, and you have fresh strawberries and peaches, oranges, mangoes, bananas, coconuts, watermelons, and several kinds of grapes. Your store is like a fairy tale."

The manager smiled. "Take as many pictures as you want."

Before leaving the store, Michal spent his remaining cash on samples of 'exotic' food. He bought a can of lima beans, bag of marshmallows, box of Kellogg's cereal, package of processed cheese, a coconut, box of cake mix, packet of Kool-Aid, bag of cashews, three packages of instant pudding and Jell-O, big Hershey chocolate bar, box of Salada tea bags, jar of freeze-dried coffee, and five packs of chewing gum. He also bought two cans of beer in the beer store, packed it all into a box and sent it by surface mail to himself at the Prague address of his parents.

After paying the postage, he had exactly $4.55 left. It did not make much sense to bring dollars to Prague. He even left his chequebook in Matheson's office. He knew that, on arrival to Prague, his luggage would be searched and it would cause endless troubles to explain why he kept a bank account in Canada while returning to Prague.

64. OVERWEIGHT LUGGAGE

On Friday afternoon, Allan took Michal to the Ottawa airport. "Where are you going, buddy, to the Arctic?" he laughed at Michal's two sweaters and his winter coat.

"I hope not to one of the Siberian Gulags," Michal said.

"Thank you for everything!" he waved one last time, and entered the terminal building.

Inside, the airline agent attached a label to his suitcase. "In Montreal, please, check-in again with Air France," she said.

In Montreal, Michal found the Air France counter.

"Place *both* your bags on the scale," the agent said.

"This is only a carry-on," Michal objected. "On my flight to Canada, I had the same bag, and it was not included."

"Sorry, sir, we have different regulations."

The agent had a small mustache, polished fingernails, and a high pitch voice with a French accent. He looked like a waiter.

Michal placed both bags on the scale, and the needle went far beyond the red 20 kg mark.

"7.5 kg overweight, that will be $75," the agent said without looking at Michal.

"I don't have $75," Michal opened his wallet and shook out its content. "I'll give you $4.55, that's all I have."

"Then we can't take you. The overweight charge is $10 per kilogram."

In his mind, Michal saw Danna at the Prague airport. She waited and waited, but Michal did not arrive. She began to cry.

He was not an experienced air traveller. He did not know that the airline would get him to the destination even if he missed the departure. He thought that if he did not board the plane, he would forfeit his ticket.

"I will try to do something," he said and walked away from the counter.

"The flight departs in thirty minutes," the agent called after him.

Under the layers of clothing, and walking with the heavy luggage, Michal was getting hot. After a short search, he found a bank that was still open.

"I am short of $75 for the overweight luggage," he said out of breath. "I have an account in the Bank of Nova Scotia."

"This is the Bank of Montreal. Have you got your cheque-book with you?"

"Sorry, I don't. I didn't think I'd need it."

"Then we can't help you."

Back in the lobby, Michal found a uniformed man snoozing under the sign INFORMATION, and he tapped on his shoulder. "Excuse me, sir ..."

The man woke up, evidently pleased that somebody needed his help. "You could send your bag back to Ottawa," he said, "but you don't have any money, and the post office is already closed. Putting it into a safety locker would not work either. Unpaid storage is removed daily and, after two weeks, it is sold in an auction.

"I bet that all your possessions are not worth $75," he said after thinking for a while. "Why don't you dump the heaviest articles into the waste basket?"

The man could not know that, after arriving in Prague and paying alimony to Zora, Michal would not have enough money to buy a pair of socks.

"Thank you for your advice," he said, and returned to the airline counter. He was perspiring under the two sweaters and the winter coat. The clock above the counter showed five minutes past the departure time, but the agent was still processing passangers

"Isn't there some other way to send the luggage?" Michal said when it was his turn.

The agent looked at the ceiling, and answered slowly: "Perhaps, if someone gives you his weight quota." He looked straight at Michal. "The flight departs in five minutes!"

A well-dressed young man with a coat over his arm overheard

the conversation, and placed his ticket on the counter. "I have no luggage, you can give him my quota."

"Aren't you lucky," the agent said and began to work on Michal's ticket at a deliberately low speed. The stranger smiled at Michal, and strolled toward the gate.

"Your suitcase may get there with the next plane," the agent said ironically. "They won't be able to load it. Also, this is only to Paris. There you will have to find another donor."

"I don't care which plane." Michal grabbed his ticket, and ran through the hall. If he had ever been close to a heart attack, it was then. After the stress of getting his luggage through, he ran through many halls and moving pathways in all those clothes and with the heavy bag over his shoulder.

Unlike in Prague, there was no security or immigration check of departing passengers. Michal was the last one to board the plane; the door closed immediately behind him.

65. LANDING IN PRAGUE

Michal had never flown in a 747 before. When the plane began to descend to Paris, Michal began to worry. The sound of the engines had changed and the huge wings vibrated. It seemed to him that all small aircraft had left the area and the traffic had stopped, waiting for the big bird to land. The pilot announced they were forty-five minutes late.

How will I catch the connection to Prague? he worried again. Can I find another passenger without luggage while rushing from one plane to another, using my broken French?

The plane landed, the engines stopped, and the attendent called first in French and then in English: "Passengers Steward, Lallonde, and Sedmý, please contact our agent outside the gate. The Prague flight is waiting for you."

The agent gathered the three passengers, took them to a car waiting outside the building, and drove them across the runways directly to the waiting plane.

"What will happen to my luggage?" Michal asked shyly.

"It's just being loaded," the agent shouted over the roar of the engines.

Only when the plane took off the ground, did Michal finally relax. He was approaching Prague at a speed that matched his heartbeat. He sat thinking about Danna, trying to imagine her face. He smiled like a fool and quickly composed his face when he noticed other passengers staring at him with odd expressions.

Several planes arrived in Prague at the same time, and four massive lines formed at the immigration checkpoint – quite a contrast to Montreal where Michal departed without showing a single piece of paper.

The lines moved slowly; some passengers sat on their suitcases and read newspapers or books. Michal noticed people from Britain, Italy, and India, but most passengers were Czechs. He recognized them instantly – they were weary and sad and looked down as if in fear of something. They had already surrendered to the atmosphere of the country, while foreigners thought this was only an uncomfortable wait.

One rebellious individual shouted: "Look at us idiots, waiting here like a flock of sheep! Once we pass through that door, we'll never come out again."

Nobody responded to him. We all know that, Michal was thinking. If these poor people had their spouses and children with them, they would not be waiting in this line. They would be staying in Sweden, Britain, Canada or wherever, definitely not returning to Prague.

Some of people smiled to themselves at the man's outburst, but Michal pretended not to hear it. There could be communist spies coming from abroad, and STB are watching through some peepholes or cameras, he reminded himself. Even a smile can lead to a trouble. I am going straight to the lion's den, and I will bring Danna out, he thought. That's something beyond the imagination of these unfortunate people around me.

Andante Cantabile

66. PORK ROAST

From the Customs area, Michal saw the mass of people waiting at the barrier. His eyes searched for Danna, but could not find her at first. Then her head popped up behind the people, again and again, as if she were playing volleyball.

He dropped his bags and signaled with both his arms. Her head bobbed up again a couple of times. He grabbed the bags, pushed his way through the gap in the barrier, and she ran into his arms.

"You came, you really came!" she sobbed, tears running down her cheeks.

"Not only did I come," he whispered into her ear, "I am going to take you out of here."

Something pulled on his coat. He looked down and saw Lenka.

"I missed you," he squatted beside her, "and I have something for you."

He reached into his bag, and took out the doll. "Do you like her?"

They stood in the middle of the main flow, paying no attention to the passengers who stumbled over them with their suitcases.

"Where did you get her? She's beautiful," Danna said.

Lenka clapped her hands and grabbed the doll. "Sure I like her," she said and looked at it, face to face. "Her name will be Janinka." She pressed the doll tightly to her chest, and was ready to go.

Only then Michal noticed Olda, grinning two steps from them. "Well, welcome to Prague," Olda said.

Michal gave him a hug. "I did not expect such a big welcoming party."

"At least, I can give you a ride. Besides," and Olda winked at Danna, "we have a surprise for you."

He took Michal's luggage, and started toward the exit.

"Where are you taking me?"

"I am sure you did not have dumplings and the real Pilsner for two months," Olda said. "Think of a crisp pork roast with sauerkraut. We are taking you to a restaurant first."

In the back seat of the car, Michal and Danna held hands behind Lenka who wriggled between them. "Shouldn't we drop off my luggage at Lída's, or at least call her to tell her I am here?" Michal said.

"You can't go to Lída's," Danna said in a hard voice.

"What happened? Why not?"

She looked straight into his eyes. "Are you blind? She loves you."

Michal let go of her hand and said quietly: "Do you remember the night before my departure – how she invited you and Lenka overnight? That would be the ultimate sacrifice someone in love could do."

"She loves you that much."

"That makes things even worse. What can I do for her?"

"Just stay away from her. Don't give her any hope."

"But where are we going then?"

Danna took his hand again. "That's the surprise we have for you ..."

"Here is the restaurant." Olda interrupted them.

After lunch and back in the car, Michal noticed how the two months in Canada had changed his thinking. The familiar streets, shops and houses now appeared foreign, neglected and grey. He understood that people who lived in this city loved it and were proud of it, but he did not belong to this country any longer.

"Now tell me, where are you taking me?"

"I bribed the lady at the advertisement agency," Danna said. "She found an apartment, but it's pathetic and one hour from the city."

"You've got a place where we can stay? Together?" he shouted. "You are a wizard!"

"After Canada, this will be a real shock," she warned him. "I did all I could, and Olda helped me a lot."

"You can commute by train," Olda added without taking his eyes from the truck ahead of them. From his occasional wink of the eye or knowing expression in his face, Michal and Danna always understood that Olda knew they wanted to defect but, mostly for his safety, they never gave him even a hint that that was indeed the case.

67. ŘEVNICE

After driving through several villages, Olda stopped in front of a grey, two-story villa with a neglected garden.

"We are in Řevnice," he announced and turned off the key.

Michal stepped out of the car. Unfinished stucco exposed raw bricks on a large section of the exterior wall. Scaffold was still there, rusty and weathered, clearly not used for a long time.

Danna entered through the rusty gate in the forged iron fence, and Lenka, Michal, and Olda followed her through the backyard littered with old paint cans and broken crates. A frightened yellow cat streaked out from the entrance, and the two chickens sitting on the stairs began to cackle. The stairs were slimy and green.

Inside, a bare bulb poorly illuminated the entrance hall with large, shale tiles that had not been swept for weeks. Dirty rubber boots stood beside the door; an old raincoat and a hat hung on the wall. The air was musty and stale.

Danna knocked on the first door and led Michal into a large room which – judging by its size, style of furniture, and the level of disorder – looked like a poorly managed farm kitchen. A woman in a black skirt, black sweater and with a black scarf on her head was washing dishes.

"Welcome, sir," she wiped hands into her black apron. "It's an honor to have such educated tenants. My Lord, two graduated engineers! Is it true that you can speak English?

"My husband and I, we were still young and strong, when we began to build. Then he suddenly died and left me with two little boys. Since then, everything has been dreadful. I've brought the boys up, but could not finish the house. At least we had a roof above our heads and did not have to pay any rent ..."

She took two photographs from the dresser. "This is my older son. He is already married and has his own family. The younger one here is serving in the army. And I am left here alone, a tired old crow."

Michal noticed that the sink on the kitchen counter had no faucet, and several pails stood beside the door. No running water, he concluded.

"I apologize for asking, but this is a matter of reputation," the woman said. "Are you going to get married?"

Michal glanced at the cross on the wall. "As soon as possible," he said.

"Come on, I want to show you my room," Lenka pulled on Michal's sleeve.

"Excuse us," Michal turned to the woman. "This is important."

"I envy you having her around," the woman said. "She is such a happy and bright child."

Lenka took Michal's hand and led him up the steep spiral stairs.

"The movers could not pass through with the furniture," Danna said. "The beds and wardrobes went on ropes through the windows and over the balcony."

On the second floor, Lenka opened a door into an unfinished attic with bare brick walls and a pile of construction lumber. The room had no floor, only loose planks that formed a pathway between two doors.

"Don't get scared, this is only the entrance hall," Danna said, grinning. Olda followed them in. The next door opened into a freshly decorated room, with curtains and neatly arranged furniture.

"You are indeed a wizard," Michal said and kissed Danna. "You made a cozy home literally from nothing."

Besides Danna's double bed, there was her old fridge, coal-burning stove, and an improvised kitchen with a two burner portable electric range. A chair with a washbasin and two pails of water stood in the corner. A large dining table with four chairs formed the center of the room. The decorations, curtains, range, fridge, even the tablecloth was white, and gave the room a sensation of brightness. A vase of fresh flowers stood in the middle of the table.

Michal opened one of the two windows and looked outside, but could not see any houses – only brown fields sloping gently up toward a crest of mixed woods on a small hill. The wind was bringing the scent of burning wood. "It's like a dream," he said.

"This is the last row of houses in the village," Olda said.

"You haven't seen my room yet," Lenka dragged Michal to the adjacent room.

"Here is my little bed, my own stove, and all my toys. Mommy gave me her desk." A large teddy bear peeked out from a half-open drawer. "These two wardrobes belong to Mommy and you, but otherwise, everything here is mine," she showed Michal proudly, all the time carrying the new doll under her arm.

"You should have seen the place when we started," Danna said. "It was just raw construction. Even the floor isn't properly finished, we just painted it over. We also had to paint the doors and the window frames."

"You know too well that finding an apartment is close to impossible, and we wanted to surprise you," Olda winked at Danna. "It's getting late and I have to go. Enjoy your little nest, lovebirds!"

They walked with Olda to his car and, on the way back, Danna opened the bathroom door under the stairs. This is the worst part of the house," she confessed. "You'll use it only when you really have to. It stinks."

The concrete cubicle without a window or ventilation was unpainted and wet. Both the toilet and the cast-iron tub had large brown stains of dubious origin. Danna stepped over the puddle in the narrow space between the bathtub and a dust-covered coal boiler. "The boiler doesn't work. There is no heating and no mirror. Only an ascetic can take a shower here. For a chamber pot, I keep a pail in the unfinished attic," she said. "Walking down here in the middle of the night gives me creeps."

68. NIGHT FIGHT

The next morning, Michal awoke to a big commotion. A car blew a horn outside; Danna was already up and dressing Lenka. It would have been two a.m. in Ottawa, but outside the sun was rising.

"It's Ivan," Danna said. "This week, he has Lenka on Sunday."

In all his plans, Michal had completely forgotten about Ivan. He thought Ivan was history, a ghost of the past, but suddenly he was there, and uncomfortably real.

"What? " Michal jumped right out of the bed. "Is he coming up?"

"You can go back to sleep," Danna pushed him back, laughing. "He waits in his car until I bring Lenka down. It's always the same routine."

Michal pulled a sweater over his pajama top, and peeked from the window, hiding behind the curtains. Ivan was sitting at the steering wheel and, from the rear seat, his parents were looking curiously toward the upper floor windows.

Lenka was already standing in the middle of the room in her winter coat, holding Janinka under her arm.

"Danna, what about the doll?" Michal said. "Shouldn't she leave her at home?"

Lenka held her doll tightly. "It's all right," Danna said softly after two seconds of thinking. "Ivan loves Lenka; he wouldn't hurt her feelings."

Michal returned to bed and listened to the sound of Danna's and Lenka's feet trotting down the stairs, the metal click of the gate, the slamming of the car doors, and the vanishing sound of the car engine. Danna came back to join him in bed. Her feet were cold and wet.

They made love and slept, sat leaning against the pillows and talked about what had happened during the two long months. Michal told her how Dr. Matheson promised to keep the fellowship open for a year, and he described the meeting with the mysterious Mr. Wellington – doubtless an important security agent who promised help, for all three of them, with entering Canada. And she burst out laughing when he told her how he negotiated the loan for the three airplane tickets at the Bank of Nova Scotia. Then they made love again and slept, got up for lunch, left the dishes on the table, and went back to bed.

Danna looked at her watch: "It's already evening. Six thirty, and Ivan is coming at seven."

Just when they finished making up the bed, the car horn sounded. Danna put on a coat and went down, while Michal sat quietly waiting for the sound of engine to start and drive slowly away. But it did not come.

Danna returned with Lenka. "Ivan would like to see you."

"Why? Is it safe?"

Michal wished Danna would give him some reason for not going, an excuse, but she was relaxed and calm. "He said he'd like to have a chat with you. He saw the doll, and Lenka told him you returned from Canada."

When Danna saw his hesitation, she added: "He didn't look upset, and he's alone. I don't think there's any danger. It's probably about Lenka ..."

Hesitantly, Michal put on a sweater and went down. It was already dark, no street lamps, and the few windows with the lights on cast no light. Drizzle was falling.

"Ivan, where are you?" he asked.

At the length of his arm, he could see a dark silhouette. "It's the time of reckoning." Ivan's voice vibrated with anger.

Is he armed? Michal thought instantly. Oh, Danna, why did you send me here? "Aren't you and Danna divorced?" he said.

"You had an affair with her when she was still my wife. That shouldn't remain unpunished."

"I would never interfere with two people in love, whether married or not. I only picked up the pieces of your already broken marriage."

Ivan did not answer. They began to circle like two tomcats.

"How do you want to fight?" Ivan asked. "Since I am challenging you, the choice of style is yours."

That sounds better, Michal thought. He has no weapons. Worst case, it means a good thrashing, hopefully not death yet. Never in his life had Michal been less inclined to fight. After making love all day and tired from jetlag, he felt at peace with the entire world. He was not angry with Ivan – he was sorry for him, and saw no reason for hitting him. He remembered the karate strikes, but was standing there with rubbery arms and unable to hit. What amazed him even more was the absence of fear. His brain worked calmly like a clock.

"What can you gain by fighting now? It's too late," he said.

"A personal satisfaction," Ivan growled.

The words of the karate teacher began to circle in Michal's head. "The brain is your weapon of choice. Use it; try to avoid the fight."

The window upstairs opened: "What's going on? Are you all right, guys?" It was Danna.

"We are just talking," Ivan said, and the window closed.

"Take your glasses off," he said. "Yes, right now." The fight seemed inescapable.

Michal placed his glasses at the bottom of the fence, and the circle in which they moved began to close. Suddenly, a car passed by. The car lights blinded them first, then the dark mass of the vehicle passed between them and broke the close contact. The car transformed into red taillights, and vanished around the corner

They began to circle again. To run away would be easy, but Ivan could interpret it as leaving Danna to him. Michal would rather face the beating. He also felt his strength recovering, his adrenaline building up. He felt he could strike, but it crossed his mind that, perhaps, Ivan was in a similar shock.

He remembered the karate teacher saying, "Use your mind, talk him out of the fight ..."

"I don't care how we fight," he said. "Any style you want. Whether you win or don't, it's not going to change anything."

Ivan was breathing heavily and did not answer.

"It's easy for you. You are much taller, much stronger. You have been doing sports since you were a little boy. Just serve yourself, beat me up."

"And you are just bullying me," Michal added.

"What do you mean?" Ivan said, and took a step back.

"I taught you math," Michal said. "If I challenge you in solving differential equations, would you have a chance?"

Ivan stood silently for a while, then spat on the ground, said "damn you!", turned around, took three long steps toward his car, jumped in, turned the ignition key, and drove off like a madman.

With drizzle falling on his face, Michal stared into the darkness and listened for the sound of the car crashing into something, but the roar of the engine quickly diminished until complete silence surrounded the road. He picked up his glasses, and walked up the stairs like an old tired man.

"What happened?" Danna said. "What took you so long?"

"He wanted to fight, but I talked him out of it."

69. COMMUTER TRAIN

The next day, Michal got the first taste of his new life. At 04:45, the alarm clock went off, and rang for a long time before Michal found the source of the terrible noise and pushed the stop button. When he got up and opened the window, damp predawn darkness surrounded the house. The birds were not singing yet, and a cat sat in the middle of the road, motionless and silent.

He returned to Danna sitting on the side of the bed. "This is not a decent hour ..."

"You'll get used to it," she comforted to him. "You go to bed earlier, and you rise earlier."

"I see," Michal kissed her. "I am already up."

First Danna then Michal, each poured a gallon of cold water from the freshwater bucket into the basin, washed face and chest, moved the basin from the chair down to the floor, finished the bath, and poured the remaining water into the wastewater bucket.

The fire in the stove had long since died, but the room was not completely cold yet.

"Your body is unbelievably beautiful," Michal said, "like of a wild cat."

"You know I have not built my life on my appearance, but it's a good feeling you like me the way I am," she said and planted a kiss on his mouth.

They wiped up the puddles, laughing.

The tea kettle began to whistle and Michal prepared to shave, using water that had warmed up in a pot on the other burner.

Gently, with sweet words, Danna woke Lenka and carried her in from her room.

The child's limbs hung down limply, and her eyes kept closing.

"Here, have a drink of milk," Danna offered.

"Let me sleep, I don't want anything ..."

In less than five minutes though, Lenka's mouth was in full gear. She kept asking questions and reciting nursery rhymes while she ate breakfast, while being dressed, and while perched on Michal's shoulders on the way to the train station. In between, she talked to her doll: "Watch out! You are spilling your cereal. And take your red coat 'cause it's going to snow."

Like a black-and-white photograph, the predawn light accentuated the branches of shrubs and trees, and the mist condensed into ornaments decorating the wet, black bark. A branch full of red berries hung over the fence.

When they reached the station, Michal lowered Lenka to the ground, shook the water off his coat, and rubbed his hands. The station and its surroundings – especially the rail yard – hovered in the grey mist. Michal took a deep breath. The air had the scent of steam engines, of hot oil, and of sulfur from trains that had passed through for decades.

Inside the waiting room, the same atmosphere prevailed.

Colourless, sleepy people huddled around a big stove with a red, glowing pipe. Lenka squatted opposite the stove and watched the flames inside through a small mica window.

Michal stood behind her, his arm draped across Danna's shoulders, all three of them absorbing the heat with their entire bodies.

"You may be sorry if we don't make it to Canada," Danna whispered into his ear.

"I am with you and nothing else matters," Michal whispered back. "Besides, there is a profound beauty in everything around us."

Brakes screeched and a cloud of warm steam came from under the wheels as the train pulled in. Car doors banged, and conductors yelled. The three climbed into an empty car.

"The seat is cold like a block of ice," Lenka said and rubbed the seat of her pants.

Danna opened the small suitcase she brought for Lenka, and pulled out a blanket. "Wrap yourself in this and have a short nap."

Lenka sat between them, watching the bleak countryside and the streaks of embers from the steam engine that flew past the window. Her eyes closed, as the train hummed ahead with an assuring certainty.

At the frequent stops, more people boarded the train, until every car was crowded – bricklayers with large, bruised hands, tanned road labourers already in their work clothes, and steel workers with grey wrinkled faces and opaque eyes that had seen too much fire.

They were packed shoulder-to-shoulder, their drying coats smelled of tobacco, sweat, asphalt, and engines. The train was heated only by human bodies and the windows were closed.

"Hey, little birdie," an old man poked at Lenka. "Where are you going so early?"

"To my aunt ..." Lenka said with pride. "She tells me stories and we sing together to make the soup cook faster. We take her dog for a walk and feed the pigeons in the park. I take a nap after lunch, and then we go back to Řevnice. I like trains."

"My, oh, my!" The man smiled and pushed his cap with one finger.

"What do you have over there?" Lenka pointed to a large, bulging pocket of his coat.

"That's my lunch." The man took out a packet wrapped in brown paper.

"Do you want a bite?"

"No, I don't," Lenka shook her head resolutely, and pulled back between Michal and Danna.

The train reached Prague five minutes after seven, and crowds stormed the waiting streetcars.

Danna and Michal, carrying Lenka, pushed their way in. Now every minute counted.

"Come on, sweet girl," aunt Mara opened her arms for Lenka. "And you two," she nodded to Danna and Michal, "off you go, and enjoy your work."

"Bye, bye," Lenka waved behind them. "Pick me up after work. Don't forget!"

Then came another ride in a crowded streetcar, holding onto each other, whispering and joking. A quick stop at a dairy store for a bottle of milk and fresh buns, and they arrived at the office by eight, exhausted.

"Michal, be most careful what you say," Danna said before entering the building. "You were away for two short months, but everything has changed. Hard Communists and Soviet sympathizers are in power. We are back to the oppression of 1950s. Say one wrong word, and you may lose your job or go to prison."

"Those two months were not short – they were terribly long," Michal took her around her shoulders. "Don't worry. I will be diplomatic and patient."

They ate the second breakfast at their desks pretending to read some papers, gradually recovered, and began to function. In the afternoon, this travel repeated itself in reverse. When they arrived in Řevnice, it was already dark, but the grocery store was still open. Together, they cooked a quick dinner and went straight to bed.

70. BACK IN THE OFFICE

An apparition of Vladimir Iljic Lenin or of Napoleon Bonaparte would not have stirred up more curiosity than Michal's sudden appearance.

"Have you seen? Michal is back," the news ran from one office to another.

Before talking to anybody else, Michal went to the director who put down his reading glasses and looked up at Michal, bedazzled: "What are *you* doing here?"

"I took a leave of absence, comrade director. I'd like to marry Danna. I trust you understand."

"No, I don't understand," the director grew angry. "We are a research institute, not a pigeon house where everybody flies in and out as he pleases." He was turning red. "Do you know how hard it was to arrange your exit visa? Since the inception of the Institute, nobody has received such an honour. And you come back in only two months? Do you have any sense of responsibility? What will the Canadians think of us? And who is going to pay your airfare?"

"I bought the ticket from the money I saved."

"You saved enough money in two months?"

Michal could see that, in his mind, the director made a fast calculation and concluded that even with his exceptional salary it would take the director many months to save for such a trip.

"All your colleagues would be eternally grateful for such an opportunity, and here, Your Majesty comes back on a whim." The director cooled down a bit. "You should have finished the fellowship first, and then marry Danna."

"Comrade director, have you ever been in love? I'd rather cancel the fellowship than live without her for another year."

"You want to take her with you?" the director began to breathe heavily again. "I tell you something: Your fellowship is a part of the cooperation we'd like to establish with the West. It must be properly executed and that is your duty. I am not going to discuss any conditions with you," he rose from his chair.

"Yes, comrade director." Michal placed the bottle of Canadian whiskey at the edge of the desk, and backed out of the office.

The secretary, who overheard the end of the conversation and saw Michal's exasperated face, laughed when the director's door closed. "Give him a couple of days. Did I hear correctly? Are you going to marry Danna?"

"Yes, but don't mention it to anybody."

71. LOST CAR

Next, Michal called Zora. She was even less pleased than the director.

"Like an idiot, you leave Canada, return to this messed up country, and you are telling me that instead of one hundred dollars a month, you will be sending me a lousy one-thousand-nine-hundred-twenty Czech crowns ..."

"I'd like to have my car back ..." Michal interrupted her.

"Forget the car. What you left at the airport was a wreck – I barely made it home," she blasted Michal. "I paid a fortune to repair it; I need the car for the children. You can't have it."

"Zora, this is not fair. The car was in perfect condition, and I left it with you in good faith. It is my car."

"The car does not belong to you any longer," Zora produced her last trump. "My mother contributed to the original down payment, and she wants her money back. Where are you going to live now? With that whore of yours?"

The dream of easy commuting was dissolving into thin air.

"What do you suggest then?" he asked.

"I suggest that you get a good lawyer. The car has to be sold, and the proceeds divided between you and me."

"Didn't we agree that you keep the apartment and the furniture, and I keep the car?"

"Yes, we did, but long time ago. We already have a buyer for the car – he is a friend of my mother's."

Michal could see through the plot. On paper, the price would be low, and the mother would collect the difference privately.

If Rita, Filip and Líza could visit me, he thought, I'd gladly forfeit the car.

"When can I see the children?" he said.

"Never! I told you already. You are a born loser ..." and she hung up the phone.

"I talked to Zora," Michal told Danna at noon. "I guess we won't have the car."

"I expected something like that," Danna said. "Let Zora swallow the car and choke on it. We will manage without it."

72. BOOKING THE WEDDING

Living together without being married caused complications at every step. When Michal dropped in at the police station to have his new address recorded on his ID card, the country constable in a greasy hat frowned. "You live together without being married? What kind of morality is that?"

"We are going to marry," Michal blushed. "I just arrived from Canada. We haven't made the arrangements yet."

The same day, Michal went to the coal depot to order winter fuel. At the end of the railway station, two women in quilted work coats sat in a wooden shanty, surrounded by papers. Michal opened the door, and the papers began to fly. "Vanda, close the door quickly," the woman behind the typewriter shouted..

Michal closed the door. "We just moved to Řevnice. Is this the place to order fuel?"

"Complete the application form," she said without interrupting her typing. Michal sat down, and filled in his and Danna's previous residences, the amount of fuel they had ordered over the past five years, and under what name.

Vanda looked the form over. "This is a difficult case. You are neither two singles nor a family, and you have a child living with you," she said and passed the form to the second girl. "I am not sure what is the right quota."

"Last year, you both lived with other families," the other one said. "Those families will continue receiving coal this winter. . All we can give you is two hundred kilograms of lignite."

"You're kidding – not even decent coal, and only two hundred? It takes at least five-times as much to keep warm for the entire winter!"

"With each shipment, we leave some coal for free sale. Come every Saturday with a cart or a potato sack. When we see how much you need this year, we'll increase your quota."

At the grocery store, the cashier whispered to an old lady across the counter: "Do you see those two with the little girl? He came from Canada and, imagine, they live together without being married."

These were just inconveniences, but Michal knew that no hotel would give them room unless they were married. Being married was also crucial for bringing Danna and Lenka to Canada. Already on the way from the airport, he had asked Danna what kind of wedding she would like to have.

She had laughed, slapped her knees, and hugged Michal. "Any kind of wedding. Let's have it soon – not fancy, a simple but nice wedding …"

Under the communist system, only the civil marriage was legally valid, and the nicest place for the wedding ceremony was the historical Old Town Hall that, with an acoustic organ and decorations of red velvet and gold, looked like a king's chamber. After the ceremony, the newly married couples entered the sun-flooded cobblestone square crowded with tourists waiting for the sound of the famous clock, who now watched with curiosity the picture taking, the shyness of the newlyweds and pigeons walking around their feet.

No Czech, even as little nationalistic as Michal, could think of the Town Hall without recalling the German revenge at the end of the war – their tanks blasting this symbol of Prague into ruins when their army was already defeated. The Hall had been reconstructed to its original splendor.

"We are booked solid for six months," the receptionist said. "If you need it sooner, call the National Committee in your district."

"It won't be in historical surroundings," Michal told Danna later. "I don't know what the hall looks like, but we are booked in Prague-Dejvice for December fifth, at ten-thirty."

"The day before St. Nicolas," she looked at the calendar. "It's only nineteen days! We'd better get everything ready."

73. GETTING READY

Lenka knew nothing about the wedding and, from the time she woke on December 5, she kept asking about St. Nicholas. "Is he coming tonight? Will the Devil and the Angel be with him? And will I get any presents?"

"Depends on how good you were over the past year," Michal teased her.

"I was good, really good," Lenka said, but then she went quiet for several seconds and began to look worried. ". . . most of the time," she said.

"Except for losing your mittens, wading through mud in your new shoes, singing at meals. . . . And who peeled all the leaves off our rubber plant?" Danna asked.

"That was an accident," Lenka declared. "That isn't enough to get a spanking from the Devil, is it?" she turned to Michal.

"No, definitely not. You were quite good. St. Nick will bring you candies, apples, and nuts, perhaps a few pieces of coal or a raw potato, but certainly no spanking." By this time, they were already riding on the train.

"I wouldn't mind a bag of coal," a man sitting across the aisle said. "What I get isn't enough to heat a single room."

"The Devil has a whip ..." Lenka started again.

"Only for nasty children ... You were most pleasant and helpful. You don't have to worry."

Lenka became more comfortable. "Why are we travelling with two suitcases today?" she said.

"We have some clothes for the cleaners," Danna said and winked at Michal. The larger suitcase contained Michal's new suit and Danna's wedding dress. As on other working days, they traveled in jeans and hiking boots.

Michal looked from the window. Wet snow was falling and melting on the ground. "Where are we going to get the masks for St. Nicolas and the Devil?" Danna whispered into his ear.

"The stationery store next to our office always has them," Michal whispered back.

74. THE WEDDING

At nine a.m., without telling anybody, Michal and Danna sneaked out of the office. Olda was already waiting outside with the suitcase in his car. "This is exciting," he said. "A secret wedding!"

"It's tight," Michal looked at his watch. "Drive first to Danna's friend Běla, where we will change into our wedding clothes. We have to pick up the flowers and be at the hall by ten-thirty."

"Your parents do not mind?" Olda asked while fighting the traffic.

"Strangely," Danna leaned forward from the back seat, "our mothers were happy about not going. Both would need a new dress, which would be hard to get at a short notice. It would also be expensive."

"My parents invited us for dinner next weekend," Michal said. "We'll have more time to talk when everything is over."

"Where is the house," Olda said. "I can't see the street numbers in this rain."

"Over there," Danna pointed her finger.

Olda was already dressed in a black suit with a smart tie. "Look what I bought for the occasion," he pulled out a pair of white gloves as they entered the house. "I also washed the car inside out, but it's now plastered with mud."

"I solemnly promise," Danna kissed him on the cheek, "that if *you* marry again, we'll wash our car and wear white gloves for the occasion."

"I know, if you ever get another car," Olda laughed, referring to the car usurped by Zora.

When Michal and Danna began to undress in Běla's bedroom, Olda barged in: "Hey, sweethearts, have you ever seen a groom and a bride changing in the same room before the wedding? Please, ladies in one room, gentlemen in another."

"Come on," the two laughed, but just for the heck of it, Michal took his armful of clothes and moved to the adjacent room.

They worked fast, like characters in an old silent movie. Michal was finished first. He called the flower shop to confirm that the bouquet of six large white calla lilies was ready. He also checked his and Danna's documents, the vinyl record to be played at the ceremony, and the wedding rings, now in his pocket and sharing the original Canadian box. In exactly eleven minutes, all four assembled at the door, Běla and Danna putting the last touches to their hair.

Michal watched Danna in front of the mirror. She wore a simple dress without ornaments or folds, which loosely followed the contour of her body. Its collar, a straight horizontal slit, closed at her shoulders, the straight long sleeves ended with a short vertical slit without buttons, and the skirt reached just below her knees, as was fashionable that winter.

The light and smooth woolen cloth that she had chosen for her dress was blue, a happy cobalt blue. She was slim at the waist, broad across the shoulders, and radiant like a mountain sky on a sunny March day.

She wore no headpiece or jewelry, and Michal was quite certain that even her underwear was functional and simple. She was what she was and needed no frills.

Danna glanced at Michal, at how handsome he was in his new dark-grey suit with blue tie which complemented the hue of her own dress. She also knew that each square of his subtly checkered suit contained a thin blue thread, visible at a short distance, and that this thread united his suit with the dress she wore, warm against her skin.

"Let's go," Olda said and drove fast without saying a word until he stopped in front of the flower shop where Michal ran in and returned with the flowers. After fighting the traffic for another five minutes, Olda finally parked the car under a NO PARKING sign in front of the Hall.

"Dash for the door," he said. "We have no umbrellas or raincoats."

"Just in time," Běla looked at her watch. "It's ten twenty-eight." The professional photographer Michal had arranged was waiting at the door.

"Get ready," Olda told Michal. "I go with Danna, you go with Běla."

When the door opened and the music began to play Tchaikovsky's first piano concerto, Michal broke into tears, but he dried his face, collected himself, and resolutely stepped forward. Danna smiled at him. This was their music.

Rows of red seats formed a theater with a small stage and a life-size wood sculpture of two lovers, embracing and kissing. It was not a frugal and simple hall designed for party meetings as Michal expected. It looked more like a small modern theater. Its atmosphere was intimate and pleasant. "This is much nicer than the Old Town Hall," he whispered to Danna.

They stopped, facing the pedestal. The district clerk, impeccably dressed and with a carnation in his buttonhole, was already waiting. He smiled at them, and opened a leather bound folder.

With curiosity, Olda studied Běla's face, turned his eyes to Danna, then back to Běla. Běla was looking at the floor, as if not sure whether marrying Michal was the best thing Danna could do. Michal could smell the calla lilies, and Danna's hand was trembling.

The clerk began solemnly: "Dear friends, we have assembled here for a special occasion, on which the present couple decided to enter the state of matrimony ..."

Just be patient, Michal told himself. He watched the light bulbs in the reflectors and the golden pins on the clerk's cuffs. There will be the part on the social purpose of marriage, the importance of children, and how the husband and wife should cherish each other until the death do them part.

He stretched his neck trying to see into the folder the clerk was reading from. He must know it all by heart, he thought. How long is it going to take?

The clerk verified the identities of the bride, groom, and both witnesses, and he closed his folder. "You both are mature people," he said. "You know enough about marriage, and you have not decided blindly. I wish you from my heart to find everything you are seeking, a new purpose in your lives. Michal, do you want to marry Danna?"

"Yes," Michal said. He had waited for this moment for a long time.

"Danna, do you want to marry Michal?"

"Yes, I do," Danna said with an absolute certainty. All three smiled.

"I declare you husband and wife. You can exchange the wedding bands." The clerk passed forward a velvet tray with the two rings, united again, side by side.

"Sign the marriage contract here," the clerk said. "You can kiss now, if you wish to do so."

Michal kissed Danna and lost his senses for a second. When he opened his eyes, he saw Olda's face, grinning. The music played the part of the concerto, where the piano sings like church bells, for the entire world, reaching the heavens. It was not just a success, Michal felt, it was a complete victory.

"Congratulations," the clerk shook Michal's and Danna's hand.

75. AFTER THE WEDDING

"You stay inside the car." Olda pushed away Michal who was scraping the snow from the car windows. "I am the driver."

"Look, the police department left us a present." Olda pulled out a parking ticket from under the wiper. "I will include it in my expenses."

Inside the car, Běla rubbed her cold hands. Now that the

ceremony was over, she was more relaxed and cheerful, as if something had resolved in her mind. "Time to go for lunch," she said.

For a long minute, Olda sat quietly behind the steering wheel without starting the engine, as if in a trance or meditating on something. Then he said slowly: "Well, Danna, how does it feel to be married?"

Without waiting for the answer, he turned the ignition key and began to race through the city. Cars blew horns at them from every direction. "Come on, slow down, you don't have to kill us just after we've gotten married," Danna implored from the back seat.

Michal had reserved a table in the restaurant of a five-star hotel. The waiter seated them at a meticulously arranged table, placed Danna's flowers in a crystal vase already prepared there, and brought a huge silver tray loaded with Hungarian salami, black forest ham, cognac pate, smoked fish, caviar and shrimp rolls, Emmental and Spanish goat cheese. A feast and utmost luxury in contrast to what was available in the stores.

"What are you going to drink?" the waiter asked.

"Danna and I will drink mineral water, and Olda is driving," Michal said. "Běla, do you want any wine?"

"A wedding without wine?" Olda said and looked at Michal and Danna, but neither of them answered.

"I will also have water," Běla said with a smile.

"I am not sure where to start," Danna said.

"Don't eat too much," Michal warned her. "They have fabulous desserts."

Outside, the sun broke through the clouds. Huge snowflakes danced behind the windows, making the room cozy.

The dessert tray surpassed the first course in both quality and size. The aroma of fresh espresso coffee lingered above the fragrances of vanilla, chocolate, fine fresh pastries, whipping cream, and fresh strawberries.

"I am sorry to mention this," Michal said when nobody could eat more. "We should be in the office before the lunch break is over."

"I ate so much I can't walk back to the car," Běla laughed.

They changed back into jeans at Běla's, and arrived at the Institute at five to one. In a hurry, they bought the masks of St. Nicholas and the Devil in the stationery store, and rushed up the stairs.

The office was still empty. Michal placed two bottles of wine on Radim's desk, Danna arranged one calla lily beside it, and they sat down at their desks, pretending they were working.

Radim came in, began to take off his coat, and noticed the bottles. He moved closer and stared at them for several seconds.

"Three Gracias? We drank this wine in Jachymov. Michal, show me your hand."

Michal showed him his new, spotless wedding ring.

Radim opened the door to the hall, and shouted: "Everybody come here, Michal and Danna got married!"

People from other offices rushed in with congratulations and best wishes, went out to the store, returned with more bottles and, within minutes, the entire institute had stopped working. They drank and sang and partied until four when, of course, everyone had to go home.

76. ST. NICHOLAS

Michal and Danna picked up Lenka, and when they arrived in Řevnice, it was already dark and the apartment was freezing. Danna unwrapped the flowers and put them into a vase. "Lenka, come here, we want to tell you something important."

Lenka trotted left and right, and landed at Danna's lap.

"Guess what?" Danna said. "Michal and I, we were married today. I am his wife and he is my husband."

Michal sat across the table and watched Lenka, worried about her reaction.

Lenka thought deeply for a while, looked at Michal, and then at

Danna. "Does it mean that I can call Michal *my father*?" she asked with a smile.

"I would love that," Michal said. "Now you have two fathers, Ivan and me."

"Great," Lenka jumped down, and clapped her hands. "We can go downstairs, and tell the old landlady."

"A good idea," Danna said. "We'll take her one flower. Here," she took one lily from the vase. "You can take it to her."

Lenka marched solemnly down the stairs with the large flower in her hand. "Good evening," she said when they entered the kitchen. "My father and my mother got married today."

"God bless you, and such a charming flower. I wish you many happy years together."

The landlady wiped her eyes with her apron.

"And what about you," she turned to Lenka. "Did St. Nick bring anything to you?"

"Was he here already?" Lenka looked at her, deeply worried.

"I haven't seen him yet," the lady consoled her. "But it's getting late. He must be coming any minute now."

"We'll look for him, but it is already dark outside," Michal signaled to the old lady from behind Lenka's back. "Can Lenka stay here for a few minutes?"

"Of course," the old lady interrupted her work. "Lenka, come here and tell me what you did in Prague today."

Michal and Danna slipped out and tiptoed upstairs. In minutes their costumes were ready. They made a bishop's hat from computer paper and marked it with a big cross. Danna threw a white bed sheet over Michal's shoulders, taped a beard of cotton around his mask and under his ears, and stuffed a large ski sock with apples, candies, and nuts. In the unfinished fore room, Michal found a rusty chain and an old broomstick. He straightened a coat hanger, wrapped it in toilet paper, formed a spiral, and attached it to the end of the stick. With a bit of imagination, it looked like bishop's cane. The chain was for the Devil.

In the meantime, Danna wrapped a large-format book in aluminum foil, and turned her imitation fur coat inside out. Michal helped her in and buttoned the coat on her back. She put on the Devil's mask, Michal attached a tail of a thick rope to her back and they were ready to go.

They came down with a thundering noise. The knocking of the cane shook the house and Danna dragged the chain down the stairs. At one point, Michal's mask shifted over his eyes and he almost lost his balance.

When they opened the door, Lenka was standing behind the old lady. "I have been a good girl," she declared courageously, and stepped out. Her voice was trembling. Soup was boiling over on the stove, but nobody noticed.

"Eh, eh," Michal said in a deep voice, and opened the photo-album. "Everything is recorded in this book. You were good, indeed, except ... who did not want to eat spinach on November 28? And on February twenty-third, you scribbled with crayons on the wall."

Lenka did not listen. She was staring at the toes of Michal's shoes that protruded from under the bed sheet.

She recognizes my shoes, he thought but continued his role and passed the ski sock to her. "Here, some goodies for you ... You were a good girl."

Danna and Michal tiptoed upstairs, took off their costumes, stowed them away, and ran downstairs again.

"You know what happened?" Lenka said excitedly. "St. Nicolas was here!"

"Did we just miss it? I can't believe it," Danna said.

"And did he bring you anything?" Michal added.

"Yes, this sock of goodies, but you should see his shoes!"

"What about them?"

"He had such enormous feet – just like a troll."

77. COAL DEPOT

Michal and Danna treasured weekends because they had them completely to themselves. If you saw them running with Lenka outside their house and catching large, slowly descending snowflakes into their mouths, you would have had no doubt they were the happiest family in the entire world.

They also did all their chores together, and even such nuisances as the trips to the coal depot were part of their weekend fun. Every Saturday, they dressed Lenka, put her on a sled, and took off with a laugh. Michal ran with the sled and made sharp turns while Lenka screamed "faster, faster" until they both ran out of breath.

With Lenka's assistance and supervision, they shoveled two sacks of coal from the pile in the coal yard, avoiding dust that only choked the fire, picked up by hand the best pieces of coal, and dragged the sacks to the scale. Sometimes, the clerk would sell them a pack of coal briquettes, or a roll of dry kindling.

With this load on the sled, Danna pulled on the rope and Michal pushed until they reached the top of the hill. Facing the ground, Michal watched the infinite strip of dirty snow unrolling before his eyes, with stretches of bare ground, blobs of horse manure and pieces of coal others had dropped on the way home.

"I can't walk anymore, my toes are freezing." Lenka pulled on his coat.

"Lenka, I can't carry you now. Push with me, it will warm you up."

78. LENKA ILL

Next Monday, on the way to the train, Lenka fell asleep on Michal's back, and woke with a sneeze. A fit of hacking coughs shook her little body. It was still dark, minus twelve degrees Celsius, with a blustery wind.

"I feel a pain in my chest when I hear her," Michal said.

"Her temperature was normal when she woke up." Danna touched her forehead again. "I should have stayed at home with her."

"I am worried about her," Michal said. "We live like pioneers in the Canadian forest. The toilet froze this morning, and I had to thaw it with boiling water."

After work, they stopped at Michal's parents to warm up before boarding the train.

"You two can survive any hardship," his mother said, when she heard Lenka's cough. "But look at this poor thing. She needs better treatment."

"What can we do?" Danna said. "We can't find a good babysitter in Řevnice."

Mother brought in hot lemon tea and took Lenka on her lap. "Why don't you use my car until this cold spell is over?"

"You spent all your savings, waited for three years, and with your sore hip, you need a car," Michal said.

"It's only a car and her health is at stake," she pointed to Lenka. "Take the car with you today."

Father came in from the piano room. "Come here. Before you go, we'll play something for you."

Mother and Father sat side by side at the keyboard, smiled at each other, and began to play. The music started with one voice quietly telling an old, almost forgotten story. Then the second voice joined the first and added more details, the voices embraced and rejoiced, lost in their rapture. Michal understood this was all about love, love so deep that words could not tell. Without looking at each other, Mother and Father played, their hands singing, and their hearts united.

When they took their hands off the keyboard, everybody including Lenka sat quietly for several seconds.

"That was most wonderful," Danna said. "What was it?"

"Franz Schubert, Fantasia in F-minor."

"I know why you played this for us," Michal half whispered.

"We thought you would," his Father said.

79. SNOWSTORM

"I like my new grandma and grandpa," Lenka said on the way to Řevnice.

"You are lucky to have so many grandparents," Michal told her. "I remember only one grandmother."

"Why?"

"They all died before I was born."

Lenka was quiet for a while.

"I know why people die. They are born as little babies," she said and showed a centimeter size with her fingers.

"They grow and grow," she stretched her arms wide, "until they are like you. Then they begin to shrink, and they are smaller and smaller, until they are like this," her fingers almost touched.

"And what happens then?" Danna asked.

"Then they vanish," Lenka clapped her hands and smiled.

They brought the car to Řevnice but, after three days, snow began to fall. By the morning, it covered the landscape and smoothed the contours of ditches and roads. The car was buried up to the door handles.

Without breakfast, they put on ski pants, and waded through the deep snow, following the track, which had already formed from house to house toward the train station. Initially hard to navigate, it improved rapidly with each person who had joined it before them.

After work, Michal cleared a rectangle around the car and began to shovel a path toward the main road. He whistled to himself, happy to be outside and, before he went to bed, he finished a 30-meter long strip, wide enough for the car to pass. He paced the distance to the corner and calculated that, at that speed, he would reach the main road in 3.6 days.

Overnight, the wind picked up, and snow filled every crevice in its path. When Michal awoke, he had to open the window to see outside. Snowdrifts covered the road and buried the car. The plows did not come. They could not handle the snow or were working in another part of town.

The trains still worked though. From his office, Michal called his mother to report the situation.

"Don't worry about the car," she said. "Cold spells don't last long in this part of the country. If they don't remove the snow, it will eventually melt. It won't hurt the car.

"But listen," she continued. "Why don't you move in with us? This commuting from Řevnice is ridiculous."

"That would be fantastic, but how does Dad feel about it? The problem isn't the number of bedrooms, but the small kitchen, one bathroom, and the lack of privacy."

"It was his idea," Mother said.

The snow melted in a few days, and the movers came to Řevnice again. The furniture went through the narrow staircase, on ropes over the balcony, and into a van that made it through the remnants of the snow. Danna had bribed the receptionist of the moving company to let her into the manager's office, had bribed the manager to send the movers before Christmas, and had paid each mover individually for coming so far out of town. Then she cooked them a good lunch and they worked carefully without breaking the furniture. Michal supplied the beer.

80. CHRISTMAS

After the upheaval of moving, the young family spent a quiet Christmas with Michal's parents. Together, all five of them decorated a tree, sang carols by the piano, prepared a festive meal, and sat by the hot stove, reading the books they had found under the tree. Lenka enjoyed her new grandfather. She talked to him, listened to his stories, and sat under the piano when he was playing. She helped him polish all his shoes and, hand in hand, they went to the city park to feed the squirrels.

After Christmas, the postman brought a large, battered parcel with many declarations and stamps.

"Michal," his mother looked at the postage stamps, "how did you know two months ago that you would live here?"

"I didn't," Michal laughed. "I had no other address to mail the parcel to."

He carried the box to the dining-room table and cut it open. Everybody rushed in.

"Look, cookies, and such nice packaging," Father took off his glasses to read the small labels. "And it's all in English and French. These cans of beer must be for me."

Lenka rolled the coconut on the floor. "That's a strange ball," she said. "Hairy and still so hard."

Mother took out her best china, made four cups of the instant coffee from the jar she found in the parcel, and poured milk for Lenka. Father divided the almond-and-raisin chocolate bar into five equal parts, and they munched it, savouring every morsel.

"I sent this as proof," Michal said, "That this magic land *is* out there, and it is waiting for us."

"You're a born adventurer," Mother put down her coffee cup. "With you, I always worry what will be next."

> *"You can negotiate anything."*
> (Herb Cohen)

81. OATH TO THE DIRECTOR

When the endless negotiations about the fellowship had not produced any results by the middle of January, both Michal and the director became impatient. The director had reached his limits. What he had promised to Michal would have already caused him problems inside the Party, and Michal was refusing to leave without Danna.

It was a surreal situation: To everybody involved, including the director, Michal appeared reluctant to go, while the director, normally opposed to anybody travelling to the West, was pressing Michal to leave. This made it easier for Michal to negotiate, but the director's interest in his departure worried him immensely.

Why would the director care about what Canadians would think about the Party? He cares about his superiors, but why would they want me to leave? Why are they ready to take the risk that I might defect and remain in Canada? Perhaps, what a horror, they need me for their intelligence operation in Canada. Perhaps the director only hopes that, sometime later, he will visit Canada and my contacts will help him.

On Friday, January 16, Michal and Danna arrived at the office, and Michal saw a note on his desk: 'Comrade director wants to talk to you. He is waiting.'

Michal ran downstairs to the secretary, who pointed to the open door. As Michal entered, everything slowed down.

The director made a half-hearted effort to lift himself from his chair. "Please, take a seat."

The office with its massive black furniture and the upholstered door looked like a funeral parlor.

The director sunk back into his armchair, and paused.

"I got this memorandum from the Deputy Minister," he pounded a sheet of paper on his desk. "The International Department keeps calling me. We have to do something about your fellowship."

"Comrade director, you know my situation. I have just married Danna, and we don't want to separate for the entire year."

"I've told you already. You can't just drop everything and desert your fellowship." He leaned on his elbows and, as he talked, his elbows were spreading wide. He looked like a toad.

Michal did not think that was the true reason and shrugged his shoulders.

"Michal, can you swear to whatever is most precious in your life that you won't defect to the West? Give me your hand, and look into my eyes."

Michal did not react instantly, and weighed his words carefully. I have no choice, he thought. A "No" could send me to jail.

"If you let both of us go to Canada, together and for the entire year," he eventually said, "I swear we will return in due time, and under any conditions."

If he helps us that much, I can't betray him, he thought. We'll stay in Canada for one year, prepare everything, and return to Prague. If we defect later, he would not be responsible.

He took the director's hand.

The director stared into his eyes, probing, then slowly let his hand go. "Well, I have a new proposal. The Federal Minister of Energy and Mines suggested that if you leave now, Danna could visit you in the summer."

After all the negotiations in good faith, Michal felt suddenly overwhelmed by despair. The purpose wasn't to bring Danna to Canada for a short visit. The purpose was to be together with her, away from all these people. He did not care about the director, about the stupid business trip from which he could not defect unless he sacrificed the career and safety of Radim, the director, and perhaps of his own mother and father. Then, in a flash, he realized that the oath he just had given did not include a short summer visit. Like magic, this could bypass all the police screening required for the exit visa.

"Can we arrange her exit visa now?" he said cautiously. "Just to make sure there won't be some unexpected obstacles …"

The director smiled as if he had anticipated the question. "I will send a letter to the Minister today. If he signs it, and I expect he will, it should be a matter of days."

His face was glowing, as he shook Michal's hand vigorously. "Remember what you promised. I trust you!"

Michal backed through the door. "Thank you, comrade director," he said, not sure whether he had made the right decision. Except for the short visit, he would be separated from Danna for the entire year.

"I don't like it," Danna said when Michal told her what happened, "but let's go along for a while. You can always cancel the fellowship."

82. LETTER TO THE MINISTER

In two days, the secretary called Michal that the letter was ready. The envelope she gave him was not sealed. Michal took out the folded paper and recognized the letterhead of the Federal Minister of Energy and Mines and his signature below. He read, holding his breath:

> To the Department of Interior, Section of Foreign Travel
>
> Recommendation.
>
> We recommend that permission be granted to Comrade Danna Sedmý and her daughter Lenka for a family visit in Canada this summer. She will visit her husband, Dr. Michal Sedmý, who works in our research division and is going to be in Canada on a one-year business assignment.

Michal brought the letter home with two visa application forms, but as he started to fill them in, he put his pen down and called Danna. "Come here. This is terrible! Ivan must sign Lenka's application. What are we going to do?"

"I'll talk to him when he comes for Lenka tomorrow," Danna said.

The next morning, Ivan parked across the street and waited in the car. Danna took Lenka down, and Michal watched from the window again.

He saw Danna helping Lenka into the car. Lenka's mouth repeatedly opened and closed, as Danna was trying to adjust the tangled seatbelt. Then Danna leaned forward, deeper into the car, and said something to Ivan, who climbed out of the car as if something annoyed him. They talked face to face for a short while, then Ivan made a wide gesture with both his arms, turned around, got into the car, and drove away fast. The street was empty, and Danna stood at the edge of the sidewalk as if she wanted to say something more.

When she returned, Michal did not have to ask what the reply was.

In the evening, when Ivan returned with Lenka, Michal went

down to talk to him. "I am sorry to harass you," he said. "I know you'd rather avoid these discussions."

"You bet," Ivan growled.

"Why can't you sign the application? It's just for a summer vacation. Are you trying to give us a hard time?"

"If you take Lenka across the border, I will never see her again. Whatever your plans are, you would not tell me anyway."

"We cannot defect even if I wanted to – my boss would go to prison. We must return no matter what."

Michal looked up at Ivan's face. When Ivan was mad, his face bloated, and his eyes crossed slightly.

"I have nothing to gain. Why would I take chances? Danna always …"

He wanted to say that Danna always wanted to leave the country, but did not finish the sentence because it would accuse her of a criminal offense. Instead, he continued: "… she was always looking westward. What you are saying may be your intention now, but when you get there everything will be different."

"Do you derive some perverse pleasure from manipulating us, from being able to decide about my fellowship, about the vacations we take?"

Ivan hesitated before he answered. "You are wasting your time. I want to keep Lenka."

83. ADOPTING LENKA

Discussions like that went on for the entire week. Michal was methodical and persistent and Ivan stubborn like a wounded animal.

On the following weekend, both sides avoided the matter. On Monday, Michal called Ivan again.

"I told you a hundred times," Ivan replied. "I will not sign that paper, except …"

"Except for what?" That was the word Michal was waiting for.

"Except if you adopt Lenka. You mentioned you'd like to do that."

Michal could not believe his ears. He had contemplated about this remote possibility many times and, suddenly, it was hovering right in front of him. Think about every word, was his first thought. Don't spook it. It would solve so many problems.

It was natural for him to take Danna's daughter automatically as his own child, and he already loved her. At the same time, he thought about his children. He would never give *them* up, and he did not want to pressure Ivan or trick him. It would have to be solely his decision.

"Are you serious?" he said, "I'd love to adopt her."

Why did he decide so suddenly, Michal thought. It cannot be for the three-hundred Czech Crowns he pays to Danna every month. That is a marginal fee, and he loves Lenka.

"How soon can we do this?" he continued. "Today?"

He did not expect Ivan would act that fast, but the surprises seemed to have no end.

"Why not," Ivan said. "Let's get it over with quickly. Come to the District Court at ten, and bring Danna with you. She has to sign all the papers."

"There is one problem though," Michal said meekly, afraid to spoil his luck. "The visa application must be signed this week. The adoption will take longer than that."

"When you release me from the alimony payments, I will sign anything you want. See you at ten sharp."

When Michal and Danna arrived at the court, Ivan was waiting with the forms ready. Within a single hour, the forms were signed, certified by a notary, and Ivan signed the visa application for Lenka. Michal felt as if the world was suddenly moving fast, so fast he could not follow what was happening.

"Ivan, thank you for both Lenka and me," he offered Ivan his hand. "You've done us a great favor."

Ivan did not accept the hand and waved as if there was nothing to speak of. It was clear though he did not want to touch Michal's hand.

"Take good care of Lenka," he said with tears in his eyes, turned away and, after a short moment of disorientation, headed toward the exit.

"Danna," Michal said on the way out. "I am the happiest person in the world, but this is not what I expected. Why did he do that?"

"I bet it was his father," she said. "I remember him saying that, after a divorce, it's better for children to have one mother and one father, one happy and closed family. Poor Father," she shook her head. "He loved Lenka so much. If he had only known this would apply to Ivan and me one day!"

84. EXIT VISA – PHASE 1

The only police office that handled applications for exit visa was in a former butcher shop. At any time of the day, a line stretched for the entire block. Waiting people chatted, laughed, and squinted into the sun, or huddled in the rain while blocking the narrow sidewalk of the dilapidated Old Town street. They all were anxious, yet pretending to be cheerful supporters of the regime.

After two hours of waiting, Danna and Michal reached the counter. The sergeant glanced over the application and looked at Danna as if he had never seen anything so absurd.

"We never let the family out before the husband is abroad for at least a year. And both wife and the daughter? That's out of question."

"But look at the attached letter," Danna said.

The sergeant reluctantly took the application. "Come back in a week. You'll see, it will be rejected."

"Perhaps we'll never make it," Danna mused on the way back to the office.

"If we can't go to Canada," Michal said, "we'll go to the Soviet Union. I've had enough of this little country and its mediocre people."

Danna stopped in the middle of the sidewalk. "To where did

you say?"

"To Novosibirsk – a top scientific community surrounded by wild nature. Soviets have developed the H-bomb and sent Sputnik into orbit. They are not as stupid as many people think."

"You are not serious?" Danna looked at him with a worried expression.

"I am driven by insatiable curiosity. I want to invent new things."

They began to walk again.

" I would not make a pact with the Devil," she said with a smile on her face. "You know the story of Dr. Faust, who lived in Prague centuries ago. He wanted to know everything, just like you. In his house, they still show to tourists the hole with burnt edges. The Devil took him to Hell."

"I know," Michal laughed. "We have just one goal – to get to Canada, all three of us, safely and fast."

85. PARTY CHAIRMAN SCHMIDT

Several days later, after lunch, Michal was sitting at his desk, languid and nodding. The sun leaned on his shoulder, and the glare from the white paper blinded his eyes. The room was hot, and his head kept dropping.

What happened next woke him up instantly. Someone knocked on the door and, without waiting, comrade Schmidt, the head of the Communist Party in the Institute, stepped in.

"I'd like to look at Michal's last report," he told Radim and took a folder from the bookshelf, where all the reports were filed. He made himself comfortable on the chair beside the drawing board, and began to flip through the pages. Neither Michal nor Radim had a clue what was happening. Schmidt worked on completely different projects, and had no knowledge of higher math or programming.

Someone who held a high position in the Party could not be trusted. Such a person was either a fanatic ready to kill for the communist cause, or a crook ready to sacrifice his brother for his own career. Two people from the Institute fell into this category: The director, Schmidt, and the personnel manager, who came straight from the Department of Interior and was most likely on the STB payroll.

Schmidt was reading the report, and his fingers trembled. Michal watched his white hair and wide shoulders, bent as if carrying a burden, and tried to imagine him in England during the war, as colleagues gossiped about him – a handsome young fighter pilot admired by women. Schmidt's wife had died of cancer, and his two sons defected to the West. He lived alone like an old wolf.

How could a former officer of the British Air Force be the chairman of the Party, Michal wondered.

"Can you stay longer after work? I'd like to talk to you," Schmidt said when Radim discretely stepped out of the office.

"Of course I can," Michal said, still puzzled.

After work, when all others had left, Schmidt stepped in without knocking and, before closing the door, he checked the hall in both directions making sure that nobody was listening. He disconnected the phone from the wall, and sat on the desk close to Michal. "I have advice for Danna and you, as a good friend. Can you keep your mouth shut?"

Michal moved closer to him. "Of course I will. Please, tell me."

"Don't try to trick me. The Party trusts me a hundred times more than it ever would you."

"I never betray my friends."

"Do not believe the story about the summer in Canada," Schmidt said quietly and fast. "Even if Danna gets the visa, there always will be a reason to prevent her from leaving. Don't trust them!"

Could this be a trap, Michal thought first but intuitively rejected the idea. Schmidt was giving him the information without asking about his plans. Perhaps he was trying to help Michal as he would have helped his own son.

"I am most grateful, Comrade Schmidt," Michal used the word 'Comrade' automatically, as if it were a title.

"I can't tell you more," Schmidt got off the desk, opened the door, and checked the hall again. "I am keeping my fingers crossed for Danna and you," he signaled to Michal.

Michal sat behind his desk, thinking. Now he understood why the director had been smiling.

86. PLAN TO CONFUSE POLICE

Michal told Danna about Schmidt on the way home, but it took them until late evening to grasp the new situation.

"There are two possibilities why Schmidt gave us the warning," Michal said, when they were in bed and Lenka was already sleeping. "He may be a dedicated communist but has a soft heart for people like us. More likely, he is faking his political zealousness. As a former British pilot, he could not survive under communist rule, but as a Party chairman, he is invincible.

"I feel like an idiot," Michal continued. "We are trying to play fair with a bunch of rogues …"

"Look at the director's slimy eyes," Danna said. "He is not as nice as he pretends to be. I would not trust anybody who is a member of the Party Assembly. That's a more influential position than to be a Member of Parliament."

"From now on, it will be a different game," Michal sat up in the bed. "We are not going to beg for permission. We are going to outsmart them. We will cheat and lie as they do, and we'll get out of this damned place despite the consequences – with the exception of Radim, Olda and our parents of course.

"I chose the words of my oath carefully. I told the director: *If you let both of us go to Canada, together, and for the entire year….* I did not say *for a short summer visit.* Besides, I was not talking from my free will. I had no choice. If we defect under the current conditions, I would not even violate that oath."

With surprise, Danna watched the change in Michal's attitude. This was a different Michal from the one she knew, and the new strategy appealed to her. "Is there a place where we could cross the border to West Germany or Austria?" she said.

"There is no such place. Not even a mouse can get through. When I served in the army, I was briefed on how the border is guarded. It is a strip of bare land with two barbed-wire fences, charged with high voltage. Between the fences, the ground is freshly plowed to show intruder's footprints; it also contains land mines. Watchtowers armed with machine guns control the entire border, and guards with dogs patrol along the fence. The adjacent forest, several kilometers wide, is closed to public, and has thin wires hidden in the grass. Tripping such wire triggers an alarm and a massive search. We have to cross the border in a smart way, not in a hard way. "

"All right," she said slowly. "Let us assume that I will get the exit visa. The question is: If you cancel your fellowship, are they smart enough to revoke my visa?"

"This sounds convoluted. Why would I cancel my fellowship?"

". . . because you should not defect from a business trip. Radim signed your application, and he would go to prison. However, if you defect from a Čedok[15] holiday tour, it would be a different story – Radim would only be reprimanded."

"Isn't your visit to Canada also a business trip? It was arranged through the Ministry ..."

"I am not sure what is it, but Radim was not involved. It was initiated by the director, and we don't have to worry about him. Assume that the Čedok tour is to France. If we time it right, we can meet at the Paris airport, and continue to Canada together."

"I see you are the daughter of a great chess player," Michal laughed, "but nobody would believe that I would go for a holiday without you."

She thought for a while. "You need a separate exit visa for each trip, but you can hold only one at any given time. When issuing a new one, the police cancel the old one. My visa for Canada will include Lenka; in that case, I must not lose it. In order not to raise suspicion, we will book the Čedok tour together, but before applying for exit visa, I can cancel the tour."

"Great idea." Michal said. "The system is so complex that they

---

[15] Czech Travel Agency, run by the government

don't know what they are doing, and we'll make it even more complicated. "

"Judging by the forms you had to fill," he continued, "they probably have one computer for the business trips and another one for personal vacations, and these computers do not communicate to each other. Your trip to Canada would be on their *business* computer, but the Čedok tour would be on the *holiday* computer. They may not notice that all three of us would be travelling at the same time, and their bureaucracy is so slow that our marriage may not be recorded yet."

Absorbed in this discussion, neither of them noticed the siren of a police car passing under the windows. Normally, just like all their neighbours, they would pause and wait in fear of the car stopping in front of their house. Fortunately, the sound of the police siren faded into the distance.

"It is too dangerous to write this plan down," Michal said, "We have to memorize it."

The plan involved four steps, and the timing was critical:

Step 1: When Danna and Lenka get the exit visa to visit Michal in Canada, he will formally cancel his fellowship. At the same time, secretly, Michal will ask Dr. Matheson to keep his job regardless of the cancellation.

Step 2: As a honeymoon, Michal and Danna will book a Čedok tour to France without Lenka. Before applying for the exit visa, Danna will pretend to be sick and cancel her participation in the tour.

Step 3: Michal will depart for France. A few days later, Danna and Lenka will fly to Ottawa through Paris, and Michal will join them at the Paris airport.

"Could something like that actually work?" Danna said. "It's scary. Even the thought of communist prison gives me goose bumps!"

"We'll proceed carefully, always testing the ground. If they ask us why you did not cancel your exit visa for Canada, you can say that, after the cancellation of my fellowship, you thought your exit visa would automatically expire. And if the border guard stops either of us, we will pretend to be polite, innocent, and dumb. We can always return to Prague as if we went on two benign, independent holidays."

He continued with an amused expression on his face. "This is great! We will confuse everybody, including the police. It will be like the Lenin's Mistress joke[16]. In the office, they will think that we have left Lenka with your mother while we are on our honeymoon in France. Your mother will think that we are camping with Lenka in South Bohemia. One police computer will think that I'm in Canada and you are coming to visit me, while the other computer will think that I'm in France and you're at home with Lenka – all combinations perfectly legal."

"The most difficult part of this plan will be to get on one of those Čedok tours," Danna reflected.

"It may need a big bribe or a good contact. Leave that to me," Michal laughed.

It looked like a foolproof plan, but neither of them could have guessed how much could go wrong.

87. EXIT VISA – PHASE 2

Danna, Michal, and the director – although for a different reason, held their breath that the minister would approve the special exit visa for Danna and Lenka. He did, and it worked like magic. In a week, the police had the visa ready. Danna went in and Michal waited outside the door.

When Danna came out, she smiled and waved the passport: "I've got it!"

"Show me!" Michal studied the new record carefully right in the street. People were passing by and nobody cared what they were reading and why it was so interesting.

"It's true," Michal was finally satisfied. "You have a regular exit

---

[16] Large red poster *Study, study, study (Lenin)* displayed in all classrooms and offices led to the popular joke of the time. A journalist asks: Comrade Lenin, is it appropriate for a Communist to have a mistress? Lenin replies: It could be. Take my case. I have a mistress, and what happens? My wife thinks I am with the mistress. The mistress thinks I am with my wife. And what do I do? I study, study, study.

visa for Lenka and you, starting May fifteenth, valid for three months. I can't believe it! No conditions attached."

They walked briskly to the office and, with Danna's passport in his pocket, Michal alone knocked on the director's door. The timing is of the essence, he thought. If I talk to the director immediately, it would be impossible to establish later whether I talked to the director before or after Danna received the visa. Neither the police nor the director would record the exact time.

Michal entered, playing a determined, angry man who had decided to speak out. "Comrade director, at the police, they keep saying that Danna can't get her visa. I want to cancel my fellowship."

"Are you sure? This is an important decision," the director said with and expression of relief on his face.

He must have worried since he signed the recommendation for Danna, Michal thought.

"Absolutely sure, comrade director," he replied in a military style, "and it is not a hasty decision. I will draft a letter to Canada, explaining that I am doing so for purely personal reasons. I will bring the letter for your approval."

He hoped that the director would not call the police to cancel Danna's visa, but the director was so elated that he forgot about Danna; he thought the matter was closed.

"It's your choice, Michal, I can't do much about it," the director rubbed his hands. "And welcome back – we do need you here."

88. MESSAGE TO DR. MATHESON

It took Danna and Michal three days of feverish searching to find a foreigner willing to take a secret message for Dr. Matheson across the border. The tall Swedish engineer, Michal's casual friend from the Prague computer exhibition earlier that year, was in town again for several days. He translated the message into Swedish, penciled it in his hard to read longhand in a notebook, and recorded Matheson's name and address separately – in case he would be searched at the border.

The message read:

Dear Dr. Matheson,

Disregard the official letter in which I canceled my fellowship. Please, keep it open as long as you can. I will return to Canada, but it may take some time. The Prague office must not know about all this.

Amused by the two letters, Matheson decided to keep the position open.

89. ČEDOK

Contrasting with the January greyness of Prague streets, posters of beach girls on every corner advertised summer vacations in Bulgaria, Crimea, and at the Baltic Sea, but nowhere, absolutely nowhere, was there even a hint of any tours to the West. So, under a fictitious name, Michal called Čedok.

"We run tours to the capitalist countries," the receptionist said, "but there are very few seats. You can't get there."

"And who can get there?"

"I can't discuss that over the telephone," the receptionist said and hung up.

The next day, Michal skipped lunch and headed for the Čedok central office, which occupied the entire ground floor of a large, historic building. In most rooms, people waited in lines: a long queue for Yugoslavia, about ten people waiting for Romania and Bulgaria, and a group of high school students talking to the girl at the Soviet counter. Except the girl behind the counter, the room selling trips to East Germany was empty.

Michal opened one of the displayed brochures. All the information was there: the prices, conditions, and schedules, but only for the communist countries.

He slowly approached the counter. "When would I have to register for this trip to Dresden?" he pointed to the schedule.

"Two weeks before departure," the girl said.

"And are there any trips to West Germany?"

He said it more quietly, as if in passing, and waited with his heart pounding.

The clerk looked at Michal, and instantly grasped the situation. "We get only a few seats, and they are instantly taken.

"Ask the girl over there," she pointed through the open door to the next counter. "She has the schedules, but everything is booked."

Michal would have preferred if she spoke more quietly and without pointing her finger. Instead of going to the other room immediately, he examined the pictures on the wall, browsed through the brochures, and when the other room emptied, he casually walked in. His hands were sweating. Asking about the trips *to the West* would have made his motives painfully transparent.

"May I see the schedules for Italy and France," he said.

The girl sat behind the counter with a sandwich in her hand, and had her mouth full. Without saying anything, she reached under the counter with her other hand and passed Michal a ring file with six typewritten pages. Michal read the first page over and over several times. The costs of these trips were astronomical. Danna and he would have had to sell everything to afford such a trip.

"For every seat, we already have three standbys. The list is closed."

Michal saw that he had finally reached a person who knew how it all worked.

"Do you have any trips to Belgium or Britain?"

By now, the girl understood the game but, on the surface, it was business as usual. She pulled out another file. "All trips to the West are booked. I can't help you."

"Look here, you have just two trips to Belgium? For thirty people each? For one-point-four million people who live in Prague?"

"These trips are not only for Prague. They are for the entire country."

She took the folder from Michal's hand and looked at the trip number.

"These two trips just got canceled anyway. The bus from the last trip returned nearly empty."

"When do you open the reservations?" Michal pressed on. "How could I get on your list?"

The girl leaned forward and whispered fast. "We never know ahead of time, only a day or two. It's usually in January or February, just about now. People come here and ask daily. You can do the same thing. The night before we open, people line up outside the office. That's the only way."

90. FOREIGN TRAVEL

Michal walked back to his office, thinking about unwritten police rules for visa screening. Police do not trust anybody with relatives abroad. My aunt emigrated to Norway in 1951, and that will decrease my chances. Young men cannot go to the West before they pass the two-year military duty, and those who served in certain units are not allowed to travel for up to seven years. I am lucky – no problem at least with the army.

He laughed to himself. If I were twice as old, it would be easy to get the exit visa. Police do not prevent old people from leaving the country. If they defect, police confiscate all their property, stop their pensions, and the state saves on medical bills. The younger the applicant is, the harder it is to cross the border. As our janitor once said, "young people are easily misled by the glitter of the capitalist society."

The janitor, age fifty-five and a hard-core Communist, had never ventured further away than thirty kilometers from Prague.

Even for a holiday trip, the main problem will be our mining related jobs, Michal concluded. All the communist governments are obsessed with the security of coal mining: Coal generates electric power, it is important for steelworks and chemical factories, and the synthetic gasoline and rubber are essential for military defenses.

The sound of a horn awoke him from his daydreaming; he almost stepped in front of a big truck. The truck driver rolled down the window and shouted obscenities at him.

Michal kept walking as if he did not hear him.

"Lunatics like you should be locked up in a madhouse," the driver was yelling.

Indeed, in a madhouse, Michal thought. Before making any decisions, we have to see what happens in Čedok.

91. LONG COLD NIGHT

Every day, Michal skipped his lunch and went to Čedok. The girl in charge of the capitalist countries already knew him and waved when he entered the office.

"Not yet. Come again tomorrow," she always said and returned to her customers.

This went on for three weeks, until the day when the girl leaned over and whispered: "We've got the trips. The sale opens day after tomorrow."

"Should I ask tomorrow again? I don't want to miss another year."

"The date is firm. We'll open at nine, but you must be here well before that."

Michal understood that meant to come in the evening and to wait in front of the Čedok office all night.

"Thank you very much," he said.

No bribe or tip would be appropriate, he thought. This is the case of a decent person helping someone in distress.

At home, Danna was determined to join him. "I don't mind the cold. At least I'll keep you company."

"You'd better stay with Lenka," Michal reflected. "The police may come with vans and arrest everybody in the line. There may be a riot."

He arrived at Čedok at ten p.m., in padded ski pants over woolen underwear and wearing two sweaters and a double layer windbreaker under his winter coat. He pulled the windbreaker hood over his ski tuque, and stuck his hands deep into the pockets without taking his mitts off. Two pairs of ski socks and rugged hiking boots protected his feet.

It was minus twelve degrees Celsius, and the temperature was dropping. The gusts of wind whisked discarded tram tickets and cigarette butts mixed with light, dirty snow. In winter, cities are cold. The ground, frozen and bare, rang under his steps when he joined the line that already stretched along the wall. It looked good; he counted twenty-three people before him, all quiet and painfully aware of the long night to come.

At first, Michal felt warm, but the wind began to pierce his layers of clothes. He leaned against the wall, hiding from the wind. Some sections of the masonry were warmer, some radiated cold.

One man sat on an old office chair, and Michal wondered how the chair got there. The pile of garbage at the curb did not show anything he could sit on.

He half sat on the narrow rim of the wall, squatting at times. Sitting on the frost covered granite pavement was not practical.

In his left pocket, he held the sandwich Danna had prepared for him; a small thermos bottle with hot lemon tea warmed his right hand, and corners of a chocolate bar that he had stored in his chest pocket rubbed against his ribs.

As the night progressed, the line tightened. Complete strangers huddled together trying to conserve energy. Without saying anything, they still maintained the line perfectly.

The line grew steadily and, at three a.m., Michal stopped counting the people behind him. A two-man police patrol passed by at regular intervals, while people in the line hunched and looked away, as if they did not see the policemen, who strode unconcerned, radiating warmth and good humour, rubbing hands, and chatting as if they did not see the line.

The sounds of the morning brought new hope. The first streetcar passed through the adjacent street. The sound of keys opening houses here and there, and then the echo of the metal tools hitting the stone as janitors began to scrape sidewalks.

The dawn also brought a new chill. Michal had lost most of his body heat, and his teeth began to chatter. Cigarette smoke lingered along the line, warm and sensually pleasing. Grey and green people with baggy eyes stomped around him, and breathed into their hands.

Another two hours, and the street took on its normal appearance. People rushed to work, cars honked, and a truck driver began to unload crates at an adjacent store. At exactly nine, a key turned in the lock from the inside, and the Čedok door opened. The line began to move, but nobody rushed. The positions were established and respected. At that point, Michal was not sure what he wanted more – a trip to the West, or a few minutes inside the warm office.

Three clerks served the line, and by the time Michal reached the counter, four seats were left for France, three to Netherlands, and not a single seat for West Germany, Belgium, or Britain. After the cold night, Michal's responses were slow. He stared at the registration sheet in disbelief. So many boxes crossed out!

"A big block of seats was reserved for government and Party representatives," the girl said, "and most people before you took more than one seat."

Michal looked at the other two clerks selling the seats. He had to act fast.

"Give me two seats to France." Forget the details, he thought, any seats to France.

"Here is your registration number," the clerk said and passed him two forms. "Please, sign here that you have received everything."

Michal reached for the pen, but it fell out of his fingers. He looked at the strange, red hand sticking out of his sleeve, smiled at the clerk and, with his left hand, inserted the pen into his fingers, pressed them together, and signed the form in large, uneven letters.

With his two seats secured, he read the trip itinerary. It was exactly what he needed: Leaving Prague on May 26, three days in Paris, two days by bus through the countryside, and flying back from Paris again. The seats were not taken yet because of their cost, twice as much as the trip to Belgium, and even that was already outrageously expensive.

When he stumbled out of Čedok, all the seats had been taken, and everybody was leaving. Holding onto the reservation papers inside his pocket, he only had a single concern. His bladder had been full for more than four hours.

A cafe in a small shopping mall across the street had just opened, and Michal barged into the restroom with a feeling that five more seconds, and his bladder would burst or his pants would be wet.

He came out relaxed, shed most of his clothes, called Danna from a pay phone, and celebrated with two mugs of hot chocolate and a big breakfast.

92. SIGNATURES AND RECOMMENDATIONS

It was a pleasant, sunny day. Jubilant Michal opened the registration package from Čedok, and pulled out blue forms with numbers 451 and 452. This was not the exit visa application yet – only a preliminary confirmation that the employer will not object to the vacation on the given days, and that the employee could afford the trip.

In the evening, Michal filled the personal data, employer and the salary in both forms, signed his form, had Danna sign hers, and the next day he placed both forms on Radim's desk.

"Where will you get all this money?" Radim asked immediately. The price of the trip was at the top of the form.

Michal did not answer.

"I hate these applications," Radim frowned.

"Radim, please," Michal said. "I have to take it back tomorrow."

"You won't defect, will you?" Radim looked at Michal. "If you do, I'd be in big trouble."

"Of course, we will return. Lenka will stay here with her grandmother," Michal lied. Radim is a Party member, he reasoned to himself, not a zealous one but still a Party member. The police may question him, but they would not hurt him.

Reluctantly, Radim scribbled into the box provided for this purpose:

Comrade Sedmý is an enthusiastic worker. He participates in all political activities, and is always ahead of schedule. He has a positive attitude to our socialistic system. I recommend him for this trip.

With a small variation, he wrote a similar nonsense about Danna. Everybody, even the dumbest policeman knew that this was not true, but a repeated lie eventually becomes accepted convenience. Managers all over the country used the same phrases to recommend their employees even for benign trips to communist countries.

The grey lady at the personnel department was a part of the communist mafia, but when she saw Radim's signature, she automatically placed the institute stamp at the bottom of the page.

With the forms completed, Michal rushed to Čedok where, in exchange for the blue forms, he received two white applications for the exit visa. To a person born in the free world, it may sound like science fiction, but completing this white form was always the first, standard step when attempting any travel abroad. It asked for the following information:

[1] All the personal data, education, and military experience.
[2] A list of all trips ever made, a list of all relatives and friends living abroad.
[3] A list of relatives or friends travelling in the same party, their addresses and phone numbers.
[4] Recommendations from the employer, the Communist Party, and the Unions.
[5] A stamp from the local prison certifying that the applicant did not have a criminal record.
[6] A stamp of the State Bank certifying that seven dollars of travelling funds had been allocated.

Michal showed the form to Danna. "This is ridiculous," he said. "We should frame it and put it on the wall. This little amount of money doesn't help anybody, and the lines in the bank take the entire day."

Radim filled in his usual generic recommendation but, on the white form, the director's signature was also required. When Michal entered his office, the director was impatient and shuffled papers from one corner of his desk to the other. "Michal, be quick! I am busy."

He must be afraid that I've changed my mind, Michal thought.

"Comrade director, all I need is your signature," he said and placed the two forms on the table.

The director read the first line, and dropped the forms on his desk. "A trip to France? Are you out of your mind? After you canceled your fellowship? No, I am not going to sign that."

He pushed the forms back to Michal.

"Comrade director, this is a perfectly safe Čedok tour. It will be our honeymoon. Lenka will remain here. You know how Danna loves her daughter."

The director sighed. He read the forms twice and crosschecked every word as if he did not like the whole thing yet did not know why. With furrowed brow, he looked at Michal, gazed at the ceiling and, on impulse, signed the two forms and shoved them across the desk. "Get away quickly before I change my mind."

Schmidt, the Party chairman, looked curiously at Michal, and signed the applications without any questions. The Union representative saw the director's and Schmidt's signatures and had no questions either.

"Here comes the critical step," Michal summed it up in the evening. "Tomorrow, I am taking my white form to the police."

"And if they ask about me," Danna added, "you'll say that my form is coming in a matter of days, that I need one more signature. I will pretend to be sick later on, when we get closer to the departure date."

For several days, the two did not sleep well – all the time waiting for the police to call the office or knock on their door at night: "You have two Čedok reservations for France and exit visa to Canada. What's going on?"

Nobody called, and nobody came at night.

"We must be on the right track," Danna concluded, but Michal still worried.

"It looks like the calm before the storm," he said. "Everything is working so smoothly as if the forces of Nature were out of balance."

Then Zora struck again.

93. LETTER FROM ZORA

The director called Michal on the telephone: "Come to my office! Yes, right now." Michal had never heard him so angry.

When Michal entered, the director held a sheet of paper far from his body, as if it was contaminated with a dangerous disease. His face was red and he stuttered:

"Here is a letter from your ex-wife. I shouldn't tell you about it, but look what she writes! Oh boy, what are we going to do with that?"

He passed the letter to Michal. It read:

> *Dear comrade director,*
>
> *It came to my attention that you are planning to send my former husband, Michal Sedmý, to Canada again. I have to warn you. I know him well, and I suspect that he may want to defect.*
>
> *Sincerely yours, Zora Sedmý*

Michal did not expect something so low even from Zora. No decent person could have written such a letter. It could send Michal to prison for years. It could send him to uranium mines where his health would be destroyed. The interrogation could cost him broken bones and teeth.

What is she trying to prove, he thought. If I am behind bars, who will support the children? Is she trying to destroy me rather than have me leave with Danna?

Now he understood why the director's hands were shaking, and he began to perspire.

He read the letter again carefully. It was dated before the Čedok opened the trips to the West – well before Michal cancelled the fellowship and booked the trip to France. This dreadful woman has an incredible intuition, he thought without blinking.

"She is so jealous that she doesn't know what she's doing," he said. "Comrade director, public scandals have always been her favorite weapon. If there were even a vague reason supporting this crazy idea, she would have said it in the letter. She might have a suspicion, but there is no substance. She must be worried about my alimony payments. If I wanted to defect, why would I cancel my fellowship?"

"I cannot keep the letter," the director said. "I have to pass it to the police, but I can add my comments. As you said, it is a clear case. I will explain the circumstances."

With this, the director calmed down, but Michal did not. For several days, he expected a call from the Department of Interior, or an STB agent to pick him up directly at the office. But again, nothing happened.

94. QUESTION OF RESIDENCE

Since Michal, Danna and Lenka moved to Michal's parents, the two families shared the small kitchen of the original apartment. One night, when the parents were out at a concert, Danna and Michal were preparing dinner while Lenka played with her doll in the dining room next door.

"When we defect," Danna said, "the police will turn this apartment upside down. We can't do this to your parents."

"You are right, and we also need the money for the Čedok trip," Michal said. "If the neighbours see us selling our furniture, rumours would spread quickly, but if we sell it while moving, nobody would notice."

Danna strained spaghetti and dumped it back into the pot. "But we have nowhere to go. Even the two rooms in Řevnice are not available anymore."

"Think about this," Michal stopped stirring the tomato sauce. "Every week, we spend two or three days traveling to Sokolov. Let's reverse it. If we move to Sokolov, we would travel to Prague for two or three days instead. When in Prague, we can stay here with my parents. Nothing would change, but our official residence would be in Sokolov."

The pot began to boil over, splattering the red sauce over the stove.

"But how can we get an apartment in Sokolov?" Danna said after they had jointly cleaned up the mess.

95. HOUSING IN SOKOLOV

The road to the mine passed through the town of Sokolov, but Michal had always driven through without stopping. German signs protruded from under the whitewash, and the old, unfriendly people with heavy German accents gave him the creeps. Facades of houses, pavement, roofs – everything was neglected. The town had a musty smell and looked like an old woman dressed in rags.

On his next trip, Michal suppressed his uneasiness, stopped in the main square and embarked on foot in search of the local advertisement agency. One block from the main square, a trickle of murky water ran along the curb, and everybody walked in the middle of the road.

Hundreds of cards labeled APARTMENTS covered the agency window, many of them years old and faded from the sun. Inside, a fat, middle-aged woman wearing a black, gold-embroidered sweater sat behind a desk, knitting. With black-dyed hair and layers of mascara, she looked like a witch.

"I'm looking for an apartment," Michal said. "How much do you charge?"

"Only ten crowns, but your chances are slim. It is about a year since we had an apartment available."

"This is worse than in Prague. I thought that here – he did not want to say the word 'Sudetenland' – some older houses still might be available."

The woman laughed. "The houses left after the war fell into disrepair, and no new houses are being built. This is a God-forsaken country. The mine has its own housing development, but its employees have to wait several years."

"Please, try this," Michal said, and wrote on a blank index card:

Professional couple, both graduate engineers, with one child, looking for a sublet in the Sokolov region, out of town preferred. Urgent, reward Kcs 300.

The woman perked up. "We cannot put the reward clause on the card, but I will remember that." She put her head through the curtain in the back of the room and shouted: "Maria, listen, three hundred crowns reward for an apartment. Do you know about anything?"

"Sorry," she turned back to Michal. "Nothing right now, but we'll keep you on a special file." She typed another card, and placed it in a small metal box on a shelf above her typewriter.

Michal noticed a stack of similar cards in the box. At least fifty, he guessed.

96. BRIQUETTE PLANT 2

While Michal slept in the usual hotel the following night, the south conveyor belt in the mine broke down, and a train derailed in the north sector. By the time Michal came to work, the belt was repaired and the train back on tracks, but the entire mine operation was in a mess. The exhausted dispatcher was ready to accept help, even from a computer. "Some shovels have too many cars, and some had to stop because they don't have any," he told Michal. "Where have you been? We have been waiting for you since six o'clock."

Michal started the optimization program, but found that the dispatcher had no recent data from the briquette plant.

I will be back in five minutes," Michal said and ran to the next building. He climbed the three floors of steel stairs, and when he opened the rusty fireproof door, he saw the usual scene: In the rough concrete cubicle, three members of the crew sat around the old, beaten-up table playing cards. A fourth man watched them, a cigarette in his hand. Red emergency instructions taped on the unpainted wall increased the bleakness of the room. The metal door leading to the furnaces muffled their noise, but did not block the heat, and the air was unbearably dry.

Outside, snow covered the ground, but the men sat without shirts, streaks of sweat running down their backs. In the corner, water dripped at regular intervals into an old-fashioned cast-iron sink.

Michal took a long sip directly from the tap. "How are you doing here? Why aren't you sending any data?"

"Everything's fine," the foreman said without lifting his eyes from the card game. "Why should we send any data?"

We must collect data automatically, at least from this part of the mine, Michal thought and changed the subject. "Would you know about any apartment for rent? Perhaps an old farmhouse I could repair myself?"

The men stopped playing and looked at Michal as if he made a stupid joke. "You want to move to Sokolov? From Prague? Why would you do that?"

"We live with my parents..." Michal paused, letting each man interpret this in his own way. "I'd give everything for having my own apartment."

"Have you considered Rovná?" one of them said. "They might have something there."

"What is Rovná?" The word meant something flat – plains, flatland, or possibly tableau.

"An experimental state farm and a forest station, up in the hills. The government built apartment buildings and a school in the middle of nowhere, and few people want to live so far from civilization. With your credentials, you should be able to get something there."

That sounded like a dream.

"Where is Rovná?" Michal asked when he returned to the dispatcher's office.

"It isn't on any map yet. Look here," the dispatcher pointed to the map of the mining operation on the wall. "Follow this road and, it will take you to Rovná."

97. ROVNÁ

For ten kilometers, the narrow road steadily climbed into the foothills of the border mountains. Michal had to pull to the side when he met a snowplough and, later on, he passed through a village, where he stopped to let a calf cross the road, and he watched for chickens which ran around free, ignoring the snow.

He caught the last glimpse of the mining territory, its smoke stacks and pits engulfed in smog. The road entered a virgin forest, mysterious and dark. A mountain stream tumbled over huge boulders, through icicles and snow. He stopped the car and listened. Only the chirping of birds and the gurgling of water disturbed the silence.

He drove for another fifteen minutes and when he reached the hilltop, he saw a cluster of white, six-floor apartment buildings that appeared out of context.

Am I back at the outskirts of Sokolov, he thought first, but when he looked around, he saw hills and more hills covered with forest in all directions.

He parked in a large, empty parking lot, and had to lean against the wind as he stepped out of the car. The wind came over the early spring forest and over the ploughed fields where the snow had begun to melt. It came in cold and warm waves, and told Michal about forest clearings where the spring sun fell on freshly peeled spruce logs.

Michal set out toward the center of the settlement. My gosh, Danna, he thought, it would be great to live here.

The first person he met was a retired farmer, who touched his cap, coughed, and said in a dry voice: "The housing office is in the restaurant over there. Ask for Josef."

When the man saw the disbelief in Michal's eyes, he added: "That's our community center. It's also a library and, twice a week, they show movies. If Josef isn't there, they will find him for you."

Michal slowly opened the restaurant door. The hall stank of beer and of the previous day's ashtrays. All the chairs were up on tables, as if someone had swept the shiny new parquet floor.

A waitress in a miniskirt and black stockings ran in from the back room.

"Would you like a beer?" she took a chair down, and set it up for Michal.

"No, thanks. I'd like to see the housing chairman."

"You mean Josef? Wait just a minute."

She called several places from the telephone at the other end of the hall. Michal strained to listen, but could not hear what she was saying.

She returned to Michal. "He is coming. Are you sure you don't want a beer?" she said and left without waiting for an answer. For about five minutes, Michal studied the large floral patterns on the curtains and wondered: Who are the mysterious people who live here? Then Josef barged in.

"I am the local agronomist," he said and laughed. "This housing business is an ill-favoured hobby of mine." In a quilted vest and woolen cap, he looked like a Canadian lumberjack.

He must be younger than I am, fresh from university, Michal thought.

From the first moment, Josef and Michal liked each other and did not have to talk much.

"Three apartments are still empty," Josef said. "Do you want to see them?"

Michal followed Josef into one of the buildings. Several pairs of rubber boots, both men's and women's sizes, all covered with mud, stood outside of every door. At some doors, Michal stepped over piles of children's articles – toboggans, wet mittens, and tiny winter boots with untied laces that stretched across the hall.

On the fourth floor someone was roasting pork. The smell made Michal hungry. One door opened a bit, and the faces of a young mother and her three kids, vertically arranged, appeared at the gap.

"Isn't this great weather," she said. "The spring is coming soon." The kids had rosy cheeks and looked very healthy.

The new apartment that Josef showed him had two bedrooms, a

modern bathroom, a small, fully- equipped kitchen, and a well-functioning central heating.

"It's hard to describe what we have gone through," Michal said, "and you say it is available? Right away, no conditions attached, and without a down payment?"

"I know," Josef reflected. "Most of us here went through similar experiences. We all love it here."

As Michal drove back to Prague, he kept thinking about Rovná. He liked the atmosphere, the ordinary people helping each other, the life reduced to its essentials with a clear purpose and not a single doubt.

"Oh, Lord! Like gypsies, just like gypsies ..."
(Danna's mother)

98. MOVING TO ROVNÁ

The director liked the idea of Michal and Danna moving to Sokolov. For years, the mine management had been pestering him about the Institute research being too academic and not helping the mine with production problems. Two engineers permanently on site would be proof that the Institute took the criticism seriously.

It was also comforting for the director to see Michal and Danna putting their hearts into their project and working happily together. If they settled down in a new, modern apartment, he thought, the potential danger of their defection would be eliminated.

With the move approved at work, Michal approached his parents. He would never have lied to them, but not telling them the true reason for the move was a matter of their safety.

"We've got a new apartment in Sokolov," he said.

"But what about your jobs?" Mother asked.

"We'll remain with the Institute.   Instead of travelling from Prague to Sokolov, we will now travel from Sokolov to Prague. May we still keep a base here?"

"Of course you can," Father said, "but we will miss Lenka on the weekends."

Michal and Danna were getting used to moving. With few material possessions and unattached to any particular place, they took it more as transferring their camp from one location to another than changing their permanent abode. Movers loaded the clothes, pots and pans, blankets, and Lenka's toys first. Then came a collection of old furniture discarded by parents and friends: two rusted metal beds, broken chairs, an old faded carpet with bare spots, odd unmatched curtains, and two old wardrobes not worth repainting. After that, the movers placed the double bed as a partition, and loaded the valuable items: the fridge and stove, the TV, the Scandinavian wardrobes and armchairs, an Oriental carpet, and the teak dining table with the chairs.

The van then drove to a second-hand store, where the movers kept unloading until the double bed that formed the partition was out. They arrived in Rovná half empty. New neighbours watched the movers from the windows, and when the van's gate closed, they decided that the new family was extraordinarily poor. Fortunately, in Rovná, who owned what was not important.

Again, Danna created a cosy home with minimal resources. A workbench that one of their friends created from two-by-fours and construction plywood became a lovely dining table covered by a blue and white tablecloth. She stitched pretty curtains and bed covers from the scraps of fabric somebody had given her. Michal fixed the chairs, set up a fish tank, and Lenka organized her toys. In a festive mood, together, they washed the bathroom and the kitchen. In one week, they were settled in as if they had never lived elsewhere.

99. LARKS

The life in Rovná was like a beautiful song. Coming home from work on the two o'clock bus, Danna and Michal stepped out a dozen yards from their building. Some days, they ran up the stairs to their warm, cozy apartment, took off their clothes and made love under full view of the huge, mind-boggling winter sky – yet securely hidden from the entire world.

Other days, they went straight for Lenka and picked her up before the end of her nursery class. Laughing and throwing snowballs at one another, they ran along a field road, away from the settlement, to a vast, snow-covered plain where the wind had blown away the snow, leaving long frozen puddles, and they charged over the ice, sliding and tumbling until they were soaked.

Then spring arrived and brought the scent of forest soil and mosses. The snow melted and filled the ditches along the road, and the hills revived with the sound of water. Streams crisscrossed the forest floor, and the puddles on which the three used to slide were now full of tadpoles. With Michal's help, Lenka fished them out with a kitchen strainer, and they fed them to the aquarium fish. The fish grew tremendously and began to spawn.

In the woods, on a brook surrounded by ferns and lilies of the valley, Michal built a toy mill that moved a wooden mallet. The sound of clapping carried over the distance, and when it stopped, Lenka rushed to the spot to remove the debris that blocked the little wheel.

Larks sang from early morning and flew first low, then very high. Lenka loved their nests in the field across the road but always forgot the locations. Every day, she searched for them again and counted the eggs, eager to see whether the baby-birds had hatched.

On weekends, they picnicked in the forest. Danna stretched a blanket in a clearing protected from the wind, and lost in tall grass, they curled up and ate their lunch while watching soaring ravens and fast-moving clouds. The sun warmed up their spot and fell on strips of spruce bark left from the previous year. The air smelled of tree resin.

"Do we still want to move to Canada?" Danna said. "I wouldn't mind staying here forever."

"I love it here," Michal said, "but when I start to have doubts about Canada, I imagine the faces of the Party Chairman and the Director."

She laughed. "Yes, that cures any doubts instantly."

"A man decides but the Lord changes."
(Czech proverb)

100. TRIP CANCELLED

So far so good, Michal thought after he called the Canadian consulate. The visa for Danna and Lenka was ready, and Danna had to come with her passport three days before the departure.

Czechoslovak Airlines had opened a new route to Montreal, and Danna and Lenka could fly with them without paying in a western currency.

"We can return the two Air France tickets and reduce our loan in Canada," Danna said.

"That means we won't meet in Paris," Michal added. "You will fly directly to Canada."

He had his passport ready as well, with his exit visa and a stamp from the French consulate already in. Only Lenka, busy and happy as always, had no idea that she would have a rather adventurous vacation.

Two weeks before their departures, Michal stopped at Čedok with his passport. "I'd like to show you that I am ready to go."

The girl made a long face. "You don't know that your trip has been canceled?"

"Are you joking?"

Michal was in a state of panic. He saw disconnected details, the girl's hand and the white collar on her dress, a spider web hanging from the light fixture above her head. He began to perspire.

"Nobody has told me. This cannot be true. Can I get another trip?"

"All trips to the capitalist countries have been canceled," the girl whispered. "The buses returned empty. All that is left are three bus tours to Yugoslavia. I am sorry."

Yugoslavia is more relaxed about crossing borders, Michal thought, though it is still a communist country. But have I any choice?

Without looking at the prices, he pointed to the trip with the accommodation in private homes. "I'll take this one," he said, thinking that private accommodation will allow him to disappear without being noticed.

"Here are new blue forms," the girl said. "Have them verified at work, and bring them back in two days. The new departure date is June 26, in only six weeks."

101. CRIMINAL TENDENCIES

"It's scary," Michal said in the evening. "When I watch myself, I see criminal tendencies."

"Who do you want to kill this time?" Danna laughed.

"We're breaking the law and I thoroughly enjoy it. Isn't that another case of the perfect crime, of outwitting the police, the detectives, and everyone else? This is what bank robbers and murderers must feel."

"We aren't hurting anyone. We just want our freedom."

"The robber may think it's all right to rob a banker who doesn't deserve the money. Consider the population of all the communist countries, including China. We're breaking the most commonly used law on this planet."

"That law is immoral and wrong," Danna said.

"Do we have the right to judge that?" Michal was smiling. He liked to play the Devil's advocate.

"I also think," he said after a pause, "that our plan will work because it's two of us. Neither of us could pull it off without the other. Like most people, we need to share ideas, and I cannot imagine carrying all these secrets in my heart, alone, and for such a long time. Working together is safer; it is also more fun."

"Talking about ideas," Danna said. "Changing the trip to Yugoslavia has one advantage: In all the travel forms and visa applications, we will refer to our Rovná address. That will make it more difficult for the police to connect this trip with my exit visa for Canada, which is connected with the Prague address of your parents."

102. CHANGING ALL PAPERWORK

Patiently, Michal went through the application process again. He collected new signatures and stamps for the two blue Čedok forms, exchanged the forms for the white exit visa applications, and went back to the same people for their recommendations. The director signed the new applications with relief; he was taking much less risk than when allowing them to go to France.

This was the usual routine – no excitement and emotions involved, no fear of police, just an annoying bureaucracy one has to endure. Being patient is often more effective than bold, sudden decisions, Michal comforted himself.

The police changed his exit visa from France to Yugoslavia, and the Yugoslavian Consulate gave him an entry visa. Danna canceled her trip with Čedok, saying she needed a medical treatment, and rebooked her flight to Canada for June 22, four days ahead of Michal's departure.

"That's a good plan," Michal summed it up. " Before I attempt to cross any borders, I can go with you to the airport, and see that you and Lenka get through safely."

Two weeks before the tour departure, Michal went to Čedok.

"I am sorry," the girl said. "Your trip has been canceled."

The entire matter was getting so ridiculous that Michal did not even get upset. It's probably the private accommodation, he chuckled to himself. Too many people defected.

"Give me any other trip to Yugoslavia," he said. "That way, I don't have to go through the application procedure again."

"What about this: Travel by bus to a seashore resort five kilometres north of Split[17]. Family rooms are all gone, but I still have seats with group accommodation, all men in one room and all women in another. It departs the same day as your previous trip."

"This was meant to be a honeymoon," Michal said sarcastically, "but I'll take it."

---

[17] The town of Split is now in Croatia.

The girl gave him a strange look.

When they came home, Danna and Michal updated the plan – the plan they carried in their heads and never wrote down. It was June 8, 1970.

On Monday, June 22, Danna and Lenka will fly from Prague directly to the Kraemers in Ottawa. Michal will call them from a public post office on Thursday night. Using innocently sounding code words, Danna will let him know whether his fellowship is still available, whether he can get a Canadian entry visa, and whether the Canadian Embassy in Belgrade could help him. On Friday morning, he will leave with the Čedok bus tour. After arrival in Yugoslavia, Michal will call Danna collect and then quietly slip into Austria or Italy. In case he could not make it, all three of them will return to Prague as if they went for two independent holidays.

103. SMUGGLING THE DOCUMENTS

Early in the morning, Michal suddenly propped himself up.

"What time is it?" Danna asked, still half asleep.

"We forgot about our documents."

"What documents?"

"Our birth and marriage certificates. We'll need them for immigration, and without the diplomas, we won't get jobs."

"I can't take them with me," Danna said, now fully awake. "If they search my luggage, it would be proof that I am running away."

"I cannot take them to Yugoslavia either. There may be STB agents in my room. They could go through my luggage."

"We could mail the documents with something heavy," Danna said. "LP records are free to export, and the cover is thick."

"I could make a blind pocket inside the cover," Michal jumped out of bed, and pulled two albums from the shelf – the Tchaikovsky concerto and another record of the same series.

Except for the title, the covers were identical, the same gloss, grain, and the thickness of the paper. Michal removed the records and examined the covers inside and out. Then, with a sharp knife, he trimmed the back page of one cover and inserted it inside the other cover. The circular hole of the cover showed the same white space, but the blind pocket behind it could easily conceal multiple sheets of paper. "Where are the documents?"

Danna got up, and passed him a flat box. "The diplomas are too thick. We'll have to send the certified copies instead."

"Luckily, we already have copies," Michal pulled a large envelope from the box. "If the police open the parcel, they'll confiscate the copies, and not the original documents."

"Quietly," Danna whispered. "Don't wake Lenka."

Michal unfolded the documents and placed them into the blind pocket, spread white glue along the inner side of its edge, and placed it all under a pile of books. When they returned from work, using a metal ruler and a razor blade, he sliced off two millimeters along the edge. The cover looked like new.

Danna looked at the edge, examined the cover against the light, and flexed it in both directions: "It works. I can't tell the difference. Even without the record, it looks completely normal."

"Let's send two records, not just one," Michal added. "The probability that the police will detect the documents will be reduced by one half."

He wrapped the two records with brown paper. "It's all Russian music played by Russian performers," he said sarcastically. "That should help it pass. But who is going to post it?"

"If we post it now and the documents are discovered, they'd catch us at the border. Pavel should send it after we leave. He is a good friend we can trust and, at the same time, it's not too risky for him. We have been out of touch for several years, and police will not suspect any connection when the news breaks out that we have defected."

"We shouldn't even call him then."

"Let's pay him a visit when we are in Prague tomorrow."

104. PAVEL

Danna addressed the parcel to the Kraemers, with herself as the sender under her maiden name and the address of the apartment where Ivan lived now.

"This will confuse the police all right," Michal laughed. "And we're not lying."

The next day, after work, they rang the bell on Pavel's door. "What's going on?"

"It's a secret," Michal whispered. "We'll tell you inside."

When they closed the door behind them, Michal went to the window and, without coming close to the glass, he scanned the street below. Nobody waited outside.

"This looks serious," Pavel said after watching Michal.

"We want to defect to Canada," Michal whispered. "Walls may have ears, and apartments may be bugged. Everything has been arranged, we only need a little help."

"You won't report us to the police, will you?" Danna poked Pavel with her elbow.

"Do I look like a police informer?" he laughed.

"Here is a parcel with two classical records. One of the two covers contains a concealed pocket with certified copies of all our documents. Can you send it to Canada?"

"That's dangerous business. What is your plan?"

"After we cross to the West, we'll send you an ordinary postcard. It will say only *Best regards from a wonderful vacation, Josef.*

"On that signal, you will post the parcel from some post office across town, where they don't know your face. For sending a small parcel, personal identification is not required. It's safe.

"Things like that may turn nasty," Pavel said. "Could they discover the documents?"

Michal unwrapped the parcel and passed it to Pavel. "Can you see anything?"

"I'll post it," he said.

105. CANADIAN CONSULATE

Three days before Danna's departure, Michal went to the Canadian Consulate and passed her passport to the clerk in a routine manner: "The visa has been ready for several weeks."

The clerk, a blond, twenty-two year old girl in a fashionable blue outfit, unlocked a file cabinet and browsed through one of the files. "Sorry," she said. "I cannot issue the visa. Mrs. Sedmý is going to visit her husband, but he is still here. Are you her husband?"

Michal looked around. Was anybody listening to the conversation? Had police detected the plot? His hands were shaking.

"May I speak to Mr. Consul?" he said eventually.

Reluctantly, the clerk turned around, knocked gently on a heavy oak door, waited for five seconds, and entered. She returned, smiling. "Mr. Consul is waiting for you. Please, come in."

Michal was not sure what to say. He could not tell the truth.

A lean, impeccably dressed consul made several steps toward Michal, but stopped halfway. "Please, close the door. Your wife has a visa to visit you in Canada, but you are still here. Can you explain the situation?"

He said it in the friendliest manner as if intending to help.

"I was supposed to leave several months ago," Michal mumbled, "but there are some complications … I may leave soon, or I may never make it … "

The consul was waiting for more.

"Please, let her go," Michal continued. "She already has the exit visa, the airplane ticket, and she is ready to go. Please, don't spoil her opportunity to see your wonderful country. I have been in Canada already, and my friends will take care of her and of our daughter."

The consul quietly studied Michal's face.

Perhaps he does not want to hear details, Michal thought. The less he knows the better for him. Perhaps he heard my name from Mr. Wellington.

"Very well," the consul offered his hand. "She can go. And good luck with your trip!"

In the front office, the girl placed a stamp into Danna's passport. Lilacs bloomed in the adjacent gardens, and two motionless Czech policemen who stood across the street watched Michal stumbling from the Consulate and quickly rounding the corner.

106. PREPARING FOR DEPARTURE

Danna and Michal had the tenacity of long-distance runners, but after months of frustration and worries, they were elated to see the departure day approaching. They had no fear and no doubts. This is what they wanted, and they pushed forward while constantly on guard for unexpected obstacles or police traps.

The apartment in Rovná reflected the impending departure and its finality. There were no pictures on the walls, no curtains – only one old, discoloured rug with big holes. Toys, tools, pots and pans, the record player, everything went somewhere. "We are short of cash before our vacation," Michal and Danna offered to various friends. "We'll take any offer."

Without the tablecloth, the dining table turned back into a crude workbench. The shelves were empty, the dust marked the rectangle where the fish tank had been and, without blankets and bed covers, the dilapidated mattresses and beds stood in embarrassingly full view.

"Are we moving again?" Lenka asked while jumping on the old mattress. The mattress was ripped in two places and the padding was coming out.

"No, just going for a vacation," Danna said.

"Where am I going to have my next little bed, Mommy?"

"Sometimes I wonder about that," Danna replied with a tired expression.

She went to the next room and whispered to Michal: "I'd like to see the faces of the policemen who'll come to confiscate the property."

"Why are you sweeping the floor and dusting the shelves then?" Michal asked.

"I don't like to leave the place messy. After all, this was our home."

107. BURNING THE PAST

"The report is two weeks past the deadline, but we have finished it before our vacation," Michal said, when he and Danna placed three thick binders on Radim's desk.

Radim studied the Contents page. "Yes, everything is here – the project description, mathematical model, software documentation, the three days production test, future recommendations, but where is the code listing?"

"The programs are loaded and running on the Sokolov computer," Danna said, "and here is the backup tape. We believe that nobody else, not even yhe Americans have a comparable system."

For the last trip to Sokolov, Michal borrowed his mother's car, telling her it would be handy before the vacation.

"Here is the key," she said. "I still remember the piles of suitcases when going for summer holidays with you boys. It was just like moving."

Back in Rovná, after sunset – when Lenka was already asleep, Michal and Danna carried all their remaining papers through the back utility door, and followed the field road to a deep crevasse, which served as the local dump. Its edges were burnt, and it looked as if the Devil had split the Earth right there, in the middle of the fields.

The suitcases that they carried were loaded with old letters and photographs, payment and court records, useless documents, half-finished technical papers now never to be published, birthday cards and souvenirs. They began to pull them out, tear and crumple them so they would burn well.

Danna pulled out a draft of Michal's paper about the computer built from little cubes. "You want to burn this?"

"Yes. I already corrected the proofs. The journal will be in the newsstands within three weeks."

Danna tossed it in the fire.

They soon discovered that, at the rate they were going, they would not finish before morning. In haste, they dumped the papers out, and soaked them with camp fuel. Michal struck the match.

The bonfire illuminated the distant apartments. "I hope it will burn out before someone gets worried about the fire," Michal said.

Danna stood motionless. The tears running down her face reflected the fire. This was true burning of the past: pictures from her childhood writhed and fell apart; her school pictures and awards from the kayak races that she had won; pictures of Lenka with Ivan, Lenka's first hair, Michal's love letters and poems, paintings and technical drawings.

Some pages remained intact after they had burnt, entire words still readable, black carbon pictures with curled glowing edges – then the draught caused by the fire lifted them up, breaking them into pieces and carrying them toward the woods.

Soon the fire was over and nothing was left. "No addresses and no phone numbers," Michal said, and pulverized the ashes with a stick. "Police would harass our friends."

Danna looked at the sky. "It's sad," she said. "We'll never come back. There is no hope that Communism will collapse in our lifetime."

"In order to fly well, an aircraft has to be beautiful."
(renowned French aircraft designer,
Marcel Dassault)

108. DANNA AND LENKA DEPARTING

On the departure day, Danna and Michal rose with the light feeling as if leaving for a holiday in a far distant country. The village around began to wake up as on any other day, but they were leaving, leaving forever this world where the sun had risen, wind blew over the hills, birds sang, children rushed to school, and a group of workers waited for the bus.

After going through the empty apartment, and assuring himself that they had not forgotten anything, Michal locked the door.

Danna was already waiting outside, two suitcases beside her and her eyes closed, as if trying to tan her face in the early morning sun. Her skirt slapped in the wind and she daydreamed while maintaining a firm grip on Lenka. Lenka held the ear of a large Teddy bear which swiveled around her while she performed a strange ritual with her feet.

Michal brought the car from around the corner. Danna and Lenka climbed in, and Michal drove away quickly without looking back. "Now the Prague airport," he said.

"To the airport?" Lenka stopped playing.

"This is a special vacation. You'll fly by plane."

"And where are we going?"

"To visit our aunt," Danna said.

"Are you going with us?" Lenka turned to Michal.

"Not right away. I will join you later."

Lenka frowned.

Four dreamy hours later, Michal parked at the airport. "We have plenty of time," he said and led them to the observation deck.

Since he had been a boy, he liked to stand on this deck for hours watching planes landing and taking off, their elegant bodies and exotic markings, smelling hot metal and jet fuel, and experiencing the invisible barrier which separated him from the free world, almost at arm's reach, and yet beyond his reach. The wind, the planes shaking the entire airport with their noise and lifting their noses up into the blue – this was the place to dream about far away places.

Danna kissed him and looked into his eyes. "I feel so tiny. Will I see you again?"

"Sooner than you think. I'll call you on Thursday night. Don't forget, the timing is important!" He also wiped his eyes.

"How could I forget?" she placed her head on his shoulder.

Michal lifted Lenka onto the railing. With their faces touching, they stared at the tarmac without saying a word.

"It's hard to imagine Soviet troops landing here," Danna broke the silence.

Michal looked at his watch. "It's time to go."

He took them down to the gate, then ran back to the deck. A wall of the thick, bulletproof glass separated the deck from the departure hall, and gave him a view of the entire floor. He saw Customs officers checking the lines of departing passengers, passport counters, and the lounge where the cleared passengers waited, ready to board the planes. He watched Danna and Lenka joining the line, lifting and shifting their suitcases as the line moved. They reached the Customs belt and Danna unzipped one of her suitcases. The officer reached in several times, went through her handbag, then nodded. They passed the first checkpoint.

They joined the second line, which led to a dark corner out of Michal's sight. He stretched on his toes, watching for any disturbance in the crowd, for a guard walking across the hall, for someone moving the people in the opposite direction, but nothing unusual happened. A tall man who joined the line after Danna had already left through the exit door.

They must have passed, Michal thought and moved to the short section of the glass, which separated the observation deck from the lounge. Danna was waiting at that spot already, smiling. She looked left and right, and placed the palm of her hand on the glass surface.

Michal could read a note she kept under her hand: "Everything's fine. I love you!"

Lenka kissed the glass. Michal smiled and played a pantomime trying to tell them: you'd better go to the plane. He waved his arms as if a bird was taking off. Lenka was laughing and holding her tummy, but no sound came through the glass. Michal waved good-bye, and withdrew from the wall.

Down below, the airplane was waiting with the stairs ready. The gate underneath the deck opened, and the passengers began to spill out in bursts, some walking slowly, some rushing toward the plane. Lenka kept stopping Danna and pulling her back. Michal could see that she was asking questions. Danna smiled at Michal, and wiped her eyes with a handkerchief. She waved for the last time from the top of the stairs and entered the plane.

The plane door closed, and they rolled away the stairs. The engines started and, slowly, the plane moved to the runway. It stood there revving the engines, then began to accelerate, faster and faster. Its nose tilted up, and the plane climbed, smaller every second until it dissolved in the blue air.

One mission accomplished, Michal thought with a feeling of emptiness clutching his heart. He stared at the airfield, the wind hitting his face and shaking his clothes. It was Monday; he had to hide until his tour departure on Friday. Early next week I should be in Italy, he thought, hopefully not in jail.

> *"From a certain point onward,*
> *there is no longer any turning point back.*
> *That is the point that must be reached."*
> (Franz Kafka)

109. FAREWELL TO PARENTS

Michal drove to his parents, parked across the street, and ran up the stairs. He had lived in this house for most of his life, and he knew its every nook. He instantly recognized the scent of individual apartments – gingerbread, fresh cured leather, cats, goulash, old moldy furniture, and a particular brand of soap – and was equally familiar with the basement storage rooms and the grey attic with the trap door that led to the roof and the chimney-sweeper's catwalks high above the city. As a special treat, his mother had introduced him to this dangerous yet out-of-this-world place when he was only six years old.

"Here are the car keys," he said when she opened the door.

"We are just having coffee. Do you want to join us?"

"I have plenty of time," Michal said, reversing his decision of not telling his plans. Who knows when I will see them again? ... if I ever do.

"Danna and Lenka are flying to Canada right now," he whispered. The apartment doors were not soundproof.

"I expected something like that," she said.. "Come in."

She had baked an angel cake that morning; the scent of vanilla filled the entire apartment. It was moist, yellow, and lightly dusted with sugar.

Father joined them and they discussed the plan.

"Michal, you do have courage," he said.

"... but your plan is built on several assumptions," Mother added while staring at the black surface of her coffee. "What if some of them are not correct?"

"We have a safe backup for every situation. And if it doesn't work, as I told you, we will be back in about three weeks."

He paused looking at his mother.

"It is unlikely the police would search your apartment, but you may lose your job."

"Don't worry, I can find a different job, " she said without hesitation. "It would be worth it for you and your children to live in the free world."

Michal got up. Saying good-bye was more difficult than he had anticipated. He tried to get it over with quickly.

"See you in Canada," he held his father's hand. "Thank you for being such a fantastic father… In my heart, I always will carry your music."

"I will go downstairs with you," his mother said, and pulled something from her bookcase. They walked side by side, without a word and both of them weeping.

They stopped near the main entrance door where, at the end of the hall, anonymous lovers often stood late at night embracing each other. Strange place to say bye, Michal thought.

"I am worried about you," she said.

Overwhelmed by his emotions, Michal could not produce a sound.

"Take this with you. It always has been your favorite." She passed him an old copy of Kipling's Kim. Its binding had been broken by use, with most pages loose and worn along the edges and corners. Even the brown paper, in which the book was wrapped, was torn in several places.

"But it is your favourite, too."

"You may need it more."

Michal kissed her cheek and quickly stepped out before he would begin to sob.

110. ZORA IN HOSPITAL

He had nowhere to go and, arbitrarily, turned left. He took off at a brisk pace, his face down, eyes incoherently recording the familiar pattern of the cobblestone pavement. When he looked up, he saw something that took his breath away. Zora's mother, Mrs. Fürst, was running toward him, with his three children.

"Michal, where have you been?" she yelled. "I have been looking for you all over the place."

"I am just leaving for a vacation."

He was determined to fend off any attempt to upset his plans, and lifted his two pieces of luggage to prove his point.

"Zora is in the hospital with gall bladder colic. If you don't take the children now, I'll lose my job."

"Now?" Michal moaned. How could he hide for five days with three little kids?

"I am working this weekend. You have them until Monday," she announced. "Here are the keys to Zora's apartment."

"But what about my vacation?"

"I don't give a damn about your vacation! Here are your children."

"Best regards to your new wife," she added as she was leaving.

"May I have my car?" Michal called after her.

"It's not your car. And it is in a repair shop …"

"Hey, wait," Michal yelled, unable to pursue her unless he abandoned his luggage and the children on the sidewalk.

Líza climbed into his arms.

"Please, stay with us," Rita said while pulling on his coat. Filip watched silently, waiting to see what Michal would do.

Michal closed his eyes, and turned his face toward the sun. You know, I have been agonizing over this, he thought. When I have finally decided to leave, quietly and without saying goodbye, you bring them into my arms. I am grateful, but is this a punishment, or a temptation and a test of my resolve? I wish there was some way to take them with me!

"I will stay with you," he comforted them.

After all, he thought, Zora's apartment would be a perfect place to hide. Nobody would expect me to be there.

111. LENKA FLYING

When the flight attendant closed the door, and the pilot turned on the engines, Danna felt as if some enormous force ejected her into deep space. She was alone with all her secrets, amid strangers, on her way to people she had not seen before, to an unknown city in a far off, foreign land.

"What is that humming noise?" Lenka said. "Why is the plane shaking under my bum?"

She unbuckled her seatbelt, and stuck her head under her seat. "Where are we going? And why isn't Michal with us?"

"We're going to visit an aunt in Canada," Danna said, and glancing at the nearby passengers; nobody seemed to be listening. "Michal will join us later," she whispered.

"To Canada?" Lenka said and placed her forefinger on the tip of her nose. "Wow! I didn't know that."

She nodded her head, and swung her legs, full of energy. "I like that!" She looked happy and secure between her mother and the Teddy on the armrest beside the window.

"Wait until they begin to serve meals," Danna steered away from the dangerous subject. "Do you remember what Michal told us? Goodies and desserts, orange juice, and wine. And a steak for dinner."

"I don't care about the wine, but I would like a dessert. Is it good?"

"I don't know yet," Danna laughed. "It's always something new. But if you like it, I'll give you mine."

"All right," Lenka said and looked out of the window. "Why are the clouds under us? Are we flying upside down?"

The attendant brought them simple sandwiches and salted peanuts. This was not Air France, but the airline run by the Czechoslovak communist government.

"When are the goodies coming?" Lenka asked.

"Sorry, dear," the flight attendant told her in a false sweet voice. "This is all we serve. Do you want more lemonade?"

"No," Lenka replied with a stubborn expression and turned her face toward the window. "Mommy, are there any bears near the Canadian airport?"

112. BETTING THE LAST DOLLAR

In Montreal, Danna and Lenka passed Immigration and Customs. One of the suitcases arrived with a broken lock, its contents bulging out. "Lenka, help me get it aside," Danna said while pushing in her bra and an old heavily mended ski sock. "We'll fix it with my coat belt."

Sleepy Lenka was barely trailing behind Danna through the labyrinth of halls and moving sidewalks. They found the right gate and, safely on board the plane, she fell asleep instantly. Danna covered her with her coat and watched her peaceful breathing.

When Lenka opened her sleepy eyes in Ottawa, it was already dark. "Where are we going to sleep tonight?"

"I am not sure. The Kraemers should pick us up. Look out for a couple with a baby and a girl of about your age. The man wears spectacles with black frames; the lady is slim, has long blond hair, and a sharp nose. Do you remember the pictures Michal brought with him?"

"No, I don't. Over there, there is a lady with a sharp nose," Lenka pointed her finger.

"No, that's not them."

They stood beside the main door, looking in all directions.

"Nobody's waiting. What are we going to do?" Lenka said, and sat down on one of the suitcases. She said it in a tone, which reflected her confidence in her mother always having a solution to any problem.

"Let's wait another ten minutes," Danna said, holding onto the seven one-dollar bills in her pocket. "Perhaps, they had a flat tire. Perhaps, the traffic is heavy. It's raining."

The arrival area emptied, and the luggage belt stopped. Nobody was coming. Did they forget, Danna thought, or did the letter get lost?

"I hope they didn't leave town," she said, and searched through her purse for a card with the Kraemers' address. Then she took their suitcases to the taxi stand, and showed the card to the driver.

"How much?" she said. She was literally gambling her last dollar.

The driver said something incomprehensible. "Not understand!" Danna underlined her statement with a wide gesture.

The driver raised three fingers. Danna nodded, and helped Lenka into the cab.

After ten minutes of driving through the darkness, street lamps appeared along the road, lighted windows of small houses lost in rain, doors locked, and curtains closed tight.

Lord, let them be home, Danna said in Czech.

The cab driver made a sharp turn, eased off the pedal, rolled the window down, and peered into the rain.

"That's the house." He stopped, helped Lenka from the car, and pressed the doorbell for them.

"Madam, you have visitors," he announced when the door opened. The water was pouring in buckets from the awning above the entrance. The driver ran to the car, brought the suitcases under the roof, and took the three dollars from Danna.

Danna and Kathy were looking at each other.

"I Danna Sedmý. Mrs. Kraemer?" She pointed at Kathy.

Allan also came to the door: "This must be Michal's wife!" he exclaimed. "I remember her picture. How did you get here? And where is Michal?"

"Take her in first," Kathy laughed. "It's pouring cats and dogs."

They hung the wet clothes in the basement and put Lenka to bed. Then they sat on the carpet in front of the fireplace, and talked, using their hands, mixing broken German with broken English, sketching pictures and writing on the edge of a newspaper. Danna took out her English-Czech dictionary, and when she did not understand some word, Kathy searched for it in the dictionary, pointed to it, so Danna could read the Czech translation.

"What an adventure," Allan said, "but don't worry! You can stay with us as long as you want."

"Tomorrow, I must go to the Immigration and to the Geological Survey." That sentence alone took Danna several minutes to assemble.

"Tell me what you want to arrange," Kathy said slowly, so Danna could understand it. "Tomorrow, I will go with you, and explain what you need."

The Kraemers went to bed at midnight, but Danna kept writing for two more hours. She wrote two and half pages of sentences like these:

- *My husband is on a holiday trip in Yugoslavia. Will he be admitted to Canada?*

- *If Michal comes to Ottawa, can he continue his fellowship?*

- *Please, help us! If they catch my husband, he may be shot or sentenced to life imprisonment.*

- *Could the Canadian Embassy in Belgrade help Michal to get Canadian visa?*

113. KRAEMERS

In the morning, Lenka was up early. The sun shone through the basement window, and she sat in her bed talking to her Teddy bear.

"Mommy," she said, "Teddy didn't like the airplane food, they had no honey."

"Please, play quietly, the Kraemers are still sleeping," Danna said, rolled over, and fell asleep again.

After breakfast, Kathy organized the house, gave some instructions to her daughter and to some lady who came in. Everybody was talking, and Danna did not understand a word.

"We are going to visit Dr. Matheson," Kathy said slowly. "Our neighbour will babysit the children."

Lenka clung to Danna's skirt.

"We'll take her with us," Kathy said after a moment of hesitation.

Danna admired Kathy who drove with the confidence of a person who had spent most of her adult life behind the steering wheel. After finding a street with several large office buildings, Kathy drove around the block, and backed into a narrow empty spot. Hundreds of cars were parked along the street, but not a soul was in sight.

Kathy led them to one of the buildings and, inside, it felt like a beehive. People hurried in all directions and even Kathy was lost at first.

"This must be the Geological Survey of Canada," Danna whispered to Lenka. A young man entered the elevator with a cart full of rock samples.

The elevator stopped, and the first thing they saw was a large display of polished minerals. Lenka ran from one glass case to another. "Mommy, look – precious stones! Is this lost treasure?"

"Please, hurry, we have an appointment with Dr. Matheson," Danna dragged her away. "Come on! We can stop here on the way out."

Matheson was sitting at his desk, dictating something to his secretary.

"Please, come in. This will take only a minute," he gestured to Danna.

Kathy stopped politely at the door, staring at the piles of books and the prospecting gear. Matheson finished his dictation, dismissed the secretary, and began to remove the books from three chairs, setting them on the floor along the wall. He wiped the dust from the chairs with an old flannel shirt. "Please, sit down."

A shelf that displayed glass bottles immediately drew Lenka's attention. "Mommy, look at this," she pointed to a large purple crystal.

Kathy began to explain why Danna had come. She talked for five minutes, then Matheson asked something, and Kathy talked again. Danna caught an odd word but, to her, the talk blurred into one incomprehensible jabber.

The conversation clearly reached a culmination point. Matheson turned on his swivel chair and dialed a number. He talked for a short while, then waited for an answer. When he put the receiver down, he articulated slowly for Danna: "Michal's fellowship is good until the end of this year."

"Please, ask about the immigration," Danna turned to Kathy.

After another conversation, Matheson dialed a different number from his address book and asked for Mr. Wellington, but something was wrong. "Yes, Mr. Wellington," he insisted and spelled the name. "I know he must be at this number. ... How do I know? ... One of my people talked to him before leaving for

Europe. … His name is Michal Sedmý. … Yes, I can wait." Matheson smiled victoriously.

Danna and Kathy watched in suspense and forgot about Lenka.

"Mommy, I must go to the bathroom."

She was standing beside Danna's chair holding the bottom of her pants.

Without removing the receiver from his ear, Matheson pointed to the door and then to the right. Danna and Lenka ran out.

When they returned to the office, the call was over and Matheson smiled. "Immigration will help Michal, but he must be in Italy or Austria. Yugoslavia is a communist country."

Kathy repeated the message for Danna.

"Good luck, and let me know if you need any help," Matheson said.

My God, how he will get to Italy, Danna thought.

"Thank you very much," she said shaking Matheson's hand.

> *"Good advice is better than gold"*
> (Czech proverb}

114. BABYSITTER DESPERATELY NEEDED

"Let's take a streetcar," Michal said, lifting his luggage. Líza and Filip held onto his bags, one on each side, while Rita walked ahead, looking carefully in both directions at crossings and turning back to Michal every few seconds. People made room for them and smiled.

They successfully boarded the streetcar, and when they reached the apartment, Michal instantly slipped into his old routine. He bought groceries at the supermarket, cooked, mopped the kitchen and the hall, did the laundry, and took the children for a walk. At bedtime, he bathed them and read them a book, but he spent all the remaining time calling his acquaintances and friends.

"Do you know a good babysitter for three children, from this Thursday night until Monday morning? My ex is in the hospital, and I am leaving for Yugoslavia on Friday.

"I will pay twice the going rate," he added, but nobody was available.

One male friend offered to help, but found later that he could not take Friday off. Teenage babysitters wanted an easy job, not three busy little kids, and professional babysitters were booked.

On Tuesday night, Michal told the children: "It's already dark. You should be in your beds, but I must show you the stars."

Hand in hand, the children, a bit afraid, stepped out into the warm summer night. Michal led them past the apartment houses, through the light circle of the last street lamp where big moths flew in circles, until they finally sat down on a grassy field under the star-studded sky.

"This reminds me of a poem by Nezval," Michal said. "*The night toppled its golden hive over the orchards of the evenings, over the roofs of cathedrals and ateliers…*" He recited it in Czech, in its original rhyme and rhythm which sound like evening bells.

"Do all people see the same stars?" Rita asked.

"People in different countries see the same stars, but at different positions."

"So when you are in Yugoslavia, I can watch the stars, and you will know that I am watching them with you."

A big meteor raced across the sky. "What was that?" Filip was startled.

"A shooting star. If you wish for something and see a shooting star, it will become true. Some people believe that …"

"What did you think about just now?" Rita pulled on his arm.

"I can't tell you. It would break the spell," Michal moved closer to her.

"Daddy, are we causing you problems? I wish I were older. I would babysit the twins."

"Don't worry. Let's be grateful that we can sit here and watch the stars together."

115. BABYSITTER FOUND

Michal was in a panic: It is Wednesday, and my bus would departs on Friday morning. What will I do without a babysitter?

He already left messages with anybody he could think of, including old university friends such as Petr who he had not seen for five years. He was running out of options.

At 10:30 p.m., Petr returned his call. "I work on Friday, but my sister and my mother are ready to help. We have a spare bedroom and a large garden where the children can play."

"Petr, your family is wonderful. I have not even met them, and they offer such help. When may I bring the children?"

"Tomorrow at three."

It was not far to Peter's villa – an easy half-an-hour walk across the Bílá Hora plain of suburban grass, but there was no direct bus or tram connection between the two places. Michal was trying to hide, and taking a taxi might have left a trail of his movements.

"We'll walk to the babysitter after lunch," he told the children in the morning. "It will be a nice outing."

At noon, dark clouds filled the sky. Michal packed a four-day supply of children's clothes into a bag with a long shoulder strap, took Zora's umbrella and three little raincoats, and they were ready to go.

When they reached the trail across the plain, the wind picked up.

It was just here in 1621, Michal thought, that mercenaries of Austrian Habsburgs defeated the Czechs. And now, Czechs come here for picnics, to walk dogs, or to fly kites on weekends.

He scanned the plain. Only a few distant figures were walking, turning their faces away from the wind.

The children marched bravely at first but, in the middle of the field, Filip sat down and refused to go on. "My legs are sore. I can't walk anymore." And it began to rain.

Michal dressed them in their rain gear, took the twins into his arms, and asked Rita to open the umbrella for him. The twins seemed to be gaining weight every second.

"Rita, are you still down there?" he called, unable to see her.

"Yes still here," the tiny voice came from below. "Is it still far?"

"Not really," Michal puffed. "Do you see the white villas high above the highway? It's one of them."

Peter's sister, a tall and smart looking girl of about twenty, saw Michal from the window, and came out with her mother to help.

"Are you ever good hikers," the girl told the kids. "Come in! I will dry you and make you some hot chocolate."

Under a large cherry tree in the garden, Michal noticed a sandbox and a set of swings. "Look at that," he showed it to Filip and Líza. "When the rain stops, you'll have a good time here."

The girl led them to a beautifully arranged nursery room with three small beds, which smelled of freshly pressed linen. Under a large, bright window was a box full of toys and a potty.

"Where did you get all this stuff when you are not even married?" Michal asked her.

"My older sister has two toddlers, and they frequently stay here."

Michal pressed a stack of banknotes into her hand. "You've made my day with your offer. Here is the phone number of Mrs. Fürst. She'll come for the children on Monday morning."

The girl counted the money, thought about it, and passed it back to Michal. "I don't want any money. We only want to help you ... Besides, this is three times the going rate."

"Keep it," Michal insisted. "I'd have to pay a babysitter anyway ... but, please, call Mrs. Fürst only after I depart. She'll be furious that I have left the children with you."

"Agreed," the girl laughed. "I call her tomorrow night."

Líza and Filip explored the room and the toys, but Rita stood beside Michal, watching him closely. "I'd like to go with you," she said.

"I wish you could," Michal said, thinking about everything that was going to happen. "Will you come to visit me?"

"To where? To Rovná? I haven't been in Rovná."

"To wherever I am going to be. And don't worry about your mom. She'll be all right."

He kissed her on her head, and without disturbing the twins who chased each other around one of the beds, stepped out, and walked briskly back to Zora's apartment.

They will be all right, he told himself. This is the best thing I can do.

"The Vixen ran behind them, her fluffy tail building bridges, making valleys, and erecting mountains."
(K. J. Erben: The Fire Bird and Vixen Reddie)

116. LÍDA HELPS AGAIN

Michal opened the apartment door, and the mess reflected the hasty departure: tiny boots and slippers all over the floor, a towel, an empty potty, two stuffed toys, a crumbled cookie, crayons, and a bib. He took a long step over the apartment hall, entered the kitchen and, at the end of the counter, found his copy of Kim. He reached for it, and a page fell out. It read:

"Hmm! Thus say the stars. Within three days come the two men to make all things ready. After them follows the Bull; but the sign over against him is the sign of War and armed men." … "None - none", said the lama earnestly. "We seek only peace and our River."

He inserted the page back into the book, and thought of Mrs. Fürst. What would she say, if she knew Danna's German background?

In spite of her German name, Mrs. Fürst hated Germans. Before the war, she had owned a mountain resort near the German border. In 1938, Germans confiscated her property and gave her two-hours' notice to move inland. The fact that, later on, her brother barely escaped death in a Nazi labour camp did not improve her sentiment.

It had always puzzled Michal how the generation of his parents reacted when the war became imminent. His parents certainly knew what had been coming in 1938, yet a year later, his brother Venda was born. And Mrs. Fürst gave birth to Zora only a year after

Hitler's army with its armoured cars, black clad motorcycle riders, and marching units bearing standards decorated with fox tails had arrived in Prague.

That must have been a great leap of faith, Michal thought. The faith in the future of the world, the faith that every child would make a difference.

His mind turned to a different subject. After I call Danna, this apartment will not be safe. After all the other places, the police may come here.

He went through his address book, and found five friends who possibly could give him shelter. Zora's line may be bugged, he thought and ran to the street phone.

Out of the five friends, two were not home. The child of the third one was vomiting and had a high fever, while the forth one had a girlfriend coming from another town. The fifth one – a woman – was divorcing her husband. Having a male visitor overnight could cause her legal problems.

Michal returned to the apartment and searched the address book again. When he reached the letter L, he realized how much he wanted to see Lída. He did not know what he would tell her – a plain *sorry, it is not my fault*, or *if you ever need help, you can count on me, any time...*

He ran downstairs, and dialed her number, only to hear the recorded voice that her number had been disconnected. He frantically searched the booth phone directory, found her under a new, downtown address, and dialed the number. After two rings, she answered.

"Hi, this is Michal."

"Yes, hello!" Her voice was impersonal and cold.

"I need a place to stay tonight before departing for Yugoslavia tomorrow – a place where nobody could find me. If this is inconvenient, please tell me."

She replied instantly.

"Come here. Nobody is going to be here until Monday. I am just leaving."

Lída never stops amazing me, Michal thought. "How will I get in?"

"The key is under the floor mat. Put it back before you leave."

Michal returned upstairs, tidied the apartment, took his carry-on bag to the kitchen, added all the remaining bread, four Danishes, a chunk of salt pork from the fridge along with a two green peppers, and two baby-food jars, one filled with salt and the other with sugar.

Then he poured Zora's unfinished white wine into the sink and replaced it by water, placed the bottle into the bag, filled the remaining space with four apples, added Kim, and closed the zipper tight.

He returned to the bedroom and placed his second luggage, the small Tartan-canvas suitcase on the bed – the bed he had shared with Zora. Hard to imagine, he thought and opened the suitcase.

Besides the usual summer wear, it contained a carefully folded two-piece suit, tie, white shirt, and dress shoes that he could wear to work in Canada. The snorkel and the facemask could help him cross a guarded body of water, and the 35mm German camera would sell well if he needed money. Then there was his trusted survival kit with everything from fishhooks and compass to candles, hunting knife, sewing supplies, first-aid kit, and a magnifying glass to start fires.

He closed the suitcase, smiling. The small luggage pieces were light, yet contained everything he needed.

Again, he went through his papers. Nothing was missing: the tour package, the best map of Yugoslavia he could buy, his passport, and the Czech and Canadian driving licenses inside the same cover. He was not aware of any law prohibiting the possession of a foreign driving license, though there probably was one. If questioned about it, he was prepared to say that he had taken it in case he had to drive in Yugoslavia.

He was supposed to leave his identification card at home, but he conveniently "forgot" it in the back pocket of the jeans he had on. This passport-like book with his picture and thumbprint contained certified records of his birth, marriage and divorce from Zora, marriage to Danna, registration of his children, his employment, and university degrees. If a border guard found the card, they would confiscate it and send it to the police in Prague, who would then reprimand him on his return. If I ever return, he thought.

He opened his wallet. The three-hundred Czech crowns he was allowed to take had little value, and the large Yugoslavian bank notes he bought at the State Bank were worth of twenty dollars. He did not dare to take any Western currency, a serious crime in all communist countries. Instead, he had bought an open railway pass for Yugoslavia. Since he was on an all-inclusive tour, the police might have scrutinized his intentions, but he bought the pass through a government agency, and nobody mentioned any limitations.

He locked the apartment, left the key with the neighbours, and walked, a sad and lonely looking figure, toward the streetcar stop.

"Secret police: No external insignia."
(Czech Encyclopedia from 1925 by B. Kočí)

117. CALLING CANADA

Michal knew that he could not escape police surveillance if they were serious about him but, in his Scout days, he had learned how to shake off an ordinary follower. He was back in a playful mood and, for the heck of it, decided to go through the routine.

He boarded a streetcar, and fifteen minutes later got off at a busy stop that served many lines. It was impossible to predict which tram he would board next.

He let several trams pass by, not looking around and seemingly uninterested; then he suddenly jumped on the one just leaving the station, and immediately looked back. Nobody else was boarding in a hurry.

That should take care of an STB agent following me on foot, he thought with a smile.

Five minutes later, he got off in front of a large department store. In several long steps, he was inside, quickly pushing across the crowded floor. With his height, he could see over the crowd, and anyone following him would have to disturb the mass of shoppers. In less than a minute, he was leaving through the opposite door and onto another street. With a smile, he boarded a tram that just arrived, certain that no STB car was on his tail. He was painfully aware though that he was easy to identify by his luggage if the followers he just shook off requested help by radio.

He disembarked at a small, residential stop and, in two minutes, he was approaching Lída's address. Ahead of him, an elderly couple was entering the house. The lady was limping, and the man held the door for her while juggling an armful of brown grocery bags.

Michal strolled by, rounded the corner, turned as if he had forgotten something, and returned to the house. After a short search of the ground floor hall, he rang Lída's bell.

The hall, the other apartments, the entire building were quiet. Michal quickly lifted the floor mat, retrieved the key, opened the door, and closed it quietly behind him.

Still worried about the neighbours, he tiptoed through the rooms without turning the lights on. Semi-transparent drapes reduced the outside light to a dim, dreamy atmosphere.

Oh, Lída, he thought, where did you get all this? You must have visited my parents, all my friends …In room after room, he stared at his own paintings, large and small, old and recent, pictures he had almost forgotten. He surveyed the entire collection, and returned to a large city landscape, the last picture he had painted when he had lived with Zora. It had a tear at the place where Zora kicked through it, and though he repaired it later, the rip was still visible.

Probably my best painting, he thought. He looked at it for a while, then got up while still thinking about the painting, and found two big alarm clocks – one of them a true antique piece, and set them both for 10:30 p.m. Then he took off his shoes and, otherwise fully dressed, stretched on one of the beds without disturbing its cover.

Within seconds, he fell into a deep, dreamless sleep. When the alarm clocks woke him up, rain was hitting the window, and a street lamp outside cast enough light for him to move safely around the apartment. It was time to call Danna, and the Central Post Office near Wenceslaus Square was open all night. He found his raincoat, checked through the peephole that nobody was entering or leaving the building, sneaked out, and quietly locked the apartment door.

Like a thief, he briskly walked through poorly lit back streets, jumping the puddles, and crossing from one sidewalk to the other to avoid people.

In this rain and under the raincoat hood, nobody can recognize me anyway, he assured himself while drying his glasses.

During the day, the post office buzzed with people but now, at night, only one section remained open. The illumination, reduced to save electricity, produced an eerie light effect: Everything had a green hue -- the floor, walls, the light fixtures, even the row of counters and eight telephone booths along the wall. It looked lkke under water.

Most counters were closed, and small desk lamps illuminated the two counters that were open. Several individuals sat on chairs that formed a semicircle between the counters and the phone booths, drying their coats on the empty chairs beside them. A tall man with a cigarette in his hand paced impatiently back and forth. This was the kind of scene Michal expected. He had been in that office late at night before.

He unbuttoned his raincoat, joined the line and watched the procedure. Each person filled in a form, but did not have to show any identification.

"I'd like to place a call Canada," he said in the most businesslike manner he could produce.

"Fill this out," the girl passed him a small, half page form. "The charge for three minutes is one hundred crowns. You have to pay beforehand."

While the girl was registering the call, Michal watched people around him. They all appeared worried as if lost while travelling or as if someone had died. An old woman with red eyes was drying the tip of her nose frequently.

Am I walking into a trap?, he wondered.

"Please, wait over there," the girl pointed to the chairs. "I'll call you when I get the connection."

Michal sank into a chair and, in his mind, repeated the phrases to watch for:

visiting aunt – the fellowship is still available;
staying home – the fellowship has expired;
being healthy – Canada will accept me;
being sick – Canadian visa is not available;
going south – the Canadian Embassy in Belgrade will help;
going north – the Embassy in Belgrade cannot help me.

Danna had memorized these codes before she had left, and now she was sitting at the Kraemers' near the telephone. For her, it was 5 p.m. Lenka was playing beside her, and Kathy was cooking dinner.

"Mr. Sedmý, booth number seven," the clerk interrupted his contemplation.

Michal got up, entered the booth, and lifted the receiver. As he began to talk, he turned back watching the room behind him. He knew though that the eminent danger did not lie in the room; it was the invisible people and machines that listened on the line.

"Hi, Michal, is that you? It's as if time had stopped …"

"Here one thing follows another at an incredibly fast pace. What's new?"

"We are having a good time. The Kraemers are fantastic, they are helping me a lot. Tomorrow, we are going to visit our aunt. She is planning a camping trip somewhere far north. It will be exciting, but I am scared."

The message was clear: visiting aunt meant the fellowship was still available, and going north meant the Embassy in Belgrade wouldn't help him.

Michal could hear from her voice that she was truly afraid. "To the north, you say? Don't be afraid, I'm sure everything will be all right. And how is Lenka? Is her cough better?"

"She is healthy and well. She has made many friends already. At her age, the language is no problem. I wish I could say that about me. Please, promise me that we will never separate like this again."

That was good news – being healthy meant Canada would accept Michal.

"I do promise that," he said. "I think about you day and night, but I have to go. I've paid for only three minutes."

Danna wanted to say "For God's sake, be careful, I'd like to be with you soon but I don't want you to get hurt," but she thought about all the agents listening to their conversation.

"Good luck, I love you," she said with anguish in her voice.

"I love you, too. And don't worry about me."

The phone clicked, and the call was over. Michal waited for several seconds to compose his face. He had to move mentally from the Kraemers' house to the green post office hall. He looked around. Are any agents coming to drag me out? Did I say something I was not supposed to say?

But nothing had changed. The nervous man still paced back and forth and the clerks served the line. Michal headed for the door and walked out into the dark night. The rain cooled his hot face.

At the first corner, he almost collided with Lída. She was walking arm in arm with a man who held an umbrella for her, both of them elegant and tall, their collars up and faces together, whispering to each other.

"Hey, Lída!" Michal called after her but, strangely, she did not notice him and passed without turning her head. There was something stunning in their gait, a unity and grace as if they danced while walking by.

Michal made several desperate steps as if to catch up with them, but abandoned his effort. He felt like his own ghost, watching the scene without being present.

I don't belong in this world anymore, he thought and returned to the apartment. He set the two alarm clocks to 4:30 a.m. and, within seconds, was fast asleep.

Presto

"Je chante pour passer le temps."
(Leo Ferré/Louis Aragon)

118. HOTEL PRIMORE

The little two-story hotel stands in silence. Here, at the shore and a few kilometers north of Split, the sea is whispering. A breeze moves the red-and-white tablecloths under the majestic chestnut trees, and soft music oozes from the speaker suspended amidst the rows of paper lanterns connecting their branches. Michal is staring blindly at the horizon.

My gosh, what should I do first?

A long island shelters the bay. On the other side, above the village rooftops, stretches a chain of mountains – green at the bottom, then abruptly changing into grey fields of loose rock all the way up to the limestone cliffs that touch the sky. The sky is perfectly blue without a single cloud, and the white walls of the houses around the hotel reflect the sun's glare with unforgiving forcefulness.

I have only two weeks, and every second counts.

After the thirty-hour bus trip and the big lunch of cabbage rolls with good local wine, most travelers have retreated to their rooms or left for the beach and fallen asleep there. The breeze has taken away the scent of their coconut oil and suntan lotions and all is quiet again.

The hotel personnel have not removed the dirty dishes, paper napkins and empty glasses yet. Only Michal and Milovič, the new Yugoslavian tour guide, are sitting at their tables – Michal leaning on his elbows, Milovič sitting straight and watching a boat, which slowly moves across the bay. The light reflecting from the sea surface dances on his face.

Michal moves his chair closer to him. "Excuse me, sir, may I leave the hotel area? I'd like to explore the town." He is thinking of calling Danna from a post office.

"Of course you can – this is a free country," Milovič laughs and points away from the shore. "That street leads to the bus stop. Buses to Split run at fifteen-minute intervals."

The street takes Michal through the village past the last row of houses and to a paved road peppered with potholes. The road separates the village from an olive grove surrounded by a rough-stone wall. Cars and trucks speed by in both directions, leaving a trail of hot draught and exhaust fumes. Yellow bus-stop signs mark opposite corners. One reads SPLIT, and the other one, AIRPORT.

Before calling Danna, he thinks, I can check the airport.

The bus arrives with only two villagers who disembark at the next stop, and the temperature is soaring. The conductor is sleeping in his booth with his mouth open. The driver appears to enjoy the wild ride through narrow streets and sharp turns. Waves of warm and cool air rush through the open windows and, in Michal's mind, all the images are fusing – houses, olive groves, and glimpses of the silver sea.

The view widens and, with a screech of the brakes, the bus stops in front of a low modern building. The conductor opens his eyes, calls "AIRPORT" as if the bus was full of passengers, and changes the sign above his head. It now reads SPLIT.

Michal steps out and squints at the sun-bleached building. The elaborate bus terminal with platforms and metal guard rails is empty; even without looking at the flight schedule, it is clear that no plane will depart for hours.

Michal enters the door, and the sterile, air-conditioned atmosphere is shockingly different from the sea, mountains, and the sweltering heat outside. The large modern hall is empty except for a clerk idling at one of the counters.

"Do you have any flights to Italy from here?" Michal asks in a casual voice, while staring at the big metal emblem on the clerk's chest. Is he an airline employee, Customs officer, or a soldier?

"We have two flights a day," the man says. "I'd like to see your passport."

Michal panics. How far is it to the exit in case I have to run? Their eyes meet.

"Here, I am a Czech citizen."

The clerk flips through it. "Without an Italian visa, I can't sell you the ticket."

No threat of jail, only a plain refusal.

Michal is getting bolder. "Where could I get the visa then?"

"The Italian Consulate is in Split, but you can't get the visa."

"Please, tell me," Michal ignores his comment, "if someone sends me a ticket through the Air France office, for a direct flight to Canada, can I pick it up here?"

That is too much for the poor man. His eyes open wide, his face reddens, and his mustache quivers. "To Canada? With Air France? Sir, you would have to be in Belgrade."

He points at the passport with his finger and raises the voice. "I have to warn you, it will not help you if you get the Italian visa. You cannot cross the border with this passport."

Michal would like to ask other questions but the clerk is clearly getting impatient.

"Thank you," Michal says, puts the passport back in his pocket, and rushes out the door.

119. SPLIT

Back on the bus, Michal worries about other Czechs boarding the bus at his hotel, but nobody does. He gets off in Split, and buys a city map showing both the post office and the Italian Consulate.

He wants to see the consulate first, and follows the ancient ramparts that cross the town in that general direction. The wall merges with old houses where locals still live, zigzags through the town, and leads Michal to a dead-end street with identical four-floor houses, all painted in army green. A large Yugoslavian flag hangs above the entrance, and two soldiers sit on the third-floor windowsill, tanning in the afternoon sun.

So there is a large military presence, he thinks.

The town that is full of surprises. A few blocks down the hill, he arrives at an Oriental market bustling with people, tents, spilled beer, carts, and improvised stands, and villagers selling everything from baskets to live chickens. Wasps circle waste bins, buyers and sellers bargain loudly, and the smoke from barbecues blends with the scent of horses. A group of musicians in native costumes begins a wild melody, and people dance as if they have lost their minds.

He pushes his way through the madness until he reaches a wharf, where well-dressed tourists and locals politely stroll along the quay and watch the stevedores unloading the ships. Seagulls scavenge under their feet, and flags flutter in the breeze. Sailboats gliding across the bay fit the festive atmosphere, as tanned local boys fish over the railing.

Souvenir shops and stores selling sophisticated dresses line the street. Michal passes them uninterested until he comes to the window of an Italian shipping company. He moves closer to the glass and examines the posters with sleek steamers and pictures of tastefully decorated cabins. A large map shows the ship routes across the Adriatic Sea and the Mediterranean. Unable to resist, Michal enters the office.

"May I see the price list of trips to Italy, please?"

"The ferry for Pescara departs daily at three p.m.," the clerk says while handing him a price list.

In his head, Michal converts the Italian prices to Yugoslavian currency. *The trip costs more than all the money I have.*

"I don't have an Italian visa yet," he hears himself saying. "Do I need a reservation?"

"You can buy the ticket just before departure. The ship is never full."

With new hope in his heart, Michal continues past the commercial piers and warehouses and up the hill through residential streets with impeccable gardens.

In front of the Italian Consulate, four boys are playing street soccer, and the ball rolls toward Michal. He kicks it back to them and reads the brass sign. ITALIAN CONSULATE, OPEN MONDAY TO FRIDAY, 10:00 to 15:00.

It is Saturday, and the gate is locked. He is staring at the stone path leading to the house. *What is it like inside,* he wonders. *What would the consul say if I told him the truth.*

In a sudden burst of energy, he turns away from the gate and runs back down the hill. Now he can call Danna.

> *"The postilion blew his horn, and horses rode to the meadows to make the stars cry. My song is a rainbow, march to it ...."*
>
> (V. Nezval)

120. POST OFFICE FIASCO

The post office swarms with people waiting for telephone connections, and all chairs are taken. There is no place to stand without touching someone else. After Michal takes a number, he waits near the door, while watching the crowd with a hopeless feeling of urgency and precious seconds ticking away.

After twenty-six long minutes, the clerk finally calls his number, and Michal hands over his phone request on a slip of paper.

"I want to call collect," he says in Czech.

"What did you say?" the clerk asks irritably in Croatian. Except for the wide-open door, the room has no ventilation.

"I want to call <u>collect</u>, R-*gespraech, un appel a fret vire, zvonok s oplatoi za schet otvechayuschei storoni*," he repeats the phrase in German, French, and Russian.

"All right, all right, I understand," the man frowns. "A collect call to Canada. It may take several hours."

Michal understands, Croatian is similar to Czech.

"I can wait," Michal says and retreats to his spot beside the door, glancing at people around him. He is afraid that people from his group could report him.

After two and half hours, he finally hears: "The call to Canada, booth number two."

Michal rushes toward the booth, while everybody stretches their necks to see who is it calling such exotic place. Idiot, flashes through Michal's mind. He could have called me by my name.

"Danna, how are you? Tell me quickly!"

"May I speak freely?"

"Yes. And even if they tape our conversation, they cannot translate it on line. Nobody recorded my address."

"Then here is what I have found: Matheson and Wellington are both ready to help you. Your fellowship is still open, but to get the Canadian visa, you have to be in Italy or Austria. The Canadian embassy in Belgrade can't help you. Yugoslavia is still a communist country.

"What worries me most," she says in one breath, "is what I would do if they catch you at the border and put you in jail. If I don't get any warning and return to Prague, they will be waiting for me. And if I don't return, they can use it as proof against you. And if they get Lenka, they will send her to a boarding school to re-educate her against her defector parents ..."

"Please, stop! I won't risk any danger. I have found the Italian Consulate right here in Split. With an Italian visa, I may cross the border as a tourist. If there are any problems, I will just say I did not want to do anything against the regulations. As you see, I can call you collect, and we can coordinate our plans."

"What are you going to do next?"

"On Monday, I'll go to the Consulate. Until then, I can't do much. I will ask local people what's the best way to travel, and I must get a good sleep. I need to be fresh. But tell me, how did you speak with Mr. Wellington? In English?"

"Yes, in English, but it was extremely hard. Kathy is helping me a lot."

"You are great. What would I do without you ..."

"You've reached three minutes, do you want to continue?" the operator interrupted.

"Michal, I love you.

"I love you too."

"I'll call you again soon," he says quickly, hangs up, and leaves the booth aiming for the door.

"Hey, you, over there!" the clerk is shouting from behind the partition and pointing at Michal.

Michal stops and returns to the counter. "What's wrong? It was a collect call."

"I made a mistake. I can't place collect calls to Canada. You have to pay."

The figure he shows Michal is ridiculous.

"What? And you tell me now? I don't have enough money." Michal is furious.

If I pay that, Michal is thinking, I would be instantly penniless. I could not afford the bus ride back to the hotel. I could not call Danna again, and there isn't any other phone where I could receive her calls.

People gather around Michal and peer over his shoulder. "What's going on?"

"I can present the case to my supervisor," the clerk says. He can sense Michal has the money. "You'd have to leave your passport here though."

That is the last thing Michal is willing to do. Slowly, he pulls out his wallet and shakes out its entire contents.

The clerk watches him victoriously. Defeated, Michal scrapes the remaining coins into his wallet. He will hitchhike back to the hotel.

121. MEETING STANIA

Before arriving at the hotel, Michal decided to play the role of an absentminded professor. Tonight, he will show up one hour after dinner and pretend he did not know the restaurant hours; tomorrow he will arrive one hour before they start to serve and demand his meal. He will not drink the free wine, will stuff his pockets with the buns from the breakfast table and fail to come for lunch.

He already walks around with his hair uncombed and with a book under his arm, and interrupts his meals to sketch formulas and diagrams on smudgy pieces of paper he keeps in his shirt pocket. He swims early in the morning when others are in bed, but leaves the beach when they are coming out.

I must stay away for long periods of time, he decides. Others will get used to my absence, and when I eventually defect, it will take days before they notice.

It is not difficult for him to play the strange character; he only has to exaggerate his natural tendencies, forget his upbringing, and enjoy being weird.

When he arrives for dinner that night, he cannot find an empty seat in the layers of smoke that fill the room. He sees turtle lady at one of the tables, and avoids eye contact with her. The only empty chair is far in the corner, where three men entertain a young woman. Two empty bottles stand on the table and a third is already half finished. Beside the free chair sits a small girl who pays no attention to the adults. With deep concentration, she is folding a paper napkin.

She must be six years old like Rita, is his first thought.

"I am Michal. Is this spot free?"

"Yes it is," the woman says, but she continues in her conversation as if Michal did not exist.

He eats quickly with his eyes down, but he cannot close his ears. The woman has been granted a divorce and she is celebrating. The girl is her daughter.

Michal is watching the little hands folding and turning the paper. "What is it going to be?"

"I have done a steamboat, a sailboat, a slipper and a horse, several times each. Do you know anything else?"

"I know a swallow that can fly." He repeats the folding sequence until the girl can do it herself. "What's your name?"

She lifts her eyes: "Stania." She has eyes of an adult with a shade of sadness. "Can we play more?"

"I have to leave now," he says as if talking to the entire table. "See you tomorrow."

"Good night," the adults reply mechanically, clearly happy he is not staying longer. Stania says nothing, only waves with the paper bird. Michal goes straight to bed, and is asleep before the other men, one after another, begin to retire.

122. BREAKFAST WITH STANIA

A cool breeze descending from the open window wakes Michal at daybreak.

It's Sunday, is his first thought. What can I do before the Consulate opens tomorrow? I need money.

Selling my cherished 35mm camera is the only option, he thinks with sadness in his heart.

Three men snore, each at a different pitch and frequency of groan. The bed beside him is still untouched; its owner has not arrived yet. Another man sleeps on his back, fully dressed and with his shoes on. Quietly, Michal gets up, changes to swim trunks and, with a T-shirt and sandals in his hand, he tiptoes out of the room.

Dew glistens on the empty beach. The low tide has exposed the perfectly flat sand and calm clear water hugs the shore. While watching the rising sun, Michal scoops water into his hands, tastes it with his tongue, and swallows a bit. He likes the taste of the sea.

On the beach, he finds fresh footprints of a large dog. Having no particular direction, he follows the dog track to the paved area behind the hotel, where the lawn chairs and half-folded sun umbrellas remain frozen in the same positions the guests left them the previous day. This is the muddy part of the bay, and large boulders protect the village from erosion.

Stania is standing in the murky water, probing between the slime-covered rocks. She is delighted to see Michal. "Come here, and look what I have found!"

She leads him to a heap of treasures, and lifts them one by one with pride – an old rubber boot, a tattered nylon rope several feet long, two empty wine bottles, and three live clams covered with mud. All the time, she is talking and holding a dead fish by its tail behind her back.

How could Stania's mother allow her to run around alone like that, Michal shakes his head. "Stania, you shouldn't walk here without your shoes. Look at the broken glass around you!"

"Can you find me some shells?" she pulls on his arm. "Please?"

"Let me get my snorkel and mask. We'll see what I can do."

Michal runs to his room, quietly opens the door, takes the mask and the snorkel from the suitcase under his bed, and tiptoes out again. Stania is waiting on the beach.

"Can you swim?" he asks her.

"Not yet, but I learn fast."

"Then you'd better stay here; I will bring everything I find."

He swims off in a long straight line. Quiet water with spiral plants passes under him, then a school of fish, and then another one. An old wooden beam protrudes from the white sand and next to it several medium-sized shells. Michal raises his mask above the water, and looks back at the beach. Stania is signaling with both her arms that she can see him. He takes in air and goes for a long dive. After collecting more shells than he can carry in his hands, he stuffs some in the side of his trunks. When he emerges, Stania waves at him excitedly.

"What have you got? Oh, they are beautiful!"

Michal goes back several times before he decides to quit. "Aren't you hungry? Let's have breakfast together."

They stick their wet heads through the kitchen door: "We know it's too early, but can we get some breakfast, please?"

The cook looks at them and has to laugh. "Take a seat in the dining room, we'll make you something!"

In a few minutes the waiter brings them fresh coffee, milk, buns, butter, and jam. When they have eaten the last crumb, Michal stands up. "I have to leave now."

"Why? May I go with you?"

She is so much like Rita, he is thinking, she must be missing *her* father.

"Stania, you shouldn't leave without asking your mother. You know, there are some bad people …"

"But you are not a bad person."

"I am not, but sometimes it is hard to tell. Besides, I want to explore those mountains over there," he points to the peaks above the village roofs, "and it may be dangerous. You'd better stay here until your mother comes."

Then when he sees how sad she is, he adds: "After lunch, I will teach you to swim.

"Agreed," she salutes like a soldier, and runs out toward the spot where she had hidden the shells under some bushes.

123. FIELD ROAD

With his mother's book under his arm and the camera around his neck, Michal walks through the village, past the bus stop, and up the field road that leads through the olive grove and away from the beach. The surface of the red, sandy road has been molded by the hooves of donkeys and the wheels of the carts they pull. The warm sand keeps filling Michal's sandals, so he takes them off and continues barefoot. A strange-looking tree is growing beside a stone bridge over a dried-up creek. In its shade, an old, one-eyed man dressed in rags sits on the stone railing and munches on a pear-shaped fruit. His black-and-white goat grazes on the bottom branches of the same tree. The man has only a few teeth.

"What is it?" Michal points to the fruit.

The man smiles. "You don't know figs?" The expression of his face says that nothing can compare with the taste of fresh figs.

Michal knows only dried figs they sell in supermarkets.

The man reaches for another fruit, and splits it open. "Here, try it."

Michal touches the strange fruit with the tip of his tongue, then takes a careful bite. It tastes refreshing and sweet.

The man gets up, ready to continue toward the village, but catches Michal's stare at his lame leg. He points to the leg, and makes a gesture as if aiming a rifle. "Fascists …" he says, "… long time ago. Enjoy the figs," and he limps toward the village dragging his foot behind him.

The field road turns several times, then ends at a big, divided highway. This must be the shore highway, Michal decides. There are no bridges or underpasses as far as he can see.

On the other side, the road ascends rolling pastures and gentle hills until it reaches a plateau some thirty meters wide with a centuries-old linden tree in the middle. A row of beehives has been set along the edge of the plateau.

Michal sits down on a stump, facing the sea. The view is breathtaking. He can see the entire coast from the far left to the far right, villages and ports, boats at sea, white lines of roads, and toy-like cars. There is no sound except for buzzing of the bees. The linden tree is blooming, and the sweet fragrance saturates the air. Behind him, white peaks of mountains rise sharply toward the sky.

He opens *Kim*, and it reads: *He who goes to the Hills goes to his mother.*

Strange coincidence, he is thinking. She said I will need this book more than she does.

A fresh breeze brings the scent of the sea, and the story of Kim blends with his own adventures. Like Kim, he meets many people who help him or he helps them, and then they part never to meet again. What looked like a haphazard mosaic of disconnected events begins to make more sense. Michal knows, just as Kim did, there must be an opportunity to grab. If he only knew how …

This is the real thing, he thinks about his own predicament. Everything is at stake. I have to throw in everything I've learned. I have been training for this all my life – with the Scouts, at the university, and with my parents. I just have to focus, and everything will work. Oh, Danna, how I do love you!

124. BELLBOY JANO

The position of the sun has changed, and Michal is getting hungry. He closes the book and watches the view again. The sea has a new colour, reflecting more sun now. The air still smells of honey and bees, and the tiny pink flowers he did not notice before grow beside his feet. Reluctantly, he gets up, stretches, and begins his descent to the world of people.

He swings by the fishing pier not far from the hotel and, with aching heart, sells the camera to one of the souvenir merchants. It's a fast deal and Michal leaves with more money than he originally paid for the camera. Minutes later, he realizes that he sold the camera with a roll of film on which he had pictures of Danna and Lenka departing from the Prague airport, his last pictures of Rita, Filip and Liza, and a few snap shots from this trip he had taken for Danna. He rushes back to the pier, but the souvenir shop is closed and nobody knows where the owner went.

When he reaches the hotel, the public areas are deserted, and everybody is sleeping. The beach and the dining room are unbearably hot. Lunch is over, the dishes have been cleaned, and the curtains hang motionless. All the hotel staff is gone except for the bellboy.

The hotel has no reception desk, and the bellboy sits in the entrance hall, which widens under the stairs – enough to accommodate two sticky leather chairs, and a short black counter with the only telephone in the resort. Several doors, most of them open, connect the area with other parts of the building – the kitchen, the dining room, the entrance hall and, through the utility door, the narrow street, which runs under the window where Michal has his bed.

When Michal enters, a hot draught is rising through the well of the staircase. The bellboy has pulled both chairs closer to the counter, enough to reach the telephone, and is resting comfortably with his feet up, surrounded by books. He is alert and absorbed in his reading, jotting notes on a sheet of paper. A glass of cold water covered with dew stands beside him.

Michal comes closer and examines the titles: Machiavelli, Marx, Keynes, and several other authors that Michal does not know. Some books are printed in Russian.

"That's heavy reading for a hot Sunday afternoon. Do you speak Russian?"

"We all do, just as you Czechs do. I am a student of political science - this is only my summer job," the bellboy moves his feet back to the floor.

"These books read like a mystery," he is all excited. "There is no decent theory on how to run a government. Communism sounds great on paper but, in reality, it is a mess. And I am determined to figure it out. My name is Jano," he smiles and offers Michal his hand.

"I am Michal, and I admire your spirit. One day, you may lead your country or the entire world."

"Can you tell me what happened when the Soviets invaded Prague? Was it a military takeover?"

"I would be glad to tell you everything about it, but it may take hours."

"We have all the time we need," the bellboy says, and pushes his books aside.

Michal takes a chair, begins with the history of Czechoslovakia, and ends with the dream of a new, better society, and how that dream has been crushed.

"What I don't understand," the bellboy interrupts him, "is that you let the Soviets in without any resistance. You had your army, your police ... To surrender without a single shot? How could you do that?"

"We wanted to prove there wasn't any uprising. We did not want to overthrow the government; we wanted to stay in the communist block but have more freedom."

"I don't want to insult you, but it sounds to me like a bunch of cowards." He takes a long drink from his glass. "Yugoslavian people would never surrender like that. Soviets could burn our entire country but, like Germans, they would never defeat us."

"Would you help a Czech who is trying to do something against his government?" Michal asks cautiously.

"That would be my pleasure." The boy's eyes sparkle.

Suddenly, Stania's head appears at one of the half-open doors. "Michal, you promised me a swimming lesson."

"Well, we'll continue tomorrow," Michal turns back to Jano." We've barely touched the subject."

125. ITALIAN CONSULATE

On Monday, Michal had a quick breakfast, jogged to the shore highway, hitchhiked to Split, and opened the door at the Italian Consulate five minutes after ten. The waiting room is black and cold like a morgue. A tired-looking man huddles at the corner of the long sofa, cigarette in his hand.

"Where should I report?" Michal asks him in English.

"Are you from Prague?" he replies in Czech.

I don't need another Czech around, Michal is thinking.

"Just sit down," the man says as if he could read Michal's thoughts. "The secretary comes out every five or ten minutes. Are you also trying to cross the border?"

"I'd like to make a short trip to Italy."

"We all say that," the man nods his head. "But it is getting tough. I don't know what I am going to do. What have you heard?"

"I arrived on Saturday, and I don't know anything. I asked at the airport, and they told me I need an Italian visa."

"My Yugoslavian visa expires today. If they refuse me here again, I will go over the hills. Someone I've met told me about a small town, up in the mountains on the Italian border. A railway station and a bus station, close to each other, are directly on the border. The border is guarded, but not between the two buildings. If you are dressed like a worker and have no luggage, you can cross there and nobody will notice. But it must be during the day, the soldiers shoot at night."

"What's the name of the town?"

"That's the main problem – I don't know! The border is one hundred and fifty kilometers long. It should be easy to find."

One of the doors opens, and a dark Italian girl comes out and hands the man two sheets of paper. "I am sorry, sir, we cannot give you the visa."

"I know, I didn't expect it anyway. Thank you." He stubs out his cigarette in the ashtray, and gets up.

"Good luck to you," he looks at Michal with pity and leaves.

"How can I help you?" the girl turns to Michal. She looks at him as if extending a warm handshake. For a second, they measure each other up.

"I'd like to apply for an Italian visa," Michal says firmly.

"You're not a Czech, are you?"

"Yes, I am. Does it matter?"

"I am sorry, it does. Dozens of Czechs come daily. We cannot give you the visa."

"But I am not an ordinary case. I left Canada last fall, and they expect me to return. I have a job in Ottawa. I have to finish my project. Please, could you help me?"

If this girl will not help me, he thinks, nobody will.

"Mr. Consul does not want to be disturbed."

Michal senses she wants to help him, but faces some mysterious obstacles. He trusts her.

"This is a matter of life and death. My wife is already in Canada. Let me tell you my story …" Hastily, he compresses his situation into a three and a half minute narration, constantly looking at the door, afraid that another Czech may burst in.

"Wait here, I'll try my best. If he gets mad, it will be your fault."

In two minutes, she returns smiling. "Please, come in."

The consul is a worldly man. His face is perfectly tanned and without a blemish, and he is busy writing behind a large oak desk covered with letters and forms. White cuffs show out of the sleeves of his grey, hand tailored suit, and Michal watches his aristocratic hand working swiftly with the pen. The only imperfection Michal can find is the thinning hair at the top of his head.

"I told Maria we cannot give you the visa," he says in English without interrupting his writing. He does not even lift his eyes from the paper. "I am not allowed to. And even if I give you the visa, they would not let you across the border."

It's not clear what the rule is, but Michal does not dare to ask about it. Instead, he tries to explain his situation in a few sentences and completely fails. The consul keeps writing, and what Michal is telling him makes little sense.

"If you already had a visa for another country, for example Austria, I could give you a five-day transit visa," the Consul says impatiently.

"But I *had* a visa for Austria..." Michal is reaching for the last straw. The Austrian visa, which he got when the Soviets invaded Prague, is still in his passport; the Czech authorities did not bother to cross it out because it has expired. Michal hesitates for a second about how to present all this, but the Consul interrupts him: "Show me your passport."

Michal pulls out the passport, finds the Austrian visa, and passes it to him.

The consul reads the page, and points to the bottom. "What is this?"

Michal looks closer. The line reads: EXPIRY DATE: 24. UNORA 1970. The name of the month is in Czech. It means EXPIRY DATE: FEBRUARY 24, 1970. The visa is expired by more than four months.

Michal grabs the chance of his life. "It means September, sir, EXPIRY DATE: AUGUST 24, 1970," he says with a face of stone.

The Consul stares at him probingly. "Why is it not in German? This is an Austrian visa."

"I have no clue. It was issued in that turmoil two days after the Soviet invasion, with thousands of people waiting in the line. Perhaps the clerk's date-stamp broke down and he just grabbed a Czech stamp that was on his desk. It is a two-year visa, Sir."

"All right," the Consul says with a tired expression. "Maria will help you to fill in the form. Leave your passport here, we have to send it to Rome. It will take three days, but I cannot guarantee anything. Good-bye." And he is busy writing again.

Maria listened to the conversation through the half-open door. "You are lucky," she whispers.

"Thank you so much. You were fantastic!"

She just waves her hand.

<u>126. SNAKES</u>

Lost in his thoughts, Michal walks back to town, stops again at the window of the Italian shipping agency, and stares blindly into the glass that reflects the passersby who stroll behind him.

His plan is now taking shape. On Thursday morning, he will sneak away from the hotel with all his luggage. After he'll get the visa, he will proceed from the consulate directly to the pier, and board the three o'clock ferry. He finds it hard to believe he may be departing for Pescara in the beautiful ship shown in the window. He holds his breath in excitement, yet he is infinitely worried.

What if the Italians read more carefully and find that my Austrian visa has expired? Could they accuse me of forgery? Would they inform the Czech or Yugoslavian authorities? And if someone asks me for my documents before Thursday, how would I explain not having my passport? And even if I get the visa, why did the consul say they would not let me across the border?

The image of the bus and railway stations standing in the middle of the forest returns to his mind, and he looks up toward the mountains. What is beyond these peaks? The dry rolling hills we saw from the bus?

As he enters the hotel, a group heading for the beach is pushing through the door, and he notices how much these people who arrived with him annoy him with their only two interests – a uniform tan and the dinner menu. When he hears their transistor radios, he longs for a solitary silence.

Besides despising them, he also fears them. He is not a good liar, and he feels that his visit to the consulate and his intentions must be written on his face.

Thursday is still far off, he decides. I should explore the mountains.

Without going upstairs and changing his clothes, he leaves through the back door, and takes the familiar road over the stone bridge, past the olive groves and the fig tree, across the highway, and up to the plateau where he had read the book the previous day. However, he neither stops there nor glances back at the village, but presses up the hill toward the mountains.

Large trees obscure the view, stones and knotty tree roots protrude from the road surface. Dry blobs of donkey chips mark the road in regular intervals.

Somebody must live up there, he thinks, but the road gives no other clues. It rises steeply, but he maintains the same pace. It feels good to expend energy in a vigorous hike.

Dense thorn bushes replace the trees, and he can now see ahead. The curly green cover stretches over a big part of the slope and then abruptly ends. From there, the path zigzags through dry grass until it reaches loose rocks. Above that line, and he has to bend his neck back to see that high, is a low structure built of rough stone.

Does it have a roof? Hard to say from where he is standing. There is no sign of life in the bare openings that must be windows and doors. Is that the place to which the donkeys travel? Is somebody living up there like an eagle, hauling food and water to the top of the mountain?

He wishes to meet that person, whoever he is, and takes off with new energy, making long steps along the path that now resembles a crude staircase and is eroded in places. The first snake he sees is a two-meter long viper five centimeters thick, stretched across the path. He freezes, then makes two slow steps back. The snake is dead. He pokes it with a stick, and when it does not move, he steps over it.

Now he continues more cautiously. Sandals and shorts do not offer much protection, and he gradually becomes aware of dry noises, as if the snakes were rubbing their skins against the rocks and the dead leaves. He checks the ground before every step.

Only much later, when surrounded by bushes, it strikes him what the noise is: The snakes are not on the ground. They hang at the height of his shoulders, wrapped around the bushes. He would have screamed with horror if it could bring him any help. He stands and does not dare to move. The temperature is soaring. The stone house has lost its charm; even he begins to retreat.

Now that he knows about the snakes, his descent is painfully slow. The white top of the mountains has turned pink then slowly dark red; purple shadows cover the shore. When he arrives at the hotel, the lights are already on.

Hopefully, there will be a better way to cross the border, he thinks. This would be my last choice.

> *"Sea, you punish those who do not understand*
> *that seafaring above the depths is a cinch,*
> *that only the depths*
> *give us the feeling of the amazing lightness,*
> *which I love so much in certain poems."*
>   (V. Nezval)

127. LONG SWIM

On Tuesday after lunch, Michal comes to the beach with his snorkel and mask. He wants to test how far he could swim. The water is warm, and he skims along the surface like a seal without straining his neck.

How long would it take to the island – perhaps an hour or two?

He returns to the beach, and walks to the fishing pier where village men sit, smoking and watching the sea.

"Is it safe to swim across the bay?" he asks them. "Are there sharks or strong currents?"

"No sharks and no currents," the oldest man says. "The bay is shallow."

Michal leans on the railing, trying to estimate the distance. The sun is in his eyes.

"On a bright day," another man says, "the island appears closer than it is. I don't remember anybody swimming that far. You are not attempting to do that, are you?"

"Oh no, I am just curious," he says and strolls back to the beach.

"I want to swim across the bay," he tells Stania. "Just as a precaution, from time to time, please, look in my direction. You could call for help, if I run into problems."

Stania's mother is watching them with a smile.

Stania, proud of her task, sits on a towel and watches Michal swimming away, but when she sees his slow progress, she returns to her sand castle and only now and then interrupts her play and looks across the bay.

Michal swims with his face down, occasionally raising his head above water to correct his direction. Under the water, objects appear closer than they are. Michal can see the bottom sand, starfish and large pink shells. He tries to dive for them, but cannot reach the bottom. The pressure squeezes his head, and after fighting the pain, he quickly gives up. Why risk anything so far from the shore?

He swims steadily, taking a break every few minutes. When he is in the middle, fear begins to creep in. Both shores far away and he is getting tired.

He reaches the island exhausted, grabs a shore rock, and relaxes in the water before climbing out. He has lost all sense of time. All he needs is a rest. The sun is getting low.

After resting awhile, he climbs up the bank, planting his feet carefully between the weeds and prickly brushes. He does not see any snakes, but he knows that in this country deadly vipers are common.

Within a minute, he can see the open sea. The island is a narrow strip of dunes with crippled weather-beaten brushes that grow between the boulders and in the crevices of the rocks. Two people sun-bathing in the nude scramble for their clothes and, embarrassed, Michal returns to the inland shore. Stretched on a warm rock, he feels his body recovering its strength. The hotel and the beach appear discouragingly distant. Without his glasses, he can see neither the hotel nor Stania on the beach. Carefully, he slips into the water and begins to swim back.

After the rest, he feels strong again and, with each stroke, the shore is coming closer. But the sun is already low, and when he looks down he cannot see the bottom. The blue, transparent water has turned to pitch black. He is cold, and his teeth chatter. He massages his calves to prevent cramps.

Purple and covered with goose bumps, he reaches the beach

when it is getting dark. All the guests have left for dinner, only Stania sits beside a big hole she dug in the sand.

"I'm glad you are back," she says. "I was worried about you."

"Thank you," Michal takes her by hand. "I knew I could rely on you."

As they walk back to the hotel, he concludes that swimming to freedom would not be easy either, especially at night.

> *"I have now lived a hundred and nine*
> *winters in this world and have never*
> *yet met any such thing as Luck."*
> (C. S. Lewis: The Horse and His Boy)

128. TWELVE MONTHS[18]

It is Wednesday after lunch, and Michal is sitting at one of the tables under the chestnuts watching the sea. Three senior women are talking to Milovič, and their questions seem to have no end. Michal is waiting until they leave; he wants to approach Milovič alone.

For two days, any time Michal was alone, he kept reciting the Czech months in the wrong order, preparing himself for the Italian consul questioning again the expiry date – something like saying *January, August, March, April, May, June, July, February, September, October, November, December* in one breath and without the slightest pause.

Finally, the three women leave for the beach, and Milovič, with sleepy eyes, is sipping a lemonade. Michal casually moves to his table.

"I have met three friends from Prague . . . they are driving along the coast, and they offered me a ride. May I join them for two or three days?"

---

[18] Czech months have poetic names, and they are not as long as their English translations: Month-of-ice, In-the-borrow, Gestation, Oaks, Blossoms, Blushing, Full-red, Sickle, Glow, Deer-rut, Falling-leaves, Praying (or Begging).

Milovič chases away a wasp and appears to have difficulty making the decision.

"Yes, you can go," he eventually says, "but let me know if you change your plans. In case you get stranded or have an accident, I should know about it."

"Thank you," Michal gets up and places his chair where it was before. "We'll take off tomorrow."

Michal is already up, ready to leave before Milovič changes his mind. Milovič watches him as if wanting to add something, but then closes his mouth.

Michal enters the hotel and goes straight to the bellboy.

"Jano, do you remember our discussion about freedom and governments?" he says in Russian.

"Are you ready to continue our discussion?"

"Not now! I'd like to ask you for a favor, but nobody should hear this …"

Michal checks behind all the doors in the hall, making sure that nobody can hear them.

"Go on," Jano says.

"I have a plan to defect to Italy," Michal whispers. "If I don't make it, I'll be back in two or three days, but nobody must know."

"Have fun," Jano pokes him. "And you are telling me this in Russian?"

"Please, be serious! I need your help tomorrow morning. I'd like to get my luggage from the hotel without being seen by anybody from my tour."

"What do you want me to do?"

"When nobody is around, I will bring my luggage and hide it behind your counter. You will carry it out through the back door, and I will meet you several blocks away."

"That is not difficult," Jano smiles.

"I told Milovič that I would be traveling with a group of friends along the coast. He approved my trip for up to three days. If people ask about me, please, tell them that I am fine and will return soon. If I am not back in three days, tell them I am probably delayed and there is no reason for panic. I don't want the police on my tracks."

"I will do my best."

129. LEAVING THE HOTEL

It's Thursday morning, and Michal watches the erratic movement of people around the hotel. Someone is always climbing the stairs or coming down for a morning walk, people who forgot something upstairs or children tossing their toys and calling their mother. The lavatory is still full of half-naked men humming while shaving themselves, and even when the hotel staff begins to serve breakfast with the constant banging of the kitchen door, the traffic does not cease. Some people got up late while others finished breakfast earlier, some come out with bathing suits and towels, but many of them return. This waiting is aggravating.

By ten, the hotel finally quiets down. Only now and then a door opens upstairs, or someone passes through the lobby. The dormitory is empty, with most beds still unmade. Michal is sitting on his bed and, through the open door, listens to the sounds of the hotel: An older couple is making their way down, then there is a sudden bang of the kitchen door and the rattle of a garbage can out in the street. Someone yells "Anna, where are you?" from a second-floor window, and then nothing for a long time. Only the sound of the breeze, and the murmur of the sea.

He pulls his small suitcase and the worn duffel bag from under the bed, tiptoes over the hall carpet and is under the stairs in three seconds.

"Here I am," he says out of breath, and slips both pieces of luggage under the counter.

"Well done," Jano says without putting down his book.

Michal steps out and checks the back street and all hotel windows.

"It's all clear, go!" he says as he returns to the counter.

Jano drops the book, takes the luggage and casually walks out the door. Michal waits looking at his watch, ready to stop anyone who would be heading in Jano's direction. Then, in exactly two minutes, he leaves through the same door.

Jano is sitting on a stone wall two streets away, merrily swinging his legs. When Michal comes, he jumps down. "Good luck, you may need it!"

"Thank you so much. I will never forget this."

"Neither will I. Have a nice journey."

With this luggage, I should not go by bus, Michal decides. It will be safer to hitchhike.

He peeks at the bus stop from behind the corner, and when nobody is there, he darts across the intersection and down the field road. After the first curve, he is out of sight.

> *"The truth prevails"*
> (Czech national motto)

130. ITALIAN CONSULATE AGAIN

It is a perfect summer morning and, at the consulate, the secretary is smiling. Michal's passport is on the consul's desk with a long visa form inserted in it. Even from the door, Michal can see the large seal at the bottom of the form. The visa has been approved.

"Good morning," the consul says, opens the passport, puts in a large stamp, signs it, waves the passport in the air until the ink is dry, and hands it to Michal over the desk.

Since Michal was a small boy, he has been taught to tell the truth. At his parents' home, at Scouts, at school, lying had been a crime. John Hus, the Czech national hero, had burned at the stake for telling the truth. "He who lies, steals," his mother used to say.

This man is helping me, Michal is thinking, and I am feeding him lies. He looks at the smiling consul unaware of the emotions that may destroy his entire plan, and he hears himself saying: "Sir, I am sorry, but I have to tell you the truth. My Austrian visa is not valid. It expired in April. The name of the month is April, not

September."

Immediately, he can see the grave mistake he has made. Transferring the responsibility to the consul is the most ungrateful thing he could do, and he can't take it back.

"What?" the consul turns red, and jumps from his seat. "Show me the passport!"

"Here, sir," Michal points to the bottom of the page, most reluctant to let the passport out of his hand.

"Then I can't give you the visa." The consul grabs a ruler and is ready to cross the visa out.

"Sir, please, it's already in. My wife is in Canada. How could you do that to me?"

Twenty minutes later, they are still standing on opposite sides of the oak desk and discussing the matter, but the situation has changed. Michal can see that the consul is not sure what would cause him more trouble – to let his superiors know that he has made an error, or to let Michal go. For a moment, consul's eyes reflect a spark of compassion.

"I am sorry," Michal says. "You were so good to me. I did not want to cheat you. I considered you a friend."

The consul's hand that holds the passport falls lower. He takes a deep breath, looks at Michal, and shoves the passport across the desk. "Get out of here quickly!"

He does not have to ask Michal twice. "Thank you, sir," and Michal is out the door and passing the secretary. "Thank you, I would not have made it without you …"

"You are welcome," she says, but Michal is already out of the door and does not stop for two blocks.

He is out of breath and the sun is in his eyes. It is almost noon, and the street is empty. Nobody seems to notice the silly young man who was rushing so much and then suddenly stopped.

What's next, he asks himself. The ferry leaves at three.

Standing in the street, with his luggage resting at his feet, he thinks of Danna. One day, she will laugh at what happened here.

Perhaps, I am losing my mind. Perhaps the stress is stronger than I think.

While running from the consulate the tail of his shirt has pulled out of his pants. He tidies himself up and takes off toward the pier, pretending to be calm.

I have to board the ferry without delay. The chances of meeting someone at the quay are too high. He tries not to think about anything else, not even about Danna. I must not make another dumb mistake.

He enters the Italian shipping agency without looking at the street window, and sets his luggage on the floor.

"One ticket to Pescara, for today," he says impatiently.

The girl slowly takes a large book from under the counter and begins to search through the time table with her finger.

"Last time I was here," he adds, "you told me that I can come just before departure."

"Do you have an Italian visa?" she looks at him.

"Yes, I do." He pulls out his passport, but the girl does not want to see it.

"It's all right," she says and begins to fill in a ticket. "It will be six million seven hundred thousand liras, sir."

"How much is it in dinars, please?"

She stops in the middle of her writing. "We do not accept Yugoslavian currency, but you can pay in dollars or West German marks."

"I don't have those either," he sighs. "Where can I exchange my money?"

"I don't think you can. What should I do with the ticket?"

"Please, hold it. I'll be back soon."

131. LEAVING SPLIT

The money exchange kiosk on the pier is a glass booth similar to those Michal knows from airports. Among other countries, the display shows conversion rates for Italy, Germany, the U.S.A., Yugoslavia, even Czechoslovakia.

"I'd like to exchange twenty-five thousand dinars into liras," he says.

The cashier sticks his head out of the window to have a better look at Michal. "Sorry, we exchange only liras into dinars, and not the other way."

"Could I pay in Czechoslovakian crowns?"

"I can't do that either. We don't sell Western currencies."

Michal understands. Yugoslavia is freer than Czechoslovakia, but it is still a communist country. The rules about foreign currencies are identical.

He rushes to the Oriental market, and joins the crowd milling around the tents. After studying the faces of several vendors, he chooses the one with a Turkish face and a big mustache.

"Would you sell Italian money?"

"To exchange money?" the man shouts and covers his ears with his hands. "Oh no, I can't! I don't have any." He pulls his pockets inside out to show that they are empty, and begins to shake, playing a pantomime of repulsion.

The second man Michal turns to just snaps back: "I don't have any Western money," and he quickly turns away.

A village lady selling sweets asks how much he could pay, but then she says: "I can get you liras, but it will take three days."

Hel is sure that most people there have some Italian money in their pockets, but nobody trusts a stranger. By three o'clock, hel can see that he has literally missed the boat.

A deal like this needs privacy, he decides as he strolls along the main street. He does not dare to enter any of the stores until he comes to the goldsmith. A goldsmith deals with a lot of money, and the door displays little Italian, French, and British flags.

He pretends to be interested in watches displayed in the window until the only customer inside walks out.

"May I see the black diver's watch you have in the window?" he asks after he enters.

The storekeeper takes out a slim box from his counter, opens it, and passes it to Michal while watching him suspiciously.

"You wouldn't know by chance who would sell Western currency?" Michal asks while examining the watch. When no answer comes, he looks up, and sees the puzzled goldsmith's expression. "I want to go to Italy, but the shipping agency accepts only liras. I'd pay any price."

"I can't sell you Western money, it could cost me my business license," the storekeeper says, then thinks awhile. "Why do you insist on going with the Italian shipping line? The Yugoslavian ferry leaves Zadar for Italy every morning. There you can pay in dinars."

"Where is Zadar, and how do I get there quickly?"

"Zadar is a seaport further up north. You can reach it by bus. Going by sea would be less expensive, but ..." he looks at his watch, "the boat for Zadar is leaving in ten minutes. I doubt you can make it."

Michal knows that going north means getting closer to the Italian border. "Thank you very much," he grabs his bags and darts out of the store and toward the pier where a small passenger boat is getting ready for departure. He runs to the booth and buys a ticket while watching the boat over his shoulder. A few long steps, and he is on the boat. A crewman lifts the wooden bridge, the engines go full throttle, waves begin to splash between the boat and the mooring, and Michal's heart is singing.

132. CRUISE TO ZADAR

After climbing metal stairs into the cool breeze of the upper deck, Michal is looking ahead, into the wide mouth of the harbor. Like a myriad of little mirrors, the sea is reflecting the sunset. Flying fish and sardines leap into the air, adding their glitter to the pink sea. The serenity of the surroundings calms his soul, but then he suddenly realizes how hungry he is. He has not eaten for the entire day.

After a search through his bag, he takes out a can of sardines and a loaf of bread. Without losing anything or spilling the oil in the strong wind, he picks up the sardines with the knife and chews on the bread. When he has finished the fish, he wipes out the oil with pieces of bread until the can is dry. Feeling better, he thinks about dessert, opens the duffle bag again and takes out a can of condensed milk, punches two holes with his knife, and begins to suck the sweet contents slowly, one mouthful of milk and one mouthful of tepid water from the wine bottle he had filled in the hotel before his departure. Without the label, the bottle has lost its identity. It is transparent and plain, but the water tastes good.

He stops when the can is half empty. After taping the holes with first-aid tape, he sets the can carefully into his bag. He sits with his feet on the boat railing, and watches the mountains slowly moving aft. Birds accompany the boat, which smells of diesel fuel and fresh paint. It is an old beaten coaster that serves the shore route, connecting fishing villages and little resorts. The engine shakes the boat, which sways only slightly in the sheltered waters.

When darkness falls, Michal still sits in the same position, his hair flying. His lips have a taste of sea, and the skin of his face stretches under a thin layer of salt. Small drops of dew condense on the surface of his sweater but, inside, it is still cozy and warm.

Gradually, other passengers move to the cabin sheltered from the wind, but Michal wants to see and hear everything, the silhouettes of the mountains, the lighthouses, foghorns, and the lights of the settlements far in the distance.

An oasis of light with the sound of Dixieland music appears ahead, and it is growing bigger as the boat prepares for landing. People dance under the stars, and the dock, decorated with lanterns, reflects in the harbour.

What are they celebrating?

The intoxicating night is tempting him to disembark and join them. It is like a dream, an illusion that is so close but never to be touched. He watches the scene and his body is responding to the music, but then the boat sounds its horn, the island of light floats away and, along with all the music, it fades into the dark night.

So many people in the world, so many faces and fates, he is thinking. People I've never met, people I'll never see again. The stars appear colder – I'd better catch some sleep.

He descends into the cabin, a large oval room with wooden benches along the walls. Most seats are already taken by people asleep in various positions. A young village woman nurses her baby, and an old drunk stares curiously at him. The room is warm, perhaps too warm with so many people.

He finds a section of the bench long enough for him to lie with his knees tucked to his chest, slips his suitcase under the bench, and folds himself against the wall using the duffel bag as a pillow. Now he understands why that section of the bench was empty – the boat engine must be directly behind the wall. Its roaring and shaking penetrates his body and brain. He feels pistons moving and working hard as the boat struggles against each wave. The bench shudders.

How long can I take this, he wonders. At two a.m., a harsh voice wakes him up: "Everybody out. Zadar!"

133. NIGHT IN A CAGE

Michal rubs his eyes, then gathers his luggage and follows others to the main deck, where he finds himself waiting with a small group of sleepy, half-conscious individuals. While he was sleeping, most passengers disembarked at various ports along the way.

With a jolt, the boat lands, and the group spills onto a large, dusty square littered with paper. Diffused light of tall port lamps illuminates the area. Shacks, trailers, and temporary buildings form three sides of this square. The fourth side, sharp and clearly lighted, is a low wall guarding the black darkness of the sea.

Is this entire place under construction, or is it a commercial port? Everything is closed, but beside the trailer where the tickets are sold, a red board with white letters displays departure times. The first line reads: 08:00 - FERRY TO ANCONA, ITALY.

The trailer has a window and, while Michal tries to see what is inside, the other passengers trickle away. He turns around, and everybody is gone.

Where can I go now? It's almost dawn.

He crosses the square to a wide street running parallel to the shore. A tractor-trailer roars in with its high beams on, blinds him for a few seconds, and disappears at the other end of the street.

He contemplates spending the night somewhere under a tree, and he walks determined to reach the end of what looks like a small, provincial town. The street is dark, except for a flickering red light above the entrance of a small hotel, and even that door is closed with an iron bar and a big padlock in the middle.

It makes no sense to walk further, he decides, and takes a side street toward the sea. He wanders among warehouses and dockyards until he finds a small city park between the sea embankment and a low office building with the sign ZADAR PORT AUTHORITY. Except for the circles of light under the few street lamps, the park is dark, and all objects appear grey.

He looks over the seawall and feels, more than sees, the deep wet space with oily, rough boulders at its bottom. It smells of fish and stagnant dockyard water.

He finds a park bench in the dark corner of the park and, using his belt, suspends the suitcase horizontally under the seat to protect it from rats. Then he lies down with the duffel bag under his head, reasonably secure that nobody could steal his luggage without waking him up.

Jasmine blooms nearby, stars flicker, and the soothing sound of the sea comes over the distance. He turns his wedding band three times to remind himself of Danna, and quickly drifts into a dream.

In less than an hour, he wakes with a searchlight pointing into his face. He does not know where he is, and someone is shouting at him in a strange language.

He covers his eyes, pleading: "Put that light away! It hurts my eyes."

The light moves from his face to his stomach, and he sees a policeman in a black uniform.

"What's wrong?" Michal says, and puts his feet down.

"May I see your passport?"

Michal pulls the passport out of his pocket, and the policeman examines its first page under the flashlight. "You can't sleep in the park like this," he said. "Someone may kill you."

"But where can I wait for the next ferry?"

The policeman escorts Michal back to the pier where, near the ticket trailer, someone has set four garden tables surrounded by a temporary fence. It looks like a prison or a big cage. Michal does not like it a bit.

"Do I have to sit inside that fence?"

"Yes, inside," the policeman insists and closes the gate behind him.

Inside is an interesting collection of individuals: One beggar, two drunks - one talking to himself and the other one singing loudly, two stranded tourists, and an old man sleeping with his face on the table in a puddle of beer. Michal sits down, and places his luggage on another chair. The ground is wet, and he loathes even to step on what may be urine. Or vomit. With his feet up, he stares into the night.

134. FERRY TO ANCONA

The sun rises into mist, and when the ticket trailer opens, Michal dares to leave the cage. The gate is not locked.

"Good morning," he says. "One ticket to Ancona, please."

The sleepy clerk sells him a ticket without asking questions.

"Where do I board the ship?"

"You have to go through Customs," the man points to the fence across the square. "Most likely, they are still closed."

Michal buys two buns and a carton of milk at the coffee shop that opened at the next trailer. The buns are two days old, but when Michal drinks a bit of milk after each bite, he can swallow them easily. The question of Customs preoccupies his mind.

The sooner I board the better, he thinks as he walks casually toward the fence. A huge white ship, its stern gate open, towers in the background. Everything is quiet, no people are in sight.

Then, as if in a dream, he watches himself passing through the fence gate and entering the first barrack. Inside, a small group of passengers is silently waiting beside a long wooden counter. He does not see any officers, crosses the hall, and exits through another door. Two armed guards stand outside, one on each side, but Michal does not look at them and continues straight for the boat. Aware of being watched, he walks like a somnambulist on a tightrope, trying to reach quickly the other end while remaining calm, not looking back at those two rifles, the distance to the gate decreasing ever so slowly.

Two girls in blue uniforms greet him at the entrance. "Your passport, please."

One of them compares Michal's passport picture with his face, and drops the passport into a cardboard box on a table beside her.

"You'll get your passport before you disembark in Italy," the other one says when she sees the worry in Michal's eyes.

Michal has never been on a ferry. He stumbles over rails and rusty chains through the cavernous garage, finds his way to one of the spiral staircases, and climbs until he reaches the top deck. There he moves forward, as far from the entrance as he possibly can be.

Nobody else is there yet. Dew covers the railings and the deck, and he huddles on a cold, metal bench behind one of the life rafts, trying to warm himself up in the weak morning sun. He has a perfect view of the loading area. People and cars are boarding in a slow procession.

There is no significant flow of passengers, but by eight o'clock when the ship begins to prepare for departure, the deck around him is crowded with people. Colorful clothes, women's scarves fluttering in the wind, the white paint of the ship and the Mediterranean sun – all contribute to the festive mood. The big diesel engines start, and the wind tears the fumes from the slanted smoke stacks. The whistle blows the departure signal, and bridges begin to lift. He watches seamen running along the shore and working with the lines.

Something else is also happening on the far side of his deck. The crowd stirs up and divides in the middle.

Someone has fainted, he thinks at first, or it's a vendor selling drinks.

He stretches on his toes, but does not see the source of the commotion until it is too late.

Two soldiers in green uniforms emerge from the crowd. One holds a small book, looks frequently in it and around at the people. It is his passport!

The soldiers come straight for him.

He looks the other way, but they recognize him instantly. "Mr. Sedmý, please, come with us."

Each soldier takes him under one arm, and they half-carry him through the crowded deck and down the spiral staircase.

"What did he do?" people ask, but the soldiers proceed silently.

"You don't have to hold me like that," Michal says. "I'm not going to run away. What's wrong?"

"Your visa is not valid."

"What do you mean? The visa was issued by the Italian consulate in Split."

"That's exactly the reason. Too many Czechs were defecting to Italy, and your government threatened to cancel all holiday tours unless we do something. The new regulation is that only those Czechs who received their visa in Prague can cross to Italy."

Michal looks at the uniforms of the soldiers and bulky handguns on their hips. He cannot recognize their ranks. "Where are you going to take me?" He hopes not to jail.

"Just off the ship," the soldier says with a face of stone.

Michal's courage returns. When they enter the narrow staircase with nobody else around, he pulls out his wallet: "Sir, I do not have much money, but I would gladly give you everything I have. This trip is very important to me."

"To bribe a border guard is a crime," the soldier says firmly.

"Personally, I would let you go, but I would lose my job. Your name is on the passenger list. If you are missing, the two of us would be blamed."

They reach the bottom of the garage space, by then full of cars. One soldier escorts Michal to the car entrance, gives him the passport, and helps him over a plank they placed there just for him.

"Sorry," the soldier calls after Michal, "the ticket office will refund your fare." The ship is already departing.

135. BUS TICKET

Two things are good, Michal is thinking. I am not in jail and, finally, I know the new regulation about crossing the border.

He stops a few meters short of the ticket trailer, assessing the risk. He needs the money, but the teller could also report him. Then he asks him to get a refund on his ticket.

"Something's wrong with my visa," he explains.

The teller nods approvingly, places the banknotes neatly on the counter, and returns to his work inside the trailer.

With a feeling of emptiness, Michal collects the money. The world is again monstrously large, and all directions seem equally futile.

He turns to the nearest object, the display of departure times beside the trailer. He does not read the letters. His mind needs some time to reorganize itself, and with his face toward the board, his blank stare is less conspicuous. The new rule is clever. The Italian Consulate in Prague obeys Czech regulations, and they would make no mistake about the expiry date.

The idea of crossing the border up in the mountains returns to his mind. Where is that little place with bus and railway stations directly on the border? How could I get there?

He also remembers the snakes and thorn bushes he encountered near Split. It's going to be tough, he concludes, but that is to be expected.

Slowly, his mind is returning to where he is standing, and it occurs to him that he is staring at a schedule of buses departing for Italy. The next bus will leave at midnight, arriving to Trieste by six the following morning.

He gathers his courage, and returns to the ticket counter. "One ticket to Trieste for the next bus, please." It is the same teller.

Is he going to be angry, Michal wonders. Is he going to swear and chase me around the square? Or could he call the police?

The teller glances at Michal as if he has never seen him before, passes him the ticket over the counter, takes the money, returns the change and, without saying a word, turns back to his books.

At least, the bus should take me to the border, Michal thinks. The guards will pull me out again, but if the Czech fellow from the Italian consulate was correct, the railway station will be right there. If not, I have to find some other way …

136. ZADAR POST OFFICE

Twenty-four hours have passed since Michal left the hotel. He has a painfully vivid vision of the two unpleasant characters from his tour asking Milovič: "And what happened to Mr. Sedmy? We have not seen him since yesterday morning." He also thinks about Danna and imagines her worried face. Even if it costs me all my money, he decides, I have to call her. She must know my new plans.

The main street has changed since last night: The doors of the stores are open with displays of fruit and newspapers along the sidewalk and people are rushing to work. A shop owner directs Michal to the post office, which is indistinguishable from other, mostly residential houses on the street. He enters the grey vaulted hall, and even there he finds no post office sign – only two political posters and an old, partially torn display of postal rates taped on the wall. This is not the main post office or Zadar is a very small town, he concludes as he opens the door leading into an irregularly shaped room with a short counter, a square opening with a scale for weighing large packages, and two telephone booths. A large table with two benches stands under two opened windows.

The room is full of American students who sit on the table and benches swinging their legs and shouting at one another. Three girls in shorts sit on the dirty floor, playing cards and swaying their bodies to the rock music blasting from a transistor radio. Michal looks at the whole scene in disbelief. Of course, they all are without shoes.

"Excuse me," he wedges himself on the bench. The boys shift to make more room without looking at him.

He begins to reorganize his luggage, and works carefully, thinking about each item. For crossing through the woods, everything has to fit into the small duffle bag. He hesitates about Kim, a bulky large edition, but places it into the bag beside the English dictionary. He adds all his food supply – the unfinished can of evaporated milk, two chocolate bars, the remaining bread wrapped in plastic, the bottle of water, a can of tuna and a can of sardines.

The bag begins to overflow when he adds even the most essential clothes. I can either wear the sweater or fold it over the bag, he decides.

Comfortable in his jeans and the red flannel shirt, he examines the thin fabric of his running shoes. His little toes show through, but for hiking in the mountains they will be better than his sandals or the office shoes.

He closes the suitcase, and takes it to the counter: "I'd like to send this to Split."

"Today is Friday," the postman says. "It will be there by Wednesday."

"How fast would a letter be?"

"By Monday, or special delivery by tomorrow."

Michal returns to the table where he works on the letter for a long time. He knows that this piece of paper may become court evidence, and whether the court would sit in his presence or absence, it must compromise neither Danna nor himself. He hopes to gain more time for crossing the border, while allowing a safe return in case he doesn't make it. The final version reads:

To: Mr. Milovič, Čedok representative,

hotel Primore, Koštel Stari, Split. (Special Delivery)

Dear Mr. Milovič:

As I have told you, three Czech friends took me for a car tour along the coast. We are having a good time, but our Škoda-car broke down, and the required engine parts are not locally available. I have to hitchhike back to the hotel. I am mailing my suitcase to your address. Please, keep it for me until I return.

Thank you, Michal Sedmy.

P. S. Please, do not worry, if I do not return in three days as originally planned. I am well and on my way to the hotel.

He submits the letter, and asks for a call to Canada.

"You have to pay first," the postmaster said. "Also," and he points to the American students, "all these people are waiting for overseas connections. It may take a long time."

"I can wait," Michal says and returns to the bench.

The girls are playing a card game he does not know. He watches them awhile, then turns to the boy sitting next to him: "I've been in Canada."

What he means is *I've been in North America, I am your friend.* The students may know something about the border, he thinks. They could take a message for Danna.

The boy looks at him with a dumb expression. "In Canada? I've heard it's cold up there. We're from Texas."

There is no hint of interest in his voice. For this boy, Canada is equally remote and exotic as Yugoslavia.

When the first American gets his connection, his voice carries across the room:

"Hi, Mom, how are you? What's new? ... Yes, we're having fun . . . You should see our suntans! ... We left Italy yesterday, and we're in Yugoslavia, heading south. It's beautiful here, and it is a real bargain. ... No, I haven't written any postcards or letters. We are too busy. But I will. I promise! ... Mom, I have only one problem. Please, could you send more money?" Then a long pause.

The student is sweating, and Michal is getting curious what the result will be.

"One hundred dollars would do. Please, send it to Split, it's our next stop. Bye, Mom, and thank you! Say 'Hi' to Dad."

The boy hangs up, and the others grinn at him. "Good job," one of them says.

At two o'clock, Michal approaches the counter again: "Sir, I'd like to buy some food in the grocery store next door. It will take me a minute. If the connection comes, can you hold it for me?"

The postmaster nods. Michal asks one of the boys to watch his bag, runs out to the store, grabs a carton of milk, loaf of bread, two buns, a small jar of honey, and a package of cheese, pays in a hurry, and runs back. Nothing has happened there. Flies crawl over the windowsill, and everybody is waiting.

One after another, the students get their connections and chatter about nothing. This is not fair, Michal thinks. So much depends on my call, and I can't get through because of these spoiled kids. He returns to the counter.

"I told you it would take a long time," the postmaster shrugs his shoulders. "I can't do anything about it."

I could send a telegram, Michal is thinking, but he is not sure how to describe his situation without using words that could alert police.

One minute before six, the postmaster places Michal's deposit on the counter: "Mr. Sedmy, I am sorry but we are closing. Come again tomorrow."

"Tomorrow, I won't be here," Michal says angrily, and scrapes the money from the counter.

"That's not my problem," the postmaster closes the wicket.

137. BUS TO TRIESTE

Michal spends the evening walking up and down the main street, poking around and doing nothing in this unfriendly town. He is usually at home wherever he goes, but here he feels like a useless speck of dust. Even Danna does not know where I am, he tells himself while looking at the evening sky.

At half past eleven, he boards the bus, takes the seat behind the driver, and watches the other passengers climbing in one by one – all short and stocky, peasants and road labourers with dark skin and rough hands. Who they are and where they are going is a mystery to Michal. The man who takes the seat beside him smells of garlic, and seconds after he sits down with a grunt, he is snoring with his cap shifted over his eyes.

Exactly at midnight, without any fuss, the driver closes the door and dives into a roller-coaster run. The bus thunders through sleeping villages and towns, taking sharp turns, plunging up and down the hills along the coast. It takes an hour before Michal stops worrying and relaxes enough to sleep.

He does not sleep well though. Flashes of light and the roar of the oncoming trucks, the jolting of the bus, and his own thoughts keep waking him. Half dreaming, he revisits his previous border crossings. After seeing each attempt several times over, a clear pattern emerges: His passport is full of records from his previous travels. Other travelers get a stamp and pass within seconds but, in his case, the border guard flips through many pages, and when he finally finds the appropriate visa, he reads it carefully.

What could I do to make them more casual and relaxed, Michal is wondering. He pulls out his passport, and bends it many times inside out at the page with the Italian visa. Then he tries the entire sequence – he inserts the passport into his shirt pocket, pulls it out and, indeed, it opens on the right page. Satisfied with the result, he puts the passport back into the shirt pocket, but he can't sleep any longer.

The dawn arrives slowly. First, the air and everything around the bus thickens with fog permeated with silver light from within itself. Then, slowly, objects like trees or houses along the road resume meaningful shapes. Michal is sleepy and tired, yet mentally alert. He analyzes his feelings, and cannot detect fear. Why, he wonders.

Instead of being afraid, he is primed up for action and his eyes scan the road.

The closer he is to the border, the more excited he is, but when a sign reads "ITALIAN BORDER 10km," he puts his head back and closes his eyes. He pretends to sleep, glancing through the narrow gap between his eyelids every few seconds. "ITALIAN BORDER 5km, ITALIAN BORDER NEXT EXIT."

He memorizes the bus route, the last stretch before the border where he could hike after they throw him out of the bus. He sees red and white bars across the road, and a silhouette of a soldier standing, legs wide apart and gun in a ready position.

The bus stops, and another Yugoslavian soldier climbs in: "Italian border. Passports and Customs documents."

With his eyes completely closed, Michal is waiting, and when he feels the shadow of the officer standing above him, without opening his eyes, he reaches into his shirt pocket, pulls out the passport, and passes it to him.

The passport opens on the right page, the soldier places a stamp under the visa, and returns the passport into Michal's hand. Without opening his eyes, Michal puts the passport back into his shirt pocket. His heart is singing and jumping with joy, but he pretends to be asleep and uninterested in what is going on in the back of the bus.

After a few minutes, the soldier returns through the aisle and tells the driver: "Everything's all right. You can go." The red and white bar lifts, and the bus slowly enters no-man's land.

Michal opens his eyes and watches his fellow passengers. Are there any communist agents? Once I am on the Italian soil, they can't take me back, he assures himself. I would run out and yell for help.

The Italian checkpoint looks similar. Small barracks, a bar across the road, only the soldier has a different uniform. Michal looks at his face trying to assess his mind, but the soldier gives signs of neither friendliness nor cruelty. He has no soul or hides it well, like a robot on duty, with a big silver emblem on his chest.

Michal passes him the passport, which again opens on the right page. The soldier nods approvingly, and puts the passport in his pocket. Then he goes through the rest of the bus, and stamps everybody's identification card. The Yugoslavian citizens do not need passports when traveling to Italy.

The soldier leaves the bus with Michal's passport in his pocket, heading back for the barracks. "Is everybody OK?" the driver asks, ready to go.

"No!" Michal shouts. "He took my passport with him."

The bus is waiting with the door open. Two minutes, five minutes, ten minutes. What should I do now? Michal is thinking feverishly. Should I run out and beg for political asylum? Should I go to the barracks? Are there communist agents on this bus?

He looks back. The bus is inside Italy, out of rifle range of the Yugoslavian guards.

"What's going on?" the driver looks at his watch.

"I have no idea," Michal says trying to filter the panic from his voice. "Can you find out, please? You speak Italian."

Reluctantly, the driver gets up from his seat and heads for the barracks. Michal sits tight, his eyes fixed on the door. In seconds, the driver comes out, with the passport in his hand.

"Thank you, what happened?" Michal is relieved.

The driver turns on the engine. "Bastard – he needed a different stamp for you and forgot the passport in his pocket. He was reading a newspaper. Let's get out of here."

138. ITALY

Once safely across the border, Michal does not have to pretend that he is sleeping. He is up and acutely aware of everything around him – of the bus descending the narrow winding road, of the breathtaking view of the Trieste harbor and its pale blue water, of the grey vegetation alongside the road. The colour of the air is different. This is Italy.

He is happy and overflowing with emotions, and when the bus stops in front of the Trieste railway station, he jumps out and walks away quickly. When nobody grabs my shoulder or asks me for my documents, I know that I have really made it.

The other passengers from the bus enter the station, leaving Michal alone on the sidewalk of a circular plaza with empty buses parked at the curb.

The facades of the houses catch his attention and he moves closer to the wall. His fingers probe the old weathered stucco from the last century.

Just like my parents' home, he whispers to himself. Even the small patches of the grass along the bottom. I have gone full circle – so far yet finding the same thing. His eyes fill with tears.

He circles the plaza and, near the station entrance, he finds a large post office, and a money exchange booth. The post office door is locked, and a sign reads: OPEN SATURDAY 9-5.

Damn, I need a telephone.

He jerks the cold brass handle once more, and turns around. A payphone is right next to the door.

Before I call Danna, I should have a clear plan. Let's try something else.

He dials zero and the operator comes on in Italian.

"Do you speak English?" Michal asks

"Yes, I do."

"Where is the nearest Canadian embassy or consulate, please?"

"Just a minute… The nearest consulate is in Milano, and the embassy is in Rome. Both would be closed on the weekend. Which number do you want?"

It's always better to be close to the central office, he thinks.

"The embassy in Rome," he says. "Please, give me the street address as well."

"The address is Via Zara 30, telephone 863-4950," the operator dictates slowly. "Do you want me to connect you now?"

"No, thanks. That's all I need."

139. TRIESTE

The money exchange is open, and Michal trades all his cash, including the 300 Kcs he was supposed to bring back to Prague.

They convert to only a small amount, but he needs every cent.

Inside the train station, the entire wall is plastered with timetables, and Michal analyzes them for a long time. Fast trains connect Trieste to Rome through several routes. The timetables list towns with magical names, places he always had wanted to visit: Venice, Ferrara, Sienna, Ravenna, and Firenze.

"How much is a ticket to Rome?" he asks at the wicket.

The cashier has a dark complexion, and Michal watches his big mustache moving up and down, as an incomprehensible stream of Italian pours from behind the glass.

The cashier sees Michal's exasperated face, stops, and writes the amount on a slip of paper.

Michal has the money, but if he pays for the ticket, not much would be left.

"How much is it through Venice and Ravenna?"

All that time, Michal is speaking in English, and the cashier in Italian.

"The same," the cashier nods.

"And can I stop-over? Stop-over," Michal repeats. Aside from the possible sightseeing, stretching the trip and timing it properly would solve the problem of finding shelter for at least one night

"Yes, you can," the cashier is getting impatient.

"Please, give me a ticket to Venice-Ravenna-Firenze-Rome," Michal says. He knows that the next train for Venice departs in two hours.

Now, with a firm plan, he tries the payphone again. It is two a.m. in Ottawa.

He listens to the ringing tone, and imagines Danna waking in her basement room and running to the telephone at the top of the stairs. In his mind, he is in the Kraemers' house with her.

"Hello?" She is short of breath

"It's me, Michal. I am in Italy."

"Where have you been for so long? I have been crying wherever

I go. For a week, I haven't heard a word from you. This was the longest week of my life. In my dreams, I've seen you in a pool of blood. I've seen you in prison." She begins to sob.

"Please, don't cry. This is a time to celebrate! Do you hear me? I'm in Italy."

"Yes, I do! I'm the happiest person in the world but, please, don't do this to me again! How soon can you be here?" She is calming down.

"I'm in Trieste, leaving by train for Rome in two hours. I'll be at the Canadian Embassy by Monday morning. Please, tell this to Mr. Wellington, and ask him to arrange my Canadian visa. I also need some money. After buying the train ticket, I don't have much left. I had to sell my camera in Yugoslavia already. And, please, don't forget the airplane ticket. Send it through the Air France office.

"Don't worry, I am writing it all down. But how did you get to Italy?"

"With a bus of Yugoslavian labourers, but that is a long story. I will tell you later."

"By the way, happy birthday!"

"I completely forgot about it." Shivers run down his back. A birthday is an important day in astrology.

"I love you."

"I love you, too."

Michal returns to the train station and, in a tobacco store, buys a stamped postcard with a view of the Trieste harbour. He smiles as he writes "Best regards from a wonderful vacation, Josef," and addresses it to Pavel in Prague. The card is the agreed signal for Pavel to post the parcel with the documents.

He drops the postcard into the airmail slot on the post office wall. Such an unreliable way to send this important message, he thinks as he walks to the pier where all the small boats are moored. Oil patterns colour the calm water, and seagulls hover above him. He sits himself comfortably on the seawall with his feet high above the water, takes out some food, but finds he cannot eat. He thinks about what happened at the border and watches the image of the sun reflecting on the water, then covers his eyes.

Behind him is a long row of shops, but no there are no people on the street, and all the shops are closed. He throws a piece of bread in the water. No fish shows up, but gulls have noticed the bread, and dive for it quickly. He gets up and takes a deep breath looking ahead, beyond the boats to where the sea meets the sky. It is the beginning of a new life, and it has started gracefully.

140. SUITCASE

The train for Venice dashes through the plains alongside the mountains. The countryside is different from Yugoslavia, more Mediterranean in a white and blue haze and slanted back with the speed of the train. Houses and gardens, fields, and trees flash past the window. Michal has never been in Italy or France, and he suddenly understands certain details from Paul Cézanne's paintings – details that puzzled him for years; they appeared artificial up north, but make sense now in the southern light.

He is leaning on the window, his hair flying, and eyes open wide.

The train is almost empty, and all the windows are down. The wooden benches polished by the pants and skirts of generations of travelers reflect the sun, and particles of dust dance in the air. Outside, the wind bends poplars planted along the road, and the window curtains crack, drumming on the wall. The wheels rumble: "Going, going to Rome, going, going to Rome, going ..."

Michal absorbs everything he can see, colours of objects, the landscape repeatedly unfolding into the most beautiful compositions, leaves and flowers, trees in the wind, a woman in a garden and her fluttering skirt, window shutters painted green and only half open.

Suddenly, he hears some voices and turns back. Three young men are making their way through the car. The empty carriage sways, shaking them between the walls of the narrow aisle. They laugh and shout to each other.

"Are these benches empty?" one of them asks in English

"Yes, they are," Michal says, wondering why, from the whole empty train, they selected his compartment

The youths throw their suitcases into the overhead net, and drop onto the bench opposite Michal. The train jerks, they lose their balance and fall over one another, but shift immediately apart trying to sit properly. All that time, one of them munches on an apple. Their pressed clothes and the air of freshness around them indicate that they had just started their journey. Both Michal and the three strangers stare silently at each other.

The silence does not last long. "Going for a vacation?" the second lad asks and bursts into laughter.

"We are studying journalism in Belgrade," the third one says as if to apologize for the crazy behaviour. "This is our summer assignment. Where are you from?"

"I am an engineer from Prague," Michal smiles. "You can call me a defector. I came to Yugoslavia with a tour and crossed the border this morning. My wife and daughter are already in Canada."

"You have to tell us more," the three move closer, catching every word from his lips.

If there was initially any barrier, after an hour of chatting and joking it has completely dissipated. "What you have told us would make an interesting story," one of the students says.

"Please, don't write about it. My parents and friends still live in Prague.

"I've got an idea," Michal continues after a moment of silence. "I have an open train pass for Yugoslavia. Do you want it?" He pulls the pass out of his bag. "I have no use for it ..."

"Are you kidding? If we could do something for you ..."

"You could. Before I crossed the border, I mailed my small, Tartan-canvas suitcase to my hotel in Primore. When you return to Yugoslavia, the suitcase may still be there. If you can retrieve it, could you mail it to my Canadian address?"

"What if the police have confiscated the luggage? Would the hotel release it to us?"

"You could try. I have no other chance of getting it anyway. I'll give you a receipt indicating that you bought the suitcase from me."

One of the students takes out a sheet of paper from his notebook, and Michal writes, trying to keep his hand steady:

Yesterday, I mailed a Tartan-canvas suitcase with my nametag to hotel Primore, Split. The suitcase contained my personal belongings, clothes, shoes, and snorkeling equipment. This letter is to certify that the luggage including its contents has been sold to Mr. J. Zito, permanent address ul. Zlota 47, Belgrad, for the amount of 120 (hundred-and-twenty) dinars.
    Michal Sedmý

The train is entering Mestre and begins to brake.

"Quickly, you have to change for Venice here," the students rush Michal out. "We are continuing to Milano."

In a hurry, he scribbles the Kraemers' address on another piece of paper. "Thank you, and good luck!"

141. MESTRE TO VENICE

Michal transferred to a local train between Mestre and Venice, and he can see that what appeared as a short stub on the map of Italy is still a considerable distance. He leans from the window trying to see ahead, but the scenery consists of a causeway built on rough boulders across a murky bay with tiny, remarkably regular waves. The mysterious town lays ahead, still out of view.

A melody of a Bach's gigue goes through his head. He can hear every note without producing a sound. He had studied the piece for a school concert when he was sixteen, but he is still able to listen to it in this inner form; this time the music springs to his mind involuntarily, expressing his mood, and going on as if measuring time by its impatient beat.

The train stops in Venice. Everybody rushes out except Michal who pauses at the exit door, his eyes slowly adjusting to the bright sunshine. He is standing above a square bordered by ugly old houses. Under his feet, old train tickets and cigarette boxes cover the stairs.

He feels sick of houses and people, of history and kings. He longs for fresh air and large open spaces, but his curiosity prevails.

After some hesitation, he follows a small arrow with the sign "St. Mark's Cathedral."

Picturesque streets and narrow passageways lead him over the canals, but even from a distance, the water smells putrid. He walks faster and faster, finding great pleasure from his body slicing through the air, his toes barely touching the ground. He is not looking left or right; his mind is focused forward.

He can already see the steeple of the cathedral, when a strange feeling interrupts his rapture. It feels as if he lost his right foot. He stops, leans on one of the houses, and examines the foot. He has never seen anything like it. The sole of his shoe is cracked in half, with its front and back parts dangling independently on the old canvas cover. He tries to fix the shoe with a string but the front part of the sole flaps clumsily, exposing his foot and pinching his toes.

He has not noticed a store since he left the train but, far ahead, he can see a covered bridge with a souvenir stand beside it. He limps to it and, amid plastic tomahawks and monkeys made of rabbit fur, he finds a pair of cheap flip-flops with a thong between the toes, made in Hong Kong.

My feet need fresh air, he consoles himself. The largest pair they have is a bit shorter than he needs, but it fits his foot fairly well and costs only a dollar. He tears off the plastic flowers that decorate them, puts the thongs on, and stuffs the old sneakers into a nearby garbage can.

Walking at a more leisurely pace now, he tests the new footwear. It feels good to be unattached and traveling across the globe with only a small bag over his shoulder.

When he comes to the cathedral, a fresh wind tosses his hair, and he instantly knows what he wants to do. Without looking at the cathedral and its stained-glass windows, he aims through the flocks of pigeons straight to a boat waiting at the edge of the square. Its motor is already running.

"How far do you go?" he asks the seaman helping people over the gangway.

"Very far, very end," the seaman tries to find the English expression. He waves his arms as if the boat would go to the end of this world. "One island," he says and points down to the ground, then walks with his fingers in the air. "Another island," he points down and walks with his fingers again.

"All right," Michal smiles. "I will go."

142. ISLAND HOPPING

The boat is crowded. Tourists and locals fill both decks shoulder to shoulder, and the boat takes off. Muddy and shallow, the sea is more like a lake with the shores uninteresting and distant. After fifteen minutes, the boat lands, and everybody pours out. Michal follows the crowd to a paved road and across the island to another boat.

This repeats several times. Michal submits to the ritual, which gradually eliminates the tourists. He is now traveling with men and women dressed in black, all talking fast and carrying baskets. He feels at home on their flat islands with weathered homes and shores bleached by water and sun.

The only tourist attraction on the last island is a row of souvenir shops along the seaway where the boat landed. After a brief excursion through the village, Michal returns to the boat. On the gangway, an old local man watches the reflection of the sun changing its shape on the surface of the water.

"How do you make your living here?" Michal asks him.

"By fishing," the man says without lifting his eyes. A shroud of sadness is hanging around him. Perhaps there isn't enough fish. Perhaps the tourists have taken over his village..

On the next island going back to Venice, Michal steps off the road and climbs a concrete seawall. Once over, he is in a different world. He is alone with the sea. The sound of human voices does not come over the wall.

He rests on one of the boulders that form the shore, and pulls out his old bread. From the boat, the sea appeared calm, but here gentle waves come and leave with hypnotizing regularity. Cautiously, a small crab crawls out and, after a moment of waiting, dashes across the stones. A rowboat rounds the island. Two fishermen pull nets into the boat, smiling at each other. It is impossible to swallow the dry bread without a drink, and the water from his bottle which he refilled at Zadar post office, does not taste good.

He looks at the reflection of his face in a pool the web tide left behind. Why am I wandering through all these places like a madman? I'd like to be with Danna. My body and soul tell me to forge ahead, but being in Rome before Monday would not solve anything. It would just create more problems.

143. RED LIGHT HOTEL

Back in Venice, the night is approaching. Purple shadows grow longer every minute, and a strip of yellow light marks the western sky. The city appears haunted. Streams of tourists converge on the railway station from all directions, and he joins the flow. The square in front of the cathedral is already deserted.

He cannot go on for another day without a good night's sleep, and he peeks between the boards nailed over the ground-floor windows of the next building. In contrast to the outside glitter, the cellars hide construction lumber mingled with dirt, grey broken furniture, old paint cans, and fallen stucco ceilings. These are not houses but ruins.

He takes the train to Mestre and leaves on foot northward. Northward means inland, away from tourists and traffic, he hopes. The street turns into a busy road, which leads past garages and welding shops, then enters a neighbourhood of small, working-class family houses. It is Saturday night and all the stores are closed. Two residents gesticulate and shout at each other, but what at first looked like a domestic fight is just a friendly chat between neighbours. On the next corner, six teenagers sit on a car and drink beer.

Michal does not have enough money for a hotel. Thinking again of open fields and possibly of a haystack where he could rest overnight, he turns into a side street, but quickly returns to the main road. Every house has a dog, and they all bark and lunge at him from behind their fences.

He has not had any dinner, is getting weak, and his thinking begins to blur. He has to concentrate on walking straight, and dodging crazy Italian drivers who speed through the winding road. The road has no sidewalks anymore.

At the next curve, an illuminated window attracts his attention. Paint peels from its frame, and road dust covers the glass. Under a bare bulb, a red sign reads: ROOMS AVAILABLE

It looks like the kind of hotel he would not normally stay in, but he shyly enters the backyard, where he finds a bar with three patrons sipping wine. The tablecloths, curtains, and the runner are all red, and everybody looks up at Michal. There is no clerk or registration desk.

"Do you rent rooms?" Michal asks the bartender.

"For how long?"

"Just for one night, something inexpensive," Michal makes his situation clear.

"One large room is left," the bartender says. "You can have it for the price of a single." He writes a figure on a slip of paper, less than half of what Michal has, and he decides to take it. The bartender gives him a large rusty key with a rough plywood tag, which has a large figure seven penciled on both sides.

"It's upstairs," the bartender says, and points to the ceiling.

Michal's family name Sedmý means 'seventh' in Czech. Perhaps, the key will bring me the luck I need, Michal thinks and ascends the narrow staircase. The old wooden steps creak under his feet, and when he turns on the light in his room, he cannot believe his eyes. A weak single bulb on the ceiling illuminates the room painted in a poisonous shade of yellow. There are two metal beds with no night tables, no bed lights, one chair, no curtains, and a cracked washbasin with a tap on the wall. Bare wood shows through the brown floor paint, and a scent of mold saturates the air.

The room would not be his first choice. It could drive a man insane, Michal is thinking referring to Vincent Van Gogh. He probes the beds, but the linens are clean – no wrinkles, hair, or stains. He opens the window and looks for the toilet in the hall. When he returns, he locks the door, leaves the key in the lock, sits on the chair and listens. The house is quiet. No shrieks, no squeaking beds, no radios, no snoring. Only the yellow light penetrates the night.

He turns the light off, takes off all his clothes, and washes his entire body, from his face down to his toes, part by part, without flooding the floor. Only a person who has traveled in the heat of the summer for days without access to water could appreciate his situation. He works in complete darkness except when headlights of passing cars illuminate the room. He has to stand on the chair to wash his backside, manages to wash his feet without breaking the basin from the wall. Shaving hurts after three days of growth and with a dull razor blade and in cold water, but he works fast, not thinking about the pain. Then he wipes the floor with the hotel towel, puts on his jeans without underwear, turns the light back on, washes his shirt, underwear, and socks with the hotel soap, and hangs them over the chair.

He is hungry but needs sleep more than anything else. He turns the light off again, takes off his pants, and slips into the bed.

144. WHY RAVENNA

Michal wakes with the sun shining into his eyes and he has to laugh. It's as if his room completely changed. In the daylight, yellow walls please his eyes. Birds sing on a branch that touches the window, and the garden outside is full of flowers.

He washes his face, gets dressed, and fills his wine bottle with fresh water. His shirt and underwear are still damp, but quickly adjust to the temperature of his body and, with his new footwear, he does not need the socks. He stuffs them into the side pocket of his bag and bounds downstairs, full of energy and ready to go.

As if by magic, the sleazy bar has turned into a cozy breakfast room filled with the aroma of freshly brewed coffee. With his mouth watering, Michal examines the selection of pastries displayed on the counter. He could eat the entire tray full, but restrains himself to buying one Danish while taking plenty of cream with his coffee.

He eats slowly, thinking about his next stop in Ravenna. He has to exorcise his demons. On their honeymoon, Danna and Ivan went for a tour of Italy. "I love Ravenna, those mosaics were spectacular," Danna mentioned several times. "especially the two doves."

The last time she added, "we have go there together," but when Michal heard about the doves, he felt a wave of jealousy. He imagined Danna and Ivan climbing the ramparts and, in a secluded section, tanning on the grass growing among the ruins. He imagined the quivering air of the hot summer day, and the two of them, naked, above the red tile roofs of the ancient city.

I want to be a part of everything she likes, he has decided. I must love all of her, including her past.

He finishes the coffee, and walks to the station – amazed how close it is once he is rested. He catches the next connection, and by noon, the train is approaching Ravenna.

Searing air smothers the countryside. Even simple thinking is difficult. Four passengers arrive with him – two peasants who drag their baskets through the side door and disappear immediately, and two students with knapsacks who meet their parents, embrace them, and follow them to a car waiting outside

Michal studies the waiting room posters. Beside the train schedules, he finds an announcement for a French opera, a list of church services, and a township notice he cannot translate. There is no tourist information, no map.

He knocks on the cashier's window. "Please, could you tell me, where to find the church with the mosaics?"

The cashier looks at him over his thick glasses. "All churches in Ravenna have mosaics. Which one you mean?"

"The one with two doves."

"I don't remember any doves," the cashier scratches his head

"The big church, the most famous one," Michal says.

"That would be St. Apollinaire in Classe, but that's out of town," the cashier looks at his watch. "All buses have already left."

"I prefer to walk anyway," Michal says. He cannot afford the bus.

"You want to go now, in this heat?" the cashier shakes his head. "Turn left, and stay on the main road. It is an hour's walk."

Michal follows the directions, trying to stay in the shade. With the sun directly overhead, houses cast narrow shadows, and walking along the walls is not practical because of all the open doors and doorsteps.

The asphalt sidewalk is melting, and Michal walks on the concrete curb, where he can avoid stepping on the asphalt with his thongs. After a while, he comes to a small restaurant. Its freshly painted, green louvered door between two flowering rhododendrons is wide open. From where Michal stands, he can see the perfectly set tables inside, white tablecloths, gleaming silverware, and crimson napkins folded in wineglasses. He comes closer, and reads the menu.

Just to see the prices, he tells himself, it's going to be expensive.

He reads the exotic menu line by line until he reaches the bottom of the page: Spaghetti - L 2000. Unbelievable, he thinks. Even I can afford that!

He enters, and sits down at the table next to the door. He has not eaten a cooked meal for three days.

When nobody shows up for two minutes, he lifts a fork and touches his glass gently. Instantly, a waiter rushes in with a basket of fresh bread and butter, and pours Michal a glass of ice water.

"Hello, sir! How are you, sir?" "What can I bring for you, sir?"

Michal pretends to be reading the menu. "Spaghetti, please."

The waiter makes a step back. "Spaghetti with what, sir? Spaghetti with meat sauce, spaghetti with eggplant, spaghetti with chicken. We do not serve just spaghetti, sir."

Michal feels his face turning red, and begins to rise. "I am sorry," he says and opens his wallet. "I did not know. I have only this much."

With a friendly smile, the waiter pushes Michal gently back into his chair. "Sir, we can make an exception. I'll bring you spaghetti." He rushes away, and Michal quenches his appetite on the butter and bread. When the waiter returns, the basket is empty.

The waiter brings an enormous dish loaded with spaghetti and tomato sauce, and pours Michal more water. "Here you are, professor."

"How did you guess?"

"People carry their professions on their faces," the waiter smiles.

When Michal pays, the waiter refuses a tip.

145. ST. APOLLINAIRE IN CLASSE

Michal resumes walking. Gravel shoulders have replaced the sidewalks, and the road continues through open fields. Under an old crooked tree, the ground is full of green, spotted apples. Michal wipes one on his shirt, and bites into it. It is sour but edible, and he stuffs more apples in his bag.

He has been hiking over an hour when the silhouette of a monastery appears ahead. He quickens his pace. Something attracts him to this structure built of large brown stones under a gently sloping roof. Tall cypresses surround the building.

Five more minutes, and he passes through the gate, crosses the yard, the door, and immediately notices a postcard with two white doves. I've found them, he thinks, but the back of the card reads: *Ravenna, Galla Placidia (VI century), Drinking pigeons.*

Danna was wrong, he thinks. They are not doves, and I am in a wrong church, but he still pays a small admission and enters.

The impression is so overwhelming he almost loses his balance. He has not expected a room so vast and yet so plain. The stone walls stretch to a ceiling high enough to let clouds form inside the building. The rough stone contrasts with pine benches and a simple altar without ornaments or carvings. The hall is square like a barn, but built on a superhuman scale.

And above, just under the roof, a row of square windows opens toward the sky – the sky or the Heavens, deep gentle blue. Shafts of light coming through these windows gently disperse and illuminate the hall. It does not smell like a church. Roses grow outside, and their scent permeates the air. He also detects the scent of gardens and of recently watered soil.

A small group of visitors arrives shortly after Michal. Some stand with their mouths open, some move humbly across the terra-cotta floor trying to suppress the echo of their footsteps. Michal is looking at cool, abraded tiles and imagines processions of monks who had prayed and crawled on their knees across this floor. He has no doubts. This is a holy ground. Then he looks up.

A huge, striking mosaic above the altar depicts a complex landscape with green hills, lush pasture, bushes, and trees and inhabited by tiny animals – sheep, rabbits, birds, and deer. Field flowers everywhere, and a large Jesus Christ suspended in the middle – his aura as natural as the feathers of the birds. As any object of true art, the picture maintains its own life, folding and closing onto itself.

Oh, Danna, Michal thinks. You have brought me to an amazing place.

Absorbed in the picture, he moves closer and studies the details, then steps back and analyzes the composition. It is quite modern yet, at the same time, subject to mysterious rules. He sits down on a bench and stares at the mosaic until he can see every detail even with his eyes closed.

On the way out, he looks back once more and has to stop. He returns and absorbs the masterpiece again. He cannot afford to buy any prints or postcards; he must record everything with his eyes.

46. EMBASSY IN ROME

It is Monday morning, five after nine, and Michal is at the door of the Canadian Embassy. Yesterday afternoon, before he boarded the train again, he visited five more churches in Ravenna, including Galla Placidia.. Around midnight, he spent hour and twenty minutes wandering through the empty streets of Firenze looking for famous sculptures, but he did not find any and all the churches were closed. He boarded the express for Rome, and slept sitting in a compartment crowded by construction workers returning to work.

As his fellow-travelers recommended to him, he disembarked at a small suburban station, bought a city map, and took a bus to Via Zara. He thought that the money from Danna should be here tomorrow and decided to pamper himself. He bought bread, milk, and the least expensive cheese, and had breakfast on a park bench.

From the outside, the Embassy looks like an ordinary villa but, as he enters, it is a showcase of luxury reminiscent of a Renaissance castle – mirrors, gold chandeliers and a huge staircase with a red carpet. The staircase with a carved railing curves like a seashell, opening wider as it ascends. There is no music or any other sound, and the light oak door at the top of the stairs is closed.

A small baroque desk covered with papers sits under the stairs. A lamp beside it is on, but nobody is around. Michal waits a minute, then hesitantly climbs the stairs and knocks on the door. Nobody answers. He knocks again and slowly opens a narrow gap before daring to enter. He is facing a young bearded man sitting behind a desk.

The difference between the man and Michal is striking. Michal is tanned, in jeans and thongs, the old duffel bag over his shoulder, sure of himself but down to earth. The clerk – or whatever his rank is, wears a black, three-piece suit that emphasizes his soft, white hands with massive rings. His every hair is perfectly trimmed and, at first glance, he seems ignorant about anything except his career. A golden letter knife and a pen with ornamental handle lie beside his papers. Michal can smell sandalwood incense.

"What do you want?" the clerk says.

Michal feels as if he has entered the wrong place, disaster hanging in the air. "Good morning, sir. I interrupted my fellowship in Ottawa last November, and I would like to continue. I need a Canadian visa."

The man is tapping on the desk with his forefinger.

"Before I left Canada," Michal continues, "I talked to Mr. Wellington from Immigration Canada. He said that if I mention his name, any Canadian Embassy would help me. Do you know Mr. Wellington?"

"Never heard the name." The clerk looks at Michal as if he had made up the story. "How did you get here?"

"I crossed the border in Trieste on Saturday. I have a five-day transit visa for Italy."

"Transit to where?"

"Transit to Austria, but my Austrian visa had expired," Michal is trying to be honest this time.

The man leans backward in his chair. "You are a typical case of permanent immigration. To process your application, we will take at least three months. With your five-day visa, you'd better ask for political asylum."

"How do I do that?"

"Go to the central police station, and when you have your papers ready, come here."

147. ITALIAN POLICE

After a short, brisk walk with map in hand, Michal is standing on a narrow cobblestone street, bewildered. He checks again the sign on the building and his position on the map.

Why would they keep the police station in such historical surroundings? No vehicles can pass through this street blocked by pedestrians and carts. Except for the narrow windows in the walls, the inside looks like a post office or a bank. Perhaps the choice of the building is not accidental. The walls are over a meter thick. This is a true fortress.

Wood and glass partitions surround the public area, where short lines of people cluster around the counters, Italian style. People jump lines, push in, and everybody talks. He joins one line, and stands quietly with his ears and eyes open. All he hears is Italian, and no East European faces are in sight. He glances back. Those immediately behind him could overhear what he is going to say at the counter.

He also studies the face of the police officer serving his line – a slim dark man in a light brown uniform without a cap and with a wide leather belt across his chest. The officer seems intelligent and efficient. The old woman before Michal leaves the counter.

"Do you speak English?" Michal opens the dialogue.

"I do. How can I help you?" Officer's English is impeccable.

Michal looks left and right, and leans over the counter. "I am a citizen of Czechoslovakia, and I want to ask for political asylum."

"Please, come to another counter," the officer's face is tense.

"Are you serious?" he says when they are alone.

"Yes, I am. I have to wait for my Canadian visa, and I have a five-day transit for Italy."

"We can grant you political asylum, but you will have to go to a refugee camp in Trieste. After six months, you can apply for the Canadian visa, and that takes additional three months."

Back to Trieste? To stay in Italy for nine months? Michal's hands are trembling.

"My wife is already in Canada, and she has no job. She does not even speak English! In nine months, my fellowship will expire!"

"I'm sorry, sir, but we make no exceptions. It is your choice – if you ask for political asylum, you have to go to the refugee camp."

"But how will I get there? I have no money."

"We'll take you there in a police van."

Michal's brain works feverishly. "I still have three more days," he eventually says.

"Take your time. You can apply any time before your transit visa expires."

Michal leaves the police station in shock. He needs Wellington's help, and he needs it fast.

> *Prokop found himself saying*
> *"Why all this happened to me?"*
> *The old man reflected. "It only seems like that.*
> *What happens to a man comes out of himself;*
> *it winds out of you as if from a skein."*
>
> (K. Capek, Krakatit)

148. CALLING FROM ROME

By two p.m., Michal is still waiting for the telephone connection at a tiny post office on a busy pedestrian street. This is annoying, he thinks, just like in Yugoslavia.

The office, cool during the morning, has warmed up. Michal has his chair close to the door, and watches the street. Every half-hour, the street vendor outside sprays his stand from a hose and rearranges his fruit under a rainbow he has created. Droplets of water roll down the fruit and trickle around the cobblestones, sending off waves of cool air.

Keep your head clear, Michal is telling himself. He has already eaten the leftovers from his breakfast and runs out for a drink of water from the street fountain. He is constantly hungry and the question of how to sustain himself on his low budget is always on his mind. Why does it take so long to get the connection?

The two men waiting there with him are equally impatient. The big chap with a German accent has inquired several times about a connection to Barcelona, and after hours of nervous pacing, he finally sits down and begins to snooze. The short Italian-American delivered a long speech on how everything in Italy is disorganized, then calmed down and now preoccupies himself by catching flies that land on his knees.

"Is there a tourist camp in Rome?" Michal asks the American. "I am looking for inexpensive accommodation."

"The camp on Via Salaria costs four hundred Liras a night," the German wakes up and answers the question. "You can't find anything less expensive in the entire city."

"Where is it?"

"Everyone knows the place. Near highway thirty-five," the

American adds.

"I don't have a car. I don't even have a tent. How do I get there?"

"Take the Via Salaria bus until the terminal loop, and ask someone there, it's a short walk."

"The collect call to Canada," the postmaster calls. Michal springs up, and runs to the booth. "Danna, how are you?"

"It's great to hear your voice! We just got up and are getting the children ready. Remember, the time difference is six hours. Over the weekend, everything was closed, but now we have an appointment with Mr. Wellington at ten o'clock…"

"How did you manage to arrange an appointment with him over the weekend? "

"He gave us a special emergency number. After seeing him, we plan to stop at the bank, wire the hundred dollars that Kraemers lent me, and send you the airplane ticket from the Air France office. The Kraemers are fantastic! I could not do anything without them."

Michal feels dreadful to spoil her enthusiasm. "If I don't get the Canadian visa until Thursday, I will have to apply for political asylum, and that would mean nine months of sitting here and doing nothing. And there's no guarantee that I would ever get the visa …"

"Mr. Wellington promised to wire the visa as soon as we see him. Trust me, you're not an ordinary case. Tomorrow, you will have the visa, money, and the ticket. Make a flight reservation for Wednesday!"

"I can't make any reservation until I have the ticket. Besides, from here, the situation looks bleak. The embassy clerk has never heard of Mr. Wellington, and the police adhere strictly to the rules. I'll call you tomorrow at two in the morning your time, and you can tell me if there is any hope."

After a pause, he continues. "You know, I haven't eaten well for several days. I am dead tired, my feet are sore, and my teeth are starting to hurt. Sometimes my eyes fill with tears as I walk through the streets. Sometimes I wonder whether I will ever see you again.

Perhaps not everything we have done was right. Perhaps, this is our punishment."

But Danna's confidence is unshakable: "We are all working on getting you out of there quickly. You will see tomorrow. I have to go now."

149. TOURIST CAMP

Following the German's recommendation, Michal rides the bus to the end of the Via Salaria line. As he gets off, the afternoon sun is in his eyes. The pavement and the walls of the surrounding houses radiate heat, and he does not see any signs indicating where the camp could be. What puzzles him most is the regular city street and the four-story houses. A tourist campground can't be in this part of the town!

He opens his city map only to find that he is beyond the map boundary.

A few steps from him, a fat old man with a white apron and crimson fez sits on a crate at the entrance to a small neighbourhood grocery. When Michal asks about the tourist camp, instead of answering, the man jumps up, grabs Michal by the shoulder, and points with outstretched arm as if pointing to a boat on the horizon or to a wild goat far in the mountains.

Michal, shocked by the physical contact with the stranger, follows the man's finger from the opposite side of the terminal loop to a four-lane highway across a bridge and toward a wooded hill a considerable distance ahead. Michal can see two cars with trailers climbing a winding road, and he understands where the campground must be. He thanks the man who pats Michal's back and returns to his crate.

Michal runs over the bridge dodging the cars, and instead of following the highway, he takes a shortcut directly up the hill. A tall chain-link fence encircles the summit, and Michal follows it through the woods until he finds the gate. A billboard lists the prices for various vehicles. The last line reads TENT LOT - 410 LIRAS.

Michal stops, and counts his cash. Including the coins from both his pockets, he has 2,120 Liras. It is three nights until Thursday when he has to leave Italy or go to the refugee camp.

If I stay here, it would leave little for food, he thinks and withdraws from the gate. Whether I sleep on the ground inside the fence or outside the fence, it makes no difference to me.

He trots down the hill and explores an abandoned section of the road. Weeds poke through the pavement, and the slope is dense with thorny undergrowth. He thinks at first of sleeping behind a pile of telephone poles, but they leak tar and broken glass litters the ground. When he begins to search under the trees, a police siren sounds nearby and, after some commotion in the bushes, two prostitutes in high heels dart across the road and disappeared under the growth.

Not a good place to sleep, he decides, and walks on.

The road takes him to a resort area with modern villas, each with a swimming pool complete with chrome trimmings and elaborate slides. The crystal water reflects white, red, and green umbrellas, and automatic sprinklers water the lawns. With pleasure, he walks through the curtains of water that reach the sidewalk. His jeans and shirt are soaked and his glasses are fogged, but the weather is hot and he dries in minutes.

In this part of town, every square meter is landscaped and fenced, and the railway underpass, a low concrete tunnel behind the houses, is smeared with shit. When Michal throws a stone into the dark space, a rat runs out. Staying at the campground seems like a good idea.

He returns to the camp, and pays at the gate. On the garbage pile behind the store is a large plastic sheet that, with some ingenuity and hoping for no heavy rain, could serve as a shelter. The plastic is not long enough, is ripped in several places, and has the inconvenient shape of the large crate it originally covered. Michal cuts it with his knife, and reshapes it into a low tent with scraps of the masking tape he also found on the garbage pile.

The tent is less than three feet high, and Michal worries about a car accidentally running him over. After a short search, he finds a nice little spot surrounded by tree trunks that would prevent any car from entering his tiny territory. He marks the spot by placing his bag and the folded plastic in the middle, then changes to swim trunks, and runs to the showers. Using his soap bar, he washes all his clothes including the jeans, rinses them and hangs them on a string between two trees. Then he returns to the showers, washes his sore feet, and stands under the hot water streaming over his head until his entire body softens and the skin on his fingers wrinkle.

"That shower itself is worth of four hundred and ten liras," he tells two students entering the showers just as he is leaving.

Dressed only in swim trunks, happy and relaxed, he buys a small can of meat in the camp store. He knows that, after this purchase, his money would not last until Thursday, but he trusts Danna that tomorrow will be better.

He sits down at his spot, takes out a writing pad, and composes several letters, laying words carefully down, and rewriting each paragraph several times over. The result does not reflect exactly the truth, but it protects parents and friends. He knows that authorities in Prague will arrange a mock trial where, in his absence, these letters will be presented as court evidence.

150. LETTERS TO PRAGUE

As Michal knows, the letter of resignation from the position at the Prague Institute will be forwarded to the police:

Dear comrade director,

I would like to inform you that Danna and I have left the country permanently. Nobody knew about our plans, and nobody helped us, and only we should be blamed if there are any legal consequences. Note that we defected during our vacation, not from a business trip.

We are not leaving for political reasons. We want to start a new family, and if we have children in the West, it will be financially easier — both for our former spouses and for us.

Prior to our departure, we completed our projects, and we are ready to help those who will take them over. Please, send our remaining salaries to Zora Sedmý.

We thank you for everything you have done for us. We both resign from our positions in your Institute. This letter is our joint statement, Danna approved it by telephone.

Sincerely, Michal Sedmý

*

The purpose of the next two letters is to inform both parents before the police would summon them for questioning. They could use the letters as proof that they knew nothing about the plot.

Dear Mom and Dad,

As you see from the postage stamp, we (Danna, Lenka, and I) are in the West. Our 'vacation' plans were not what we told you; we are going to stay here permanently. I know that you will not approve of our decision. Please, understand that we want to get away from our past and start a new life. We only hope this will not cause you too many difficulties.

It is a strange feeling having to depart without saying good-bye. You have gone through uncounted troubles because of me already. All I can do this time is to apologize again. I am sorry!

Your loving son, Michal

*

Dear Mom,

I am not sure how to tell you this news; it will upset you greatly. We did not go for a vacation to South Bohemia as we told you. Danna and Lenka are in Canada, and I will join them soon. We will not return to Czechoslovakia. Danna asked me to write you on her behalf. Please, don't be angry with us.

I know how much you care for Danna and Lenka, but I cannot give any details yet. We will write again soon. We are not going to have a permanent address for several weeks, but when we settle down, we will let you know immediately.

With apologies, Michal

*

The purpose of the fourth letter is to eliminate problems in Rovná.

To: Mr. Josef Smutny,

Chairman of the Housing Committee, Rovná.

With apologies for not ending our lease properly, I left the keys to our apartment under the floor mat. We have decided to leave the country. The other keys, including the keys for the basement locker are in our apartment hall, on a hook beside the door.

We left nothing of any value in the apartment, and I assume that the police will confiscate whatever is there. Our Institute should pay for the last month's rent, as usual.

We are sorry if our departure will cause any inconvenience. Rovná is a wonderful place, and we liked it very much.

Best regards, Michal and Danna Sedmý

*

The purpose of the fifth letter is to block Zora's demands for alimony payments from Michal's parents:

To: District court, Prague 6

Subject: Alimony

I have decided to leave Czechoslovakia permanently. This may create confusion about how I will continue the alimony payments to my former wife Mrs. Zora Sedmý, born Fürst, as ordered by your court, decision number 246/69, dated September 3, 1969.

I will support my children from wherever I am, and will continue my payments. I will let you know my permanent address when I have one.

Sincerely, Michal Sedmý

*

The last letter is a courtesy to Zora's mother, but it also reinforces the previous letter:

Dear Mrs. Fürst

I have decided to leave the country. Is Zora still in the hospital? She will be better off financially, and she will have the children to herself as she always wanted. I will be sending her $100 monthly, as I promised before my first departure for Canada.

I instructed my former employer to send her my last salary. I may be late with my next alimony payment, because I am traveling across Europe and have no job or income.

Unfortunately, I had to leave at a critical time when you needed my help. I considered postponing my departure, but it was simply impossible.

Yours, Michal

For several minutes, Michal is trying to imagine Mrs. Fürst's face. He is not sure whether she will be smiling after reading this letter or livid with rage.

> *"May the Great Spirit make the Sun rise in your hearts!*
> *With that our campfire has ended."*
>
> (North American Indians)

151. LITTLE CAMPFIRE

Shadows grow longer and the warm evening is descending quietly with the sky turning red behind the trailers and the trees, but Michal does not see anything except his papers. He works on the letters until there is no light, then moves closer to the store and finishes the last page sitting cross-legged on the ground under the floodlight that illuminates the back loading door of the campground store.

It is dark, but not his bedtime yet. He is mentally exhausted, and slowly begins to distinguish his surroundings. To fight the creeping loneliness, he makes a miniature campfire from match-sized twigs and tiny pinecones, and keeps it going under the protection of his hands. The flames grow and jump from one twig to another, warming his hands and sending streaks of smoke through the ends that are not burning yet. The little light dances in the evening air, and Michal thinks of Danna and Lenka, of the campfires they made and of the places they will go together yet.

Watching the fire gives him peace of mind. He imagines the expressions of the director and of the police agents after reading his letters, and he is glad that he has left that part of the world. The evening breeze, originally warm, begins to feel damp.

He lets the fire die out and watches the embers glow; then he smothers them with a single cup of water. He expects a cold night, and puts on all his clothes: two pairs of socks, both briefs, jeans (still wet in the seams), the T-shirt, the checkered flannel shirt, and the black woolen sweater. Then he stretches his nylon raincoat on the ground inside the tent, and crawls into this lair.

His bag, which by now contains only the dictionary, the book, and the square box with the emergency kit, does not make a great pillow, but sleeping on it will protect its contents.

He falls asleep instantly, but wakes soon perspiring and hot. There is not enough air between the raincoat and the plastic. He opens a bigger gap but soon wakes up again, shivering and wet. The temperature is dropping, the plastic is too short, and dew has condensed on his sweater and face. Either his feet or his head stick out, and all his joints ache.

At five a.m., he throws the plastic back and listens to birds, then warms himself in the hot shower. The camp is still asleep when he tiptoes through the gate.

> *"August walked through a summer street*
> *with the sun in his eyes —*
> *the time of the boys with the fishing rods,*
> *the time of the bees and butterflies."*
>
> (Jindřich Balík)

152. EATING A CAT

Michal comes to the bus stop, and counts his money again. He has to mail the letters, keep enough for two nights at the campground, and at least buy some bread. That leaves forty liras — not enough for the bus fare.

He looks at the map. The campground isn't there, but it shows the bus terminal loop. Just eight kilometers to the Canadian Embassy, he tells himself and begins to walk.

At noon, he is sitting in the city park near the Embassy. The sun is standing in flames, and his brain is refusing to operate in such heat. He tries to recollect what happened during the morning, but he only remembers fragments out of context and time.

He recalls his long walk through the streets of Rome, the call to Danna who insisted that the telex from Mr. Wellington had been sent and that the money must be waiting at the Bank of Rome. At the Embassy, the receptionist treated him like an old nuisance.

Who would expect the Bank of Rome to be closed on Tuesdays and, at the Air France office, they did not know anything about his airplane ticket.

Slowly, he eats the dry bread, and drags his feet to the fountain in the corner of the garden. There, in the cool shade, a trickle of water from the mouth of a stone face representing the Sun is falling into a large basin overgrowing with algae. A gargoyle's head shows under a thick cover of ivy. Michal watches its eyes before he bends over to reach under the spout. He knows this spot already. Discarded paper cups float in the basin but, as in most fountains in Rome, the water from the spout is cool and potable[19]. He drinks until his teeth tingle and wets his hair to cool his head.

Ready to take a nap, he returns to the bench, when a cat appears and rubs against his legs. It is a city puss from a rich neighbourhood, well fed and self-conscious, with no fire in its eyes. Michal likes animals, especially cats, but as he strokes this one behind its ears, his thoughts surprise him. He imagines a cat carcass roasting on a skewer, and his fingers explore the cat's muscles as one would test a good steak. Never before had Michal even dreamed of eating a cat.

He remembers reading a newspaper article about a French restaurant famous for its rabbit meals, and how workers discovered a pile of cat skulls in the nearby sewer. The cat would taste good, he assures himself and his mouth waters.

He looks around. Nobody is in sight. It would take one blow over head, and I could hide the dead cat in my bag. Or perhaps pet it, carry it away in my arms, and kill it where nobody could see it. Without the skin and the head, it will look like a rabbit.

Then he imagines a group of mad Italians yelling and chasing him through the streets, and a policeman with a grave face pulling the dead cat from his bag.

He lets the cat go, and stretches on the bench looking up at the sky. The sun shines through the trees, and he can feel the water rolling in his empty stomach.

---

[19] This was true in 1970, but may not be true at the time you read this novel.

153. AUSTRIAN CONSULATE

After an hour of dreaming, he jumps up with a new idea: When my five-day transit visa for Italy expires, I don't have to ask for the political asylum. I can move to another country and wait for the Canadian visa there, but to which country? Of course to Austria! I still have the expired visa, and Austria opened its door to all Czechs when the Soviets invaded.

It takes him ten minutes to find a payphone where the phonebook has not been stolen, and once he has the address of the Austrian Consulate, he is on his way, checking his bearings against the map.

Excited about the idea, he walks fast, ignoring famous museums and churches. The address takes him to an old apartment building with a dark hall. A small paper arrow points upstairs.

He follows the arrows to a small, disorganized office crammed with old metal furniture and stacks of paper. The office has no windows, the light fixture in the ceiling has been broken, and a bare bulb gives a weak, yellow glare. A middle-aged, motherly woman sitting behind an ancient Underwood typewriter, occupies half of the remaining space. If more than two people entered the room, they would have to leave the door open.

Michal takes a step back, and reads the sign again.

"Don't mind the mess, we're moving," the woman says. She is cheerful and happy and seems to levitate behind the typewriter. She is so stout her stool is invisible underneath her body.

"I am Czech," Michal says. "Could I get a tourist visa for a few weeks?" He is getting bolder.

"Do you have your passport with you?"

Michal passes her the passport, and she opens it ready to put a stamp in. "It will cost you nineteen hundred liras."

"I forgot my money in the car," he says, shocked by the speed with which everything is happening. He does not have a car, and he does not have the money.

"Come again later," she smiles. "We are open until three."

154. MELONS

Michal descends the staircase with mixed feelings. He has solved one problem only to encounter a new one. How could I raise the 1,900 liras? I have already sold my camera and have nothing of any value. My sweater has holes at the elbows, my 20-year-old watch is scratched and corroded, and nobody would buy an old Czech-English dictionary in Italy. I am not allowed to work here without a permit, and I don't speak the language. He walks back to the Canadian Embassy.

"No telex," the receptionist says before Michal even opens his mouth.

Michal begins his retreat, the two-hour track back to the camp. The sun presses on his shoulders, and the pavement is searing. His body aches, his feet are sore, and only his will makes him walk. All he can think of is some shade, of having no worries, and eating a good dinner. He hopes for a miracle – a banknote on the pavement or someone offering him a job.

The street widens as he reaches the suburbs. Large trucks thunder in both directions, each bringing a new wave of hot, oily air. This part of town has no street fountains, and Michal is thirsty. His mouth is dry.

Suddenly, an old farmer sitting beside a pyramid of neatly stacked watermelons materializes ahead. He grins at Michal long before he is close enough to talk.

Michal loves watermelons. The farmer must have sprayed his melons recently, and the cool water drips from lush waxy skins. A sign reads: 200 Liras.

"Would you sell a slice, just a small slice?" Michal says, but he sees that the farmer does not understand English.

He imitates cutting a melon with his hand.

"Oh, no, signore," the farmer shakes his head, and says something long in Italian.

"It is too big for one person," Michal points to himself, and raises one finger: "Uno."

The farmer shakes his head, takes a striped melon, and juggles it in front of Michal's face. Michal understands the farmer saying something about a rich man and two hundred Liras, and he closes his eyes. He imagines the woman at the Austrian Consulate, and continues toward the camp.

155. GLASS SHARDS

He walks on, concentrating on his sore legs. They hurt all over, but the soles of his feet are worst. The beach thongs are not good for the long hikes he does twice a day.

He takes a rest on a low garden wall, and examines the ball of his foot. He does not have blisters, but deep parallel cuts, as if he cut himself eight times with a razor blade. His foot is dirty and bleeding. He looks at the left foot – the same thing.

He stares at his feet in disbelief and probes the inside of the already worn thongs. They seem to be smooth, but when he pushes more, a sharp edge cuts his finger.

The rubber foam collected pieces of glass that worked their way through. This is the last straw. He cannot continue this torture. He has no money for the visa. He has no water to wash his wounds. He cannot afford new shoes.

He is sitting on the fence and staring at people passing by without noticing his tragedy. After a while, he pulls himself together, and bends the thongs back and forth, paying no attention to how strange this would appear to passersby. He pushes the glass out, and pulls it with his fingernails and his knife, fragment by fragment, until the sole does not hurt even under pressure. The glass collected in one small area of each thong and, after thirty minutes of patient work, he can walk again.

At the campground gate, he wonders again: Can I afford this luxury?

He pays 410 Liras and enters.

156. MINISTER FROM IOWA

After taking a shower, he pulls the folded plastic from the tree, where he hid it before his departure in the morning. He stretches it on the ground and can see again how useless it is. Could one of the campers have a spare blanket?

The evening camp is crawling with people. Like penguins, each group or family claims its territory marked by canvas barriers and clotheslines along invisible boundaries.

Michal follows the road through the camp, and imagines the campsites behind the trailers and tents. He can smell barbecues and camp stoves, hot dogs and hamburgers. Parents cook and shout at children who play hide-and-seek while tripping over the lines and knocking down the tents. A group of teenagers relaxes on the grass drinking beer.

Except for a lone biker who plays a guitar for himself, the entire camp is shaking to the rock 'n' roll music that blasts from numerous radios, each station different but all just the same. This sound and the scent of suntan lotion create a beach atmosphere, though this camp is on a wooded hill, far from any river or lake.

Three lots down the road, an entirely different music is coming from a small transistor radio hanging on a trailer beside a playpen with a toddler wearing only diapers. The boy's face is dirty, and his diapers are wet. A young couple is trying to start a camp stove on a picnic table.

"That's wonderful music," Michal says, realizing how much he has been missing good music. "Would it disturb you, if I sat here, out of your way, and listened awhile?"

"We would be delighted. Please, join us." They look like Italians, but speak English with American accents.

The man offers Michal a lawn chair, but Michal prefers the ground beside the radio, where he can sit lost in the music, indifferent to his surroundings. The voices of instruments talk to each other like two gentle lovers. They embrace, pause, and take off in an all-sweeping dance. Michal can see his father playing, his fingers scaling the keyboard, sees the frowning face of the composer, and he wonders where all this beauty came from, with its tremendous strength that makes him so happy yet he has to weep.

When the hosts see Michal's concentration, they move quietly around him. "What was it?" the man asks, when the music stops. "It reminds us of something, but we can't recognize it."

"Dvořák's Piano Quintet in A-major. My father is a pianist and, once a week, he plays chamber music with his friends. When they play this piece, it is a special day, almost as special as Christmas."

"Your father must be a superb pianist if he can play this."

"He is. I am sorry you can't hear him playing."

Michal is thinking how he could express his gratitude. "Would you have a sheet of plain paper and a pencil, please?"

After a search inside the trailer, the woman brings a sheet of typewriter paper, a pencil, and an old magazine on which he could write.

Michal sketches a portrait of the boy standing in the playpen.

"Look at it," the mother is ecstatic. "It's just like him!"

"It's only a sketch. Please, keep it if you like."

"Would you like to join us for dinner?" she asks after a short eye contact with her husband. "It's nothing fancy. We're not very rich."

Michal can see that from every piece of their clothing, from the broken webbing on the lawn chairs, from the rusty car, even from the expressions of their faces. They have the muscular but not athletic bodies of white, untanned people who work hard but have no time for sports.

"I'd be grateful for any kind of food," Michal says and joins them at the table. The man lowers his forehead, and prays quietly. They eat without a word, sharing a loaf of bread and a single can of vegetable soup, diluted enough to suffice for three people.

"I am a Presbyterian minister from a small Iowa town," the man says.

"And I am a Czech engineer, on the way to Canada."

"Why did you leave your country?"

Michal has told his story several times before and, this time, he starts calmly, trying to remain organized, and narrating events as they happened one after another. But each part of his story has its own logic and is connected to many other things. He entangles himself in these details and finds it impossible to describe, in a reasonably short time, what has happened to him. He does not want to torment his new friends with a long and complicated story, but his heart overflows with emotions and he is talking faster and faster. The two Americans listen with their mouths open. They cannot understand – there still is a country that does not allow its citizens to leave. They do not even know what an exit visa is.

At last, in his narration, Michal comes to his visit at the Austrian consulate. The sun shines and the smell of the barbecue lingers from the adjacent campsite. Both Michal and his new friends sit without saying a word.

"What a story," the woman finally says, takes the boy into her lap, and wraps him into a blanket.

"Only nineteen hundred liras?" the man articulates slowly, as if thinking hard, and he reaches into the trousers that hang on the trailer, and counts the money.

"Please, don't be offended," he says when he sees Michal's hesitation. It's less than three dollars."

"I can't take money just like that," Michal says. "If I could do something for you ..."

"You are plain silly! You would not accept money from a good friend?"

"I came to listen to the music. Why did I ever mention money?"

They stand looking at each other, both smiling.

"I am most grateful for your offer." Michal finally says. "May I borrow the amount from you and send it when I get to Canada?"

They shake hands.

"God bless you on your way," the minister says.

157. PROGRESS AT LAST

On Wednesday, after another night under the plastic, Michal packs his bag, and begins his morning journey across Rome. He knows the route by heart, and walks without the map. By tomorrow, I have to leave Italy. Except for the 300 liras I put aside for the Austrian visa, I have a few coins left – not enough for another night in the camp.

The morning is fresh and colorful, and he throws away his worries. At the Austrian consulate, he climbs to the upper floor where the same lady in the same brown dress is typing as if she had not left the office since the previous night. Dust and stucco particles cover the piles of paper, and the small table fan hums helplessly without improving the air.

"You want a tourist visa," she remembers. "For how many days?"

"Can you make it for six weeks?" Six weeks feels like infinity, but why not ask for more.

"No problem," she says with her strong German accent, finds a blank page in Michal's passport, and imprints a large stamp. While Michal holds his breath, she fills in the dates and signs at the bottom.

"I made it for two months," she says. "The fee is the same."

Elated, Michal dances into the sun-flooded street. At the Bank of Rome, the clerk places a small stack of ten-dollar bills on the counter as if the money has been sitting there for at least a week. At the Air France office, they have no indication that the airplane ticket would be coming, and the Canadian Embassy has not received the telex from Ottawa. Still good progress, Michal is thinking, and the receptionist treats him like a harmless lunatic.

With a feeling of utmost luxury, he buys a real ham-and-cheese sandwich, and eats it in the park before his afternoon nap on the bench. He tries the Embassy again before closing, but the telex isn't there yet.

Finally on Thursday – the day he has to leave Italy, things truly begin to move.

At the Air France office, the message arrived only minutes before Michal comes in. "The ticket you originally bought was from Prague to Ottawa?" the girl says. "Do you want to change it from Rome to Ottawa?"

"No, thank you. I am taking a train to Vienna, and will fly from there."

"That's even better. You can fly from Vienna at the same price."

Only at the Canadian embassy nothing has changed.

"I have to leave Italy today," Michal reminds the receptionist. "May I see the clerk, please?"

The receptionist, happy that this daily nuisance will stop, leads Michal upstairs and opens the door for him. The clerk, already displeased that someone opened the door without knocking gets even angrier when he sees Michal.

"The receptionist has told you we have not received any telex. What else do you want?"

"I have to leave Italy today, but I have a two-month visa for Austria. My contact in Ottawa confirmed that the telex should come any time now, but the only train to Vienna leaves in three hours. May I call you from the train station just before departure?"

Michal's confidence has transferred to the clerk who, though not trusting Michal completely yet, senses there could be something to it.

"Call at noon, and ask for the secretary. She will also give you the address of the Canadian Consulate in Vienna."

Michal spends exactly one hour and ten minutes at the post office. He knows there isn't enough time to get a connection, but at least he is trying. When the wall clock reaches the position he has set as the ultimate limit, he cancels the call, collects all the letters that he had written to Danna while traveling through Italy, places them in a large yellow envelope, and scribbles on the last page:

I have received both the $100 and the Air France ticket, but the Canadian visa has not arrived yet. I have to leave Italy today. I am taking the 1 p.m. train to Vienna. I tried to call you, but have to leave now. I will call you from Austria.

I am sending this letter as a precaution in case I disappear or have an accident. I love you, Michal.

> *"Across the trunks of pines, fine streaks of mist.*
> *I asked the boy where the Master is.*
> *Far away in the mountains, collecting herbs.*
> *Mist covers him, and where he is nobody can tell."*
> (Mathesius, The songs of old China)

158. IRANIAN PROFESSOR

Michal arrives at the Rome Central Station with a big brown bag full of groceries. The express for Vienna is ready with steam rising from beneath its wheels. All luggage has been loaded, and several late passengers scurry along looking for their cars. Only Michal is standing on the platform beside a public phone. He has checked that the phone works, and he is making sure that nobody will attempt to use it before he does.

Exactly fifteen minutes before departure time, he enters the booth and dials the Embassy number. "This is Michal Sedmý," he says. "Have you received the telex?"

"I can't believe it myself..." It's the receptionist. "The fax just arrived. The trouble is that we can't process it today. Mr. Ambassador says that you should take your train, and contact our consulate in Austria. We'll forward your papers to Vienna immediately."

"Can you do it by fax, please? I will be there by tomorrow morning."

"Yes, we will do our best."

Michal can see a conductor closing the doors and moving along the train toward the end where he is standing.

"Thank you and good bye ..." He hangs up and runs for the nearest door. Seconds later, the train is already moving.

The train is far from full, and Michal walks through several cars until he finds a window seat. The compartment is empty except for a man in a three-piece suit who sits stiff and erect and, from time to time, stretches his long fingers adorned with jewels, and observes his perfectly trimmed nails. The white cuffs of his shirt complement the expensive suit, and even his black lacquered shoes are without blemish – they must be brand new.

More than by the man's attire, Michal is puzzled by his face. His pale ivory skin contrasts with his black hair, thick but not curly, and after careful consideration Michal rejects the idea the man is an Egyptian. He has a Swiss watch, and custom-made spectacles that look like real gold.

Michal opens his bag of groceries with an apology: "This is my first meal since last night."

The man does not say a word, only smiles as if he knew how Michal must feel when behaving like a child who gets thirsty when the train begins to move. The man observes with polite curiosity what else Michal will fish out of his bag.

"Would you like one?" Michal offers him an apple.

"Thank you, look how pretty it is," the man holds the apple in front of his face, and turns it in his fingers. Then he wipes it with an embroidered handkerchief, and cuts it with a tiny pearl-inlaid penknife he took out of his pocket. "I stopped at a restaurant before the train departed, but this will be my dessert. Traveling far?"

"To Vienna."

"I too. We'll keep each other company."

From English, they switch to German, then they try French, briefly Russian, and return to English where they both feel most comfortable. They speak about politics, music, and ordinary, everyday life. Two electrical engineers, one from Teheran and the other one from Prague.

"I've never met an Iranian. Are you a university professor?" Michal says.

"I taught for several years, but I am now in business." The Iranian retrieves a tiny leather container from his pocket, takes out a card with a golden coat of arms, and passes it to Michal.

Michal studies the card – the name with many titles, and a London address; no company name.

"The address isn't valid anymore," the Iranian says. I am just moving to another place, possibly a different country."

"I didn't take my cards with me, and I don't know my future address either."

"The world is an interesting place."

They both sit contemplating, until Michal starts again: "Our native tongues, religions, and backgrounds are quite different. Why do I feel so close to you? We even like the same music. It can't be just our profession."

"We come from the same old culture," the Iranian reflects, "the culture that learned what's important in life. How did you like North America?" He looks at Michal with a curious expression.

"I was only in Canada, but it was as if I reached my destiny – an instant, perfect fit. No other country has wide open spaces and pristine nature like Canada."

"But you don't live amongst nature. You live amongst people. After six months in New York, I decided to leave. America is still too young. Money isn't everything ..."

"For me, nature *is* important," Michal interrupts him. "And in Ottawa, you can live in wild nature and commute to work. People are friendly and respectful regardless of your income. I saw a country of immigrants who are helping each other."

"Interesting," the Iranian says quietly as if talking to himself, "such contrasting experiences."

"Ottawa is the capital city," Michal says, "but it still has the ambiance of a small town. Large cities dehumanize their inhabitants.

"Young or not, people in America are free, and that's what drives both of us," Michal continues. "You left the rightist military regime that jailed and tortured people, and I am running away from the leftist communist country which does the same.

"You must be very well off," Michal changes the subject. "Why are you traveling by train?"

"I've been to Vienna many times, but I've always travelled by plane. I've never seen the Alps."

Before the train reaches the foothills, night arrives with layers of rain and fog. All that the two travelers can see is a quivering yellow rectangle, the projection of their compartment window onto the banks alongside the tracks and on the tunnel walls through which the train is passing. Michal opens the window and listens to the echo returning from the valley they must be crossing. There is nothing to see.

The Iranian sleeps covered by his coat without taking his jacket off or loosening his tie. Michal shakes his flip-flops off, and curls on the bench with his bag under his head.

When he wakes up, it feels as if the train is flying through a thick morning mist. He pulls down the window, and listens. In the distance, a cow is mooing.

Then the train breaks through the cloud, and the view opens. "This is the prettiest countryside I've ever seen," Michal whispers, "like a fairy tale, but it changes too fast to sketch it. I wish I had my camera!"

Like a centuries old painting in gold and brown hues, graceful hills are dotted with peaceful villages. Cattle and sheep are grazing, and majestic oaks are spreading their branches with every leaf in exactly the right position.

The Iranian also absorbs the view with intense concentration.

Perhaps this is the country I always wanted to go to, Michal is thinking. Perhaps I like it because it is much like Bohemia. Perhaps my ties with Bohemia are stronger than I am willing to admit.

The train enters suburbs of a large city, and Michal is in Vienna, exactly on time. It's Monday, seven in the morning.

The new friends descend from the train and walk toward the station hall.

"Good luck, and see you again – some other place, some other time," the Iranian says.

"And good luck with your new job, wherever you end up."

159. CONSULATE IN VIENNA

Entering Vienna is like stepping into yet another world. As if some magic carried Michal from the sun-scorched streets of Rome into this grey city submerged in drizzle and cloud. Austrians do not rush like Italians. They are organized, and everything works well. The train station has a small post office, and Michal gets a phone connection to Ottawa in two minutes.

"Where are you?" Danna says. "We have been worried about you."

"I'm in Vienna."

It takes several seconds before she grasps what he just said. "What? Where? How did you get there?"

"By train. I have a two-month visa for Austria. I tried to call you several times, but couldn't get through."

"What happened to the telex from Mr. Wellington?"

"It arrived only minutes before the departure of the train. The Embassy in Rome is transferring my papers to Vienna. Please, call Mr. Wellington and let him know."

"And what about the money and the airplane ticket?"

"Thank you very much, I've got both, but I'd better go now. I will call you again after I visit the Canadian Consulate."

Michal's journey has brought him full circle. He is in a free country, but only 75 km from the Czech border, and this proximity worries him greatly. He constantly watches for certain styles of clothing, for Czech or Russian accents, for facial expressions that could identify an agent. He does not dare to ask for directions except from older pedestrians who, judging by their appearance, have never lived elsewhere. Vienna reminds him of Prague: Nineteenth-century grey apartment houses, cobblestones, street layouts, the sound of streetcars, parks, sparrows, cafes and pubs, the linden and locust trees along the curbs. For three centuries, both cities had been important centers of the same empire, and many store signs display Czech names like Novak, Liška, Polatschek, or Sowa.

The Canadian Consulate occupies the entire fourth floor of a modern office building and is buzzing with Turkish and Greek labourers, who are milling around and helping each other fill out forms. Michal looks over the shoulder of a Turk in an oil-stained jacket with a torn sleeve. A pen is falling from his stubby fingers with short broken nails; large uneven letters run across the lines on his form.

"Fill in this application, and join the line," the receptionist tells Michal.

The line is long, and moves slowly – most applicants speak neither German nor English. One man is refusing to leave, and he keeps repeating the only English sentence he knows: "I want to go to Canada."

"My name is Martha McClellan," the clerk says when Michal reaches the counter. "What can I do for you?"

She has the businesslike manners of American diplomats, the same style of dress, and blond short hair with a wave to one side. There is a faint, almost undistinguishable scent of perfume around her.

Looking straight into her grey eyes, Michal says: "I just arrived from Rome. The Embassy there promised to transfer my visa to your office. It may not be here yet, but I thought I'd better drop in and tell you about it."

"Wait a minute. What visa? Why from Rome? You have a Czech passport."

"It's a long story. Last September, I started a post doctorate fellowship in Ottawa ..."

"You were in Canada last year? What's your name?"

"Michal Sedmý."

She steps back, opens a file cabinet, fingers through numerous files, and pulls out a folder. "Michal Sedmý, born on July 6, 1937 in Prague?"

Yes, at 7:05 a.m. - Michal chuckles to himself.

"You entered Canada on September 15. How did you get here?"

Michal is aghast. How could she know all that?

He narrates his story, and McClellan listens intensely. When he is finished, she closes her eyes, and reflects: "What you need is a permanent entry visa. By all regulations, that takes three months. Do you have any money? I would advise you to rent a room. We will get you the visa, but it will take three months."

"Is it safe around here? I've heard many stories." If there is anyone Michal trusts in Vienna, it is McClellan. He looks over his shoulder. The grinning Greeks do not appear dangerous.

"It's not too bad," she says quietly. "From time to time, someone disappears and nobody knows why. It doesn't happen often, but keep your identity hidden. Don't send any letters to your old country. Avoid visits to this consulate – use the telephone instead. But in general, you don't have to worry. You are neither a diplomat nor a high-ranking army officer."

<u>160. FRAU MESSINA</u>

Michal steps out of the building into a major storm. Considering what McClellan said, he does not want to wait at the consulate entrance. He runs for some other shelter, but after a few seconds he slows down. It makes no difference. The torrential rain and the gusts of wind have torn his vinyl raincoat. He is soaked to the skin. Just as this begins to really annoy him, he sees the open door of a crowded cafe.

He enters, shaking the water off. The room is packed and the air is saturated with a scent of coffee, wet coats, and goulash soup. Michal drapes the remains of his raincoat over a free chair, sits down, and dries his glasses with a serviette. He has nothing dry on him, even his pockets are full of water.

He searches the menu for something inexpensive. Let's see whether the wiener made in Wien tastes different. He also orders a hot tea.

The talk and laughter of people around him mixes with tinkling of glasses and silverware with the Viennese music in the background. The vaulted ceiling transforms it into a noise with a specifically German grunt, a noise of happiness from good food and being in a dry place.

"So you are looking for accommodation?" the tuxedo-clad waiter says with a smile, after Michal asked him about a rental agency. "It's only two blocks; turn left when you enter the street."

As soon as the rain stops, Michal strides to the agency. It's sunny and pleasant, and when he gets there, he has to laugh. It looks exactly like the rental agency in Sokolov – a small store with a window full of sun-bleached cards, but as he comes closer, there is a remarkable difference: Most cards start with APARTMENT FOR RENT!

He is excited about having so many options. He begins to read, but does not understand the German abbreviations on the cards. Also, the reflection of his skinny face with large sunken eyes haunts him. He enters the store and an old lady behind the counter smiles at him.

"… we don't have anything under sixty dollars. At least not at the government standard we are allowed to offer."

"I don't care about the standard. I need a simple room until my Canadian visa is ready. I can help with the housework."

"Now that you mention it, I have a friend who may have a room just like that."

She writes an address on the back of an index card. "It's around the corner."

Michal looks at the name. "Frau Messina, is she Italian?"

"She was born in Vienna, as far as I know. Tell her I sent you," she winks at Michal.

After finding the third floor apartment, Michal rings the bell beside the door. A large woman in an embroidered housecoat opens the door, and she stares at Michal without a word for a good thirty seconds. She looks like a countess from the previous century.

"The lady at the rental agency gave me your address," Michal says.

"Why are you looking for a room?"

"I have to wait for my Canadian visa."

She still does not trust Michal, but decides to show him the room: A large brass bed, a washstand with a basin, and two large windows overlooking the street.

From the first moment, Michal likes the room. Compared to the stale street through which he came, it is like entering a garden – it is full of sun, and the fresh air coming through the open window carries the scent of flowers.

Another female figure of the same proportions, younger yet not young, appears in the doorway.

"This is my daughter," Frau Messina says. "Not married yet, still hanging around here."

"Hopefully, this will be only a short stop. My wife is waiting for me in Canada."

Without acknowledging what Michal just said, Frau Messina continues: "Please, use the washstand in your room. With two women, the bathroom is in high demand. The phone is in the kitchen, but no long distance calls, please."

"And what is the rent?"

"If you wash dishes every night, it will be thirty dollars per month."

For that price, Michal would take anything. He pulls three ten dollar bills from his pocket, afraid she may change her mind.

"When will your bring your luggage?"

"This is all I have," Michal laughs and slaps his bag.

Again, she looks at him suspiciously. "You must register with the police, and rent your linen and towels in the laundry across the street."

After calling the consulate and leaving his new address and phone number, Michal calls Danna collect.

"This is like calling you from my office in Prague, with Radim watching me. I'm standing in the kitchen of my new place, and the witchlike landlady and her witchlike daughter are watching me. Fortunately, they do not understand Czech ..."

After he hangs up, still trying to keep a straight face, he runs to the laundry, stops at the police and, on the way back, buys basic food supplies. Excited about cooking his own dinner and having his own bed, he strolls with the apartment key in his pocket, and feels as if he had lived in Vienna for years.

He arrives at his new place, knocks on the kitchen door, and waits.

"Come in," Frau Messina calls.

When he enters, she is leaning back in a comfortable armchair and smiling at him over the newspaper she is reading. An enormous pile of burnt pots and sticky dishes covers the stove, sink, and the adjacent counter – an accumulation of cooking and eating over a week or two.

This rental may not be the great deal I thought, Michal thinks while scrubbing the pots. But if I do this every night, there will not be so many.

161. LOOKING FOR WORK

On Saturday morning, Michal wakes up early. The bed is too soft. He is thinking of Danna and how nice it would be if she were beside him, and how they would have to whisper so that Frau Messina would not hear them.

Through the open window, the sun shines directly on his face. The chirping of birds is unusually loud. The street below is quiet. He jumps out of bed, and does sit-ups and push-ups until he falls to the floor exhausted.

He has a simple breakfast from the supplies he stores on the windowsill, tiptoes out of the apartment, and takes the first streetcar that comes. He rides across the city into the suburbs – to places where family houses mix with commercial gardens and warehouses, and where rail yards with coal and lumber stockpiles border on abandoned fields.

He is close to being broke again. Three months is a long time, he thinks, but at least McClellan seems to know what she is doing. I'd rather find some work than ask the Kraemers for another loan.

He asks at three gardens, but they do not want any foreigners, and a sign posted on the rail yard gate declares in long-winded, official German that *Only the citizens of Austria or owners of a working permit may work on these premises.*

Sunday night, the pile of dirty dishes in the kitchen is again enormous. Am I washing the dishes for all the neighbours, Michal wonders. But as he scrubs the pots, he analyzes the leftovers. It is clear. The two women manage to burn anything they touch, and when the food begins to burn, they just use another pot.

162. GOOD NEWS

On Monday morning, Michal is sitting in his room and writing a letter to Danna, when a sound of knocking interrupts his thoughts. "Mr. Sedmý, telephone call for you. I did not know you are a doctor."

"Nobody is supposed to know my phone number," he murmurs on the way to the kitchen.

"Hello," he answers without identifying himself.

"Dr. Sedmý? This is the Canadian Consulate."

"Yes, this is me."

"The problem with your visa has been solved. We'll reinstate your visitor visa from the last year. That will allow you to enter Canada and to arrange permanent immigration later. All documents will be ready tomorrow."

"That's fantastic!" he yells. "When tomorrow?"

"Tomorrow after lunch."

He is so excited he does not know whether to turn somersaults or lift Frau Messina and dance a waltz with her around the kitchen. Then he calms down, dials the operator, and asks for a collect call to Canada.

He tells Danna the news, and without even thinking of breakfast, he takes off for the Air France office.

"I don't know how I should explain this to you," the clerk shakes her head. "We only have two transatlantic flights per week – Tuesday and Friday. If you want to fly on Tuesday, you have to be at the airport by nine a.m."

"I want to fly on Tuesday, but my visa won't be ready until the afternoon."

"It's clear. You have to fly on Friday."

"I can't wait so long," Michal says like a stubborn child. "Could I fly on Tuesday night with another airline? Do you know how long I have been waiting for this?"

Michal can see what she is probably thinking about him: a nut, or maybe an artist.

"Your ticket doesn't allow a change of carrier," she continues calmly while filling out the ticket for Friday. Make sure that you're at the airport well before the departure."

Michal steps out of the airline office, not sure what to do. Three days of waiting, nothing to do, nothing to speed up his departure – perhaps he should visit some museums and galleries he may not have a chance to see again. On foot, he wanders through old streets, gardens and city parks, until a sound of an organ stops him in his tracks. An obscure little church and the music of J.S. Bach, the same fuge that enchanted him in Prague when Danna was in Finland.

He enters the church, tiptoes to the last row, sits down and closes his eyes. The music comes down in waves, soothing his soul. The piece ends, some people come in, some leave, and the organ starts again. How long he listens he does not know, but when he finally gets up – he is ready to wait, three days or whatever it takes.

When he returns to the apartment, Frau Messina has already found a new tenant. "If you wax all the floors," she says with a smile, "I will give you back half of your deposit."

Michal plans to spend a day scrubbing and waxing the floors, but when he asks for a pail and soap the next day, she tells him only to "dust the floor, wax it, and polish it with the machine."

That does not make much sense, but he follows her orders. He sweeps the floors, waxes over the dirt, polishes them with the machine, and is done with the entire apartment in less than three hours.

"Please, drop us a line," she says when Michal is leaving on Friday. "We'd like to keep in touch."

"The thousand miles, the thousand miles,
the single aim, the single goal ..."
(Czech lyrics to the song
"Five Hundred Miles" by H. West)

163. FLIGHT TO CANADA

If it had been a century before, Michal would have raced his horse across Europe, covered with dust. He would have left exhausted steeds, foam at their mouths, and switched to fresh horses until he reached the ocean. Without dismounting, he would have galloped onto the first ship and, in spite of an approaching storm, he would have sailed out with all the sails on, faster and faster, as fast as he could.

Instead, he is sitting on a jet and a stewardess brings him a steak. Every muscle in his body is tense; he cannot eat, he cannot sleep. All he can do is to count the remaining minutes until his arrival in Canada.

"Is there anything I can do for you?" the stewardess asks.

Michal smiles at her. "Please, ask the pilot to fly faster."

Two men in the seats ahead of Michal speak Russian and their blue suits are unmistakable. They are no refugees, but rather diplomats or intelligence agents, most likely both.

The plane prepares for landing and Michal can see the familiar pattern of the two rivers. His heart is jumping with joy, his eyes fill with tears. Home at last.

He rushes through the halls of the Montreal airport, and reaches the immigration counter before any of the other passengers. He is so glad to be there that he could kiss the immigration officer on his big moustache.

Once I pass this point, he thinks, I am safe.

The officer pages through his passport and routinely asks with his French accent: "What is the purpose of your visit to Canada?"

"I am coming to finish my post doctorate fellowship in Ottawa."

The officer's eyes scan Michal, starting at the dirty toes protruding from the worn flip-flops, over the jeans with holes on their knees, to the small bag with both handles broken and tied into a knot. His eyes stop at Michal's tired face. Michal has not shaven that day and has not had a haircut since he started his journey.

"Is this the only luggage you have?" the officer points to the bag, and pierces Michal with his eyes. "You are a *doctor*?"

He closes the passport. "Please, go to that door, and report your arrival."

"But I am in a hurry," Michal objects. "My plane for Ottawa is leaving in fifty-five minutes. My wife and daughter are waiting for me at the airport."

"The question is whether you can enter Canada or not," the officer says in a stern voice. "Please, report at that door."

Two other officers begin to question Michal. They ask for additional documents, but Michal does not have any. They want to know how he has gotten the visa. They ask for addresses and phone numbers of Canadians who could confirm his identity.

"His story is so absurd it cannot be true," one of them says.

Question follows question for thirty five minutes. Michal fights for his life.

"We called Dr. Matheson," the officer says. "There is no answer on the phone number you gave us."

"He has probably left his office, just like Mr. Wellington," Michal looks at his watch. "It's five-thirty."

"We tried his home number. He isn't there either."

"He lives far from the office. He may not be home yet. Perhaps he went shopping."

"Do you have anything on you to prove your story?"

"I've told you already," Michal says. "I ran illegally through several countries, I could not take any documents with me."

He looks at his watch again. The plane for Ottawa is leaving in

20 minutes.

"The only document I have is my Canadian driver's license."

"You do have that?" one of them says, and they simultaneously reach for the little piece of paper. One of them examines it from both sides.

"You can go," he says.

Michal clears out of the room, but he feels as if he has aged by twenty years during the last half-an-hour. He is close to fainting. During his journey, all the time, he was ready to fight, to run under fire, but not now, now when he has reached home. It was a blow he did not expect.

He is the last passenger boarding the plane. "Hurry up, we're closing the gate," the attendant shouts.

In Ottawa, Michal is ascending from the plane like a victor – straight and glowing. He stops for a second, scanning the mass of people at the barrier. And then he sees Danna.

They run into each other arms, touching each other from toes to lips, breathing each other's breath, until they realize that Lenka is also trying to get Michal's attention. She is so excited she can hardly speak. "Daddy, Daddy!" she says. They lift her up and embrace, all three of them together.

"Look, the Kreamers are also here," Danna says.

Smiling Kraemers stand beside them. Michal hugs them and follows them to their car.

"And I thought it would be just a couple of days," he says when he climbs in after Danna and Lenka.

"These were the three longest weeks of my life," Danna says and puts her head on his shoulder.

*"He was so angry he wanted to smash the entire world.
Instead, he chose words that landed like boulders."*
(V. Vancura) [20]

164. WHAT HAPPENED AFTER

What happened after would be another book – about the immigrants who had nothing except the loan from the bank to be paid off. They rented a small, unfurnished apartment, placed two mattresses on the floor, and used cardboard boxes from the supermarket as shelves along the wall.

Mrs. Matheson arrived with a carload of items collected from her neighbours: three plates, three forks, three knives – each different – old pots, an old sofa with one torn cushion, and three lawn chairs. As in Rovná, rough workbench covered with plastic served as a dining table.

Before Christmas, the Tartan suitcase arrived in the mail. Inside, on the top of his suit, Michal found a note from the Yugoslavian students: *With some difficulties, we retrieved your luggage. Good luck in your new country.*

In Michal's and Danna's absence, the Czechoslovak government staged a trial against them. For the crime of leaving the country without a proper permit, they were sentenced to the loss of civil rights; Danna to two years of jail and Michal to five. All their property was confiscated.

The court record read: *Their decision to leave was not a result of a momentary weakness or whim. It was a carefully planned and orchestrated criminal act, which deceived the police and the authorities. Michal Sedmý has two university degrees and speaks several languages. He is intelligent and dangerous.*

The police turned the Prague Institute upside down. "It looked as if we would never travel abroad again," Olda wrote from Hungary four years later. "We all had to sign a declaration that we despise you, will never contact you, and if we did we would be immediately fired." Olda printed the message on a postcard, and

---

[20] Czech physician, historian, and writer, tortured and killed by Nazis at the beginning of the WWII.

signed it: "Your friend O."

Michal's article about the computer composed from little cubes was never published. The editor-in-chief decided that he could not publish an article of a defector, and the journal appeared in the newsstands with eight pages missing.

As a possible security hazard, Michal's mother was dismissed from her position in the international trade organization. She could not find a professional job and worked as a low-paid typist until she retired.

Ian Watson, the loan manager at the Bank of Nova Scotia, was smiling when Michal appeared at the door. "I was afraid I'd never see you again," he said. "Your account ran out of money, and we are just adding interest to your loan hoping you would show up one day."

From his first salary, Michal sent three dollars to the minister in Iowa.

He never met the Iranian engineer again.

Within one year, Zora married a well-situated government executive. Since Michal had lost his civil rights, the court allowed her new husband to adopt their three children and change their names and birth certificates without even informing Michal. That did not prevent Zora from keeping the support money Michal sent every month for the next 15 years.

Both the director and the Party chairman Schmidt died of heart attacks within four years of Michal's and Dana's departure.

Radim remarried, and remained in the same position until his retirement at sixty five. He is now dedicating most of his time to his hobby farm with sheep, rabbits, and vegetable garden.

The class clown Olda rose through Party ranks to a deputy position.

To Lenka's delight, Michal and Danna had a baby girl a year after they arrived in Canada, and a baby boy later.

The Kraemers had a serious car accident, separated, and divorced.

Lida achieved recognition and honours in her scientific career, but never married again.

Michal and Danna wanted their parents to join them or at least come for a visit. Michal imagined his father taking the children for a walk along the Ottawa River, playing the piano, and telling them stories.

Since his father was already retired, he was the first candidate for a visit. As a financial burden to the communist government, most seniors were free to travel, but not in this case. Every six months, he applied for the exit visa and, as a punishment to Michal, the application was always rejected. His father died in 1973; the permit arrived only a week later. Since then, both mothers have visited Canada many times.

In a 1975 ceremony, Michal, Danna, and Lenka received their Canadian citizenships.

Michal never had any doubt that he would reconnect with his children one day. The relations began to build when the children married and had children of their own. Without calling each other father, daughter or son, they simply became precious friends. Today, Michal and Danna exchange emails with them almost every day.

APPENDIX

Brief history of Czechoslovakia
that you won't find in any textbook.

The republic of Czechoslovakia was proclaimed in 1918, after the end of the WWI, and the Versailles peace treaties confirmed it in 1919 and 1920. It combined Czech lands (Bohemia and Moravia), Slovakia, and Sub-Carpathian Ukraine. For three centuries, these lands had belonged to the Habsburg (Austro-Hungarian) Empire, and had a significant German and Hungarian population.

Thanks to its extensive industry (coal mining, smelting, iron works, machine-tool production, glass works, textile, breweries, sugar refineries, chemical production) and to its democratic government, the new republic instantly became one of the vibrant, modern states of Europe.

When Hitler came to power in Germany, Czechoslovakia with its Czech and German universities became a haven for the Jews and freethinking Germans trying to escape the persecution. Czechs were known producers of armaments, and the young republic had a small but modern army. Concrete fortresses protected the border with Germany, and the country had defense treaties with both France and Britain.

In 1938, Hitler demanded German annexation of the large border area with its predominantly German population, called Sudetenland. Czechoslovakia mobilized its army, but France and Britain approved Hitler's demand in the infamous Munich Treaty. With the border territory, Hitler took over the border defenses and, in March 1939, the unopposed German army occupied Czechoslovakia. The country was split into the Protectorate of Bohemia and Moravia, and a semi-dependent Slovak State. Czech universities were closed, and German became, once again, the official language of the country. The oppression by Germans was brutal. Thousands of Czechs, the best minds of the nation were imprisoned, and those who survived the torture were sent to concentration camps.

When the war ended, the Allied Command allowed the Czechoslovakian government to relocate the German minority (2.7 million, about 30% of the country's population) to Germany.

When planning post-war Europe, the Jalta agreement (1944) assigned the original Czechoslovak territory to the Soviet sphere of influence. In 1945, the new democratic Czechoslovakia included the original territory except for the Sub-Carpathian Ukraine, which was taken by the USSR. In 1948, a communist coup established a new government backed by the Soviets. All industry and large farms were nationalized and their owners sent to jail. Small farms and businesses had to join government owned cooperatives. A series of mock political trials, a system of torture and forced-labour camps, the elimination of personal liberties, and the terror organized by the secret police (STB, similar to the Soviet KGB and German STASI) lasted throughout the Cold War. Soviets plundered all the resources including the best uranium deposits in the world (Jachymov).

Under Alexander Dubcek, during the "Prague Spring" of 1968, Czechs attempted to establish "Communism with a human face" – a system which would guarantee personal freedoms and gradually revive democracy while keeping the safety net of the Socialistic government. This was to be established within the Soviet Bloc, with no intention of separation.

In August 1968, the Soviet Army occupied Prague and forced the government back to the dark ages of communism that lasted another 21 years. When the Soviet Empire began to crumble, in 1989, the bloodless "velvet revolution" returned Czechoslovakia to democracy and ideals of the Prague Spring.

In June 1991, the Slovaks asked for separation. Czechs approved it in January 1992, and that dissolved Czechoslovakia. Neither side held an election or plebiscite. The Czech Republic and the Slovak Republic are now independent states, both members of the EU and NATO.

This novel briefly mentions the 1968 Soviet invasion of Prague and runs through the subsequent two years of the depressing communist rule.